# EVERGREEN

## A NOVEL

First Printing: 2017

ISBN-13:978-1981561421

ISBN-10:1981561420

Edited by Stephen R. Willis
www.stephenwillis.co

Published by Thomas J. Torrington
torrington@protonmail.com
www.thomasjtorrington.com

For My Children

"Everything I could hope to teach you can be found within these pages."

To My Wife

Thank you for helping me to realize greatness.

# Acknowledgements

I acknowledge with gratitude all of the family and friends who have helped and supported me throughout this process. In particular, my wife who suggested that I should pursue my dream; my parents, Rawn and Judith, who have been my example of hard work and perseverance; my wife's parents, Robert and Sally for reading my draft and making notes for me; and the rest for of her family for their encouragement.

Thank you to all of my wonderful beta–readers, especially those that went above and beyond. Malain Collins, Leo Dymkowski, Karen Lee, and Rich Williams — your feedback was of greater help than you could possibly know.

A special thanks to my editor, Stephen R. Willis, for putting up with my neuroticism, my impatience, and my desire to craft something as close to perfection as possible. It is hard enough to find someone who understands your vision. It's far more difficult to find someone to help you bring it to life. I found both in you as an editor. *Evergreen* would not be the book it is without your help. I know how much you like short sentences. So, thank you for everything.

# EVERGREEN

A NOVEL

Thomas J.
## Torrington

# 1

"I went to the woods because I wished to live deliberately, to front only the essential facts of life, and see if I could not learn what it had to teach, and not, when I came to die, discover that I had not lived."
—Henry David Thoreau, Walden

The snow fell softly and came to rest on the pine boughs, collecting until they drooped under the added weight. The air smelled clean and fresh, as it always does during a new–falling snow. This was a gentle snow, the kind that gets caught on tongues and eye lashes. This wasn't the kind of snow where the animals hunker down, but rather the kind where the birds still dart down from the trees and scratch looking for morsels under the soft flakes. This was the first real snow of the season.

Down a lonely dirt lane, there were several small houses. The first of these was the Marshall house, quaint in its simplicity. It was a white cape–cod with two small bedrooms upstairs, both with dormer windows overlooking a small stream out back and to the woods beyond. The stream, when it wasn't frozen over from the winter chill, flowed east and fed into a pond several hundred yards away on the Peterson farm next door. The Peterson's place was a typical old farmhouse, large and plain with a porch on the front which was perfect for balmy summer mornings. To the south of the farmhouse was the barn, which in its heyday was the home for half a dozen cows but now held only two horses: an old Arabian mare and a younger Shetland pony. Together, the two households were the epitome of rural Maine: simple and honest, hard and strong.

Outside the smaller of the two houses, Buck Marshall was piling freshly chopped firewood under the shed he'd built on the west side of the house. The shed would keep the wood dry until it was burned in the fireplace.

The man whose real name was William, but who was called "Buck" because he had neither the look or demeanor to be called "William" or "Bill," was a grizzled old man. His hands were worn and calloused by hard work and suggested an age far beyond his years. His hair and beard were white and woolly, and his face was cracked and tired. Everything about Buck suggested that he was far into his twilight years. That is, everything except his eyes. Blue and thoughtful, his eyes suggested a youthful fire, a curiosity — even mischief. To know Buck Marshall was to know the meaning of life, for the two are equally mysterious and equally profound.

Much like the meaning of life, people thought they knew Buck Marshall when they didn't. That is to say that people knew of Buck. They knew of his generous spirit, his propensity for hard work, and his thoughtful nature, but they did not know the soul encased in the ragged shell they saw in his appearance. Other than his wife Margaret, or Maggie as he affectionately called her, no one truly knew Buck Marshall.

Maggie was a simple woman, with simple beauty. Her dark hair, kind eyes, and the crooked smile she constantly wore, would warm the hearts of everyone she met. While not particularly smart in the usual sense of the word, she had an uncanny knack for reading and understanding people. Perhaps that's why she understood and loved her husband when no one else could possibly know him. She could see past the hard exterior to the child still living in his heart, and she loved him dearly for it.

It was November and Buck had stored enough wood to keep the house warm through December. He would have to see Jim Peterson about storing more in the unused part of his barn for the remainder of the winter, since the makeshift shed was nearly full. He placed the final few logs on the pile, and was just about to head over to the Peterson's farm to talk to Jim when his wife called from the porch.

"Buck, lunch is ready. Why don't you come take a break?"

Buck came around the corner, smiled, and said in his Down–East accent, "Your timing couldn't have been bettah, Maggie. I just put the last log on the pile there, and I think some dinnah would suit me just fine."

He kissed her on the cheek, and she smiled as he walked past her and into the house. She'd gotten used to his accent over the years and still loved when he called lunch "dinnah," even if she'd never fallen into the trend herself. She was from Ohio and had no predisposition to drop the "r" from her words. But she found the diction, like the state, to be quaint. She'd met Buck in New York shortly before he was discharged from the military, and had fallen instantly in love with the man only she would ever truly know.

Buck ate his lunch in silence, as he often did. Grilled cheese and tomato soup with crackers was a staple of winter living in Maine, and a glass of milk topped off a perfect meal. Maggie stood by the sink doing dishes as she watched her husband finish off his lunch. Silently, he rose with his glass, plate, and silverware, and joined her at the sink. He took the sponge she held in her hand and proceeded to wash each of the items in turn, and handed them to her to dry and place back in their proper places. After they finished, Buck kissed Maggie on the cheek and walked out of the kitchen with a smile. He turned down the hall, out the front door, and headed towards the Peterson farm to talk to Jim about storing firewood for the winter. He was sure Jim would agree. In reality, there was really no need to ask since they'd had the same arrangement for the past seven years. Buck could cut trees from the forest on the Peterson's property and would store wood in their barn, and in turn Jim could split and use what he needed for the winter. Still, Buck stood on ceremony. Every year he would walk to the Peterson's and ask Jim if he could store firewood in the barn, and every year Jim's reply would be the same.

"Of course, Buck. Same arrangement as last year?"

"That'd be fine," would be Buck's retort.

With that, Buck would turn and head home. Jim would smile and call after him, "Talk to you later, Buck."

This year was no different. With the tradition fulfilled, Buck turned and retraced the footprints he'd left in the snow, back to his easy chair by the fireplace.

The snow continued falling throughout the evening, covering the entire world with white and leaving the air fresh and new. Buck and Maggie spent the evening by the fire. Not a word passed between the two, but a glance in his wife's direction and a twinkle in his eye, was all that was needed for Maggie to know how much Buck cared for her.

# 2

**P**aul Marshall paced nervously back and forth across the hospital waiting room. The tension of the moment was etched across his face and a million thoughts raced through his mind. Not twenty minutes earlier the doctor had asked to talk to him in private. It was in that moment that his heart skipped a beat and the world seemed to stop spinning. His wife, in labor some twenty hours, was having a difficult delivery and the baby was now in distress. An emergency C–section was planned and an OR prepared. The doctor stressed that they were confident that both Paul's wife and child would survive. But somewhere deep down, Paul knew different. He had a sense, in a dark place he couldn't understand, that events beyond his control were unfolding that would change his life forever.

Paul was a tall, lanky man of thirty–two. His hair was slicked back, neat, and representative of the image he portrayed to the outside world. A professional. A businessman. Paul believed that the way others saw him was integral to achieving success. He was dressed in a blue business suit, the jacket of which he had thrown over the back of a chair. His collared shirt was unbuttoned at the top, his tie loosened, and his armpits stained with the sweat that let slip the secret anxiety he fought to keep hidden. The son of Buck Marshall was the exception to the rule, an apple that had fallen far, far from the tree that bore it. His hands were smooth and callous–free, suggesting that manual labor was something he had never tried. In truth, Paul neither felt the need nor saw the use in working with his hands. Paul was of the school that "working smarter not harder" was the way to get ahead in the world. There was always a big deal ready to be made around the corner: a prospective fortune that would set him for life. Now, however, finances and the business of making money didn't seem to matter, with his wife's life and the life of the baby she carried in jeopardy.

The activities of the hospital went on around Paul, barely showing any notice of his existence. Every now and again the receptionist would flash him a sympathetic glance and then return to her work. Paul finally stopped pacing and sat down in one of the stark waiting–room chairs. His head fell into his hands as he wrestled with the strain of the moment. For what might as well have been an eternity, the world for Paul disappeared; it was only he, the hall, and the agonizing minutes alone with his thoughts. His stomach in knots, Paul decided he would get a cup of coffee. It was more the task than the beverage itself that he needed to occupy his mind. If nothing else, he needed a brief reprieve from the torturous spinning in his head.

He walked to the cafeteria and purchased coffee, black, in a small styrofoam cup. Once he returned to his seat in the waiting room, he stared blankly at the swirling black liquid in the cup between his hands. He looked up briefly from time to time to glance hopefully at a nurse, orderly, or doctor coming down the hall. He wrongly thought they might bring news regarding his wife and child, struggling to survive in the OR not far away. Time passed, the coffee became cold, and Paul's face remained unchanged: sullen, hopeful, fearful, and confused. His world was collapsing.

Once time had lost all meaning, a doctor emerged to deliver the final blow to Paul's happy existence. Paul stood, a condemned man, resigned to receive his final judgment and have his punishment carried out. He caught only snippets of sentences containing words about complications, hemorrhages, bleed outs, cardiac arrest, resuscitation, and condolence. All Paul understood was that his wife had passed, and while the baby had survived it had been moved to the N. I. C. U. and that the outlook was not good. From that moment on, Paul was in a daze.

He was led to a plain grey room with a gurney, covered by a sheet, to say his final goodbyes to his loving wife. The doctor pulled back the sheet from the face and left the room quietly. As Paul gazed down at the woman he loved, he was moved to tears, only now grasping the gravity of the situation. He fell into her and grabbed her hand as he began sobbing. He kissed her lightly on her forehead and tried to speak. His words were obscured by the tears as he tried to choke them back.

"I don't know how to do this without you."

He lingered for a while, trying to find a sign of the soul that was so connected to his own. There remained only an empty shell. His wife was gone. The strain of holding on eventually wearied him to the point that fatigue broke his grasp, and he exited the room.

Still wiping tears from his face, Paul was whisked to the N. I. C. U. to view his newborn from behind a glass wall. Human emotion is not meant to survive such drastic swings, and the effect on Paul was clearly visible. He mourned for his wife and hoped for his child, not knowing how he would raise it alone. Deep down, part of him wished the child wouldn't survive, only because he didn't know if he could bear to have a constant reminder of his wife. It wasn't until then that Paul found out he had a son. The doctor may have mentioned it, but Paul had been in such shock in the waiting room the news had escaped him. Now the blue blanket in the crib, from which the tubes and wires exited, was enough to let him know the truth.

A son was to be cherished, and Paul knew that it would be up to him to raise the child, should he survive. He set his mind in a single second to do just that.

The doctor reappeared to inform Paul of the baby's condition, knowing that initially Paul had been overwhelmed. He started into a speech about how the hospital was doing everything in its power to save the child's life when Paul stopped him.

He spoke slowly and deliberately, as though the words were fact. "My son will survive. He will survive, and I will raise him because that is the life fate has chosen for me. I will be his family because that is my duty and that is what I owe to my wife: to raise our only child."

He paused for some time. The doctor, incredulous at Paul's certainty, said nothing. They stood there in silence for several minutes before Paul spoke again.

"His name is Brandon, Brandon Marshall."

It was two weeks before Christmas, 1960, when Paul Marshall left Massachusetts General with his son, Brandon, and returned to his now lonely apartment in Cambridge. The funeral of his wife, as well as his son's battle to live in the hospital, had clearly taken its toll on Paul. His face was scraggly and unshaven. His hair was mussed, and his face drawn in and sullen from lack of sleep and from depression. He had spent the majority of the last two weeks either at the hospital with Brandon, or drunk at home alone. Meals over those two weeks had consisted of what he could get in the hospital cafeteria or whatever he could scrounge up at the apartment. That is, when he remembered to eat at all. His skin was stretched over his thin frame from lack of nourishment, and had the stench of someone who badly needed a shower. It was not a promising start for the man who had vowed to raise a child to the best of his ability. Little did Paul know, his situation was not about to improve anytime soon.

# 3

**O**ften, it is the smallest of details that set forth a chain of events that help to shape the future. Jim and Nancy Peterson were set to attend a New Year's party across town, but the cold December air rendered their car battery useless. Rather than bother to jump it, they decided to spend the night at home alone. Nancy prepared a meal of chicken and rice with green beans and homemade apple sauce. As she worked, Jim stoked the fire in the fireplace and added several logs, fueling the flames. He then opened a bottle of red wine the two had been saving for a special occasion.

The happy couple made a picnic of their meal on the floor in front of the stonework. They ate silently, watching the flames flicker in each other's eyes. Jim's gaze slowly slid down to where Nancy's thighs snuck out from under her skirt. She caught him in the act and a wry smile came over her face. Sliding closer to her husband, she took his hand. He again peered into her eyes and this time, the flicker was born from within and had the burn of desire. As a few flurries of what would become the first nor'easter of the season began to fall outside, Jim and his wife Nancy succumbed to temptation in front of the fireplace. They made love softly in front of the flames, and then Jim carried his wife to the bedroom, with the fire still licking at the hearth.

It was Buck Marshall who noticed the red glow and the smoke billowing from the Peterson's chimney that first of January. He and Maggie were returning from town and the New Year's party, when the light from the chimney alarmed him. He parked the car in the drive, told Maggie to call for the fire department, jumped out of the vehicle, and began running towards the Peterson farmhouse. He made his way, struggling through the wind–blown drifts, onto the Peterson's porch. The wind did its best to silence his screams and the sound of his fists pounding on the door. The Peterson's had a chimney fire, and only Buck Marshall could get the two out in time. Jim and his wife were oblivious to the trouble. The effects of their love making and the wine had lulled them into a very deep and contented sleep. Outside, Buck was kicking at the door, trying desperately to open it or wake the owners inside.

As Maggie stood outside the Marshall's door yelling through the wind that the fire department was on its way, Buck finally broke through and entered the Peterson farmhouse. Smoke and flames were spreading inside the home, and there was no telling when the fire department might arrive. Choking on smoke, Buck tried to yell for Jim and Nancy, but received no answer.

# 4

Cambridge had long been a beacon for learning and intellect. Many of the brightest minds from all over the world congregated at Harvard University and MIT to study, teach, and otherwise drive the wheels of academia. Truly, the very epitome of opportunity, it was brimming with a wealth of knowledge and the means to convey it to each young vessel with the desire to learn.

That winter was particularly peaceful. College students traipsed with some trepidation the snowy walkways, sidewalks, and paths. The trees along the Charles River glistened in the winter sun. Silence fell softly from the sky, blanketing the world in white as if to suggest rebirth, hope, and the sense that all that was once bleak could be light once again.

Paul however, was oblivious to the world outside his tiny apartment as he lay passed out in his chair. The talk–show host on the television hollered loudly, despite no one in the room listening. Little Brandon wailed in desperate hunger from his crib in the corner of the room. Paul heard neither the child nor the pounding of his next–door neighbor on the apartment door. She yelled in the vain attempt to find out if everything was all right inside. It wasn't until the Cambridge police arrived that Paul stirred from his drunken slumber.

Paul jumped slightly when the officer rapped on the apartment door. In his confusion, it took him nearly a minute to realize where the sound had come from amidst the crying and the prattling talk–show host on the TV. He reached the door as the officer began to knock again and opened it, obviously irritated.

"What do you want?" he asked. Then realizing it was the Cambridge police, he instinctively checked, and righted himself to the manner in which he presented to the outside world. "Oh, hello officer. What seems to be the problem?"

"We got a call from your neighbor. She heard the baby crying but was unable to get anyone to answer when she knocked on the door. She was concerned and decided to phone it in."

"Ah," said Paul. "I had the television on pretty loud there, must not have heard her."

The officer, sensing Paul's discomfort and smelling the liquor on his breath said, "Everything all right, sir?"

"Yeah, yeah, everything's fine." Paul answered, closing the door slightly.

"Have you been drinking today, sir?"

"Well — yes, I mean one or two. You see officer, I lost my job yesterday. I've been a little stressed out about it." The officer looked at Paul sternly. Paul continued, "My wife. Uh, my wife… she died giving birth, and I'm left with the little guy over there." Paul motioned over his shoulder to the crib. "I don't know what I'm going to do."

The officer peered past Paul into the dingy apartment. It smelled of booze and cigarettes and looked like it hadn't been cleaned in quite some time. It certainly didn't look like the type of environment a child should be raised in. He looked at Paul somewhat pitifully and said, "Sir, I'm going to have to call this into Child Services and have them stop by to make sure that you're providing properly for the baby. Now, drinking in your own home is by no means a crime. But in my opinion sir, you should be keeping yourself in a state where you can adequately care for that infant over there. In my estimation, you've had more than your fair share to drink today. My recommendation is to put on some coffee, sober up and tend to your little one. If you need help with child care there are a number of services I can recommend."

"No, no that'll be fine officer. I'm sure I can handle everything here."

Paul was somewhat startled by the officer's estimation and decision to send Child Services. He felt the need to defend himself.

"Officer, I really don't see the need to get Child Services involved. I'm just going through a rough patch. I'm sure things will turn around soon."

"That may be, but it's my job to report any potentially dangerous situations that I may come across."

"Oh, I see," Paul said.

"Someone will be by to see you in a day or two. In that time, my suggestion is to clean this place up a bit and get yourself together."

"Okay. Thank you, officer," Paul said apprehensively.

With that, the officer left, telling Paul to have a nice day. Paul closed the door and returned to the crib. Baby Brandon was still crying for food. Lifting him gently, Paul carried him into the kitchen to prepare his formula. As he looked into the baby's face, he couldn't help but see the face of his wife looking up at him. The baby continued to wail. Paul's mind wandered and heard instead the screams of his wife in labor some two months earlier. The horror of the loss rushed back to him and he reeled. He staggered, but returned to the present in time to regain his balance.

With the bottled warmed, Paul checked the temperature on his wrist like the nurse had taught him. Convinced it was right, he presented the bottle to his son, who began to suck greedily.

The truth of the situation was that Paul had lost his job not long after he and Brandon had returned home from the hospital. His boss had called Paul into his office on a Friday and released him. It was true that Paul had once been the model employee, but through his depression his work had fallen below par. He had begun showing up to work unkempt and reeking of alcohol. The burial of his wife and the mother of his child had only fueled the fire of desperate unhappiness in Paul's heart. It had in fact been almost a month since he'd been let go. He had to release his caregiver shortly thereafter. Paul was left with nothing to occupy his time other than listening to the screams of his son, equally unhappy without his mother to care for him. And so, he had drunk and wallowed in the squalor which so represented the chaos of his soul.

In every man's life, there comes a point where he has to make a decision: a crossroads at which his life can potentially take two very different directions. It was in this moment holding his baby son, that Paul realized he was at such a crossroads. He rocked Brandon gently, patting him on the back until the newborn let out a burp. As soon as Paul placed him lovingly back into his crib, Brandon quickly fell into a contented sleep. Paul then went into the bedroom and pulled a suitcase down from the top shelf in the closet. He packed a number of items very carefully, then closed the lid, zipped the contents inside, and returned to the living room. Brandon didn't stir as Paul picked him up, wrapped him in blankets, and placed him lovingly in a basket. Father, son, and suitcase then exited the apartment and made their way together down to Paul's car parked on the curb.

The car was reluctant to turn over in the frigid Massachusetts air. Paul turned the key repeatedly until the engine finally squealed to life. Driving slowly through town, Paul watched the students trudge home from class, bundled as warmly as they could be. In them he saw hope, he saw promise, and it broke his heart.

One quick stop, for which Paul made sure that Brandon was adequately covered in blankets before he left him in the backseat, and then father and son were again moving over the snow–laden streets towards the interstate, now with a brown paper bag sitting in the passenger seat.

In the winter, driving up I–95 from Massachusetts to Maine as dusk falls is a very peaceful and surreal experience. On a quiet evening, such as the one Paul and his son were blessed with, there are so few cars that it can feel like one is the only soul left on this earth.

Brandon slept soundly in the floor of the backseat as Paul negotiated the icy road. The two met only a handful of other travelers and several trucks plowing the interstate. As father and son crossed the bridge and entered Maine, Paul let out a sigh. It had been well over a decade since he had been in the state he grew up in.

There is something about Maine — the woods, the coast, the mountains; even when one has been away for years, the state makes you feel like your heart never really left. The old–timers say that the land gets in your blood, infects you, and no matter where you go, you bring a little piece of it with you. Regardless of the real reason, Paul felt like he was returning home.

He left the interstate in Augusta and headed west on Route 202. In Winthrop, he turned and headed towards Wayne on Route 133. By this time, darkness had set in and the towns were asleep but for a few lights scattered in frosty windows. A few miles past downtown Wayne, he turned off the main road. It was only a short time before he turned down the quiet dirt lane, and arrived at his childhood home. All the lights were off in the small two–bedroom house, which was just as well because Paul didn't want to raise any attention just yet. He pulled off to the side of the road just at the end of the driveway, turned off his lights, and looked somewhat sadly at the place where he grew up.

Paul knew the stream out back would be frozen over by now. The forest beyond would shine, glistening in the winter moonlight. He had played in that forest as a child, and in the winter, had made snow forts between the trunks of the trees from which he would battle imaginary armies with well–thrown snowballs.

He reached into the glove compartment and brought out a pen and a notepad on which he wrote four lines. After he tore off the top sheet, he got out of the car. Paul opened the back door, retrieved the suitcase, and picked up Brandon in his basket, making sure he was wrapped sufficiently against the cold. Father walked, carrying son and luggage, briskly up the drive to the front step. Paul kissed his son's sleeping face, and then with tears in his eyes he placed the note in the blankets and set Brandon carefully on the step next to the suitcase. With a deep breath he knocked on the door, loudly enough to wake anyone sleeping, and then retreated hastily to the car which he had left running.

As Buck Marshall opened the door, nothing could have prepared him for the bundle he found waiting for him. He picked up the basket and child, and a piece of paper fell to his feet. Car lights disappeared around the corner of the dirt lane just as he stood up from retrieving the note. Buck brought the child inside, placing both basket and baby gently on the kitchen table. He put the suitcase on the floor, and then opened the piece of paper. On it was written simply,

*This is your grandson, Brandon.*
*I know you will succeed where I have failed.*
*Please forgive me.*
    *–Paul*

One of the plow–truck drivers called in the abandoned vehicle to the state police. They found the car parked on the side of the road between Wayne and Winthrop. Paul Marshall was lying thirty feet away, down an embankment. Underneath his lifeless body, the police found a brown paper bag. There was a 9–mm pistol still in his right hand. He had put the gun in his mouth and pulled the trigger. It had been less than a year since Brandon had been conceived. Even the noblest of hearts can succumb to insurmountable grief. Paul Marshall was proof of that.

# 5

**B**uck was still hovering over the bundle on the kitchen counter when Jim Peterson, who had been woken by the knock at the door, came down the stairs and walked in.

"Who was that at this hour?" Jim asked.

Buck moved out of the way and handed the note he held in his hand to Jim. Jim read it silently, his mouth agape. Maggie and Nancy entered the kitchen together, and seeing the baby, the two were shocked and pressed Buck for information. Buck shrugged and pointed to the note that Jim was reading through again, now for the second time.

Jim and Nancy had been saved the night of the fire. Buck managed to get the two out of the house by kicking in the door and climbing the stairs to their room. The fire department had arrived in time to save the physical structure of the home. The inside, however, was badly damaged, and it would need to be repaired before it was safe for Jim and Nancy to live there. Buck and Maggie had extended the courtesy of letting the Petersons live with them until the farmhouse could be cleaned and repaired. Living space was tight already in the small Marshall home, and now a baby would complicate things further.

The note and the child were the first contact either Buck or Maggie had received from their son Paul since he had left home as a young man, many years ago. The extreme circumstances left Maggie feeling bewildered, and a bit lost for words.

"What should we do, Buck?" she asked, looking at her husband.

Buck looked down at the child, silently reached down, and lifted him from the basket. The boy shifted, but did not wake.

"Well," Buck said, "I suppose we should find a place for the little guy to sleep tonight, and tomorrow I'll head into town and buy some things he'll need." With that he handed the baby to his surprised wife.

"We can't take care of him!" Maggie exclaimed.

Buck shrugged again. "Seems we'll have to. I'm headed back to bed. I suppose he'll have to sleep in that there basket until we can get him a propah crib. G'night, Jim, Nancy."

With that Buck headed back up the stairs, leaving the other three looking at each other in disbelief.

"What are you going to do, Maggie?" Jim asked.

Maggie of course already knew what they were going to do. Her husband's response along with his actions had stated the facts to her loud and clear. He had weighed all the options, and there was no question in his mind that the two of them would raise their grandson together.

Maggie looked at the tiny bundle in her hands and said, "I guess I'm going back to bed, and we'll have to figure it out in the morning. No sense staying up trying to figure things out now."

There was, in fact, nothing to figure out, but it was easier to say so than try to explain in the middle of the night that the decision had been made. She placed Brandon back in the basket and carried him upstairs to bed. Jim and Nancy retired as well. The only one of the four adults that got much sleep the rest of that night was Buck, who snored loudly and seemed to wear the slightest smile on his face.

The next morning, Buck headed into town with Jim to buy supplies for the baby. Maggie and Nancy did their best to make Brandon comfortable and give him something to eat. There was some formula in the suitcase, much of which they had used the night before. Maggie prepared and fed him what they had left and patted him softly on the back until he burped. When Brandon spit up on Maggie's shoulder, she simply wiped it up with a rag. She didn't bother to put the baby down, but just shifted him to the other shoulder. Nancy admired how at ease Maggie was around the child and was about to comment on it when she felt nauseous. She rushed to the bathroom and vomited.

As Nancy wretched over the bowl, Maggie stood in the doorway holding Brandon. "Looks like we might have another little one around before the year is out," she said.

Nancy looked up, her eyes wide. "No, no. I probably just ate something that didn't settle right."

"Dear, I've been around enough pregnant women to know one when I see her."

Nancy's mind raced at the possibility. If she really was pregnant, things could get very uncomfortable. They wouldn't be back in their home for several months at this rate. Buck and Maggie had Brandon to care for. The house was cramped as it was. How much more cramped would it feel with a baby and a pregnant woman in it?

Maggie seemed to read her thoughts. "Now don't you worry… We're going to take care of both you and this little guy just fine. Don't you give it another thought."

Buck and Jim returned a little before noon, the truck loaded down with supplies. They brought diapers and formula, clothes and blankets, along with other necessities for the baby inside and had lunch with their wives.

Buck cleared the table after the meal, washed the dishes, and handed them to his wife to dry. Brandon, in the meantime, slept quietly in his basket in the corner.

After lunch, Buck and Jim were leaving the house to head over to the farm when they spotted a state trooper pulling into the driveway. Buck told Jim to head over without him. As Buck approached the car, the officer got out.

"Buck Marshall?" the trooper asked.

Maggie watched the exchange through the front window as the trooper put his arm on Buck's shoulder and spoke to him. Buck didn't seem to react beyond nodding slowly. After a couple minutes the trooper and he shook hands and the officer was then on his way. Once the trooper's car disappeared from sight, Buck walked slowly back up to the house. Maggie met him at the door.

"What was all that about?" she asked.

Buck led her up to the bedroom. It was there that he told her the news. Their son was dead, and had taken his own life. Maggie broke down into tears, and Buck held her for several minutes, until her sobs subsided. He looked lovingly at her and said that they would handle their son's arrangements the day after tomorrow, but for now he had to go help Jim with something. She nodded, knowing that work would help Buck to settle his own mind. He kissed her on the cheek and left the room. At the bottom of the stairs, he bumped into Nancy.

"Is everything okay?" she asked, concerned.

Buck told her she could go up and Maggie would explain everything. With that, he opened the door and left.

Buck backed his truck up to the Peterson's barn where he and Jim disappeared inside for the rest of the afternoon and into the evening. They only emerged for supper, and afterwards quietly returned to the barn until well after dark. The wives looked together out the window at the glow from the barn wondering what in the world their husbands could be up to. It wasn't until late the next day that they discovered the truth. Buck and Jim came up from the barn late the next afternoon with a crib the two had built. Maggie laid cushions in the bottom and blankets on top of them and placed little Brandon inside. The crib was much like its maker: rough to the appearance but soft and perfectly suited to its purpose on the inside.

The next day, Buck and Maggie tended to their son's final arrangements. There was no funeral and no service for Paul. Years later the only indication he had lived would be a simple stone bearing only his name.

After that, the five settled into a routine quite well considering the tight living conditions. Maggie and Nancy took care of the baby while Buck and Jim worked on repairing and cleaning up the damage from the fire in the Peterson farmhouse. The weather outside was rather mild for February, so the work progressed quickly. It looked like the Petersons might be able to move back in sooner than expected. At least it looked that way — until the blizzard.

A few days before Valentine's, there were two days of wind and snow that forced the five to stay indoors. Nancy had often been sick in the morning, and had missed her monthly cycle by several weeks. She had accepted Maggie's assertion that she was pregnant, and waited for an opportunity to break the news to Jim. Just such an opportunity presented itself one afternoon when Buck and Maggie were taking a nap. Jim and Nancy were alone together with Brandon in the living room, and Jim was enjoying playing peek–a–boo with him. Nancy decided that was the right moment.

"He's cute, isn't he?" She asked coyly.

Jim looked up from the game. "He is. Alert too. He seems more aware of people than I would think most babies are at this age."

Nancy looked down at the knitting in her lap. "What would you think about us having a baby?"

Jim looked at her abruptly. He didn't speak.

"I'm three weeks late. I've been sick a lot in the mornings. Maggie seems to believe, and I'm starting to agree with her — I might be pregnant, Jim."

The emotions on Jim's face moved with his heart, from shock and fear to excitement and pure joy.

"Well, that's great news! I'm going to be a father! I'm going to be a father!" he exclaimed.

"Shhh, shhhh." Nancy tried to quiet her husband. "You'll wake Maggie and Buck!"

But it was too late. They had already woken to the noise and soon joined the two in celebration downstairs. Maggie of course already knew, and Buck was far less surprised than perhaps he should have been.

He simply smiled and said, "Well, isn't that wonderful news?"

Once the storm cleared, Jim and Buck dug out the two homes and then settled back into the routine of working on the farmhouse. The weather turned cold from the February warm spell, and as a result the work on the Peterson farmhouse remained slow. Buck always took a pragmatic approach to the work anyway, insisting that it be done properly regardless of the amount of time it took.

"You have a place to stay until it's done, so it needs to be done right. Besides, you have an extra room you need to put in there now," He said.

"What extra room?" Jim asked.

"Well, the nursery of course. Can't have a baby around without one."

The warmth of spring arrived in April, and mud season began. Jim got the truck stuck in the mud down by the barn one day trying to move lumber up for the farmhouse. It took him, Buck, and the tractor an entire afternoon to get it unstuck. Work on the house was nearly complete, and the Petersons were eager to move back home. Buck and Maggie had been gracious hosts and had epitomized the axiom of "help thy neighbor."

It was late April, and Nancy was just beginning to show when she and Jim were finally able to move back into their home. Buck and Jim had done a fantastic job fixing the place up. Many who had seen the home in the past said it was even better than new. Nancy broke into tears upon seeing the new nursery, which had been added without her knowledge so as to keep it a surprise.

Mud season drew to a close as the rains subsided, the flowers began to bloom, and the earth turned green. A stressful time in the lives of the two families had been faced and conquered. As is the case with challenges however, there are always more to be had around the corner. It is often the way with life that when we stop to catch our breath, fate reminds us to keep moving.

# 6

**F**ormula, diapers, wipes, clothes, toys; everything costs money. It seemed to Maggie that their expenses had doubled since little Brandon came into their lives, and that just may have been the case. The Marshall's bank account was being depleted faster than it was being added to, and that was a concern. Maggie spoke with Buck about their dwindling assets one early summer night over dinner. She wasn't sure how the two could possibly continue to support Brandon in their current financial situation. Buck was still working from home as an auto repair man and doing general handyman work as well, but it simply wasn't bringing in enough money. Her concerns were not falling on deaf ears. Truth be told, Buck had been thinking about the potential for financial problems since Brandon had arrived but hadn't realized money would become so tight this soon. He put on a brave face and told his wife he would take care of things.

The next morning, Buck got in his pickup truck and headed into town looking for work. He drove to the hardware store, parked, and went inside. Speaking with the boy behind the counter, he requested to see the general manager. After some discussion as to what this might be in regard to, the boy went and found him. Buck explained that he was in need of work and would be willing to do just about anything the manager needed done. He said that he was familiar with tools, building, and repair, and would be a valuable asset to the store. The manager stood patiently listening and waited for Buck to finish. Buck was well liked and respected in the community by everyone. This was exceedingly clear because for anyone else, the manager would have cut them off near the beginning to explain that there simply was no work to be had at the store. As it was, he let Buck go on for the better part of five minutes before finally expressing his deepest regret that he couldn't help him. Dejected, Buck left the store.

He was just about to climb back in his pickup and figure out where to head next when he heard a voice behind him.

"Buck?" It was Jim Peterson.

"Jim! How are ya?"

Jim just so happened to be in the store that morning and overheard what Buck told the manager. He was upset that after all the Marshalls had done for them when their house had been damaged by the fire, that Buck hadn't asked him for help when they were in need.

"Well," said Buck, "no need to go bothering you about our problems."

"After what you did for Nancy and me, I owe you and Maggie the world. I have plenty of work around the farm you can help me with and I would be glad to pay you what you need for Brandon."

Buck was skeptical that there was enough work for him to earn what he and Maggie needed, but Jim was insistent.

"With Nancy pregnant, I'm going to need the help. There are horses to water, stalls to clean, hay to cut and bale. Quite frankly, Buck, I'm going to need some help, and it's even better that I can do something to repay you and Maggie for your kindness in the process."

Buck accepted Jim's kind offer and agreed to start the next morning. He climbed back in his pickup and drove home to find Maggie waiting in the kitchen with Brandon. When he told her what had happened at the hardware store her heart lifted. She was glad that not only would their financial stress be lessened, but also that Buck would be nearby should she need him.

Early the next morning, Buck went over to the Peterson farm, and he and Jim made their way down to the barn. Jim went over the daily routine that Buck was to follow, which included letting the horses out to pasture, and ensuring that they were fed and watered. He then offered to show Buck around the farmland. Buck realized, to some chagrin, that in all the time he'd lived in his home, through the different owners of the farm next door, he had never walked any land outside of the woods across the stream. He accepted, and the two set off.

The Peterson farm was separated into four distinct areas. The first area included the house, the barn, and a small paddock for the horses. The paddock was just east of the barn and accessible out the back door. This was the area where Buck would spend the majority of his time working. He would have to clean stalls, do some repair work, and generally care for the horses.

The second area was southeast of the paddock and adjacent to the pond south of the barn. This was the pasture–land where the horses could run freely and exercise. Buck would be responsible for seeing that the fence around the pasture was properly maintained and that the horses didn't get out.

The third area included three hay fields: one each to the north, east, and south of the pasture. Each was separated by a belt of trees and a stone wall. In all, the Petersons had close to 50 acres of hay fields which needed to be cut and baled every summer. While this wouldn't be a daily activity for Buck, he would be expected to help out during haying and baling, as well as in storing in the top of the barn what wasn't going to be sold.

The final area of the Peterson farm was the one area where Buck was most familiar. On the south side of the stream sat the woodlands that used to be cattle fields. Two owners before the Petersons had kept cattle in that area, but it had since grown up and been covered in trees. Remnants of the old cattle wade could still be seen down at the stream, but a small bridge had been erected nearby for Buck to cross with the tractor. It was in these woods that Buck Marshall cut his firewood every year. The woods now extended from where the cattle fields used to stand all the way to the end of the Peterson farm, where they had stood as far back as history could remember. In those far woods was excellent hunting for white–tailed deer and the occasional rabbit.

Jim and Buck walked the land slowly, talking about all that had happened since December the year before. Jim tried to broach the topic of Paul's note subtly, as subtly as one can do with such a subject. Buck was reluctant to talk about it himself, but was satisfied to let Jim give his thoughts.

"It must be hard without any explanation." He said. "I know his wife passed, which has to be difficult, but to give up… I can't imagine the state of mind. She's buried down in Cambridge, right?"

Buck slowly nodded in agreement and let Jim continue. But rather than continue, Jim posed a question.

"Were you and Paul close?"

Buck let out a sigh. The two men passed from the pasture into the first hay field and made their way towards a break in the trees to the second. Neither spoke for several minutes until Buck broke the silence.

"We were close only in so much as we were family. We never quite understood each othah."

Jim started to say something, but stopped himself. When a man speaks as little as Buck Marshall, it's best to listen when he's willing to talk.

"Life will often try to break a man, and it will if he lets it happen," Buck continued. "Paul broke. It's a terrible thing, but it brought Brandon to us. I am thankful for that much."

Jim wanted to press Buck for more. Did he forgive Paul? Why didn't they understand one another? Why hadn't they had a funeral for their son? He had so many questions, but knew better than to ask any of them. The two walked without speaking through the second hay field and through the belt of trees into the third. Eventually, the silence was too much for Jim, and he had to ask if Buck and Maggie would be allowed to keep Brandon.

Buck again was slow to answer the question. He admitted that the authorities had found a will in Paul's things, naming Buck and Maggie as legal guardians. Adoption was raised as an option for the two, should they choose to pursue it.

"Are you going to pursue it?" Jim asked.

Buck looked down and slowly nodded. He didn't like the idea of anyone else raising his grandchild. The very night Brandon had arrived on the doorstep Buck had made that decision. The decision to keep Brandon at all costs. It was that decision that Maggie had read in his eyes and had accepted without a word.

The two men came to the far end of the third hay field, and Jim started to turn and head back towards the south end of the pasture, but Buck stopped.

"What's the matter, Buck?" Jim asked.

Buck nodded his head towards the woods that used to be cattle fields on the southwest of the farm.

"No reason to go in there." Jim said. "We don't use that for anything."

"Sure you do." Buck replied. "That's where we get the wood for wintah. Why don't we take a look at it?"

"All right." Jim said, and the two turned and headed for the woods.

Buck walked even slower than he had through the fields and Jim wondered if he still had something on his mind. Every now and again Buck would stop and look up at the trees as if deep in thought. Jim was just starting to think what a strange person Buck Marshall was when Buck decided to speak.

"I've been thinking about the trees a lot lately."

"Been thinking about how many we need to cut for winter?" Jim asked.

Buck shook his head.

"No, just about how they are — their charactah," He continued looking up at the trees around him.

"Their character?"

"Yeah, their charactah."

With that, Buck looked at Jim and began walking again towards the farm. Jim just chuckled to himself and starting walking alongside Buck towards the edge of the woods and the stream.

"Well, Buck, you think this arrangement will work for you?"

"Sure," Buck said as he nodded.

The two soon emerged from the woods and crossed the small bridge near the old cattle wade and made their way back up to the barn. Jim left Buck with instructions to repair a section of fence they had seen down in the pasture and headed back up to the farmhouse. Buck gathered some tools and set to work mending the fence. He was glad to have some work to do and to have a way to earn some money to take care of Brandon. The best part, he thought, was that he could continue his job of fixing cars and doing handiwork on the side without neglecting his work for Jim and Nancy. The summer certainly looked like it was going to be a blessing for both households.

Jim never had cause to regret hiring Buck. He did quality work and he did it fast. In fact, Buck kept the farm running so smoothly that Jim hardly helped out at all. He spent most of his time with Nancy, helping her during her pregnancy. When it came time to hay the fields, Buck worked like the equivalent of three men, and Jim found they finished the work in a quarter of the time it would normally have taken him. Jim was amazed that a man many years his senior seemed to have an unlimited supply of energy.

In reality, Buck returned home every evening exhausted, but satisfied with the work he had done. His auto repair work and job as a general handyman had gone better than expected too. He and Maggie had built their savings back up, and there was little doubt they would make it easily through the winter.

As summer began drawing to a close, Buck turned his attention to the woods and to storing enough firewood for the winter. He wasn't sure why, but he felt in his bones that this winter was going to be colder than normal. He was glad the loft was full of hay for the horses and that they would have plenty to eat. He also knew that with a newborn in the house, the Petersons would need more firewood than was typical. Of course, Brandon was less than a year old as well, and they too would need to keep their house a little warmer than normal. Everything suggested that Buck needed to get started harvesting wood, or they wouldn't have enough. His building the shed on the side of the house now seemed more like providence and less like the convenience it had merely been meant to be.

# 7

A brisk wind blew in out of the north, sending a chill whistling through the fall foliage. Through the cold, the hills
burned red and orange from the color of the changing leaves.
From an opening in the forest, Buck emerged riding a green John
Deere tractor, towing a trailer laden with wood he had cut for
winter. An icy blast rode down and met him face–on, causing him
to shiver slightly and pull up his collar around his neck. The cold
spell had come early that year and that day it was particularly
fierce.

In the distance, smoke poured from the chimneys both at the
Marshall house and the Peterson farm. Buck steered the tractor
across the bridge that spanned the stream south of the property
and up the hill. He stopped the John Deere next to the wood shed
he'd built, and began unloading the wood one piece at a time.
Next to the shed was a chopping block and his old axe with a
worn handle laid against it. He would place each log on the block,
split it, and place it neatly in the shed.

With the cold spell the two families had begun burning wood
for heat earlier than normal that year and Buck was working to
catch up. As the cold grew, so did his fear that winter would

arrive before he had a chance to finish. He would have to work faster to make sure both homes could be heated until spring. Normally in such a situation, Jim Peterson would have been glad to give Buck a hand, but his wife Nancy was very pregnant and nearing the time of her delivery. Buck understood. Jim needed to stay at home with his wife while awaiting the arrival of their first child. In the meantime, Buck continued logging, cutting, splitting, and stacking.

When his most recent load filled the wood shed next to the house to capacity, Buck removed his gloves and set off on foot to the Peterson farmhouse. As always, he was determined to officially agree to their yearly arrangement to store wood in the barn.

Buck knocked on the door of the farmhouse and he heard Jim yell from inside, "Come in." He opened the door and entered into the living room. The wooden floorboards creaked under his steps as he walked. He found Jim and Nancy sitting on the couch. Nancy was knitting with a ball of yarn in her lap, and Jim was reading but put his book down as Buck entered.

"Buck! How's it going? Getting enough wood stored? With this cold I'm afraid we're going through it as fast as you're cutting it."

"I think I've caught up. The shed beside the house is full and I wanted to ask you about storing more in the barn. You're welcome to what you need for the house, of course."

"Buck, you've worked here all summer. You know you're more than welcome to store whatever you need in the barn. And we're happy to let you cut what you need from the woods when you're stocking for both of us for the winter. You really don't have to ask."

"Well, I feel bettah about the whole thing hearing it from you every fall. Sometime folks get into a deal they can't get out of, and it can certainly put a strain on neighbahs if that happens. I wouldn't feel right without checking first."

Jim smiled. "That's fine, Buck. Why don't you…"

At that moment Nancy caught her breath and a put her hand on her belly.

Startled, Jim asked, "Nance, you all right?"

"I think my water broke!" She exclaimed.

Jim helped his wife to her feet, and sure enough the spot on the couch where she had been sitting was wet. Buck helped Jim get Nancy to the car, and husband and wife drove off to the hospital. Buck promised to look after the place until they got back and keep the house warm for their arrival.

Buck headed home and told Maggie the exciting news. She made soup for lunch, and talked excitedly while Buck ate. Maggie loved the idea of having two babies around, so little Brandon would have a playmate, and wondered whether it would be a boy or a girl. Buck smiled as he ate. He enjoyed seeing his wife's excitement, but didn't offer any thoughts of his own. When he finished, he rose and washed the bowls and silverware and handed them to Maggie to dry and put away. He kissed her on the cheek and said that he was going back to work. He hoped to get a couple loads of wood into the barn before the end of the day.

Buck managed to haul two full trailer loads of wood into the barn and stack them in one of the horse stalls before dusk. He worked after dark by the light in the barn to split about half of it and move it onto a separate pile, ready for use. When he returned home, Maggie had a hot dinner ready and on the table. The two ate and Maggie continued to talk about the excitement of having another baby around as Buck and Brandon, sitting in his high chair, listened. After dinner, Buck washed the dishes and handed them to Maggie to dry and put away. He kissed her on the cheek and headed for his chair in front of the fire when Maggie stopped him.

"I was thinking about heading in to the hospital to see how Nancy is doing."

Buck nodded and told her to take the truck. He decided that he would stay with Brandon and keep an eye on the Peterson's. It was after seven when Maggie pulled out of the drive and headed to the hospital to see how Nancy Peterson was getting along.

Buck settled into his seat in front of the fire and placed Brandon in his playpen on the floor next to him. He was weary from the work he'd done all day, and his mind wandered over the events that had taken place in less than a year. Life was moving with the fury of a galloping horse, bounding over hedges, crashing through streams, disturbing the serenity of the surface of the water, and pounding the ground underfoot. How could any man manage to grasp hold of the reins and slow the thunderous rush? It seemed to him something wild and unstoppable that would run until it tired on its own. He resigned himself to the fact that the world around a man could change rapidly, and that it would change the man too, if the man let it. That's when Brandon began to cry. Like fall leaves from the branches on a windy day, Buck was loosed from his thoughts and blown back to the moment. Buck Marshall got up from his chair, bent over and picked up his grandson.

As he rocked Brandon in front of the fire, Buck Marshall set himself against the roaring charge of life. He would remain unchanged. He would stand resolute against the trials that life presented him and would be the stability his family needed. Brandon's bright blue eyes were still wet with tears when Buck looked down.

"Now don't you worry, Bud. Life can be hard, but I can be harder. You just quit your worrying. You're in good hands."

Brandon looked up at his grandfather and stopped crying. Buck continued to slowly rock him side to side.

"That a boy, Bud. You just go to sleep and let the world change if it wants to."

Maggie returned after midnight to find Buck asleep in his chair with Brandon in his arms. She smiled and quietly took Brandon, and carried him upstairs to his crib. When Maggie returned downstairs, Buck stirred in his chair and woke. Maggie shared the news that the Petersons had given birth to a healthy baby girl whom they had named Teresa. Nancy was tired, but doing very well. The doctors had said that if everything went well she and Teresa would be able to come home the day after tomorrow. Maggie's eyes widened with excitement as she spoke.

"And of course, it's already tomorrow, so the day after is just one day away!"

Buck smiled at his wife's excitement. He suggested that they do what they could to make the Peterson's return as stress–free as possible. Buck said he would have a good fire going so that the house would be plenty warm for mom and baby; and he suggested Maggie make a couple of casseroles to put in the fridge because, as he put it, "New moms don't want to be thinking about what to make for suppah."

Buck headed up to bed and easily fell back asleep. Maggie knew she was far too excited to sleep, so she began cooking then and there.

The next day was extremely busy for both Buck and Maggie. Buck returned to the woods and made several more trips with firewood and stored it in the barn. He split almost two trailer loads and stacked it with the rest. He then stocked the house with wood, so that he could have a nice warm fire for Jim and Nancy when they returned home with Teresa. Maggie, meanwhile had slept for about four hours before getting up and resuming her cooking. She planned on having a week's worth of lunches and dinners prepared and in the fridge for when the Peterson's got home. Brandon helped out by sitting quietly in his chair and not making any fuss at all. That night, all three of the Marshalls slept soundly from exhaustion, but they woke early with anticipation of what was to come that day.

It was a little before noon when Maggie saw the Peterson's car coming down the dirt lane. She called to Buck, who picked up Brandon from his playpen saying, "Come on, Bud, time to go meet your new neighbah."

The Marshalls met the Petersons in the driveway next door and there were hugs, handshakes, and congratulations all around. The six went inside the Peterson farmhouse and into the living room. Nancy sat on the couch, holding baby Teresa with Maggie sitting next to her. Jim and Buck stood to the side talking, while Brandon crawled around on the living room carpet. Brandon looked up intently at his grandmother sitting next to Nancy and the newborn. Maggie, seeing him said, "Brandon, would you like to see the baby?"

Brandon crawled to the couch, pulled himself up and looked at the bundle in Nancy's lap.

Nancy looked down and said, "This is baby Teresa."

Brandon pointed at the bundle and spoke for the first time. "Bay — bee."

Everyone stood shocked and amazed.

"Yes, baby!" Maggie exclaimed! "That's the baby!"

"Bay — bee," Brandon said again.

There were smiles and laughs all around the room. Brandon just continued to stare, and then reached up with his little hand and touched Teresa lightly on the nose with his finger. "Bay — bee." He stood transfixed by the newborn.

Once the surprise settled in the room, Maggie and Buck had the chance to tell the Petersons what they had done. Nancy was overwhelmed by the amount of food Maggie had prepared and was insistent that she had done too much. Maggie waved her off saying it was simply the neighborly thing to do. Jim was most appreciative of the wood that Buck had moved into the cellar for the stove. He was grateful that he would be able to stay in the house and help Nancy for a week or so before worrying about splitting more wood or going out to shop for food. Nancy suggested that the Marshalls would have to spend Christmas at the Peterson farmhouse that year and that she would cook a big Christmas dinner as a thank–you for everything they had done. Jim nodded his agreement. Buck and Maggie could never refuse such an offer, so the matter was settled.

Buck couldn't help but think how quickly four neighbors had become six. He wondered how much more could change and how they all could possibly keep up.

# 8

A day is just a day. No single day has any meaning apart from that we each choose to give it. Still, we schedule our lives around those days that we feel hold meaning for us: anniversaries, birthdays, the Fourth of July, and Christmas. We dread days that hold negative significance such as the death of a parent, or a tragic event in history. We project our own feelings onto the days in our lives to fill those days with meaning. How we remember a day will shape our opinion of it for many years, or in some cases, for the rest of our lives.

For Brandon Marshall, the twenty–eighth of November could be remembered as the worst day of his young life. It was the day he was born, but it was also the day he lost his mother and the day that his chances of being raised by his parents in a typical home in Massachusetts faded. Just one year into his life however, Brandon's birthday became a day of celebration: it became the day that his adoption by Buck and Maggie Marshall became official. A day is just a day, but for Brandon Marshall, the twenty–eighth of November would henceforth be a day remembered both for tragedy and for joy.

The legal process had been both lengthy and frustrating for Buck and Maggie, but they were determined to legally adopt their grandson. The one saving grace was that they had been named the legal guardians for Brandon in Paul's will. Still, the government was thorough, and to the Marshalls it seemed to take forever. But finally, confirmation came. They would be able to adopt their grandson.

Maggie wanted to have a first birthday party for Brandon. Buck felt it was silly and unnecessary for a child of one who would have little recollection of such an event. He told Maggie that he thought she wanted the party more for herself than for Brandon.

"What difference does it make? We have reason to celebrate!" Maggie said.

She told Buck to ask the Petersons to come over for dinner and cake, and then she set herself to baking. Buck walked over to the Peterson farmhouse and invited the family over for a birthday celebration, which Jim and Nancy accepted.

The party was a pleasant affair. The two families drank, laughed, and enjoyed each other's company much in the same way an extended family would. Conversation centered on the excitement of Brandon's official adoption and how wonderful it would be for the two children to grow up together.

Buck and Jim moved on to discuss the onset of winter and work to be done around the farm. Jim was worried that if the winter was indeed as cold as everyone seemed to fear it was going to be, it would be difficult to provide enough fresh, unfrozen, water for the horses. It wasn't a problem getting water from the farmhouse spigot, or to cut a hole in the ice when the pond froze and pull water from there. The problem was keeping the water from freezing in the trough out in the paddock. Buck stroked his chin, thoughtfully, pondering the dilemma.

In the past, Jim would water the horses in the barn, but he had a problem with colic from dehydration. The horses simply didn't get enough to drink one bucket at a time. It would be fine to continue doing so on really cold nights, but it wasn't a long–term solution. Buck said he had an idea and that he would start working on it that coming week. He wouldn't say any more about it, but Jim knew that if Buck thought it would work, it probably would.

Meanwhile, the ladies discussed everything baby related: feeding, sleeping patterns, changing diapers, rashes, formula, and the like. Teresa woke part way through the conversation and began to cry. Nancy picked her up and fed her while she and Maggie continued talking. It wasn't until Maggie smelled something burning that she realized she'd overcooked the biscuits. She was devastated, but Buck just chuckled.

"It's all right Maggie, that's how I like them," he said.

The four adults sat down to a meal of burnt biscuits, roast beef, potatoes, carrots, peas, and squash. Maggie sat at the end of the table and fed Brandon, sitting in his high chair, mashed peas and squash. He didn't seem to care for either and ended up with more on his face than in his stomach. He followed that up with a face full of cake and frosting, managing to get a good deal of that on the floor as well. No one seemed to mind however, as the mood was generally cheerful. Maggie offered their guests coffee after the meal, and the whole party once again moved into the living room and took its place in front of the fire, which Buck had stoked to a roaring glow. Together, the two families were the picture of contentment.

Soon the conversation shifted to talk of the holidays, and Nancy reiterated their invitation for the Marshalls to join them Christmas Day for dinner. Maggie graciously accepted once again, but insisted they would not be coming empty handed. She said that she would bring a couple of pies which she heartily promised to keep an eye on and not let burn. The whole group had a good chuckle, and the matter was settled. Nancy bundled baby Teresa against the cold, and the Petersons made their way home, satisfied and content.

Maggie saw the Petersons to the door, and then she returned to the living room where Buck was still sitting by the fire, holding Brandon. Buck was dangling something on a gold chain, and the little boy was laughing playfully and trying to grab it. Maggie walked up behind them and saw a gold pocket watch that had certainly seen better days spinning in the air.

"What in the world are you doing with that, Buck Marshall?" she asked.

"It's my present for the little guy."

She chuckled. "What is a baby going to do with an old pocket watch?"

Buck glanced up thoughtfully and shrugged.

"Where did you get it from?" she asked.

"My box of things from the army," Buck said. "The one in the upstairs closet."

"Does that old watch even work anymore?"

"Depends on what you want it to do," he answered.

Brandon giggled happily as he batted the watch side to side. Maggie just sighed, and left the room to clean up. The watch glimmered in the firelight, and the worn letters of an inscription could just barely be made out as Buck watched it swing back and forth.

"*Tempus Edax Rerum*," it read in Latin. "Time, devourer of all things."

The next morning Jim and Nancy Peterson woke to the sound of loud thumping outside. Jim glanced out the bedroom window which overlooked the paddock and the barn behind the house. Outside the barn, Buck Marshall was swinging a sledgehammer to drive a post into the ground near the horses' watering trough.

"What is it?" Nancy asked.

Jim turned, held his hands up and replied, "Buck." No more explanation was necessary. Jim said he would get dressed and head down to see what the older man was doing after breakfast.

The thumping was replaced by sawing and hammering as Jim and Nancy sat to eat. Eventually, Jim poured himself a second cup of coffee, put on his boots and jacket and headed out the door to walk down to the barn. As Jim approached the paddock, the new construction around the water trough was plainly evident. Buck had built a wooden frame around the outside of the trough, leaving nearly a foot–wide gap which he had filled with a mixture of hay and manure. Jim was taking it all in when Buck came strolling out of the barn carrying another large wooden object.

"Getting an early start, are we, Buck?" Jim said.

"No sense doing latah what can be done now." The truth was Buck hadn't slept well with the plans for his creation rolling around in his mind. The thoughts had tossed and turned in his head as Buck had tossed and turned in bed. It had gotten so bad that finally Maggie's frustration with him had driven Buck out of bed and to the kitchen where he sketched his idea on a piece of scrap paper. As soon as the first light of dawn had begun to peak over the eastern horizon, Buck had dressed and headed down to the barn to get started.

"Looks pretty good," Jim said. "The idea is to insulate the trough so the water won't freeze, right?"

Buck smiled and nodded. He then placed the wooden object in his hands on top. It was a large wooden lid for the structure, and it had a hinged section that allowed it to be opened when the horses were out and needing to drink but could be closed at other times to hold in some heat.

"Very clever, Buck," Jim said. "How'd you come up with this?"

"To be honest, I got a little chilly last night when I got in bed. So, I got up and got anothah blanket."

"Well, it looks like it'll work just fine, Buck. Good job," Jim said.

The structure worked very well, as it turned out. Most mornings there would only be a thin layer of ice that needed to be broken so the horses could drink, and for all but the very coldest of days and nights the trough remained useable.

The days passed smoothly until Christmas Eve arrived. Buck had found two suitable Christmas trees in the forest and put one up in each family's home. The trees were decorated, and stockings were hung by the chimneys to complete the tradition. With small children in the house, both families felt it was important to provide a good old–fashioned Christmas experience, even though the children were far too young to remember it.

On Christmas Day, the Marshalls trudged through several inches of freshly fallen snow to the Peterson farmhouse for Christmas dinner and to open presents. Maggie carried little Brandon, bundled up and looking more like a sack of potatoes than a baby boy. Buck balanced four pies in his arms as he walked, his eyes twinkling with laughter. He had told his wife that four pies seemed far too many for four adults and two babies, but she had brushed him off as being ridiculous. After all, it's Christmas!

Nancy greeted them at the door and then quickly called for Jim to come help get some of the pies from Buck.

"Oh Maggie, four pies? It's just the four of us and the two children. I think you may have done too much. How will we ever eat all of this?" Nancy asked.

Buck smiled as he looked at his wife. She shot him a disapproving glance and said matter–of–factly, "I'm sure my husband will do his part to see them eaten."

"And so will I," said Jim as he made his way over to the others and took two of the pies from Buck's arms. Buck just continued smiling as he carried the pies into the kitchen with Jim.

Soon after that, Nancy and Maggie were in the kitchen with Teresa, bustling here and there to get things ready. Jim and Buck sat quietly in the living room watching Brandon play on the floor.

"You'd think our husbands could help out a little here in the kitchen," Nancy said.

"Would you really want them to? Who knows what they'd destroy," Maggie replied.

Nancy cocked her head and said, "Hmmm, who was it that burned the biscuits?"

The men heard the laughter coming from the kitchen and looked at each other. "Do you think we should go in there?" Jim asked.

Buck shook his head. "Whatevah that's about, it doesn't involve us," he said. "We are fah safah where we are."

"Safer?"

"When women are laughing, you're probably safe. It's when they get quiet that things get dangerous. We best not interrupt the laughtah."

It wasn't long before the women said that dinner was ready, and the men joined them in the dining room. Nancy had truly outdone herself for this Christmas meal. There was a glistening ham which Jim eyed greedily as he carved slices off of it. There were mashed potatoes, carrots, squash, green beans, apple sauce, and an assortment of other vegetables and goodies. Maggie's four pies sat on a small side table letting off a sweet aroma of apples, pecans, pumpkin, and spices. Baby Brandon tried a little of everything but was not a fan of the green beans, throwing most of them on the floor and spitting out the rest. Teresa stuck to the carrots and squash. The adults filled themselves to the brim with delicious food until they felt about ready to burst. It was then that Maggie starting putting slices of pie in front of each of them. Buck was about to wave her off when she shot him another glance and he relented.

"Looks delicious, Maggie," he said.

After dessert, the gentlemen helped to clear the table, and Nancy decided to let everything sit in the kitchen for a while and as she put it, "Let the dinner settle before cleaning up." Everyone made their way back into the living room and took a seat watching the fire.

"Did you bring over the presents?" Maggie asked Buck.

"I was carrying pies."

"Well, why don't you go back over to the house and get the presents and bring them over."

"Yes, dear," Buck said as a smirk crossed his face.

Buck rose from his seat and started putting on his boots and jacket at the door.

"Why don't you give him a hand, Jim?" Nancy said.

Jim looked at his wife and then pleadingly at Buck for an out. Buck's eyes twinkled and he just nodded.

"Yes, dear," Jim said.

Jim joined Buck at the door and donned his own boots and jacket and the neighbors opened the door and headed back over to the Marshall house. The two men walked in silence, Buck with a slight grin on his face and Jim a look of slight annoyance at having had to leave the comfort of his seat in front of the fire. The two men returned to the farmhouse shortly with armfuls of packages and presents. Buck then motioned for Jim to join him in the kitchen. Buck washed all of the dishes and handed them to Jim to dry and put away. When Jim asked why they were doing all this, Buck asked him if he heard any laughter from the living room. Jim shook his head and Buck looked at him as if to say, "There's your answer."

The men were just finishing up when the ladies could be heard chuckling.

"Is that our cue?" Jim asked.

Buck nodded and the two men, having finished the dishes, rejoined the women in the living room. And Jim was finally able to settle back into his seat in front of the fire. The women were chuckling at Brandon attempting to pull the paper off of one of his presents. When the men had once again sat back down, Nancy asked them where'd they had been all that time.

"Just doing dishes," Buck said.

"You two did the dishes? Jim hates doing dishes."

"Well, he only dried them and put them away," Buck said eyes twinkling.

Nancy laughed at that, and Buck shot Jim a quick satisfied glance. Everyone exchanged gifts, and there was a great deal of laughter and smiling all around. Years later no one could really remember who gave or got what gift, what was said by whom, or really any particular details; but everyone agreed it was a wonderful happy day, and that memory was cherished by each of them.

It is often that way with memories. It's far easier to remember the feelings than what was said or what was done or any other specific. Thinking back on a cherished memory evokes smells and emotions. The two families remembered that Christmas for the warmth and the happiness, the smells of spices, good food, and the fire roaring in the fireplace. The recalled the laughter that filled the living room and the love that filled their hearts. Years later, when asked to remember that day, the women always said they remembered the laughter. Jim would say he remembered doing the dishes. Buck would say he remembered the pie, and then he would smile.

And so, such a day can mark both an ending and a new beginning. A day is just a day, but that particular Christmas Day marked the end of the early trials for the two families and the start of a long stretch of routine that accompanies raising small children.

# 9

Time is a constant. Every second passes at the same speed. Every minute — every hour — lasts as long as any other. Every day, every week, and every year counts the same as the one before. Yet as we live those seconds, count those minutes, pass those hours, and live those days, weeks, and years, there are moments when time seems to drag slowly and painfully. Paul Marshall had experienced as much the day Brandon was born and his mother died. Anticipation, excitement, dread, and any sense of wonder about the unknown seem to precipitate the phenomenon of time slowing.

There is, however, an opposite effect to be found from routine, monotony, and foreknowledge of what tomorrow brings. In such a case, years can fly by to the point that one looks up and wonders where the time went. It often seems that way when raising small children, who depend upon routine for comfort. And so it seemed on the small dirt lane where Brandon Marshall and Teresa Peterson were growing more every day. More than five years passed from that Christmas meal the families had shared together. If you were to ask any of them, it seemed like yesterday. It wasn't until they looked up and realized that Brandon would soon be attending his first day of school, that it really hit any of them just how far they had come and how much the children had grown. Where had the time gone, indeed?

The farm was doing wonderfully with Buck working as hard as ever. The Petersons had made enough money to purchase an additional one hundred and fifty acres to the east of the hay fields. The land was forested, and as the trees were thinning from gathering firewood in the "back woods" as Buck called them, they began clearing land on the new acreage instead. As the land was cleared of trees, it was prepped and used for growing a variety of vegetables that could then be sold to generate more revenue. The new land was only partially cleared in those first few years, so there was plenty of acreage left for firewood. On the cleared land the Petersons grew corn and pumpkins mainly; but they had added a sizable garden closer to the farmhouse where they now grew potatoes, cucumbers, and any number of other smaller vegetables. Of course, they still had the hay fields and the barn where they continued to keep a couple of horses, but they had added two milking cows and several pigs. There was a new small chicken coop beside the barn as well, in which they kept some laying hens for fresh eggs. There had been so much to do, in fact, that even Buck Marshall couldn't keep up with it all. The Petersons had to hire a young man to help Buck with the day–to–day chores and maintenance. Stanley, a lanky, local boy had been brought on and was working out seemingly well.

Further down the dirt lane there was a small blue house, and a family had moved in with a son about Brandon's age. Everyone thought it would be wonderful that the children would have another playmate. The boy's name was Lance, and he was big for his age. He had dark hair and dark eyes and always seemed to be wearing a scowl on his round face. Lance's parents kept to themselves, and his father was often away on business. That left him alone with his mother, who sent him outside whenever she had the opportunity. He was often over for play dates as the children started to get a little older, especially in the summer.

Across the road from the Marshall house, a small yellow trailer–style home had been brought in. The man who bought the land and made his home there was older and rarely left the house. His name was Malcolm LaVerdier, but no one knew much more than that about him. Mr. LaVerdier had a mutt that he kept on a run next to the house. The dog was ornery and barked incessantly. It seemed to have taken on the personality of its owner and would growl at anyone that got too close. Buck had tried to be welcoming to Mr. LaVerdier when he first moved in, but the old man had snapped at Buck's invitation to dinner saying that he didn't need "handouts" from anyone. The statement seemed ironic to Buck when he saw the church food pantry delivering canned goods to the old man on a weekly basis. Buck would just shrug and say, "Can't choose your neighbahs, I guess."

Buck's auto repair work, combined with his work on the farm, had left him with little free time. He had become so busy in fact, that he'd built a garage to work out of on the west side of the driveway. He put in a small wood–burning stove, so that he could continue to work through the winter months. There was more time to do repair work then, since that was the slow time of year on the farm. The downside was that Buck Marshall never stopped working. Maggie routinely said that he was sure to "work himself to death," but Buck felt like working kept him young. As Brandon got bigger, Buck would let him help in the garage by handing Buck tools as he lay under a car that he was fixing. The two of them would walk back into the house covered in grease, and Maggie would have a fit sending them both to the bathroom before they tracked dirt all over the house. Buck would smile and Brandon would laugh as she chased them through the house to the sink to get clean. Brandon had taken to calling Buck "Pa," short for "Grandpa," which suited him just fine.

Teresa was growing into a precocious little girl. She had straight auburn hair just like her mother and her father's hazel eyes. She was polite and mannerly nearly as soon as she could speak and was known for admonishing Brandon any time he did something she felt was inappropriate. She would help her mother with daily chores and would have a near meltdown if something was what she deemed to be out of place. She was tidy and neat to the point of being obsessive about it. If something she was wearing got a smudge of dirt on it, she would immediately have to change. Buck always found it amusing when she would follow Brandon into the garage and look disgusted at the filth around her. To see a girl at four years old needing to return home for clean clothes because she got a little grease on her overalls made him chuckle.

And so, the two children balanced each other out — Brandon always acting foolish and trying to get the two of them dirty and Teresa always trying to keep him in line and never letting him get her too messy. Teresa didn't like Lance as he spent most of his summer days outside and his clothes would be covered in all manner of dirt, leaves, and mud on a regular basis. He was rude and bossy, always trying to tell the other two what to do. She tended to avoid him whenever possible. Brandon, on the other hand, got along great with their young neighbor. The two of them would splash around in the stream and come back soggy, wet messes. Maggie would sigh and strip Brandon down and throw him in the tub to get clean. Buck would chuckle and say that's how it should be for little boys.

It was in those first years that Brandon's nickname "Bud" cemented itself into the lexicon of those that knew him. Of course, it was Buck who first referred to the little boy as "Bud" when he was just a baby. Over time, the name caught on. The only two people in his life who still referred to him as "Brandon" were his grandmother, "Gran" as he called her, and Teresa, who insisted on formality in most of her interactions anyway. Bud, as was his way, would refer to Teresa as "Reese," which annoyed her to no end.

"Mother," she would complain to her mom. "He calls me 'Reese.' That is *not* my name."

"He's just teasing you, Teresa," Nancy would say.

"Well, I don't like it!"

The first realization that Bud would be attending school happened around his sixth birthday. Jim and Nancy had come over for cake and coffee, and Teresa and Lance had been over most of the day to play with Bud. The boys were racing around the house making a general mess of things, while Teresa followed them telling them they needed to put everything back. It was Buck that verbalized the thought first.

"I suppose we'll be sending Bud to school next fall."

"That's right," said Maggie. "After all, he's six now. Will you and Jim be sending Teresa? She turns six this fall also."

"We might wait a year," Jim replied.

"Really?" said Maggie. "She seems so mature for her age already."

"Oh yes," said Nancy. "She's a grown woman when it comes to being organized and bossing people around, but she's got a ways to go to understand how to listen to an adult other than her mother and father. She's very opinionated and extremely stubborn. We think waiting a year wouldn't hurt."

"It is too bad she won't be in a class with Bud though," Jim said.

"That might be for the best," Buck said. The other three looked at him curiously waiting for him to continue, but he just left his thought there.

Teresa had overheard the adults talking and got very excited. She quickly grabbed the boys and pulled them into a side room and began whispering hurriedly.

"Brandon! You're going to school next year. Isn't that great? I think so. I wish I was going too. Think of all the great stuff you'll learn and all the other kids you get to play with. I don't want to wait a whole year before I go. I wish I could go with you. Aren't you excited?"

"It's not a big deal," Lance interjected. "I go to school and it's nothing special. Just adults telling you what to do, and a bunch of learning stuff. Pretty boring if you ask me."

"No one asked you, Lance," Teresa said. "Brandon, aren't you excited?"

Bud looked from Teresa to Lance. Lance rolled his eyes and made a face.

"Umm, I dunno," Bud said. "Sounds kind of silly. I bet it is boring like Lance said."

"Ugh, boys," Teresa said, and she stormed off to be with the adults.

In actuality, Bud was a little excited and very nervous. He didn't know anything about school. When he tried to ask Lance about it, the older boy always just shrugged it off as if it was nothing and he didn't want to discuss it. Bud couldn't ask Teresa about it. First of all, she was younger than he was, so he should know more than her. Besides that, he had said he wasn't interested and it sounded boring. If he asked her she would know that he was more interested than he had said he was. As spring approached, he began to ask Maggie questions.

"Gran, how come I have to go to school? What do kids do there? What will I learn? Do I have to go? What if I don't like my teacher? Can't I just stay with you and Pa on the farm?"

Maggie answered all of his questions patiently. School was important so that he could grow up and learn everything he needed to know. Kids at school learn new things, play games, and have lots of fun. He'd learn reading, math, writing, science, history and lots of other things. Yes, he had to go. He'd like his teacher just fine, she was sure. No, he couldn't just stay on the farm.

"But why do I have to go?" Brandon asked pouting.

"You have to go so you can learn and grow up to be successful and a great man like your grandfather."

With each passing day, Brandon's apprehension for what was to come the day he had to go to school grew. His grandparents' excitement grew as well. After more than five years of time racing past them, it once again slowed to a crawl as the snow began melting and spring struggled forth over Bud's last summer before school.

To make matters worse, a late March snowstorm dumped almost two feet, which meant less time for Bud playing outside and more time cooped up thinking about school. He spent nearly a week sitting by the living room window just watching the new snow slowly shrink until a few tufts of grass could once again be seen poking through. He longed for an April warm spell so that he could get outside and try to pry some more information about school out of Lance. In the meantime, Bud's grandmother continued to try and assuage his fears about going to school.

"It's going to be fun, Brandon. You'll get up, have breakfast with Pa and me, get dressed, and then walk down the road and ride the bus to school."

"What bus? I have to ride a bus? You and Pa will ride too, right?"

"No Brandon, we don't ride the bus."

"I ride the bus alone?"

"It's ok. Lance will be riding on the same bus with you."

"He will?"

"Yes."

She smiled at her grandson who seemed comforted by the thought of a familiar face riding the bus with him. Bud did feel a little bit better, but he wanted to talk to Lance about all of this;

especially this whole bus business. It would have to wait though, as the snow was still lingering and there was another cold snap due over the next couple of days. Time seemed to crawl; and for a six–year–old boy who desperately wants something, even answers, every minute can seem like hours. But just like little boys, spring can't wait forever. Its arrival is inevitable.

# 10

**W**hen winter finally broke, it broke fast and hard. The weather went from the dreary thirties to a weekend of beautiful sun and temperatures approaching sixty degrees. The last of the snow melted rapidly and the result was a sloppy, muddy mess on the dirt lane. Puddles and mud are natural attractors for little boys, and Bud and Lance were drawn to it from their houses like moths to a flame.

At the Peterson house, Teresa was admiring a beautiful new light blue dress that her parents had bought her for Easter Sunday. She begged her mother to let her wear it outside in the beautiful weather.

"Easter isn't until next weekend, Teresa," her mother said.

"Please, Mother! I'll stay clean."

"I know you will, but don't you think we should save it for Easter?"

"It's so pretty. I don't want to wait. I want to wear it now. It's warm out. I'll just sit on the front steps and read. Please, Mother?"

"All right Teresa, but just for a little while."

Teresa sprang up to her room, put on her new dress and picked out one of her favorite books to read. She practically flew down the steps and out the front door and picked a warm sunny spot on the steps. She brushed the stair treads with her hand to remove any dirt or dust that might get on her dress, and then settled down to read.

Nearby out on the dirt lane, Bud and Lance had found each other and were making mud pies near one of the sloppier puddles. Bud was pressing Lance for information about the bus, but Lance was more interested in a worm he had found by the edge of the road.

Teresa saw, or rather heard them playing in the mud. She sighed, closed her book, and headed over to admonish them for getting absolutely filthy.

"What are you doing?" she asked.

Lance looked up from his worm.

"I could ask you the same question," he said eyeing her up and down.

"I was reading, but you boys are so loud I can't concentrate."

"Reading? Ew!"

"Yes reading, which is better than getting all dirty if you ask me."

"No one asked you," Lance sneered.

"Brandon, why are you getting yourself all muddy?" she asked.

"So what if I'm muddy? We're having fun," he said.

"Yeah, so buzz off, bookworm!" Lance added.

"Ha–ha, yeah, bookworm!" Bud said as he pointed.

"What's wrong with books? Don't you like to read, Brandon?"

"I don't know how to read. Reading's dumb," he said.

Teresa chuckled. "You don't know how to read?" she said. "Wait right here." She ran off towards her house.

Bud turned to Lance and rolled his eyes. "She thinks she's so smart because she can read," he said.

"I can read," said Lance. "I'd still rather play."

"Oh, right," said Bud somewhat embarrassed.

"She's just a bookworm. Who wants to read when you can have fun? What's wrong with playing in the mud?"

"She doesn't like getting dirty," Bud said.

Teresa came running back out of the house with a book in her hands looking very proud of herself.

"Doesn't like getting dirty, huh?" Lance said as she came running up. "But she's a bookworm, worms love the mud." He dangled the worm at her as she stopped by the road.

"Lance, stop it!"

He smirked as he tossed the worm at her. He laughed out loud as she shrieked and jumped back.

"Ha–ha! What's wrong, don't you love other worms? All worms love mud!" Lance jeered as he looked at Brandon for approval.

"Yeah bookworm, go back to your book," Bud added smugly.

Teresa defiantly stepped forward into the road to face the two boys and took up her best disapproving motherly stance.

"It's not my fault I'm smarter than you! It's not my fault I can read and Brandon can't!"

Bud's face turned bright red and anger grew inside of him. He picked up a handful of the sloppiest mud he could find and flung it straight at Teresa.

"Here, bookworm! Here's some mud for you!" he yelled as it landed on the front of her blue dress.

Teresa dropped the book as she tried to stop the mud from hitting her, but to no avail. The front of her dress was smeared with brown, and her leggings got splashed as the book landed in the puddle in front of her. Lance was laughing at the horrified look on Teresa's face. Tears began to well up in her eyes, and her hands shook as she tried to find her voice.

"I... I... I hate you, Brandon," she screamed as she burst into tears and ran back to her house, leaving the book in the puddle.

"Good one, Bud," Lance said slapping him on the back.

Just then Lance's mom called for him from down the street. He said he had to go and ran off for his house. Bud sat in the dirt feeling more than just a little bit guilty. He felt bad that he'd ruined Teresa's dress and got her all muddy, but she shouldn't have made fun of him for not being able to read. Why did she always have to be so smug and bossy anyway? He reached over and picked up the book she had been holding. It was one of those "Alice and Jerry" learning–to–read books. Bud opened the cover and noticed that Teresa had written something inside. He couldn't read it all, but he recognized his name. A horrible thought came into his head as he studied the words. Maybe she hadn't been making fun of him, but was going to try and help him learn to read instead. He jumped up and raced home, taking the book with him.

Bud opened the front door quietly, hoping Gran wouldn't hear him, and made his way towards the stairs. Halfway up the stairs, she called to him from the kitchen.

"Brandon, you better not be tracking mud into my clean house!"

He raced the rest of the way up to his room to hide the book. Managing to wipe most of the mud off of it with his shirt, Bud then stashed it under his dresser before his grandmother entered the room. She was appalled at the state of his clothes, and ordered him to the bathroom to strip them off and take a bath at once.

"Honestly, I don't know how you manage to get so filthy. Next time you strip your muddy clothes off before you go traipsing through the house. I just cleaned up in here."

"Yes, Gran," He said.

Next door, Teresa was a ball of sobbing tears as her mother tried to calm her and get both the story out of her and the muddy dress off of her. Nancy caught the words Brandon, reading, mud, and Lance and was able to piece enough together to get the gist of things.

"Sweetheart, boys don't always understand. I don't think Brandon meant to hurt you. He shouldn't have thrown mud at you though."

"I hate him. I hate him. He ruined my dress."

"There there, dear. It's not ruined. It's just a little mud. I'll clean it up, don't you worry. You just take a warm bath and forget all about it. It'll be okay."

"No, it's not okay. I hate him. I'm never talking to him again."

"Now Teresa, you don't really mean that. Give it some time and you'll feel better."

"No, I won't. He's mean. I'll never forgive him!"

Teresa sat in the bath crying as Nancy washed her clothes gently. She was able to get all of the mud out, and the dress was eventually as good as new. Teresa, on the other hand, would need more than a washing to be clean of the whole endeavor.

After dinner that night, Bud went up to his room and pulled the book from its hiding place under his dresser. He flipped the cover open to where Teresa had apparently written him a note. Bud had learned his alphabet, knew his letters and the sounds they made but had never made the leap to reading anything. "A is for apple, B is for ball," was about as far as he had made it. He sat by the window with the fading evening light shining in, and for the better part of thirty minutes he sounded out the letters until he was able to get the basic feeling of the note.

*To Brandon,*
    *This book will help. Friends forever.*
        *Love,*
            *Teresa*

While he couldn't read every word, Bud comprehended the general meaning. Teresa had been giving him something to help him learn to read, not to make fun of him as he had first thought. Her mother or father had probably helped her spell some of it out, but they were surely Reese's words. The twinge of guilt Bud had felt when Teresa had run off crying came flooding back, and tears welled up in his eyes. He sobbed quietly for a few minutes and then returned the book to its hiding place under his dresser. After getting ready for bed, he said goodnight to his grandparents, and put himself to sleep. Maggie thought he felt guilty for tracking mud through the house and tried to reassure him that she forgave him and that he wasn't in trouble anymore.

"I know, Gran. I'm just tired."

As Bud lay in his bed thinking about how much he must have hurt Teresa for her to scream the things she did at him, he made up his mind that the very next day he would get Lance, and the two of them would go and apologize to her. Pa had always told him that when you do something wrong, the right thing to do is to say you're sorry. He meant to do just that.

Immediately after breakfast the next morning, Bud put on his shoes and told his grandparents that he was going to run down to Lance's house. He raced down the lane and up the front steps and knocked on the door. When Lance's mother opened it, Bud asked if Lance could come out to play.

"Not today," she said. "I'll let him tell you why. Lance, Bud's here!"

Moments later, Lance came to the door with the same sour expression on his face that he usually wore.

"I can't come out to play."

"Why not?" Bud asked.

"I have to pack. We're moving."

"Moving? Moving where? When?"

"We're moving to Boston. We're leaving tomorrow."

"Tomorrow?"

"Yeah. Dad got a new job and we have to go. He's leaving tonight, and Mom and I are going after the moving truck comes tomorrow."

"But, you're coming back someday, right?"

"No, we're moving for good Bud. I told Mom I don't want to go, but she said I don't have a choice. So, I can't come out, because I have to get my stuff ready. Mom was going to let me come say goodbye after I packed, but I guess I should say it now since you're here."

"Oh. Goodbye, I guess."

"Bye, Bud. Maybe you can come visit me in Boston."

"Yeah, maybe."

"Ok, see ya."

"See ya."

Bud left Lance's house feeling confused, sad, and very let down. Lance was Bud's only real friend other than Teresa. Teresa! Bud had forgotten why he had run to get Lance in the first place. He ran back down the lane to the Peterson's house, up the steps and knocked on the door. It was Nancy who opened the door and looked down at Bud standing there.

"Is Teresa home?"

"Yes, she is Bud. Just a moment, please."

Nancy left the door for a few minutes before returning herself.

"I'm sorry, Bud, she says she doesn't want to talk to you right now."

"Really? Will you tell her I'm sorry and Lance is moving and I was going to come with him to say we were both sorry but he couldn't come because he has to pack but I came anyway because I know I made her feel bad and I feel bad and I hope she'll forgive me?"

"I'll try to remember all that, Bud," Nancy said as she smiled.

"Okay." Bud's eyes dropped to the porch in front of his feet.

"Hey Bud," Nancy said, kneeling so she was eye level with him.

"Yeah?"

"I think coming to apologize was very good of you — very grown up. Teresa will come around in time, okay? Keep your head up." Bud looked up at her and saw her kind smile looking back at him. He tried to put on a brave face and gave Nancy a determined nod of his head to show that he understood. "Bye for now, Bud," she said.

"Bye."

Bud walked slowly back to his house and went inside. His grandparents were still sitting at the breakfast table when he entered. He told them that Lance was moving. They could tell he was upset by it, and did their best to console him. Maggie said she was headed all the way down to Portland the next day to do some shopping and if he knew what he wanted she could pick him up a little something as a treat. In Bud's mind an idea flashed.

"Could you get me a book?" he asked.

"A book?"

"Yes, to help me learn to read. I should start learning for school."

"I think that's a good idea Bud," Buck said.

"All right," said Maggie. "I suppose I can find an early reader or two down there somewhere that will work."

"Thank you, Gran!"

Bud spent the rest of the day in his room with the book Teresa had dropped in the puddle. He sounded out letters and looked at the pictures to help him learn the words. He made slow progress but was determined to teach himself to read.

The next day was a mixture of excitement and dread as he waited for his grandmother to bring him back a book or two from Portland, and for the moving truck to come and Lance to leave forever. Bud sat by the window in his room going page by page in the *Alice and Jerry* book, watching for either his Gran's car or a moving truck to come up the lane. It was shortly before lunch when the first one appeared. It was the moving truck. Bud's stomach sank as it drove by. He slowly put the book back under his dresser and made his way down the stairs and out the front door. He sat on the front steps and waited. As he looked down the lane towards Lance's house he could see that Teresa was also sitting outside and reading in the sun. He screwed up his courage and got up to walk over and apologize in person for messing up her dress. Before he got his chance, she saw him coming out of the corner of her eye. She got up and went inside, but not before shooting a nasty glance in his direction. Bud stopped, and retreated to the steps.

It was several hours before the moving truck started making its way back down the lane towards the paved road, with Lance and his mother following behind in a car. Seeing this, Bud jumped up and ran to the side of the road hoping to say goodbye one last time. To Bud's dismay, Lance's mom didn't stop. All Bud could do was wave to Lance as he drove by. Standing there on the side of the dirt lane, watching his friend turn the corner, left Bud feeling more alone than he'd ever felt in his short life. He wanted to cry, or to run and hide in a safe place where he could shut the world out. He spun around looking for someplace to go or someone to talk to, but the only person he could think of was Teresa, and she wanted nothing to do with him. Eventually, he found himself wandering back up to his room and laid down on his bed. His face was wet with tears he didn't know he had been crying.

That was where Maggie found him when she came home. She wiped the tears from his face and got him a handkerchief to blow his nose. Then she ran him a hot bath and made him sit in it. Once he was dried and dressed, Maggie showed him the books she had bought for him. There was a whole series of *Dick and Jane* early readers that she had found, which they brought downstairs to start reading together. Buck found them by the fireplace when he came in that evening from working on the farm. Bud was sounding out words, and Maggie was praising his progress.

"I think we have a natural on our hands."

"I wouldn't doubt it," Buck said.

Over the next several weeks, Bud poured himself into learning to read. Teresa was still avoiding him, so he really had nothing else to do. He would ask for parts of the morning paper when Buck was done reading them and do his best to find words that he knew on the page. When Maggie wasn't too busy with chores, she would sit with him and help him sound out words and practice with his books. He was soon able to read the message that Teresa had left for him in the *Alice and Jerry*. He would pull the book out every night after he was supposed to have gone to bed and read it to himself. Each time he read "friends forever" his heart ached a little, and his eyes welled up. One night he finally made up his mind to talk to Teresa no matter what.

Bud had to wait several days before he got his chance, but one afternoon Teresa was sent to bring a pitcher of water to the barn for Buck and Stanley while they were working. Bud had been watching from the window like a hawk every day for any chance he could get to speak to her. As soon as he saw her walk out the front door and head to the barn, he knew this was that chance. Quickly, he put on his shoes and ran out the front door. Just in time, he caught her making her way back from the barn.

"Hey Reese, can I talk to you?"

She walked right past him without so much as turning her head.

"Reese? I'm sorry!" he called after her.

She marched back up the steps, through the front door and then it seemed to Bud that she shut it with a little more effort than necessary. Buck had walked out of the barn shortly after Teresa to get some tools from his garage and had witnessed the whole scene.

"Problem there, Bud?"

"Hey, Pa. Yeah, she won't talk to me. I just want to say I'm sorry."

"Mmm Hmmm. Let me give you a piece of advice, Bud. It might be best to let her come to you when she's ready."

"But when will she be ready, Pa?"

"Only she knows that."

"But I want to talk to her."

"She won't listen."

"But Pa—"

Buck shook his head, cutting him off mid–sentence. Bud relented. Maybe his grandfather was right. He stopped trying to talk to Teresa and just continued working on his reading with Maggie. Progress came quickly, and he was soon able to read all of the *Dick and Jane* series as well as the *Alice and Jerry*.

The April thaw had turned into early May showers. With the rain falling outside leaving him few other options, Bud continued reading. He found that he really enjoyed it. Unfortunately, all the books he now had in the house were either too easy for him, or far too difficult. Maggie said that when she went down to Portland again, she would try to find him some books that were more his reading level. Bud was excited for the possibility of having something new to read, but he would have to wait a couple weeks before he had the opportunity.

Bud was restless when the day finally came and Maggie went to Portland. It was raining once again, so he was stuck inside while Buck was out working on the farm. He tried to play with toys and look at a couple of his older books, but nothing eased his boredom. Once Maggie got home it was almost dinner time, and he didn't have an opportunity to even look at the new books she had got for him. He asked if he could see them after they ate, but they sent him up to bed. The books would have to wait until the next day, his grandparents told him to his disappointment.

When Bud awoke in the morning, the sun was shining bright outside his window for the first time in what felt like a month. As soon as breakfast was over, Bud asked his grandmother if he could go outside and read his new books. She agreed and brought him a bag with several that she had purchased. She held up one in particular that she thought he would enjoy.

"Now, Bud, this book is much longer and more difficult than what you've been reading, but I think you'll like it. It's called *Stuart Little*. You can try it if you like, but don't get frustrated if it's too hard for you."

Bud was excited. It was exactly the kind of challenge that he was looking for. He thanked his grandmother, and ran outside to find a warm sunny spot to read. As Bud began reading, he realized his grandmother had been right. This book was far more difficult than anything he had been reading thus far. He struggled over many of the words, and some of the names were basically impossible for him. He would run inside to get help from his grandmother if he couldn't figure out a word, a name, or sometimes an entire sentence. But he kept at it.

From her living room window, Teresa noticed him leaning against a tree in the sun. She was confused because he was looking at a book, but to her knowledge, Bud couldn't read. She was still determined to be mad at him, and decided she could use the opportunity to chastise him for ruining her dress and her book. She marched out of the house and walked defiantly up to him. Lost in his book, he didn't even notice her coming until she snatched it out of his hands.

"What are you looking at, Brandon?" she demanded as she held the book up.

Bud was too stunned at first to answer. He blinked in the sunlight as he tried to look up at her and stumbled over his words not sure whether to answer her question or ask her one of his own.

"It's... um... a book... hi... are you? are you still mad at me? I—"

"I see it's a book, and yes I'm still mad. *Stuart Little*? You can't read. Are you just looking at the pictures? This is a good book. My mother reads if to me sometimes at night. Why do you have it?"

"I learned to read," he said proudly.

She eyed him doubtfully. Then she sat down and shoved the book back into his hands.

"Prove it," she said. "Read to me."

Brandon opened the book to chapter one and started slowly reading, sounding out the words he wasn't sure about. He stumbled over a few, and Teresa corrected him on one or two as well, but when he finished the third sentence she stopped him.

"How did you learn to read, Brandon?"

"The book you dropped," he said embarrassed. "The one you tried to give me. I practiced a lot. Gran got me some like it, and she's been helping me. I tried to say I was sorry for the mud, but you wouldn't talk to me. I thought you made fun of me because I couldn't read."

"I wouldn't make fun of you, Brandon. *Stuart Little* is a big book. Even I can't read it."

"Gran just gave it to me today. She said it might be too hard, but I wanted to try."

"Maybe..." she paused. "Maybe we could read it together."

"Does this mean you forgive me for the mud? I'm sorry about your dress."

"No... I'm still upset with you..." she sighed. "Mother cleaned my dress. It's better now. As long as you're sorry—"

"I am! I am sorry. It's just that Lance—" Bud stopped. He remembered that Lance had moved away, and a look of sadness crossed his face. Teresa saw the look.

"Yes… Lance. I didn't like Lance, and now he's gone. Mother told me he moved. I know you liked him. I'm sorry him being gone makes you sad." Bud nodded. "Okay, Brandon, I forgive you. Let's try to read this together."

Buck noticed the two of them sitting together looking at the book as he came up from the barn to have lunch. He said nothing, but his eyes smiled at Bud as he walked past them into the house. Maggie asked Buck if he'd seen their grandson on the way up to tell him that it was lunch time.

"I did, but I wouldn't bother him right now. If you have to know why, take a peek out the window there."

Maggie looked out and saw the two of them sitting under the tree sharing the book. She smiled and decided lunch wasn't all that important. Brandon would be sure to come looking for food if he got hungry.

The two children sat together most of the day, reading in the sun. When Teresa failed to turn up for lunch, Nancy made some sandwiches and lemonade, and carried it out to the two of them to eat. It wasn't until the sun began to set and the air cooled that Teresa said she should go and said goodbye to Brandon. He thanked her for her forgiveness and for sharing *Stuart Little* with him all day. She smiled and rolled her eyes.

"We can read more tomorrow if you want, Brandon," she said. "I won't ignore you anymore."

"Ok. Gran got me other books too. Maybe we can read those?"

"That would be fun. See you tomorrow."

"Ok, see you tomorrow."

As he watched her open her front door and disappear from view, Bud couldn't help but hope that he had put things right. He felt like he needed to do something more to make up for what he had done to Teresa, but he didn't know what that something was. For now, he would have to be content being her friend again and sharing his new–found love of reading. He was glad he wouldn't have to spend the summer before his first year of school alone.

# 11

The world was reborn as the warmth spread green along the dirt lane, and into the fields. The leaves burst forth from their buds and winter lost its hold on the land. The stream running into the pond swelled with the meltwater from higher ground while the first flowers opened dotting the landscape with bright colors.

The two children, likewise, shared a renewed and budding friendship. They spent the spring days together outside reading, playing, and laughing. When the black fly swarms became too much to bear, they would take shelter in the barn or in one of their houses and share books with one another. Bud had flourished as a reader in a very short time. Teresa was amazed at the words he could read that she could not. The two of them were inseparable and their time together sped spring into summer before either of them had realized it.

A heat wave hit towards the end of July, and the air was humid and sticky. The farm animals would gather around the pond in the pasture to stay cool, and the children would settle in the shade of a tree and wait longingly for the slightest breeze to cool them off. If they were lucky, Buck would hook up a water sprinkler to the spigot on the farmhouse and let them run and play in it to cool off. Bud liked this far more than Teresa who still didn't like the idea of getting all wet and messy. She would complain that after she ran through it the grass would get stuck to her feet, and before long she would retire inside to clean up and change, leaving Bud to run through the water by himself.

One particularly hot day, Bud suggested they ask Buck to get out the hose for them, but Teresa said she would rather not get all dirty again. That was about all Bud could take of the "dirty" complaint, and it gave him an idea.

"Come with me, Reese," he said.

"Where are we going?"

"You'll see."

He led her down the hill to the stream, and then along the banks to the west below his house and beyond. They walked until they came to a culvert and the adjoining road to the dirt lane. If they had turned left the road, named Baker Street, would've taken them to Route 133, but Bud led them across it and continued following the stream from where it had entered the large culvert.

"Bud, where are we going?" Teresa asked. "We shouldn't cross the road. My mother would say no."

"Don't worry, I've done it before."

Bud led her on about another five–hundred feet to where the stream exited a small pool at the base of a four–foot waterfall. The far side of the pool ended in a steep bank at the edge of the woods, but on the side the two children stood it was grassy and gentle where it led down into the water. The bank was blanketed in sun, but the surrounding area was wooded enough that nothing could be seen for quite some distance in all directions. The effect was to give the place a feeling of security, as though giant walls of trees would repel anyone with an unsavory purpose. Bud sat down on a log nearby and started removing his shoes and socks.

"It's pretty Brandon," Teresa said. "But why are we here?"

"To go swimming," Bud said, continuing to strip down to his underwear.

"Umm, I don't think so. I'm not swimming in that!" Teresa said, looking at the little pool.

"It's really clean," Bud said. "And the bottom is nice and sandy. Plus, it's not deep. I came here once last summer with Lance. I could touch bottom in the middle. Come on."

Bud stood there in only his underwear with the sun reflecting off the pool. The doubt was etched all over Teresa's face.

"There's nothing to worry about." Bud said.

He walked down to the water and waded out to the very middle. The water came to a little above his belly button at the deepest point.

"See?" He said. "No problem. It's nice and cool. It feels good."

Teresa sighed, sat down on the log and removed her shoes and socks. She too removed her clothes, but for her underwear and stepped apprehensively down to the water's edge. She tentatively dipped in the toe of her right foot. The water was cool, but not cold, so she slid her foot further in and felt the sandy bottom. It wasn't slimy or gross as she had feared it might be, so she put her weight down and stepped in with the other foot. She waded into the water and over to Bud. Because she was quite a bit shorter than him, the water came up to her arm pits. She was very thankful she could still stand.

"I can't swim," she said to Bud.

"That's ok, I can teach you. Or you can just stand if you want to."

The two children began to splash and play in the pool. Bud even started teaching Teresa how to kick her feet and paddle with her hands. He would hold his hands under her, so that she wouldn't sink under the water. Bud could remember Maggie doing the same for him when he was learning to swim in

Androscoggin Lake two years earlier. When they were finished, they climbed out of the pool and lay on the grassy bank, drying in the sun.

"Thank you, Brandon," Teresa said.

"For what?"

"Thank you for making me go in the water. And for trying to teach me to swim. I don't even mind the grass here. Everything seems clean."

"Oh, you're welcome. We can try more tomorrow. And all summer when it's warm."

"I'd like that."

They lay in silence for some time, just enjoying the warm rays of the sun.

"Brandon," she finally said. "Are you excited for school?"

"A little, I guess. I was scared after Lance moved because I'll be alone on the bus. Now that I can read a little, I feel better."

"You can read a lot. You're a really good reader, Brandon. If you want, I could walk with you to the bus stop."

"You could?"

"Of course, if you like."

"That'd be nice Reese. That'd make me feel better."

She smiled, glad that she could do something nice in return for him helping her learn to swim.

"Brandon," she said. "What do you want to be when you grow up?"

"I don't know."

"Well, you're going to school. Don't you think you should know?"

"I guess so. Maybe."

"So, what do you want to be?"

Bud thought hard about that question. He remembered what Maggie said about becoming successful and a great man like his grandfather. "I want to be great, like Pa," he said.

"A great what? A great car repair man? A great helper on the farm?"

"I don't know, A great man, like Pa."

Teresa chuckled.

"What's so funny?" he asked.

"That's not a job, Brandon. You need a job. You can be great at a job."

"Well, what would I be great at?"

"You'd be a great teacher. You did good teaching me to swim."

"A teacher? Teachers aren't great. I want to be liked. I want everyone in town — no, in the world, to like me."

"I like you," she said quietly.

"Thanks, Reese, but you're just one person. I want everyone to like me. What do you want to be?"

"I don't know," she said. "I want to help people. Maybe I'll be a nurse."

Bud looked over at her and thought for a minute. Then he nodded. "You'd be good at that. You're very helpful," he said

"Thank you."

The two lay in the sun until they were dry and warm. Then they got up, put their clothes back on, and made the walk back to the farm. They returned to the pool beneath the waterfall every day that week, and by the end of it, Teresa was starting to get the hang of swimming. She couldn't go for very long, but she was able to keep herself afloat and move forward slowly. Bud was very proud, and Teresa kept telling him what a great teacher he was.

That was how they spent the rest of their summer. When it was hot, they'd run up the banks of the stream to the pool and swim. When it was cooler, they would sit on the bank and read in the sun. It became their place, a haven the two friends could escape to from the rest of the world and just be together.

As September drew near, Bud began to get nervous about going to school again. Teresa had asked her mother if she could walk with Bud to the bus stop, and she had agreed. That would certainly help, Bud thought, but he would still have to ride the bus and go to school all alone. Maggie had purchased him some new clothes for his first day and a bag to carry his school supplies in. Teresa was very jealous that Bud was getting to go to school and that she had to wait an entire year before she went. In his current state, Bud would've been happy to trade places with her.

When the day arrived, he rose and ate breakfast; and when he headed out the front door to walk to the bus stop, Teresa was already waiting for him on the steps. She smiled broadly, and Bud forced a smile in return. The two walked side by side down the dirt lane to where it met Baker Street and where Bud would catch the bus to school. They stood in silence until the bright yellow bus came into view down the road.

"Have fun, Brandon," she said. "I'll wait for you after school right here. You have to tell me all about it!"

"Ok," he said. "Thanks, Reese."

The bus stopped and the door opened. Bud climbed the steps and returned the driver's hello. He took a seat and looked out the window as the bus pulled away. Teresa waved and he waved back until he could no longer see her through the cloud of dust the bus left in its wake.

Bud arrived at the tiny school house and filed in to take his seat with the other children. Ms. Wing, the teacher, had each student stand and give his or her name. Bud settled in well and demonstrated on the first day that he was an excellent reader for his age. Ms. Wing was impressed and even had him read a few lines out loud to the class. Bud was very proud of himself and thought he must appear somewhat "great" to all the other students already. The day went quickly, and Bud made sure to make mental notes to share with Teresa when she met him at the bus that afternoon.

Sure enough, Teresa was standing and waiting patiently for Bud at the end of the school day. As soon as he got off the bus, she began peppering him with questions. Bud did his best to answer all of them as they walked back down the dirt lane together to their houses. He made a point to mention that he had proven himself an excellent reader. When he saw the smirk on Teresa's face, he thanked her for helping him.

"You're welcome, Brandon," she said. Her smirk turned into a full smile that didn't come off of her face the rest of the way home.

Bud shared everything he could remember, and by the time they reached his front steps Teresa was ready to pack a bag and attend school the very next day. She knew, of course, that she would have to wait a whole year. She set her mind to live vicariously through Bud so that when she finally did get to attend school, it would be as though she had already gone a full year. She said goodbye to him at the door and ran off towards her own house. Bud went inside and shared his day with Buck and Maggie. Both were glad that it was a positive experience and that his studies were off to a good start.

"An education is the most important thing," Buck said.

His grandfather didn't offer his opinion very often, so when he did Bud listened. He vowed to make education one of the primary focuses of his life from that day forward, which is easy to do when you're six years old and have no real choice in the matter.

The next day went much like the first. Teresa met Bud on his front steps and walked him to the bus. Once again, she was standing there waiting for him when he got back. It was like that each and every day during the fall. In the rain, she was there. When the weather got colder, she was there. Even in the November snow, she was bundled up and waiting. Bud never minded. For him, it was wonderful to have a friend that wanted so badly to share in his life.

The afternoon of his seventh birthday, Teresa met Bud when he came home from school, holding a cake. She started singing *Happy Birthday* as he stepped off the bus.

After she finished, Bud said, "You made me a cake?"

"I baked it with mother for you."

"Thanks, Reese."

"You're welcome, Brandon. How was school?"

They walked back chatting contentedly. When they got to Bud's house they went in and asked Maggie for a couple of plates and forks so they could try the cake.

"Before supper? You'll ruin your appetite," she said.

"Ah, what's a little cake, Maggie? Let them have a small piece. Won't hurt them that bad, will it?" Buck chimed in from his chair in the living room.

Maggie relented and the two children each had a small piece of chocolate cake. Bud thanked Teresa again before she headed home. Maggie sat down next to Bud at the table and tried a little piece of the cake herself.

"It must be wonderful to have such a thoughtful friend," she said.

"Yeah, she is pretty thoughtful."

"You should probably think about getting her something for Christmas, don't you agree?"

"Do you think I should?"

"Don't you think she'll be getting you something?" she asked as she took another bite. "A girl doesn't just bake you a birthday cake and not get you a gift for Christmas as well."

Bud thought about it. Gran was surely right. Teresa would be getting him a gift, but what could he get her?

"Buying for girls can be tough," Maggie said, almost reading his mind. "Maybe something the two of you could do together."

A light switch flicked on in Bud's mind. "I've got it Gran, but I need your help."

Christmas preparations began shortly after that. There was decorating and shopping and cooking to do. The Marshalls had invited the Petersons over on Christmas Day to once again share a meal.

Bud went with Maggie all the way to Portland to do some Christmas shopping, and they were able to find what Bud thought was the perfect gift for Teresa. When they got home, Bud wrapped it all by himself in shiny red and green paper. He had Maggie help him tie a bow around it, and then wrote his own message on the tag.

> *To Reese,*
> > *Merry Christmas.*
> > > *Love,*
> > > > *Bud*

While it wasn't the most eloquent message ever put to paper, Bud was immensely proud that he had written it all by himself.

A couple of days later, Bud went with Buck into the woods to find Christmas trees for the two houses. Buck wheezed and coughed some as they went. He had been working extra hard those last few weeks making final preparations on the farm for winter. In the middle of it all, the town manager, Mr. Wiess, had shown up with his car. It was making an awful racket and he needed it tuned up immediately. He said he had to drive into Augusta in two days for some big meeting, and he couldn't risk it breaking down. Bud noticed that important people always seemed to have somewhere else they needed to be. Buck had stayed out in the garage most of the night working on it, and the small wood stove just hadn't done enough to keep things warm through the cold night. Now it seemed Buck had come down with a bug.

Buck walked a little slower than usual, but Bud didn't mind because it gave him time to scout out the perfect tree for Teresa and her family. Once Bud picked it out, Buck chopped it down with his small hatchet. Then they found one for their own house before beginning the walk home. Grandfather and grandson carried the two trees from the forest. Buck led, holding a trunk in each hand — and Bud followed, holding each of the tops. Buck coughed and wheezed as they trudged slowly up the hill. They dropped their tree by the door and carried the Peterson's over to their house. Jim was most appreciative until he looked at Buck's face.

"You don't look so good. You feeling all right?" Jim asked.

"Been bettah." Buck said through another cough.

"You shouldn't have been out there with that nasty cough. That's my fault, Buck. I get complacent with you doing all the work around here, and I don't pay enough attention to when you need a break." Buck started to wave him off, but Jim cut him short. "You go straight home, and I don't want to see you back to work until you're at one hundred percent. You understand? I'm going to tell Maggie the same thing. You might not listen to me, but I know damn well you'll listen to her. Bud," he said turning to the young man. "You make sure your grandfather goes straight to bed when he gets home. I swear the man will work himself to death if we all let him."

Bud nodded. He and Buck headed home, and once they got the tree inside Bud told Maggie what Jim had said. With that, Maggie sent Buck straight upstairs to bed. She had noticed he wasn't feeling well and was thinking herself that he needed a little rest. She was going to suggest it when he came in anyway. What she wasn't expecting is for Buck to put up no fight at all.

That's when she started to get worried. To relent that easily was not something Buck Marshall was prone to do.

Maggie made dinner, including some chicken soup for Buck, which she carried up to him on a tray. She found him in bed, shaking and feverish. From the closet, she grabbed another blanket and covered him before going downstairs to call the doctor.

Dr. Randolph made a house call that very evening. He listened to Buck's lungs and shook his head. "Pneumonia, I'm afraid," he said. "He's not to get out of bed any more than absolutely necessary. I'm writing him a prescription for antibiotics, and you have to make sure he takes them. I can't be sure it's bacterial without doing a blood test, but I think we should be on the safe side."

Maggie thanked the doctor and showed him to the door. The prescription would have to wait until the next day when she could run into Augusta to the pharmacy. In the meantime, she got a cold washcloth for her husband's forehead and made sure he was properly covered. It was going to be a long two weeks until Christmas at this rate.

A week later when Buck still wasn't up and around, Jim suggested they cancel the Christmas dinner. Maggie shushed him and said that was ridiculous. They would have their dinner with or without Buck.

Thankfully, by the time Christmas morning came around, Buck was feeling more like himself. He was weak and tired, but his symptoms had cleared up. Maggie could see he was feeling better, but she warned him not to overexert himself and to go lay down if he started to feel too weak. Buck smiled and thanked her for being so good to him.

The Marshalls opened gifts and smiled and laughed for the first time in weeks. Bud got a bike which, while not great for Maine winters, made him very excited for spring to come. Buck got new work gloves and Maggie a new apron. They were talking merrily and enjoying the fire when the Petersons arrived.

As soon as she removed her coat, Teresa walked directly to Bud and handed him a gift beautifully wrapped in silver paper with a red and green ribbon.

"Merry Christmas, Brandon," she said.

He smiled, held up a single finger for her to wait and ran over to the tree. He retrieved his gift for her and came running back.

"Merry Christmas, Reese."

The two children tore into the shiny paper as the adults looked on smiling. They each removed the paper to reveal a book — the same book. They had both chosen another children's story by the author of *Stuart Little*, E. B. White, for the other as a gift. They looked confused for a second at their individual copies of *Charlotte's Web* and then to each other. Then they started laughing. The adults laughed too.

Buck sat off to the side in his chair just smiling, watching his grandson and his friend Teresa. Christmas is a wonderful and festive time anyway, but having a true friend to share it with makes it that much better. Maggie glanced over and saw him smiling. She made her way across the room and leaned down next to his ear. "And what are you thinking about, Buck Marshall?" she whispered.

"Happiness," he said as he smiled up at her. "And how the ones we love make it that much greater."

She kissed him on the cheek and announced that it was time to eat. The families carried the joy into the dining room and shared a delicious meal. Maggie made sure to point out that this time she hadn't burned the biscuits.

Time surged forward for the families on the little dirt lane. Buck's health returned to normal, and with it his work habit. The children shared their summers reading and swimming in the little pool in the stream as well as wandering around the farm helping Buck or pestering Stanley the handy man. Teresa started school that next fall, and she and Bud continued to walk to and from the bus together. The children grew: older, bigger, and closer together. They were inseparable, for the most part. Bud would occasionally have another boy from school over to play, or Teresa another girl; but generally, the two only played with one another.

For young boys and girls this isn't abnormal, to be so close. It isn't until they begin turning into young men and young women that they find anything strange with it. It wasn't until after Teresa had turned ten and Bud had turned eleven that she started to view him in a different light.

# 12

The robins were back. Teresa watched them as they poked around on the bare ground between the patches of lingering snow cover looking for food. She and Bud walked silently side by side, making their way home from the bus stop after school. Normally they'd be chatting about their day. But today, Bud was oddly silent. She could tell something was bothering him.

"It'll be spring soon," she offered, not sure what to say.

"Hmmph," Bud grunted in response.

"Buck said he wanted you to help out more on the farm starting this summer, right? That should be fun. He said he'd even pay you. It'll be nice to make a little money, won't it?" Bud just sighed. "I hate for school to end," she said. "I like it as much as you, but I still look forward to summer. It'll be great to have some time to ourselves on the farm and—"

"You don't get it, Reese," Bud cut her off. He stopped walking and turned back towards where the bus dropped them off at Baker Street. She stopped as well and turned to face him.

"When classes begin again this fall, I have to go to a different school," Bud said. "That means I take a different bus than you and the ride is a lot longer. I have to get up earlier and I get home later. We won't be walking together next year, and I won't be at the elementary school with you."

Bud turned and started walking again and Teresa fell in beside him. She didn't speak after that. She knew exactly what Bud was talking about. Their little elementary school only taught up to grade five. There was a regional middle school for grades six through eight that combined a number of the smaller elementary schools in the area.

Bud was like the king of their little school right now. Everyone liked and respected him as one of the oldest and smartest kids there. When Bud went to middle school, not only would he be in the bottom grade again, there would be a number of children that he didn't know and who didn't know him. It was like starting all over again. Teresa remembered how nervous Bud had been to start school all those years ago.

The arrival of spring had made Bud realize, just as Teresa had, that the school year would be ending soon. When it started back up again in the fall, things would be different. And on top of it all, Buck wanted Bud to help on the farm. That meant even less time he could spend with Teresa. The summer was sure to be too short, and then they would be spending an entire school year apart. Bud knew several kids moving on to middle school with him, but he wasn't close with any of them. Fear of the unknown had put him in a sour mood.

When the two reached Bud's house, they stopped on the steps and turned to face each other. Teresa looked up into Bud's eyes, which were normally a bright blue, much like his grandfather's. Today however, they seemed gray and sad. Somewhere in her heart there was a twinge of pain for him, and her stomach flipped slightly in a way she'd never felt.

"It'll be okay, Brandon," she managed to choke out. Then she turned and walked quickly to her own house.

He watched her go before opening his own door. He appreciated her trying to make him feel better, but somehow he knew that "okay" was nowhere near how things were going to be.

When school ended that year, most of the children ran out of the building excited to start their summer vacations. Teresa and Bud walked out solemnly side by side knowing they would never exit the building together again as schoolmates. They rode the bus next to one another and neither spoke a word, even when another boy tried to tease them about being boyfriend and girlfriend. They got off the bus and started walking down the dirt lane together. It was hot, unusually so for June, and their feet on the road kicked up little clouds of dust. Suddenly Bud stopped and turned to Teresa.

"Reese, I'm not ready to go home yet," he said.

"O... kay..." She looked at him confused.

"Follow me," he said smiling.

He half ran, leading her back down the lane towards Baker Street. At the corner, he turned left and brought her to where the stream ran through the culvert. Then they crossed the road and followed the stream up to their place by the waterfall. He sat on the log and began pulling off his shoes.

"Come on," he said. "First swim of the summer. What do you say?" He peeled off his shirt and stood looking at her waiting for her response.

Teresa looked at the boy next door that she'd known her whole life. He had grown so much, and with him standing there without his shirt on she was embarrassed for reasons she didn't fully understand. The thought of stripping to her underwear and swimming in the little pool with him made her heart skip erratically.

"I don't know, Brandon," she said finally. "It still seems a little too cold for me."

"Suit yourself." He shrugged and dropped his pants, ran and jumped in the water.

Teresa thought to herself that Brandon was growing quite handsome. She felt her cheeks flush as she watched him floating around the little pool. She bit her lip and turned away as he stood under the waterfall and let out a gasp as the coldness of the water took his breath away.

"Brandon," she called to him. "My mother is going to be expecting me home. She's going to wonder what's taking so long. I... I better get going." She got up to leave.

"Wait, what?" he said. "It's fine, just tell her we stopped to play."

"No, no, I better go." She ran off down the length of the stream towards the farm.

Bud watched her go, confused as to what had happened. He dunked his head one more time and then made his way out of the water and lay on the grass in the sun to dry. As he walked home he caught a glimpse of Teresa outside the farmhouse and waved to get her attention. She turned and quickly walked back inside when she saw him. Bud didn't understand what he'd done wrong, but he'd be sure to ask her about it and apologize if he upset her the next time they were alone.

That was the start of a lonely summer for Bud. The next day, Buck started him working on the farm helping Stanley with some of the chores. It got hot early that summer, and by the third week in June they were cutting and baling the first loads of hay. Any time Bud did manage to see Teresa, she acted funny around him. She said that he hadn't upset her, but she didn't ever seem to be able to play when Bud had free time. Combine that with the fact that Buck was keeping him so busy that his free time was reduced to a pittance of what it had once been. It all left Bud in a rather sour mood. Stanley the handyman tried to cheer him up, always talking about how no one understands girls and that it was best just not to try. Bud would listen, but he didn't think Stanley understood at all. This was Teresa after all, not just some girl that he didn't know. They had been friends their whole lives, and it wasn't like her to avoid him for no reason.

One of the worst parts was that the summer was brutally hot and that Teresa didn't once go up to the pool at the waterfall with him. Every time he suggested it, she had an excuse or suddenly had to go inside for some reason. Bud still went swimming, but it just wasn't the same by himself with no one to talk to. Bud even considered asking Stanley to go with him one time, but rejected the idea. Stanley was older, and besides, it was his and Teresa's place. Bud didn't want to ruin that.

Bud did learn how to manage most of the smaller jobs around the farm, helped with haying and some of the harvesting. He was getting much stronger, and Jim was beginning to wonder if he was going to need Stanley at all in future summers. Bud certainly seemed to have his grandfather's work ethic.

As summer dwindled and the new school year approached, Bud's apprehension about moving to the middle school grew. One day in late August he finally got some time with Teresa and expressed his concerns to her. She shrugged him off, saying he would be fine and how she wished she was going to middle school with him.

When the first day of school arrived, Bud hoped that when he walked out the front door to go catch the bus that Teresa would be standing there waiting for him. He knew that his bus came a full half hour before hers, but he thought she might get ready early so she could still walk with him. Sadly, he found when he opened the door that he would be making the walk alone for the first time — apart from a handful of days Teresa had been sick or absent in the past. He walked to Baker Street and climbed onto the big yellow bus headed for Maranacook Middle

School. That fall morning, Bud found himself in the largest class he had ever been in.

He managed fine through the morning and soon all the children were outside for recess. Bud wandered around slowly by himself watching the other students collect into groups with kids they had known from their old elementary schools. Suddenly a squinty eyed boy with mussed hair called to him from one of the clusters.

"Hey! Hey you!" he said. Bud gestured to himself questioningly. "Yeah, you. Come here for a minute," the boy continued.

Bud walked over slowly. "Me?" he asked.

"Yeah. What's your name?"

"Bud."

"Bud? Really? Well, ok then, Bud. My names Chad Smith, but everyone calls me Smitty. I'm from Mt. Vernon, where are you from?" Bud answered him carefully as his eyes shifted around the group to the other boys standing there. "Yeah, yeah, great kid." Smitty said. "Listen, you see that girl over there?" He gestured at a blonde standing some twenty feet away. "Her name's Sarah, and word is she thinks you're cute. You think she's cute?"

Bud shrugged. "I guess so," he said.

Smitty seemed satisfied with this answer and brought Bud into the conversation with the other boys. Bud had found a group willing to take him in, and for the first time in months he didn't feel alone. Smitty continued leading the conversation. He explained that if the girl liked Bud and Bud liked her that they should get the two of them together. Bud didn't really understand the whole thing, but went along with the crowd anyway.

The bell rang, and the kids all headed back inside for class. Smitty told Bud that they would work everything out for tomorrow. Bud didn't know what that meant but said, "Okay" and headed for the door.

When school ended, Bud rode the bus back to the dirt lane off Baker Street. When he got off Teresa was there waiting for him. Her bus dropped her off earlier than his, but not so much so that she minded waiting. She peppered Bud with questions about middle school, and Bud told her everything that had happened. While she said nothing, she frowned at the story of Smitty and the blonde girl, Sarah. She left Bud at his front door and went on to her own house. She suggested that she might walk with Bud the next morning to the bus stop and just wait a little extra for her own bus to pick her up. Bud grinned and told her he'd like that. He explained that he had actually thought she might have done it that morning and was sad when she wasn't there. That actually made Teresa smile, and she touched him gently on the arm as she spoke.

"Well, that settles it then. I'll be here in the morning," she said.

Sure enough, Teresa was waiting at the bottom of the steps the next morning. The two walked side by side once again down the dirt lane to Baker Street. Teresa waved as the bus to Marana-cook Middle School pulled away with Bud on it.

Smitty found Bud in the hallway before classes began and told him that they were all going to meet behind the bleachers by the ball field at recess time. Smitty winked as the bell rang and he ran off to his own class. Bud was confused again, but was glad that he had friends to talk to.

When recess began later, Bud made his way down to the bleachers by the ball field. A group of girls, including Sarah, had gathered along with the group of boys Bud had met the day before. When Bud walked up, Smitty took control. He explained that since Bud and Sarah liked each other, they would be boy-friend and girlfriend. The boys all hooted and the girls giggled. Bud turned a little red in the face as the reality of what was happening hit him.

"So," Smitty continued explaining. "Since Bud and Sarah are boyfriend and girlfriend now, it's only fitting that they kiss."

Bud started to protest, but one of the other boys gave him an encouraging shove forward towards the group of girls. The girls, likewise, nudged Sarah forward. She was looking down shyly, but she lifted her head as she approached Bud, and he saw her beautiful green eyes. The two kids stood awkwardly face to face, their skin turning all shades of red as the other boys and girls egged them on. Finally, Sarah leaned in and pressed her lips against Bud's. He felt a warmth spread through his body as he returned her kiss.

The world became muted, and Bud was completely unaware of the children cheering and hollering around him. His lips remained locked with Sarah's until a hand grabbed his collar and yanked him back away from her. It belonged to the teacher on duty, who began admonishing him as she marched him to the principal's office.

The principal explained that physical contact between boys and girls was prohibited on school grounds and that this would be Bud's only warning. Any further violation of school rules would result in detention. Bud was embarrassed and terrified at the fact that he was in trouble. He promised the principal that he wouldn't be a problem moving forward. Then, because recess had ended, Bud was told to return to class.

Teresa was waiting when Bud got off the bus. Bud was still embarrassed about what had happened and he debated whether or not to tell her about it. However, Teresa could sense that something was bothering him and pressed him for details until he explained the whole escapade. Teresa listened in silence, and it wasn't until Bud finished the entire story that she spoke.

"So, you really like this girl?" she asked.

"I don't know," Bud replied.

"You don't know? You kissed her! Why would you kiss her if you don't like her?"

"I don't know. Everyone was telling me to and watching and stuff—"

"Brandon Marshall! How could you be so stupid?" Teresa's face was flushed red and her eyes were welling up.

"I didn't get in that much trouble, Reese. I told the principal I wouldn't be a problem anymore. I didn't know it was against the rules."

"The rules? The rules, Brandon?" She stopped walking, looked at him and shook her head in disbelief. "You kissed a girl that you don't even know if you like on the second day of school, and you're worried about the rules?"

Bud just looked at her standing there with a red face and tears in her eyes. He reached a hand out to wipe a tear from her cheek, but she knocked his hand away and stepped back.

"Don't you dare touch me," she said. "Not after what you did. I don't want to talk to you right now." She turned and ran off leaving Bud standing confused in the middle of the dusty lane with his mouth slightly agape and a bead of sweat running down his forehead. She wasn't waiting to walk with him to the bus stop the next morning. Two days later, one of Sarah's friends went up to Bud at recess and told him that Sarah was breaking up with him and that they weren't boyfriend and girlfriend anymore.

Bud grew angry. He was angry at Teresa, but he wasn't sure why. He was angry at Sarah, even though he didn't really know Sarah. Most of all, he was angry at Smitty, and Smitty he could deal with. At recess, Bud marched up to him, gathered with some boys in one of the dugouts of the ball field.

"Hey, Smitty," he said. "I want to talk to you about—"

"Bud, keep it down!" Smitty said.

"No, I won't! You need to listen to—"

"Bud, seriously. Shut up and come here."

The boys were all gathered around Smitty who was flipping through the pages of a dirty magazine. Bud's eyes widened and his heartbeat raced as he thought what would happen if they were caught with it.

"Where did you get that?" he asked.

"I swiped it from the store," Smitty said.

"You stole it?"

"Let's just say I borrowed it, all right? What's the big deal?"

"You're going to get in a lot of trouble if they catch you with that! I already got a talking to for kissing Sarah under the bleachers the other day, you know? She broke up with me, by the way. So, thanks a lot for that. The last thing I need right now is to get in trouble for looking at some nudie mag. I don't think they'd let me go without detention if they found me here looking at this."

"Shhh, quiet down already. If they catch us it'll only be because you're yelling and causing a scene, all right?"

Bud's anger had quickly turned to nervous fear. He couldn't leave because the other boys would think he was soft. He was terrified to stay and get caught, but he didn't see another choice. In the moment, he forgot all about Sarah breaking up with him, about Teresa getting angry and running off, and about wanting to blame the whole thing on Smitty. He stood and looked at the dirty pictures with the other boys until the bell rang. When it did, he was able to relax a little and headed off to class, having saved face with the other boys.

Bud wanted someone to talk to about the whole incident, but Teresa wasn't an option and he didn't want to go to Buck or Maggie. Stanley was the only other option Bud had.

Stanley laughed when Bud told him the story. "You were afraid of getting caught with a smut rag, huh?" Stanley said. Bud nodded. "Eh, don't worry about it, Bud. Ain't a kid alive that hasn't been caught looking at a nudie mag at least once in his life.

Besides, sounds like you weren't caught anyway. Rules were made to be broken, after all."

Bud didn't expect that kind of reaction, but he was glad at least Stanley wasn't upset with him. It was the first time in several days that Bud didn't feel like he had done something that made someone upset. He supposed Stanley was right. It couldn't be that big a deal if all the other boys were doing it. And they hadn't gotten caught, so it was nothing to worry about. Bud was perched precariously atop a slippery slope that he knew very little about. The only people he could turn to at the moment though were Stanley and Smitty, and neither of them was going to turn him away from the edge any time soon.

# 13

The school year flew by. Things between Teresa and Bud improved as time went on. By Christmas they were exchanging gifts and walking home from school together again. By spring, things were about back to normal. Teresa was still having some trouble placing her personal feelings for Bud in terms she could understand. She still thought of him as her best friend, but felt like she had lost a measure of the trust they shared when he kissed a girl he wasn't sure he even really liked. It seemed unlike him, and Teresa's mind had trouble reconciling the event with the "Brandon" she knew and cared about. To complicate her emotions further, there was an underlying uncomfortableness in just being around Bud lately.

Bud was largely living a double life. At home, around Teresa and his family, he was the same Bud he had always been. He worked hard, read books, played, talked with Teresa, and was every bit the well–behaved young person he had always been. However, there was another side of Bud that was coming out at school with Smitty and around Stanley. That side was learning to like Stanley's statement, "Rules were meant to be broken." While

Bud hadn't done anything that had placed him in hot water, that was just because he hadn't been caught yet.

Bud and Smitty had grown close over the school year, and Bud had developed into Smitty's best friend and his unofficial second in command. The principal always said they were "thick as thieves" and was sure to keep a close eye on them. So far, their mischief had been a lot of pranks and some minor indiscretions of which teachers and other students could only speculate they had committed. There were the frogs that ended up in the teachers' lounge one day, and the time all of the erasers went missing during an assembly. Of course, no one could ever prove it was Bud and Smitty, but everyone assumed. Bud had gone from a reputation as an exemplary student in elementary school to one of a trouble maker who was too smart for his own good in a single year.

When Bud was around Stanley working on the farm, the interaction was more of an inappropriate classroom environment. Stanley would teach Bud about women, and the terminology and descriptions he used were graphic and uncouth. Stanley would provide him with dirty magazines once in a while, which Bud would hide in his room and look at when everyone thought he had gone to bed. For a twelve–year–old boy, Bud was getting the "birds and the bees" in the worst possible way. He knew far more of what types of things he could do with a girl than how to treat them or what the feelings he was experiencing meant. At the time however, Bud thought it all made him a lot more grown up. Whenever Bud would share Stanley's teachings with Smitty, Smitty thought it was great. Bud felt like his stature rose a little in his friend's eyes.

Bud was actually excited for the last day of school for the first time in his life. He was growing bored of his studies, and Smitty had said that his older brother, Gavin, was getting his license that spring and would be able to drive him and Bud around over the summer. Bud had visions of going to the beach at the coast, or down to Portland for the day, or even up to the mountains to go hiking and camping. When he told Teresa about his plans, she wasn't nearly as excited as he was at the proposition and did her best to squash his hopes.

"Won't you be working on the farm all summer?" she asked. "When are you going to find time to do all these things?"

"Maybe I can get a day or two off. Pa might let me."

"He never gave you any time off last summer. I seem to remember you wanting not to work a bunch of times and him telling you that it was your responsibility. I think you're fooling yourself Brandon, if you think you're going to have all this free time to hang out with Smitty. Besides, I'm going to be going to middle school next fall, and I was hoping you could help me get a little head start with some of the things I'll be learning."

"Ugh," Bud grunted. "More school, Reese? Really? Don't you ever take a break from the school work? Maybe if you asked, Smitty would let you come with us to the beach or something. We didn't get to go swimming at all together last summer."

Teresa's heart skipped a half a beat. She was still nervous to be in any state of undress in Bud's presence. "I don't think I trust Smitty's brother to drive me anywhere," she said.

"Now you're just being ridiculous."

"Ridiculous, am I? I guess you're just so much smarter than me now. Is that it, Brandon? Am I too dumb?"

"Woah, calm down okay? I didn't say you were dumb. I'm sorry, Teresa. I didn't want to upset you. I just thought it would be fun is all... Never mind." He looked down at his shoes and kicked some dust into the air. "You're probably right anyway. Pa is never going to give me any time off. I'll be stuck here all summer."

Her face softened a little and a mischievous grin began at the corner of her mouth. "It'll be okay, Brandon," she said. "I'll be sure to visit you while you're working. I'll bring you some water. I'll make wave noises and throw it on your head. It'll be just like if you were at the beach."

She laughed and ran off, leaving him rolling his eyes and smiling. Teresa had been right though, it was going to be a very busy summer for Bud. He would have to ask his grandfather how much he was going to need to work and what he could have for free time. He certainly didn't want to waste his entire summer on the farm if Smitty's brother, Gavin, was going to be able to drive them around to have fun.

Buck listened to Bud's entire spiel as he lay out the desire to have some time off in the summer. Bud didn't mind working some, but didn't want to have to be on the farm every single day and wanted some free time to have fun. Buck thought hard for several minutes before saying anything. The silence was harder for Bud than anything his grandfather could have said. Buck relented, saying that Bud could have two days each week off as long as they weren't haying or in the middle of a harvest. Bud was ecstatic and thanked his grandfather repeatedly. When Bud left the room with a huge smile on his face, Maggie walked over to her husband and kissed him on the cheek.

"That was very kind of you, dear," she said.

"Wasn't kindness, Maggie. The boy needs to learn responsibility. He can't do that if I'm constantly forcing it on him. I just hope he learns it quickly enough."

Bud ran over to Teresa's house and told her what Buck had said: that he could have two whole days a week off! When he saw the frown forming on her face, he quickly assured her that he wasn't going to spend all that time with Smitty, and he would be happy to tell her what to expect next year in middle school. Teresa pursed her lips and thought about that, then relaxed and smiled. Truth be told, she was excited to be able to spend some time with Bud this summer, if only to have a chance to figure out why she felt so awkward around him lately.

The last day of school, Gavin showed up in a beat–up old Buick to pick up Smitty and drive him home. He had gotten his license and bought an old beater with money he'd saved up from working previous summers. For Bud, the sight was just about the coolest thing he had seen in his life. Smitty said something to his brother, and then Gavin shouted to Bud asking if he wanted a ride home too. Bud abandoned riding the bus in a flash and hopped in the backseat of the Buick.

Teresa was waiting at the end of the lane when Gavin pulled up with the Buick belching smoke and making a horrible knocking noise under the hood. Bud jumped out and thanked him, yelling over the engine noise to Smitty that he'd be in touch for the two of them to get together as soon as he had a day off. Smitty looked over Bud's shoulder and saw Teresa.

"Who's that, Bud?" he asked. "Your girlfriend?" He stretched the word out to make it sound as mocking as possible. Teresa furrowed her brows and crossed her arms, hugging her books close to her chest.

"Her? Oh, no," Bud replied as he waved Teresa off. "She's just my neighbor." He waved goodbye as Gavin stepped hard on the gas, and the Buick kicked up a cloud of dust as the tires spun on the gravel of the shoulder.

"Just my neighbor?" Teresa said as Bud turned to her. "That's all I am? Just your neighbor?" Bud started to answer but caught himself when he saw that Teresa was actually angry. "Well, I guess your neighbor shouldn't have waited here for you to get off the bus." Teresa said. "And since you'll be meeting up with Smitty on your first day off, I guess that means I'll have to wait for whatever free time you have later. I suppose that's okay, since I'm just your neighbor." She emphasized the word each time she said it, and every one was like a tiny dagger stuck into Bud's gut.

She started to turn to walk away, but Bud reached out and gently grabbed her hand to stop her. Her heart skipped, her feet stopped, and for a moment she couldn't breathe or move. All she could do was stand and feel the touch of his hand on hers.

"I'm sorry, Reese," he said. "I didn't mean it like that." He said it so gently and honestly that, for what felt like an eternity, Teresa couldn't think. Her head swam, and she had to shake free of his grasp before she could reorganize her thoughts.

"I just... I just don't want you to forget about me," she said once she'd composed herself.

"I won't. I promise."

"What about your day off? Are you going to spend it with him?" she gestured back towards Baker Street as she said it.

"Well, I told him I would hang out with him my first day off..." Teresa frowned again, but Bud cut her off before she could speak. "But I get two days, so the second one is all yours, Reese. We can do anything you want to do."

She smiled, and the two of them started walking again. Teresa suggested that their first day that summer they should find a good book that they could read together and find a nice sunny spot to start in on it. She had just the book in mind too, *The Secret Garden*. Her mother had bought it for her, and she was just waiting for the right time to start it. Bud said that all sounded perfect. Teresa continued prattling on about *The Secret Garden* and how it was supposed to be a wonderful story as Bud walked next to her smiling and listening intently.

Bud didn't want Teresa to be mad at him. He had always left the side of his personality that came out around the other boys at school. When Smitty had goaded him, he only knew one way to react. Standing there on the dirt lane, Bud's two worlds had collided. The sparks that resulted from the contact should have served as a warning for what could happen if he allowed it to continue.

Gavin and Smitty picked Bud up on his first day off, and the three of them drove back to the Smiths' place in Mt. Vernon. They lived not far from the country store down a little side street. It was a short walk to the store and just a little further to the public beach on Minnehonk Lake. The house was small and dusty, with two bed rooms, one of which Gavin and Smitty shared.

Bud and Smitty played outside, kicking an old tin can back and forth across the road, only pausing for the rare car. Young boys when left with little to occupy themselves will generally find something to do, even if that something isn't of a savory quality. Boredom breeds bad decisions. Indeed, it wasn't terribly long before Smitty declared that he was bored and had a great idea of something fun to do.

Smitty led Bud down to the main road that ran past the country store. Instead of turning left towards it, he turned right and followed it as it meandered down the side of the lake. After about a quarter of a mile they came to a cabin perched on the edge of the water. Smitty and Bud turned off the road to the side of the cabin. The older boy started kicking at a side door to the building.

"What are you doing?" Bud asked.

"Trying to get inside, what's it look like?"

"Do you know who lives here?"

"They're summer folks. They won't be up for a while yet."

"But why do you want to get inside?"

"Just to look around, Bud. Now, are you going to help me?" Smitty was clearly getting agitated and he kept looking around nervously.

Against his better judgement, Bud took a deep breath and kicked hard at the door next to Smitty. The lock gave way, and the door swung open. The two boys looked at each other and then ran quickly inside. The cabin was rustically decorated with wood furniture and animal motifs, but everything was clearly of high quality, and the owners of the cabin evidently were very well off.

Smitty wandered around whistling amazement at the expensive knick knacks. Bud walked to the back of the cabin and looked out the window down to the dock by the water. He felt funny being in the house of someone he didn't even know, and was about to suggest to Smitty that they should leave when the other boy called over to him.

"Bud, come here."

"What is it?" Bud asked.

Smitty proudly held up a pack of cigarettes and a matchbook with a mischievous grin pasted across his face. "Ever have one before?" Smitty asked.

"No," Bud said. Buck had warned him against smoking, explaining that it was a dirty vice and that he needn't have anything to do with it. Bud had seen Stanley sneaking off to have a smoke now and again and had mentioned it to Buck who just shook his head as though there were nothing more to say.

Smitty pulled a cigarette out of the package and put it between his lips, letting it dangle slightly. "My brother has had 'em before," he said. "All the cool kids smoke. Let's try it."

"I dunno…" Bud began.

"Come on, Bud. You going to make me do it by myself?"

"No, but—"

"Good, come on."

Smitty opened the matchbook, pulling a single match out and striking it on the side of the package. He held it to the end of the cigarette and sucked in as he had seen the older kids do. He coughed as the smoke hit his lungs. Then he passed the cigarette to Bud, nodding as he continued to cough. Bud took the cigarette between his thumb and forefinger and placed it hesitantly between his lips. He took a deep breath and also started coughing just as a large figure walked through the side door.

The owner of the cabin had arrived to get it ready for the summer to find the door broken and two teenage boys smoking one of his cigarettes.

Bud stood in the living room of the cape while Maggie lectured him. The cabin's owner had called Bud's grandparents and let them know what he had found when he arrived. When Bud got home, Maggie and Buck were waiting to have a talk with him. Maggie was doing most of the talking, saying how disappointed she was in him and how she couldn't believe how irresponsible he had been. Bud stood with his head down staring at his shoes the whole time. It wasn't until Maggie had basically exhausted herself that she begged Buck to jump in.

"Don't you have anything to add?" she asked looking at her husband.

"Bud," he said taking his time. "I guess that's the last of your days off for a while."

That simple sentence hit Bud harder than anything his grandmother had said. Bud raised his eyes and began to protest. "But," he said. "But I was supposed to spend the day with Reese tomorrow. We were going to start reading *The Secret Garden* together. She's going to be really mad at me if I don't have the day off."

"I suppose you bettah go explain it to her then," Buck said.

Bud was going to try another round of protesting, but one look at his grandfather's face told him it was useless. Like a scolded puppy he turned, left the room, slunk out the front door and started making the walk over to Teresa's house.

"What are we going to do with that boy?" Maggie asked Buck after Bud had gone.

"The only thing we can do," Buck replied.

"And what's that?" She looked pleadingly at Buck for an answer. Buck walked over and sat down in his chair.

"Our best," was all he said.

To say that Teresa was really mad was an understatement. Bud got a second lecture that rivaled the first he had received from his grandmother. He may have tried to fight back, but all the fight had been driven out of him for the day. Instead, he grew resentful of everyone telling him what to do and how he should behave. Inside, Bud started to shut down. He was tired of being told he had been wrong. He was tired of being told about responsibility. He was so tired of all of it, that nothing Teresa was saying could make any impact anymore. Bud had retreated from the world to a place inside of himself where nothing mattered. When Teresa dismissed him, he turned and walked home prepared to go upstairs to his room and wait for nightfall.

After supper, Buck made his way up to Bud's room. He found his grandson lying on his bed with his hands under his head. Buck sat down gently on the side of the bed and let out a deep sigh. The last thing Bud wanted was another talking to.

"You here to give me another lecture, Pa?" Bud asked. "I get it, I messed up. I won't do it again, okay?"

"I'm not here to lecture you Bud." Buck said. "You got plenty of that from your grandmothah, and I imagine anothah good earful from Teresa if I know her well enough. No, I'm not going to try to tell you who to be or how to behave. You listening to someone tell you those things was what got you into this mess in the first place."

Bud looked up at his grandfather. Buck's tone was gentle and understanding, not accusatory. It opened him up just a little to what was being said and he began to listen more intently.

"I think breaking into that cabin," Buck continued. "I think that was Smitty. I think the smoking was Smitty's doing too. I'm not sure why you let him convince you it was something you should do too, but you did. I'm not going to tell you how to act, Bud. No one should do that — not me, not your grandmothah, not Teresa, and certainly not Smitty. You need to decide how you should act. It's up to you to decide who Bud Marshall is and how he behaves."

Buck looked over at his grandson, now sitting up in his bed listening carefully. "The world..." Buck said, pausing to choose his words carefully. "The world will slam into you from all different directions. It will mold you into something you're not if you let it, Bud. You have to know who you are so that when the world hits you, damages you, even if it breaks you, you can put everything back where it belongs. The Bud I know is kind, thoughtful, and respectful of othahs. He loves his family and his friends. He's hard working and responsible with his own belongings and those of othahs. But the Bud I know doesn't mattah. The only Bud that mattahs is the one you know."

Buck patted his grandson on the leg, stood and walked slowly out of the room. Bud had never heard his grandfather talk like that before. He sat pondering the words long into the night, wondering if he himself really truly knew Bud Marshall at all.

# 14

**B**ud was exhausted. Buck had worked him hard all summer with hardly any days off. The few days he did have off weren't all that fun either. Buck wouldn't let him go anywhere in Gavin's car, and he was only allowed to hang out with Smitty if he came to the farm, which Smitty found boring. Somehow, Smitty hadn't gotten punished at all for breaking into the summer cabin and smoking.

"My old man just slapped me upside the head and called me an idiot," Smitty said. "That was it."

Bud wished it had been that simple for him. He had tried to spend some time with Teresa, but she was still upset with him for ruining their first day together. If there was one thing that girl could do, it was hold a grudge. Bud was always amazed at how easy it was for her to completely ignore and avoid him when she wanted to. Once she decided to forgive him though, it was like flipping a switch. She went from non–existent to friendly at the snap of a finger. The two had finally found time to read *The Secret Garden*, but Bud was so exhausted that he kept dozing off. Teresa would have to nudge him to wake him back up.

The new school year was rapidly approaching. Bud was glad that he and Teresa were back on friendly terms because they'd be riding the bus together again. Teresa was just excited to be going to middle school. It would offer new challenges and new opportunities to learn, which is what she loved. Bud had told her some of the stuff that she would be covering in class her first months so that she could study a little bit ahead and really shine in front of her new classmates.

When the day arrived, she was waiting for Bud on the steps and the two walked down the lane together and boarded the bus. They sat together for the ride to Maranacook Middle School, even though Bud was a little concerned that Smitty would give him a hard time if he saw them get off the bus together. Thankfully, he was nowhere to be seen when they arrived at school. Bud showed Teresa to her homeroom and said goodbye to her.

"See you at recess, Reese," he said. She smiled and entered her homeroom. Bud walked down the hall glad to have Teresa in the same school as him.

Bud went outside when the bell rang for recess and started looking around for Teresa. He had a hard time at first, until he finally saw her sitting on the bleachers with another boy. He made his way down to the ball field and walked up to them.

"Hey, Reese," he said.

"Reese?" the other boy said looking at Teresa confused.

"Oh. Gregg, this is Brandon," Teresa said.

"Bud," Bud corrected her.

"Brandon, this is Gregg," Teresa continued. "We're in the same homeroom. He's really smart. He already reads at a high school level! We were just talking about books, why don't you join us?"

Bud stood there not sure what to say. He was upset with Teresa. She was supposed to meet up with him at recess and instead she was sitting down here talking to some guy about books.

Didn't she care that he'd been looking all over for her? He felt embarrassed by the whole situation, and as a result, anger was beginning to grow deep down inside him.

"Uh... No thanks," he answered. "I was just looking for you because I thought you might be a little lonely with it being your first day and all. Since you're clearly fine without me I'll just go and find Smitty."

He had meant the reply to be stinging and make Teresa feel bad about ditching him, but she just smiled back at him.

"Okay, Brandon," she said. "I'll catch up with you later then." She turned back to Gregg and continued their conversation.

Bud walked off fuming. He found Smitty standing under an oak tree nearby with a couple of other boys, and they had seen the whole thing. As Bud walked over to him he started chuckling.

"Looks like your girlfriend replaced you, Bud," he said with a laugh.

"She's not my girlfriend," Bud said irritated.

"Well, not anymore."

"Look, she was never my girlfriend. Okay? I would never date a dirty slut like that."

The boys' mouths dropped open. Bud had heard Stanley use the word to describe women more than once. The reaction he got having said it was enough to egg him on. At least the focus was no longer on what a fool he had been made to look like.

"That's right, a slut," he continued emphasizing the word. "That girl lives next door to me and she's always trying to do dirty stuff with me."

"Like what?" Smitty said not really believing him.

"Well, like, she takes all her clothes off in front of me and splashes around in the stream trying to get me to go in with her. And I found her kissing our handy man, Stanley one time. And she's always saying how much she wants to see me naked and touch my cock."

The other boys, including Smitty, gasped at the use of the dirty word. Bud was on a roll now. He had their attention and he could see that their interest in his story was growing. He went on describing all the dirty words that Teresa liked to use around him, and all the things she had suggested they should do. She wasn't even twelve years old yet, but by the time Bud finished his story all the boys around him thought Teresa was the most promiscuous girl they'd ever seen.

The bell rang and everyone headed back up to the school for classes. Bud started to feel a little bad about the lies he was telling the other boys about Teresa, but she shouldn't have ditched him the way she did. When school ended he headed out to get on the bus. He climbed the steps and starting looking for an empty seat where he and Teresa could sit together. He would straighten it all out with her on the ride home, he thought. Then, he saw that Teresa was already on the bus and she was sitting with Gregg. As he walked down the aisle, he caught her eye.

"Hey, Brandon!" she called. "Gregg rides our bus too. Isn't that great?" Bud gave her a dirty look and sat down in another seat before he got close enough that he had to answer her.

As Teresa sat talking to Gregg about her day, she became aware of the kids around her whispering and glancing in her direction. With no indication of what it was all about, she put it out of her mind. When she got off the bus, Bud was already quite a ways down the dirt lane and heading quickly away from her. She ran to catch up with him, but when she tried to talk to him, he just ignored her and kept walking. Giving up, she slowed to her normal speed and watched him pull away. If Bud was upset it would be best just to give him space and try to talk to him about it the next morning.

Bud got up extra early, trying to avoid having to walk with Teresa to the bus stop. He walked out his front door just as she was walking out of hers. When he saw her, he turned and immediately started towards Baker Street without her. Once again, she ran and caught up and this time she wasn't going to let him ignore her.

"Brandon Marshall," she said. "You are going to tell me why you're so upset this instant!"

"Fine!" he said. "I don't know why you had to ditch me for that Gregg guy. I was just trying to make your first day a good one, so you didn't have to be alone at recess and you weren't even waiting for me. You just left with your new best friend."

Although Bud didn't know it, but he was feeling the same emotions that Teresa had felt when she found out he had kissed Sarah on his second day of middle school. It wasn't really that he wanted to be Teresa's boyfriend, just that he didn't want anyone else to be either. He was supposed to be the one discussing books with her, not some new guy.

"It's nothing to be upset about, Brandon," Teresa said. "He's just a new friend. You'd like him. He loves books just like you and I do."

"That guy is nothing like me. If you want to be friends with him instead of me that's just fine. I don't care."

"Can't I be friends with both of you?"

Bud didn't answer. He kept walking until the intersection with Baker Street. Teresa waited patiently for him to reply. He stood for a long time, just letting the anger inside him swirl, burning his insides. It wasn't until the bus came into view and pulled to a stop in front of him that he said anything at all.

"No," he said as he headed for the opening bus door. "If you want to be friends with him, then you don't need to be friends with me."

Bud got on the bus and made a point to sit down next to another kid the first chance he got so that Teresa couldn't sit next to him. Teresa was incredibly hurt, but she knew there was nothing she could do about it right now. She would try to talk to Bud at recess if he would let her. For now, she walked down the aisle looking for Gregg. He was sitting halfway down the bus by himself, but when he saw her coming he moved close to the aisle, blocking her from sitting with him.

"Sorry, you can't sit here," he said not looking up at her.

"Why not, Gregg?" she asked confused.

"I'm sorry, I didn't know you were... that way."

"What way?" Teresa was really confused now. She was going to have to find a seat soon or the bus driver was going to get upset with her for not sitting.

"I didn't know you were... a slut," he said, barely whispering the word.

"What?!" Teresa screamed. The bus driver yelled for her to quiet down and find a seat.

Gregg turned his head away from her and wouldn't say anything else. Her mouth agape, Teresa staggered to the back of the bus where there was an empty seat. She sat down and rode the rest of the way to school with her head swimming.

Teresa cornered Gregg in homeroom and made him tell her everything. Gregg said after she'd gotten off the bus the day before, one of the other kids had told him that everyone was talking about how Bud Marshall had been saying she was a slut and did all kinds of dirty things with boys whenever she could. Teresa's face turned bright red as she denied all of it. She asked Gregg how he could believe such a thing about her.

"I don't really know you," he said. "We only met yesterday."

Teresa said everything Bud had told people was a lie and that she was going to confront him about it at recess today and clear everything up. Gregg said he was willing to give her the benefit of the doubt and that he had found it hard to believe she was that kind of girl anyway.

When Teresa approached Bud at recess, he was standing with Smitty and the other usual guys he hung out with. She walked right up to him and demanded to know why he was spreading rumors about her that weren't true. The other boys raised their eyebrows as they looked at Bud to see how he was going to handle the situation. Bud felt numerous pairs of eyes boring into him. It felt like the rays of the sun shining directly on him, and the heat was so intense he started to sweat. He knew his only way to save face in front of the other boys was to stick with the lie.

"Look, I know you're embarrassed," he began. "I'm sure it's embarrassing to be a slut. I mean, I wouldn't know because I'm not one."

Teresa's eyes widened as she realized that Bud wasn't going to take back what he said. Her mouth opened, but no words came out.

"I'm sorry that new boy that you wanted to get naked with doesn't like you now that he knows what you are," Bud continued. "Maybe you should try keeping your clothes on and guys will respect you a little bit more."

There were snickers from the boys around him aimed in Teresa's direction. Her face was reddening by the second, but Bud knew he was selling the lie to the other boys, so he kept going.

"I'm sure there are guys who like that kind of thing. I mean, heck, I hear some guys even pay for it. Maybe that's a possible career for you."

At that, Teresa found her voice.

"Brandon Marshall!" she screamed. "You are the most despicable boy I've ever known. I never want to talk to you again! I hate you!"

She stormed off as the boys around Bud started patting him on the back and saying how great it was that he told that slut off.

Bud's heart, however, was in his throat. He had made Teresa mad before over little stuff, and she had held it against him for far longer than he could have imagined. He was pretty sure this time, he had upset her enough that she might actually never speak to him again. This gave him a feeling of emptiness deep down in a place he'd never felt before.

Sure enough, Teresa refused to look at or speak to Bud at all the rest of that day, and the next, and the next. At first, Bud tried to talk to her and apologize, but she ignored him completely and walked away any time she saw him coming. After over a week of that treatment, Bud gave up altogether. He began to ignore his school work, choosing to hang out with Smitty and the other boys instead.

Bud dropped into a state of depression that he couldn't seem to shake. He was smart enough that he maintained reasonable grades, despite not ever really opening his books or listening in class. He continued to get into bits of trouble with Smitty, earning himself a couple of detentions and the ire of Maggie and disappointment of Buck. The trend continued for the entire school year, past Teresa's twelfth birthday when she refused to accept Bud's gift, beyond his thirteenth birthday when Teresa ignored him, through Christmas when she sat in the corner and didn't speak to him, and into the spring as school drew to a close.

The situation should have humbled Bud, but instead he grew resentful and defiant. If Teresa thought he was such a despicable person, maybe he was. He stopped caring about the rules and his responsibilities. His days consisted of doing what he thought would make him "feel good," but it always ended up making him feel a little worse about himself and so the cycle continued. Bud was on a dangerous path, and if he didn't do something to correct his course, he was in danger a losing himself in the wilderness.

Buck's plan for dealing with an unruly boy was simple: work, and lots of it. Bud rarely had any free time, and the little he did have he spent with Smitty. Smitty was a year ahead of Bud in school and would be attending high school that coming fall. Bud kept asking him if he was nervous to go to school with all of the older kids. Smitty would shrug and explain that his older brother would be there, and the older kids got to do cool stuff so he thought it would be all right. Bud was sorry he wouldn't have Smitty to hang out with at school for a whole year, especially with Teresa still ignoring him.

Eventually, spending his free time with Smitty seemed to depress Bud even more. Smitty was starting to hang out with Gavin and some of his high school friends, and Bud just didn't seem to fit in with them. So, on his days off, Bud would wander up the stream to the pool by the waterfall and just sit watching and listening to the water splash.

Bud didn't know it, but once when he was there Teresa came walking up along the stream looking for a place to read and saw him sitting there on the log deep in thought. She hid behind some bushes and just watched him for a few minutes. She wondered how someone she had felt so close to could have treated her so poorly and violated her trust so greatly. Teresa was the type to trust another wholly until that trust was betrayed. Once the trust was gone, it took her a long time to give that person another chance, and then it took longer still to earn the trust back. It would be some time, she thought, before she would give Bud another chance. Any feelings that had been developing for Bud had been buried under a mountain of anger and resentment so high that not even a wisp could escape the crushing weight above.

Sitting on the log watching the waters of the pool boil where the small waterfall fell, Bud felt utterly alone. He was tired too. He was tired from work on the farm. He was tired of waiting for Teresa to talk to him. He was tired of Maggie being mad at him. He was tired of Buck being disappointed and thinking more work would straighten him out. He was tired of thinking about school. Mostly though, he was tired of feeling alone.

The weariness and sadness crept through Bud slowly, gnawing at his mind. All through the next school year he withdrew more and more from the world. He had built a reputation over his first two years in middle school as a troublemaker, so any little thing he did to get out of line got him in more trouble. It could be as simple as not hearing a question a teacher asked because his thoughts had been smothered by the blackness that was ever growing in his mind. For that, he was called disrespectful and was sent to the principal. Bud discovered that reputations are hard things to break once they are set.

Maggie was the first to notice the change in Bud. He seemed withdrawn and there was no joy where it once had been. She expressed her concerns to Buck, who started paying more attention after that. If Maggie noticed something, something was there. Bud's grades had been steadily declining the last two years. Where he had once been at the top of his class, he was now firmly entrenched in the middle. But the thing that struck Buck the most, was that Bud never wanted to read anymore. Bud had loved reading and would rarely be found sitting without his nose in a book when he had free time alone. Now all of Bud's free time was alone, and he never read for fun.

On his fourteenth birthday, Bud didn't want a party or any other children around. He sat in his room staring out the window, asking to be left alone. At Christmas, he again sat in his room and refused to leave even when he was told that Teresa was there. When the school year ended for summer in '75, Bud felt no joy. He felt nothing at all. He went to work on the farm as he had the previous two summers. When Buck asked him to do a job he did it, but he did so without enthusiasm. He also exhibited a diminished work ethic from what Buck had seen from him in the past.

Maggie was very worried about Bud, especially with him starting high school in the fall. She told Buck he needed to get through to their grandson.

"He's got to figure it out for himself, Maggie," Buck said.

"He's lost, Buck," She replied. "He can't figure it out. He doesn't even know what he's trying to figure out. He needs some guidance. Can't we get Teresa to at least talk to him again. He's been this way ever since she stopped hanging around."

"I don't think anyone can get that girl to do anything she doesn't want to do."

Maggie sighed. She felt like if they didn't do something, and soon, they were going to lose Bud the same way they lost their son.

# 15

The prospect of attending high school lifted Bud's spirits a little. While Teresa still had a year of middle school left and would be taking a different bus, Bud thought maybe her not having to work so hard to avoid him would help the situation. Who knows, maybe she would even relent and allow him to apologize finally for spreading rumors about her. The thing that gave him hope was that he would once again be in the same school as Smitty, so maybe he'd have someone to talk to and hang out with again. Smitty's brother had graduated the previous spring, so he was less likely to be hanging out with that older crowd now.

On Bud's first day of high school, he decided he would leave the hallway where the freshmen had their lockers and go in search of Smitty. He wandered down towards the main office scanning faces for his friend when an older boy bumped into his shoulder shoving him into some lockers on the other side of the hall.

"Watch it, freshman," he sneered. The other boys around him laughed. "This isn't your hallway. I think you need to go back where you belong."

The boy was taller than Bud and clearly athletic, but Bud had grown quite strong from working on the farm. Confrontation wasn't something he was used to though, so he stood there with a confused look on his face for several seconds.

"Didn't you hear me, freshman?" The boy said poking Bud in the shoulder.

"I heard you," Bud replied not moving. "But I don't think you own this hallway."

This enraged the boy, and he was about to shove Bud again when Smitty came running up.

"Woah, woah, hey, Drake!" Smitty said coming between the other two. "He's just a little lost, no big deal."

"You taking his side, Smitty?" Drake said.

"Sides, why is it always sides with you jocks? You think everyone needs a team?" Smitty nodded over Drake's shoulder at the other boys standing around. "I bet you wouldn't act so tough if you were alone."

"You want a fight?" Drake said raising his voice. "I don't need any help to kick your scrawny ass!"

At the sound of the raised voices, principal LeVeque made his way out of the office.

"What's going on out here, gentlemen?" he asked.

"Nothing, Principal LeVeque," they answered.

"Mr. Smith," he said looking at Smitty. "Are you causing problems." Smitty shook his head no.

"And who might you be?" he asked, turning towards Bud.

"Bud Marshall, sir," Bud answered.

"Ah yes, Mr. Marshall. Yes, I've heard of you. You wouldn't be trying to start trouble your first day here, would you?"

"No sir," Bud answered.

"He bumped into me, Principal LeVeque," Drake interjected. The boys around him nodded in agreement. The principal eyed Bud suspiciously.

"Listen, Mr. Marshall, I know your reputation for causing trouble. I'm here to tell you right now that I have zero tolerance for that type of behavior in this school. Do I make myself clear? You step so much as one toe out of line and I will suspend you. Understand?"

Bud nodded and the principal returned to the office. Drake smirked at Bud as Smitty grabbed him by the arm and led him back towards the hall for freshmen.

"What are you trying to do, Bud?" he asked once they were out of earshot.

"What do you mean? I was just coming to find you."

"Freshmen don't just walk through the halls unless they're going to and from classes. Upperclassmen won't allow it."

"That's ridiculous."

"Ridiculous or not, you got on Drake Goucher's bad side. He's a jock, and jocks stick together. You need to just keep your head down this first year. Once you're no longer a freshman, most everyone will leave you alone."

Bud didn't understand all these new rules of social hierarchy. Smitty explained jocks were any of the guys who played sports. Drake was a star in cross country and track and field, two of the biggest sports at Maranacook High School. He was a big shot, and an honor student in academics; so not only did he have the jocks on his side but the teachers and principal would likely side with him too.

When Bud asked what Smitty was considered, Smitty laughed. He didn't fit into a category, but most of the jocks thought he was a greaser. He liked taking shop and working on cars. Bud knew a lot about cars from having helped Buck in his garage. He told Smitty he wanted to take shop too, but Smitty explained that as a freshman he wouldn't have elective periods his first semester. The teachers initially set the schedules for freshmen. Once again, Bud would have to wait before he could be around Smitty much.

The little hope Bud had found in starting high school faded that first month as he tried to keep his head down and avoid the upperclassmen. Drake, especially, had decided to make it his mission to pester Bud. Every time he saw him in the hallway he would bump into him and pretend it was an accident. The whole thing was starting to grate on Bud, but he knew that he would be blamed if things escalated.

Things back home and on the farm were starting to wind down as summer ended and fall began. Buck had things all ready for pumpkin season and was preparing to start clearing trees in the newer acreage for firewood. As Bud was in school, he was mostly exempt from farm work, unless Buck needed an extra hand on the weekend. Bud spent his free time outside, hoping to catch a glimpse of Teresa and get her to talk to him again. It was like she had disappeared though, because he never saw her. Once, he asked Jim how she was doing. Jim furrowed his brow and looked hard at Bud with understanding eyes.

"She's all right, Bud." He said. "She spends a lot of time at friends' houses these days. I know you'd like to see her again, but you know Teresa. She's not ready, and until she is you can't make her be."

The darkness within Bud continued to spread like a cancer eating away at what remained of his joy. He was consumed by weariness and anger at the world for abandoning him.

It was early October when he was first overwhelmed. The trees had turned fiery red and orange, and the leaves were falling fast. He was sitting in class pretending to pay attention through the fog of not caring while watching leaves blow by the window. The teacher asked Bud a question, but he didn't hear her. She asked again. Again, Bud didn't hear. Finally, she raised her voice and he heard. He stammered, having no idea what she had been discussing. She dismissed him to the office, calling him disrespectful and a trouble maker. Bud left the room to the sound of snickering behind him. The pit of his stomach started to burn.

As he walked down to the office he cast his eyes to the floor, knowing that Principal LeVeque would punish him simply because of his reputation. He loathed the world. As he neared the office, he didn't see Drake coming the other way. Drake saw him, though. He bumped into Bud's shoulder, knocking him sideways. As Bud looked up at him, Drake smiled a wicked smile.

"Ooops," he said mockingly.

He turned to walk away, but in that moment Bud snapped. He lunged back at Drake, grabbing him with both hands. The adrenaline surged through him, the anger fueling a power he didn't know he had. He lifted Drake into the air and slammed him against the lockers nearby. He took his fury and placed it squarely into Drake as he tossed him to the ground. Principal LeVeque came charging from his office just in time to stop Bud as he pinned Drake to the ground ready to lash out with his fists.

Bud pleaded his case, but because he had been thrown out of class for being disrespectful to a teacher and had attacked Drake, he had little chance of leniency. He was suspended for three days and was told that the next time it would be expulsion.

Maggie was so exasperated with their grandson that she couldn't deal with him anymore. She left Buck to take care of the situation, and he promised to handle it. Buck told Bud that for the next three days he would have to help gather firewood from the new acreage, split it, stack, and store it. Bud didn't bother to argue. He had told his side of the story, and that was all he could do.

Bud worked in the woods with his grandfather. They cut down trees and cut them up to be hauled up to the house. After several hours of work, Buck sat on a downed tree to take a break. He motioned for Bud to come sit next to him.

"I want to talk to you, Bud," Buck said.

"Ok."

"But I want you to really listen."

Bud looked over at his grandfather and into his deep blue eyes. They twinkled slightly in the dim forest light. He nodded, knowing that when Buck spoke at length, it was valuable to listen.

"Look around, Bud," Buck began, speaking very slowly. "What do you see?"

"Trees," Bud said looking around.

"What kinds of trees?"

"I don't know. All kinds I guess."

"There are two types of trees in the world. First there are the trees that lose their leaves for the wintah: deciduous trees. When the weather gets coldah, the days shortah, and the sun weakah, the deciduous trees wilt from lack of nutrients. They shut down, close up, go dormant. Essentially, they die inside until the world around them improves.

Then there are the evergreens: those trees that nevah change color. The ones that are steadfast in the face of impending disaster. No mattah how harsh the season, how bleak the outlook, or how scarce the availability of basic necessities, they remain green. Regardless of circumstance, the evergreen is resolute.

People are basically the same. Some will meet the challenges in life with a resolve to resist unchanged. Some will shrink from them and trust to hope that things will improve. The problem is… there's no telling when spring will come. But, for the evergreen, that doesn't mattah. The evergreen trusts only in its own charactah to survive."

Bud looked up at the trees around him with new eyes. He studied them thinking not only about how they lived, but about how they survived.

"But, Pa," he said. "The deciduous trees are the ones we call 'hard woods,' and the evergreens are 'soft woods.' Aren't hard woods stronger than soft woods?"

"That's true," Buck said smiling. "The deciduous trees are hardah, but only at their heart. They are soft on the outside, where the evergreens may have a rough exteriah but are soft at the heart. Look at how the trees that are hard at heart do in a storm — they are quick to break. But the evergreens, the trees that are rough on the outside but soft at heart, can survive strong winds without breaking. A storm has to tear an evergreen up by its very roots to destroy it.

If a man can be like the evergreen, tough on the outside and soft at heart while refusing to be changed by the world, that man can get through just about anything the world throws at him. If a man lets the world change who he is, but is hard in his heart, he will break."

Bud understood what his grandfather was telling him. He knew he was allowing the world to change him. What others thought about him had become more important than what he thought about himself. Bud now knew he had been spiraling down into a pit that he eventually wouldn't be able to climb out of. Depression had led him to the brink of despair, but he was beginning to think he had the courage to turn aside before it was too late.

Buck suggested it would be a good time to head in for lunch and take a proper break. The two loaded what they had cut onto the trailer behind the tractor and pulled it up to the house. They left it to be unloaded until after lunch and went inside. Bud sat in silence and ate the soup that his grandmother had prepared. Maggie sensed a change, almost a lightness to her grandson's mood, and it cheered her heart.

Bud watched his grandparents eat; they seemed so content. When Maggie was done, she went to the sink and started doing the dishes. Buck finished and joined her, washing each item in turn and handing them to her to dry. Bud had watched them do this thousands of times, but he had never really seen it. He added his bowl to the sink, Buck washed it, and Maggie dried it. Buck gave her a kiss on the cheek and led Bud outside and back to work.

Bud was deep in thought and splitting wood, while his grandfather stacked the cut pieces under the shed when a car pulled into the drive. Bud hardly noticed as Buck stopped stacking and walked over to meet a man getting out. Bud continued splitting wood until he heard his name.

"Bud and I will be ovah tomorrow and take care of it," Buck said.

"Thank you, Buck. It's a good thing that we have someone like you in our town," the man said.

Bud looked up and saw Mr. Pratt, one of the wealthier men in the area. He owned several lumber mills around the state and was a pillar of the community. Mr. Pratt caught Bud's eye as he was shaking Buck's hand before getting back in the car.

"Your grandfather is a great man, youngster," Mr. Pratt said to Bud. "You could learn a lot from him."

Bud nodded as Mr. Pratt climbed behind the wheel of his shiny sedan and backed out of the drive. Buck walked over and continued stacking the split wood. Bud didn't turn back to his work until he had watched the car drive up the lane and out of sight. It wasn't two minutes before he had to ask his grandfather about the meeting.

"What are we doing tomorrow?" Bud asked.

"Mr. Pratt has a problem with one of his logging trucks. I told him we'd go and take a look at it."

"He's pretty important, huh, Pa?"

"Important?" Buck asked, amused.

"Sure — I mean, everyone knows him and thinks quite a lot of him. He's rich and owns a bunch of stuff and has a lot of employees. He's one of the most important men in town, isn't he? And he said you're a great man! If someone like Mr. Pratt calls you a 'great man' that's a pretty big compliment, right?"

Buck saw the wonder in Bud's eyes as he talked about Mr. Pratt. "Bud," he said, "do you think your Pa is a great man?"

"Of course, Pa," Bud answered. "But when a great man like Mr. Pratt says it, it means a lot more than if your grandson does."

"No, Bud, I don't think Mr. Pratt has any idea whethah or not I'm a great man."

"What do you mean, Pa?"

"What do you think makes a man great, Bud?" Buck stood waiting for Bud to answer, but when he didn't Buck continued. "Do you think owning lots of land and huge companies and making lots of money makes a man great? Do you think it's being well known, or considered important that makes a man great? I don't think so. I think doing great things is what makes a man great. The actions of our lives that impact others, the things they'll remembah are what make us great."

"What great things have you done, Pa?" Bud asked. He had meant it innocently, but as soon as it left his lips he thought it sounded condescending. He wished he could take it back, but Buck was unfazed. The old man just paused from stacking wood and looked off into the distance smiling, his eyes twinkling slightly in the sun. Finally, he took a deep breath and answered.

"The greatest thing a man can do, is love anothah with all his heart. In that measure, you and your grandmothah are the finest examples of the great things I have done. If you look all throughout human history at the greatest men, they all have that one thing in common; they gave of themselves for the love of anothah. Whethah for love of a friend, a wife, a child, their country, or just a love of freedom, they gave all that they had. That's not to say they were wasteful with their life, or gave foolishly, but each was willing to sacrifice for those that he loved. That's what makes a man great, Bud."

Buck went back to stacking wood as Bud stood there soaking in the words his grandfather had spoken. He had once told Teresa that he wanted to be great when he grew up, and now he was realizing he had never truly known what that meant. He wanted it now more than ever, but how to get there was another thing entirely.

That night after dinner, Bud found a blank notebook with a dark green cover in his school things and wrote down all the things Buck had told him that day as closely as he could remember them, word for word. He knew it was too much for him to come to grips with that evening, but he wanted it all for future reference. He placed the notebook under his dresser with the old *Alice and Jerry* book that he had knocked out of Teresa's hands and into the mud all those years ago.

He hauled his school bag up onto the bed and pulled his school books out of it. He sat in the light of his bedside lamp and did his homework for the first time in as long as he could remember. He wasn't sure it was who he really was, but he knew that finding himself meant he had to try something different from what he had been doing. His reputation wasn't going to change overnight, but he was going to have to ignore everyone else and just charge ahead. "Be like the evergreen," his grandfather had said. Bud was going to try.

# 16

**T**hose first few days after returning to school were some of the hardest Bud could remember. Knowing your reputation isn't going to change overnight is one thing. Living through the difficulties of trying to change it is another. Bud started simply enough by doing his homework and being respectful of the teachers and his other classmates. He didn't speak out of turn, raised his hand, and tried to be a good student.

His first challenge was when his math teacher expressed concern that he had either copied or stolen someone else's homework. Bud responded politely that the work was, in fact, his own. He suppressed his anger when the teacher eyed him suspiciously but relented in accepting the work.

Such minor incidents Bud could get past. After all, his reputation was of his own making. However, the second incident was harder for him to accept. Several weeks had passed, and Bud's grades were steadily improving in all of his classes. When the time came for a big test in his history class, the teacher told Bud he would need to sit in a corner of the room separated from all the other students. Bud asked why, and the answer he received hit him hard.

"I just need to be absolutely sure that your improvement in this class is of your own doing and not anyone else's," the history teacher, Ms. Driscoll, said.

"You think I'm cheating?" Bud asked.

"Well now, I don't want to accuse anyone without grounds of such a thing, but your grades have been... shall we say, unusually high for you lately. If it's been your own work and you've actually been learning the material, it should be no problem producing results sitting off by yourself, should it?"

"No Ma'am, no problem at all," Bud said, forcing a smile.

While Bud scored well on the history test, earning an eighty–eight percent, his resolve was shaken. He sat on his bed later that night fuming about the whole thing. Perhaps if everyone thought he was a troublemaker and he couldn't shake the reputation even by improving his actions, then maybe he was a troublemaker. After all, what good was changing the way you act if no one accepted it?

Bud got up and walked to his dresser, and pulled out the notebook where he had written all the things Buck had told him. He read them over and then took several deep breaths and exhaled. The small act of meditation helped him to soften his heart towards those who couldn't see past his reputation. Several years of causing trouble wasn't going to be erased by a month of trying to change things. Bud knew he wasn't going to work miracles.

He opened his school bag and took out a pencil. In his notebook he found a blank page and wrote at the top "Do it for yourself" in large block lettering. The act cleared his mind and focused his perspective where it needed to be. He would never convince anyone else that he had turned over a new leaf if he didn't believe it himself.

The next week his English teacher, Mr. Gauge, assigned *The Scarlet Letter* for the class to read. It would be the first assigned book that Bud read in several years. He was actually excited for the prospect. Mr. Gauge gave the class two weeks to finish the book before they discussed it and then took a test on the material. Bud finished the entire novel that weekend. He nestled down in front of the fire with some pillows and read non–stop like he had done when he was younger.

Maggie actually smiled when she peeked into the living room from the kitchen at him lying like a little boy on his stomach, propped up on his elbows in the glow of the fire. She turned to Buck and caught a glimmer from his eye in the firelight as he watched his grandson. She felt hope for the first time in a long time, for both of them.

The story of Hester Prynne, the adulteress forced to wear a scarlet letter "A" on her clothes as punishment for her crime, was especially poignant considering Bud's current situation. He empathized with the protagonist a great deal, and so he felt prepared to discuss the book in his English class.

Bud waited anxiously for the day of the discussion, and when it arrived he had a nervous excitement he didn't fully understand. Mr. Gauge began the day by giving a brief overview of the book and the sensitive nature of the material. Mr. Gauge stated that he expected everyone to take the discussion seriously and that they should behave as adults while discussing any matter of adultery. There were some snickers that were quickly shut down when Mr. Gauge eyed the room gravely. The teacher then opened the book to discussion with a question.

"Does anyone here feel like they can identify with Hester Prynne?" Mr. Gauge asked the class.

Most of the class shifted nervously in their seats. Bud raised his hand. It was immediately met with laughs from around the room. Mr. Gauge frowned at Bud.

"Bud, what did I just say about taking this seriously?" he said.

"I am, Mr. Gau —," Bud began.

"You can head straight to the principal's office," Mr. Gauge said cutting him off. He started to turn his back to Bud to write on the chalkboard, but Bud wasn't about to give up: not today.

"Mr. Gauge?" He began.

"Young man, I am not prepared to tolerate any—"

"Sir, I wasn't trying to make a joke. May I explain?" Bud said softly.

Mr. Gauge studied him suspiciously, but Bud looked him straight in the eye giving nothing away. The rest of the class seemed to hold its collective breath as the two stared each other down. Bud's face was stoic, and Mr. Gauge was at a loss for trying to figure the young man out. Eventually he broke eye contact and relented.

"Very well, Bud," Mr. Gauge said. "You may explain how you feel like Hester Prynne to the class. Please come stand at the front of the room, but let me warn you that if you act in a way that I feel is disrespectful or immature in any way, you'll go straight to the office. Do you understand?"

Bud nodded and rose from his desk. He walked slowly to the front of the room while every last eye in the place tracked even his smallest movement. He turned and stood in front of the blackboard and swallowed deeply before speaking.

"Hester Prynne did something wrong, and for that she was punished. She wasn't just punished once, though. Hester was branded with the scarlet "A" to wear as a constant reminder of what she did wrong. Plenty of people have done stuff that was wrong before. I know I've done things that were wrong. The difference for Hester was that she had to carry that reputation with her all the time. Sometimes I feel that way. Mr. Gauge, even you assumed I was making a joke when I raised my hand. I don't blame you, I know my reputation. Even though I don't have to wear a letter on my clothes everywhere I go, I might as well be. I can try to be better and improve my grades and follow the rules, but my reputation will always be there. Hester did good things too, but that scarlet "A" was always there."

Mr. Gauge's face softened as Bud looked at him. Bud continued when the teacher didn't say anything.

"It's not even about one mistake, or several mistakes, or being punished. It's about everyone else's perception of you and how that controls how you live and what you do and what you think of yourself. Hester was brave. She could have moved, or been sad or miserable because of what she had done. Instead, she wore that scarlet "A" every day. What she had done influenced who she was and how she grew as a person. I feel like that's what I have to do. I can't be consumed with what everyone else thinks about me or the scarlet letter of my reputation. All I can do is be the person I want to be regardless of what everyone else sees. That's why I can identify with Hester Prynne."

Everyone stared at Bud, but no one dared to move or speak. Even Mr. Gauge didn't say anything. Bud slowly walked back to his desk. It wasn't until he sat down that Mr. Gauge finally said something.

"Thank you, Bud," He said. "I apologize for assuming the worst from you. I think you've summarized Hester Prynne very well for the class and I'm glad you found a way to connect with the character and make the novel personal to your own life. That's something we would all do well to achieve each time we read a piece of literature."

While Mr. Gauge attempted to continue his lesson as if nothing had happened, the atmosphere of the room had changed. Bud felt as if he had won some small victory in the war to rediscover himself. People had always said that speaking in front of a group was one of the scariest things there was to do. Bud on the other hand, felt liberated. He spoke the words he felt and believed in his heart and didn't care what anyone in the room thought about them. It was the opposite of scary; it was empowering.

Bud didn't know, and couldn't have known, but his act sparked quite a discussion in the teachers' lounge later that day. When Mr. Gauge recounted the story for the teachers assembled, it most spoke to Ms. Driscoll. She backed up Mr. Gauge's story saying that Bud was performing far better in history class, and perhaps the young man was in fact turning a corner. No one else seemed very convinced, but at the very least Bud was convincing himself, and that was all that mattered.

Momentum was finally on Bud's side, and his spirits continued to lift. His grades were steadily improving in all of his classes, and while many of the teachers still assumed Bud was somehow gaming the system or otherwise getting his work from someone else, Bud no longer let it bother him. He got to see Smitty occasionally in the hallway, and he was looking forward to the end of the semester when he could finally sign up for an elective shop class with his friend. The only person who was still able to get under his skin was Drake, and he longed for a way to turn the tides on the jock who still managed to find a way to literally bump into him in the hall from time to time.

"Why don't you pull some kind of prank on the jerk?" Smitty asked him one day when Bud was particularly upset with Drake.

"Sure, but what kind of prank?"

"I don't know, man. I'm sure you could get into his gym locker when he's not in there. Maybe do something to his clothes?"

"Like what?"

"Like put something in them, or steal them. Hell, I don't know." Smitty said.

"Put something in them, like to make him itchy or something?"

"Hey, there you go," Smitty said with a grin. "The poison ivy is nice and bright red right now. Stuff some of that in his clothes and watch the jerk squirm!"

The two boys laughed together at the thought. Then they hatched a plan. Bud would gather some poison ivy and put it in a bag to bring to school. The two of them would bring rubber gloves and ask to go to the bathroom from class at the same time during Drake's gym class. The plan was to sneak into the locker room and rub the poison ivy all over the inside of Drake's clothes. They would ditch the gloves and bag in the trash and return to class like nothing happened. The brilliant scheme was laid, and they planned to execute it two days later.

Bud sat anxiously in class on the day he and Smitty had chosen, waiting for the clock to hit the agreed upon time. When the hour struck, Bud raised his hand and asked to be excused to the restroom. The teacher agreed, and Bud left the room and made his way to his locker. Smitty met him there. They retrieved the poison ivy and the gloves and walked quickly to the locker room. When they go their chance, they found Drake's locker unlocked. They chuckled at the arrogance of the jock thinking no one would mess with his things. The boys donned the gloves and began rubbing poison ivy all over the inside of his pants and shirt. Bud ditched the rest of the poison ivy in the trash. Smitty threw away his gloves as well. Bud kept his rubber gloves, knowing he would have to wash them before returning them to their place under the sink where he had borrowed them from Maggie.

Bud and Smitty were standing at Bud's locker, laughing, as he put his gloves away. He had just shut it when Principal LeVeque came down the hallway. When he saw the two boys together laughing he walked up to them.

"Gentlemen, not skipping class, are we?" the principal said.

"No, sir," they said.

"What are you doing then?" LeVeque asked.

"I was just using the bathroom," Smitty said.

"Me too," Bud said. "Then I wanted to drop a book in my locker. I was just about to head back to class."

Smitty nodded in agreement.

"Then I suggest you get on with it," LeVeque said. "This is not social time."

"Yes, sir," the two boys said and made their way back to class.

It was late in the afternoon already, so the boys wouldn't be able to enjoy the fruits of the prank until the next day. Bud was excited to see Drake itching and squirming, but he was disappointed when Drake didn't even come to school the next day. He grew apprehensive when he was called out of his first period class to the office. When he walked into Principal LeVeque's office, Smitty was already sitting there. Bud's heart skipped when he saw the plastic bag with the discarded gloves and remnants of poison ivy leaves. Bud sat quietly in the chair next to Smitty across the desk from Principal LeVeque. Neither boy spoke.

"Well, Gentleman," LeVeque began, "which of you would like to explain this?"

Neither boy moved an inch as LeVeque held up the plastic bag of contraband by the corner. He eyed each boy in turn, but neither gave anything away by their face.

"You should know," LeVeque continued, "that Mr. Goucher is in the hospital."

He scanned the boys for a reaction. His plan had been to shock them into admitting something, but all he got was confusion from their faces. Bud's heart was pounding, but he didn't understand why Drake would be in the hospital. They had only rubbed poison ivy in his clothes. He should have a rash and be really itchy, nothing more.

"Someone apparently rubbed poison ivy in Mr. Goucher's clothes while he was in gym class," LeVeque said. "He had a very bad reaction. He has rashes and blisters covering much of his body, and it was bad enough that his parents took him to the hospital. The janitor found these items in the locker–room trash.

We've pieced enough of this together to have an idea of what happened. When I remembered seeing the two of you in the hallway together, I put the final piece in place. Which of you would like to tell me the whole story?"

Neither Bud nor Smitty looked at the other. Principal LeVeque had already figured everything out. Bud knew he was in trouble. He would be expelled. All of his hard work in turning things around was going to be for naught. This would cement his reputation. He was resigning himself to his fate when Smitty spoke up.

"I did it, Principal LeVeque," Smitty said. "Bud had nothing to do with it. I just bumped into him in the hallway when I was heading back to class and told him about it. That's what we were laughing about before you walked up."

"Bud had nothing to do with it?" LeVeque said eyeing the two boys.

"No, nothing," Smitty said.

"Very well. Mr. Marshall, you may leave us and go back to class," LeVeque said.

Bud rose slowly looking around in a daze. He glanced at Smitty who nodded at him. He returned to class still unsure of what to make of things. Smitty had taken the fall for the both of them. He was grateful for that.

Smitty was suspended for three days for the poison ivy incident. Although neither Principal LeVeque nor Drake were entirely convinced that Bud had nothing to do with the whole thing. Smitty stuck to his telling of the story in which he was the lone perpetrator. Only with Bud would he ever discuss what had actually taken place. Bud thanked Smitty repeatedly and said that if there was ever anything he could do to return the favor, he would do it.

"That's just what friends do, Bud," Smitty said. "Don't worry about it."

Thanks to Smitty, Bud's momentum wasn't stalled. When grades came out before Christmas break, Bud was climbing back up towards the top of the class. He got to sign up for second semester classes and was able to sign up for the same shop class that Smitty was taking. It seemed Bud was on a winning streak, and he was looking forward to Christmas vacation to celebrate. He thought maybe his luck would even continue and Teresa would begin to forgive him if he could talk to her over vacation. It was a prospect that even to Bud seemed too good to hope for.

# 17

"What do you mean they're not coming?" Bud asked. "They always come!"

"Jim, Nancy, and Teresa are going out of town for Christmas this year, Bud," Maggie said. "Teresa's grandfather died last spring, and her grandmother is all alone for Christmas, so they're going to stay with her in New York this year."

"I didn't know her grandfather died," Bud said looking down ashamed.

Bud had stayed in his room the previous Christmas, and the one before Teresa had refused to speak to him. This would make three straight years without the two of them exchanging gifts. Bud put on a brave face and told himself he was determined to make it a great Christmas with just his grandparents anyway. Then, Buck got sick. Buck got really sick.

Dr. Randolph made a house call and confirmed that Buck again had pneumonia. The doctor ordered lots of bed rest and another round of antibiotics. With Christmas only a week away, it seemed that the great family celebration Bud had in mind was going to remain a fantasy.

Bud helped his grandmother take care of Buck, but the mood it was setting for the holidays was troublesome. Bud noticed that he was slipping back into a depressed state and decided to say something to his grandmother.

"Gran, I know Pa can't help it, but it's really hard with him being sick for Christmas and the Petersons not being here. It makes the whole thing seem sad, when it should be happy."

"I know, Brandon. What if we invited the Steins from down the street to come have a Christmas meal with us?"

Deborah and Mitchell Stein were an older retired couple who had moved into Lance's house some time after he left. They had grown children who were off somewhere living lives of their own and rarely came to Maine to visit them. The Steins had chosen Maine to retire to because they liked the peace and quiet. They were a little younger than Bud's grandparents and seemed nice enough the couple of times he had spoken with them.

"All right," Bud said. "And what about Mr. LaVerdier?"

Maggie frowned. Malcolm LaVerdier kept to himself and never seemed very friendly. Bud sensed her hesitation, but pressed on.

"Maybe Mr. LaVerdier wouldn't be so grumpy if he had some people to talk to," Bud said.

"Ok, Brandon, you can ask him. Why don't you put your coat on and head down the road right now and invite everyone over for Christmas Day? Tell them two o'clock."

Bud got himself dressed and walked down the dirt lane to what used to be Lance's house. Mr. and Mrs. Stein were a round-faced couple that in another life could have passed for brother and sister. They had rosy cheeks, and Mr. Stein could have played a department store Santa, if only he had the beard to go with his white hair. The two gratefully accepted Bud's invitation and said they would get a hold of Maggie to see what they could bring to help with the meal. Bud left their house and came back down the road to Mr. LaVerdier's.

The yellow trailer was faded and dirty and looked like nothing had been done to it in all the years it had sat there. The cranky mutt that the old man kept tied outside growled at Bud from the end of the house. He took a deep determined breath, climbed the stairs, and knocked on the door. A frumpy, gray old man answered wearing a dirty blue bathrobe with flannel pajamas underneath. Although he was younger than Buck by more than a decade, one wouldn't know it by looking at him. He had narrow, black eyes, and a gravelly voice. He spoke in a forced whisper that was agitated and nervous.

"What do you want, boy?" He said.

Bud swallowed and took a shallow breath.

"Mr. LaVerdier, hi," Bud began. "My grandmother and I were hoping you could come and join us for Christmas dinner at two o'clock on Christmas Day. The Steins will be coming too, so it's kind of a neighborhood thing. The Petersons would come, but they'll be out of town, you know? You wouldn't have to bring anything, just yourself."

Bud had spoken quickly because he was running short on air, and Mr. LaVerdier's appearance had caught him off guard. Malcolm LaVerdier glared at Bud and then glanced towards his house across the lane.

"What about your grandfather?" he said.

"Excuse me, sir?"

"You said you and your grandmother want me to come. What about your grandfather? Buck, is it?"

"Oh yes sir, Buck, yes. He's uh, he's sick right now, pneumonia, so he won't be joining us for dinner, but I'm sure he'd be glad if you could make it."

The old man stood, thinking, not speaking, while a slight breeze ruffled the bottom edge of his bathrobe. A chill ran down

Bud's spine, and he shivered slightly. The shiver seemed to pull Mr. LaVerdier out of his trance.

"Fine, I'll come," he said as he stepped back and shut the door in Bud's face.

Bud turned and took a deep breath. He felt like he hadn't been breathing the entire time, and he felt a little dizzy as a result. He composed himself and walked back to his own house. When he told Maggie that everyone was coming, even Mr. LaVerdier, she had to catch herself.

"Mr. LaVerdier is coming? Well... Good then. I'm glad... I'm glad we could brighten his holiday," she said.

She didn't really know what to make of it, and Bud didn't actually know why he had even thought to invite the man. It had just seemed like the thing to do at the time. Now that he was coming, neither of them knew what, if anything, they should do about it.

Between preparing for Christmas Day and taking care of Buck, Bud and Maggie were kept very busy. Buck wasn't dealing well with the illness this time around. Maggie was worried that age was finally catching up with him. He was in his mid–seventies and just didn't bounce back like he used to. They kept him as comfortable as possible and did their best to keep his fever down. That was all they could do.

On the day before Christmas, Maggie was running around like mad making last–minute preparations. Bud was trying to be helpful, but kept ending up in the way. Exasperated, Maggie sent him to the hutch in the dining room to get the good candlesticks.

Bud opened several of the drawers in the hutch looking for the candlesticks, but paused when he found a yellowing envelope at the bottom of one of the drawers. It was marked on the front only with a name: "Paul." Seeing the first name of his father, curiosity got the better of Bud, and he opened the envelope.

Inside was the note Paul had left in the basket with Bud when he had been left on the front doorstep, and a police report from the day after his body was found. It read, "Paul Marshall, 32, of Cambridge, Massachusetts was found dead in an apparent suicide Wednesday morning. Road crews found his car abandoned on Route 133 just south of Wayne at approximately 2:40 AM and his body was located nearby with a single gun–shot wound to the head. He was pre–deceased by his wife and is survived by his parents and new–born son."

Bud's head was swimming as he started putting the pieces together. It was at that moment that Maggie walked into the dining room to see if he'd found the candlesticks. She stopped when she saw the envelope on the dining–room table and the two pieces of paper in Bud's hands.

"Gran, what is this?" Bud asked, raising his head to look at her.

"Oh, Brandon…" she answered, drifting off.

"You told me my parents died in an accident and that's why I came to live with you and Pa. But that's not what this says," he said, holding up the clipping.

Maggie was at a loss for words in the moment. They had told Bud what they felt they needed to when he was younger. She and Buck had always known they should one day tell him the truth, but they hoped he would be older and better equipped to handle it. Now she was backed into a corner and had no choice but tell her grandson the horrible truth.

"Brandon, why don't we have a seat in the living room," she began.

"No," he said, his brows furrowing. "You and Pa lied to me."

"We did Brandon, but please let me explain…"

"I'm waiting."

"You were still very young when we felt the need to explain that we weren't your parents. We thought the truth would be too much for you then."

"And what's the truth, Gran?"

"The truth...," she said pausing to take a breath. "The truth is that your mother died giving birth to you. Your dad, for some reason — I imagine grief — couldn't bear to raise you on his own, so he brought you to us. You were left in a basket with that note on our front steps late one night."

"Why? Why would he do that? How did my mom die? Why didn't you tell me any of this?" Bud was angry and confused.

"I don't know," Maggie said, tears forming at the corner of her eyes. "I don't know, Brandon. I don't have any answers for you, I'm sorry. I wish I did. I only know that your mom died because it's what your grandfather and I were told by the authorities as we went through all the legal issues after your father died and we worked to adopt you. Please understand—"

"Understand? How can I understand you lying about this? You haven't ever even really told me anything about my father."

Maggie's tears started in earnest at that point and she sat down at the dining room table and wiped her face with her apron. Bud's anger softened slightly at seeing his grandmother and his tune lightened.

"I'm sorry, Gran," he said. "I just want to know more."

"I know, Brandon, and you deserve to know more. I'll tell you what I can. I would like to think that your grandfather and I would've told you all of it once you were older, but who knows if we would have. He doesn't like to discuss it, even with me. If possible, I think it's harder on him."

"What is?"

"Your father, Paul, left home when he was sixteen years old. He and your grandfather had a big fight. At this point, I can't even remember what it was about. I suppose it doesn't matter, but they yelled and screamed at one another and Paul left. Your grandfather grew quiet after that day — I don't know that he's raised his voice since. It's partly my fault, probably. I was so upset and blamed him for letting his anger get the better of him. It wasn't only his doing though, not really. The two of them just never saw eye–to–eye on anything. We never heard from Paul again, at least not until the night he left you with us."

"And my mother?"

"I don't know, Brandon. Like I said, we learned she died — in childbirth. Beyond that I don't know anything about her. Her parents were already dead, and any surviving family she had didn't come forward, which made adopting you easier legally at least. I may have been told her name — but amidst the sadness, confusion, and stress it passed out of my mind. You became my — well our — whole focus after that day."

Bud placed the newspaper clipping and the note back into the worn envelope and slid it across the table to his grandmother.

"I just wish you'd told me," he said.

"I know, so do I," Maggie said. "This certainly isn't how we would've wanted you to find out. I hope you can forgive us. It was never our intent to hurt you. We just wanted to keep you safe."

Maggie rose from her seat, returned the envelope to the drawer, retrieved the candlesticks, placing them on the table. She apologized again and gave Brandon a kiss on the head before returning to the kitchen, still wiping her red eyes. There was a worry, in the recesses of her mind, that her grandson would sink back into depression knowing the truth about his father's fate. Maggie hoped he had found strength in his recent climb out of the darkness, but she decided to keep a close eye on him nonetheless.

Bud did feel a small sense of betrayal from his grandparents. He wished they had felt him capable of handling the truth about his parents, though he understood that as a small child there would have been no way for him to do so. Growing up without a father was hard enough, but knowing how his father had died added further complications to Bud's emotions. Even though Bud never knew his father, he knew it was something that he would never stop thinking about. It was something that he thought he should discuss with his grandfather, though he wasn't sure he wanted to or how to do so. For now anyway, the matter would have to wait until the holidays were over and his grandfather was feeling better.

On Christmas Day, the Steins arrived first, just before two o'clock, carrying a pie that Deborah had baked. The two were chatting and laughing happily with Maggie when there was a knock at the door. Bud walked over and opened it hesitantly. Malcolm LaVerdier was standing there in a grey suit with a long black overcoat, and in his hands, he held a simple white package tied up with twine. Bud's face was a mixture of shock and confusion.

"Aren't you going to let me in, boy?" Mr. LaVerdier asked.

"Oh yes sir," Bud said stepping aside and welcoming him in.

Bud took his coat and led him in to where the others were gathered in the living room. The same look Bud had when he opened the door repeated itself on the faces of the others.

"Mr. LaVerdier," Maggie said. "You are looking quite dapper this afternoon!"

"Well, thank you, ma'am," he replied. "But please, call me Malcolm."

He handed the package he was carrying to Maggie.

"It's a balm," he said. "It's supposed to help you breathe. I thought your husband could use it."

"Thank you so much," she said.

The gathering was pleasant, if not a little awkward in terms of conversation. Malcolm sat mostly in silence listening to the others talk, only offering his thoughts if he was asked directly for them and not elaborating beyond the shortest possible reply. Still, everyone was warm and well fed.

After the meal, they all moved into the living room to sit around the fire. Malcolm sat off to the side, again just listening to the others talk. After some time observing him, Bud made his way over to the old man.

"Mr. LaVerdier," he said. "Why don't you sit and talk with the others?"

"Guess I don't have much to talk about."

"I'd be happy to talk with you, if you'd like."

"You? Boy, what would you and I have to talk about?"

"I don't know," Bud said simply. "You could tell me something about your life. I don't know anything about you."

"Ha!" The old man laughed. "Not much to tell about my life, boy. I fought in World War Two, came home, and now I live across the street from you."

"World War Two was a while ago. Surely something must have happened since then?"

"Nothing worth talking about, boy," Mr. LaVerdier said.

"Well, then, can you tell me about the war?" Bud asked.

"I don't talk about the war with people who can't understand it. You want to hear about war? Why don't you ask your grandfather something about war? From what I understand he fought in the Great War, World War One. Ask him about that. Ask him about The Big Red One. I'm not talking about my war."

Malcolm LaVerdier stared solemnly into the fire, watching the flames taunt him, dancing around the hearth. Bud didn't know his grandfather had fought in a war. Bud wondered why his grandfather had never mentioned it, but then he hadn't said anything about his father either. Maybe he was like Mr. LaVerdier and didn't like talking about it. Like the matter with his father's suicide, he wasn't sure he wanted to bring it up. He would rather try to press a little against Mr. LaVerdier and risk angering him, rather than risk upsetting his grandfather. Malcolm LaVerdier looked up from watching the fire and caught Bud's blue eyes staring back at him. He thought he caught a slight twinkle in the firelight.

"Listen, boy, thank you for inviting me. My family wants nothing to do with me these days. They say I'm too grumpy to be around. Maybe I am. You want to know about the war? I'll tell you this: war is hell. You have no idea what you're capable of doing until you have to do it to survive. Men are animals. Men are savage animals."

The old man's face went sad and then he looked pained as though he were reliving an old wound.

"People can't understand," the old man continued. "They can't understand if they haven't been there. Your grandfather could understand. But he's dealt with it better than me. You do things you aren't proud of in war, but you do them because you have to. You see things that haunt your dreams for the rest of your life. Sometimes you want to crawl into a dark place and shut all the dreams and the memories out. I guess that's what I did. I crawled, and I hid. You can't escape them though, boy... You can't escape them."

Bud felt sorry for the old man sitting in his living room. He thought he understood now, why Mr. LaVerdier seemed so small. He was making himself small to try and hide from something awful in his past. Bud thought he must have been hiding for so long that he no longer knew how to do anything other than hide. It didn't matter that the past kept finding him in his dreams — in his memories. He only knew how to keep hiding.

The Steins and Malcolm LaVerdier left shortly before dark, thanking Bud and his grandmother for a wonderful time. Mr. LaVerdier seemed genuinely grateful to have been outside of the house for a change. Bud was glad in his heart that he had suggested inviting the old man.

Buck remained ill into the new year, but he recovered early in January. He was weak for a while, but because it was winter there wasn't much work he had to be doing anyway. Maggie was sure to feed him well and help him recover his strength.

Bud continued to forge a new path for himself both at school and at home. He made a point every day to count his blessings and remind himself who he was and what he had to be thankful for. While Bud went back and forth on whether to ask about both his own father's death, and his grandfather's time in World War One, he ultimately felt it best to wait for the right moment in either case. Bud's grades continued to improve and by the time his final report card came out, he was receiving top marks in all of his classes. Buck and Maggie were both extremely proud of the work he had been putting in. There was no question that things were turning around for Bud Marshall. The last piece of that puzzle was Teresa; and as Buck had reasoned, no one could get Teresa to do anything she didn't want to do.

# 18

**W**hen summer came back around, Bud was back to working on the farm with his grandfather. Buck was slowing down and handing more and more duties over to Bud and to Stanley the handyman. Because Bud had been taking shop class in school, Buck decided it was time to have him start learning how to care for the tractor. Buck pulled the old John Deere up to his garage to show Bud how to grease the fittings and do some general maintenance. While they were working, there was a knock on the side of the garage.

"Hello?" a female voice called. "Anyone here?"

"Come on in," Buck answered.

In walked Teresa, carrying a vase of flowers. Bud's jaw dropped. She was wearing a light blue and white sundress that danced in the light that shone through the small windows of the garage. The dress was scooped in the front with slender straps that highlighted the lines of her neck. Her hair was draped lightly over one shoulder and hung just past the cut of the neckline. Underneath, he could just make out the shape of her newly developing breasts. She wore a simple pair of white sandals which gave her a girlish and innocent look. In an instant, his heart

ached. It ached for all that he had done to her, and for never seeing what had been there all along. She avoided his eyes altogether
and focused on Buck.

"Hi, my parents wanted me to bring these over for Maggie,"
she said. "I knocked on the front door but no one answered."

"She ran into town, Teresa," Buck said. "Just leave them on
the front steps, and she'll get them when she comes home.
They're lovely."

Teresa smiled, turned and walked out of the garage. Bud
stood there, his mouth still agape, watching her hips sway in the
sundress as she left. He then turned and looked dumbly at his
grandfather.

"Well, what are you waiting for, Bud?" his grandfather said.
"Go on."

Bud jumped as though startled and hurried out of the garage
after Teresa. He caught up with her at the steps.

"Hey," he said startling her. "Sorry, hi. Why don't I take
those inside with you... so they don't get damaged out here?"

She looked doubtfully at him as he opened the door to let her
in.

"Please?" he said.

She half rolled her eyes and walked inside. He led her into
the kitchen, and she placed the flowers on the table and turned to
go.

"Thanks," she said.

"Wait!" Bud said.

She stopped and turned towards him, waiting patiently for
him to continue.

"Listen," he began. "I'm really sorry, Teresa. What I did—"

"Stop," she said firmly.

"No, I need to apologize."

"Then do it right, Brandon," she said.

"I'm sorry?"

"Do it right. You don't call me 'Teresa.' If you call me 'Teresa' I think you're saying what you think I want to hear instead of what you want to say. Say what you want to say, not what you think I want to hear."

Bud took a deep breath. He had rehearsed this speech a thousand times in his head, but now in the moment everything he'd practiced seemed wrong. How does one apologize for the worst thing he can imagine doing?

"Reese," he began again. "I miss you."

It was the most honest and simple statement he could have made in that moment. He stopped only to collect his thoughts to continue.

"I miss you too," she said.

"Wait, please, Reese. Let me finish." She put her hands on her hips, waiting. "We both know what I did was horrible," Bud continued. "What you don't know is that I was sorry the second I did it. I had no idea it would get as bad as it did, but that's no excuse. You should still be mad at me. And I don't expect you to forgive me because it's not forgivable, what I did. I'll certainly never forgive myself. Maybe things can never be like they were before, but I would like it if we could at least be on speaking terms again. I'd like to try and show you that I've changed."

"You're right that things can never be like they were before, Brandon," she said. "I have missed you. But every time I missed you and I found it hard to stay away, I just remembered what you said about me. I know you're sorry. I could see that you were sorry the day I found you sitting by the waterfall. You didn't see me, but I watched you. I had gone up there to read and I found you sitting. You looked so sad. You looked the way you had made me feel. If I were a better person I would have forgiven you that day, but I wanted you to feel as horribly as you made me feel. I guess that's not fair either. Maybe I've been wrong in all of this too. Maybe I should be the bigger person and just forgive you.

There were times that I thought staying mad at you just gave you power over me that you shouldn't have. If I could just forgive you, I could take back that power. But I couldn't do it, Brandon. Right or wrong, you do have power over me because I care about you. At least, I did care about you. It's been so long that I don't even know if I know who you are anymore. But I'm willing to try and be friends again, Brandon. That's if you can show me that you have changed and that you're no longer the boy that would spread lies about me to make himself look better in the eyes of a bunch of jerks."

"I have changed, Reese," Bud said.

"I hope so."

She turned and walked out of the house. He followed her, shut the front door, and walked down the steps. She headed for her house, and he called after her.

"Maybe you'd like to get together and talk about what's to come in high school?"

She stopped and turned to face him. A slight smile crept up in the corner of her mouth. The sunlight shone through her dress silhouetting her body, causing Bud's heart to stall and his stomach to flip for the few seconds before she answered.

"Sounds like you still know me, Brandon Marshall."

The slight smile turned into a full grin, she rolled her eyes and playfully tossed her head.

"Ok, your *first* day off this time," she said.

"*First* day." He held up one finger and smiled back.

She turned and walked back to her house. Bud watched her the whole way, stunned by how she had grown up in the time they had been apart. He then went back to help Buck in the garage. When he walked in, Buck couldn't help but notice the air of happiness that surrounded him as he walked. Buck looked at his grandson, smiled and nodded at him.

"Good," Buck said. "Very good."

"Pa?" Bud said.

"Hmmm?"

"I'm going to need a day off soon."

"Mmmm," Buck nodded again.

When Teresa entered her house, she bumped into her father by the door.

"How did Maggie like the flowers?" he asked.

"She wasn't home," Teresa said.

"What did you do with the flowers?"

"Bud let me in, and I left them on the kitchen table for her."

"Bud let you in?" Jim said looking at her out of the corner of his eye.

"Yes Dad, he did. And yes, I talked to him."

She crossed her arms over her chest and put all her weight on one foot the way she always did when she was expecting a lecture.

"Oh, that's nice," Jim said and started to head out the door.

"Wait," she said stopping him. "That's nice? All you're going to say is, 'That's nice?' All the times you and Mom told me I should talk to him and see what he has to say — and now that I have, that's it?"

Jim just smiled at his daughter, gave a nod of his head, and walked out the door. Teresa hated it when her parents were right, but she hated it even more that her father wasn't going to bother to point out that he'd been right. She let out a deep sigh and headed upstairs to her bedroom to do some reading.

Bud lay in bed awake that night, thinking about seeing Teresa again for the first time in what felt like a lifetime. It might as well have been a lifetime, he thought, for how much she had changed.

Buck had agreed to give him one day off each week so long as he "kept his nose clean" as his grandfather had put it. Bud was both excited and nervous. Teresa had grown into a beautiful young woman. She would be turning fifteen that fall, and Bud hadn't really spent any time with her since the fall she turned twelve. Three years was a long time around that age. He knew he had changed a lot, and he could see that she had changed too, at least physically. He wondered, had she changed as much on the inside? Would she even still want to be friends with him? Did he want to be more than friends?

Those and a thousand other questions swirled in Bud's mind, keeping him up until the early morning hours before he was able to quiet his thoughts enough to finally fall asleep. A single belief gave him enough peace of mind to calm himself.

"It's Reese. We've always been friends. We'll always be friends, no matter what."

He believed even the deep wound he had caused was healing and that there was nothing worse either of them could do to the other, and so there was nothing they couldn't get past. Bud was certainly never going to do anything to hurt Teresa like that again.

Jim had told Teresa that Bud was going to be having a day off, and so she was sitting outside on her front porch when that first morning arrived. Bud found her flipping through the pages of a notebook in her lap. She was wearing denim shorts and a yellow cotton t–shirt with a pair of sneakers. Her hair was tied up in a ponytail which drifted ever so slightly with the morning breeze. Bud couldn't help but think how cute she looked sitting there waiting for him.

It was late June, and the weather that morning was already fairly warm. Reese suggested they walk up to the waterfall to-gether, and Bud was happy to do so. She brought the notebook she held in her lap. When the two sat down on the log by the bank of the little pool in the stream, she opened it and began flipping pages.

"These are some of the poems I wrote for English class last year. I thought you might like to read some of them," she said.

"Why don't you read them to me?" Bud said as he smiled at her.

The two sat on the log for over an hour as Teresa read Bud her poetry, and he listened amazed by her ability to paint a picture with her words.

"You're really good, Reese," he said.

"Thank you, Brandon. I don't know about really good, but I enjoyed writing them."

"No, really good. You're a talented writer, Reese. I wish I could write like that."

"You just need to practice. Think about the books or poems you like to read and just try to write like that," she said.

Bud looked down at his shoes and shuffled them in the grass.

"I haven't done as much reading lately as I used to," he said. "But I'm getting back into it. I kind of forgot how much I used to love it."

"But you've had to read stuff for school, right?" Reese asked.

"I was supposed to, sure. Most of the time I just blew it off. I know, not very smart. I did start doing the assigned reading again this year. The only thing we had to read that I really liked at all was *The Scarlet Letter*."

"Yes, I've read that," Teresa said with a frown. "I felt a little like Hester Prynne."

Bud looked over, caught her eye, and then looked away embarrassed. He hadn't even considered that when he read the story, but surely Teresa had been ostracized in a similar way as himself, only by different people.

"And you didn't even deserve it," he said finally. "I'm so sorry, Reese. I thought I was like Hester Prynne because I had a reputation as a trouble–maker that I couldn't shake. And that was my own fault. I hadn't even thought about the fact that you had a reputation as a... well, that you had a reputation. And that one was my fault too. I guess I'm good at giving reputations. I wish I were as good at changing them."

"It's okay, Brandon," she sighed. "Really it was only the boys that were convinced I was that way. I was able to convince Gregg it wasn't true, and most of the girls believed me, so it's not like I didn't have any friends. I have a bunch of friends. I'm sure you'll meet some of them this summer, and we'll all be in the same school together next year. Tell me about high school, Brandon. Let's forget all that stuff in the past for right now and talk about the future. What's it like?"

Bud told her what he could about high school. He told her about the different cliques of students, and how freshmen can't walk the halls. He told her about the principal and some of the teachers she would have. He told her about the classes and choosing electives second semester. He answered her questions as best as he could. They sat talking until lunch time and then made their way back toward the farm.

Nancy had put sandwiches and lemonade on the porch for them, so they sat out in the sun eating. At one point, Bud reached over and placed his hand on Teresa's.

"Reese," he said. "I really missed this. I missed you. I don't want to mess this up again. I promise I won't ever do anything to hurt you again. I know I keep saying 'I'm sorry,' and I'll never be able to say it enough, but I am. I care about you."

Teresa withdrew her hand from Bud's and sat back just a little studying him closely.

"I believe you're sorry, Brandon," she said. "I think we need to just take all of this slowly, okay? We haven't spent a lot of time together, and I think we need to get to know each other again. It's going to take some time before we're really even friends again, you know?"

Bud was stung a little, but also panicked that he may have pushed things too much.

"I'm sorry," he said. "I didn't mean — I wasn't trying to — I hope you don't think—"

"It's okay," she cut in. "Let's just try being together some without disliking each other first, okay?"

"I never disliked you, Reese."

"Well, I don't think I ever gave you reason to," she said.

Bud was stung again, but he knew she was right. She wasn't going to just flip the switch this time back to being best friends, and he certainly wasn't going to be able to skip being friends and move into being anything more than that. "Do it for yourself," he thought, repeating the words he had written in his notebook.

"You're right," he said to her. "You've never given me a reason to dislike you — and so I don't. But if it takes time to rebuild your trust in me, I understand. If it takes the rest of my life, I'm going to do just that, Reese. Because your friendship is worth it."

"Thank you, Brandon," she said.

Teresa did have a couple of friends over that summer, and Bud got to meet them. There was Stacy, a lanky girl with large–rim glasses and long dark hair. Bud thought that she would have been cute, but everything about her just seemed stretched out too much from top to bottom. She was nice anyway, and smart as a whip. She could give Teresa a run for her money in a discussion, and she was sarcastic, which Bud appreciated.

The other friend Bud met was Mabel. Mabel was much the opposite of Stacy in physical appearance. She was shorter than Teresa and already had full breasts that matched her round, cute face. She had blonde hair, which she wore short, and bright blue eyes that laughed when she smiled. Bud thought she was very attractive, but she giggled incessantly, which he found annoying.

Bud was kind enough to show Teresa's friends around the farm one day when they visited and he had a day off. He was in his element as the center of attention, and he would make jokes and tell stories that made the girls laugh. Teresa hadn't seen him act so carefree in a long time, and it made her happy to see him smile so much. Bud was just happy that he could feel important without having to make up any stories or cause any trouble.

Bud left the girls at the front porch of the farmhouse after he finished his tour of the farm. Teresa had suggested he show them all the waterfall, but he made an excuse that he had some work to do inside and didn't have time. The truth was, Bud didn't want to share the waterfall with Teresa's friends. In his mind, that was his and Teresa's place and no one else's. It was special.

Teresa's friends couldn't stop talking about how great Bud was and how much they loved the tour. Stacey thought he was hilarious, and Mabel just kept going on and on about how big, strong, and handsome he was. Neither girl could believe that Teresa had never had any interest in dating Bud. Mabel especially seemed smitten with the boy. She kept asking Teresa what she thought Bud looked for in a girl and asking if Teresa thought she had made a good impression.

Teresa was a girl of her own mind, but even she had to wonder if there was more to the boy next door than she had realized. Her friends certainly seemed to think so.

Mabel kept pressing Teresa on why she and Bud had never dated, and if Teresa thought he was cute. Finally, Teresa had had enough.

"Mabel, if you think he's that wonderful why don't you ask him to go steady?" she said.

The words left her mouth before she really realized what she was suggesting. Immediately she regretted saying it thinking about Bud dating another girl.

"Oh, I couldn't," Mabel said. "I can't imagine what he'd say. What do you think he'd say, Teresa? Do you really think he'd want to go steady with me? Oh, I don't know if I could do that. Maybe you could talk to him for me."

Mabel prattled on for several minutes before Teresa calmed her down by suggesting she would talk to Bud for her.

"I'm not doing it until after school starts though," Teresa said. "He needs to get to know you a little more before I suggest the two of you date."

She hoped to buy herself some time to figure things out, but she had a feeling that she had inadvertently started something in motion that she wasn't going to be able to control.

# 19

Teresa was very excited for her first day of high school. She was waiting rather impatiently for Bud on his front steps when he came out of the door. She grabbed him by the hand and half led, half dragged him down the lane.

"Come on, Brandon," she said. "If we don't hurry we'll miss the bus."

"Calm down, Reese. We have plenty of time."

Teresa fidgeted in the seat next to Bud the whole ride. Even when Gregg got on the bus and sat across the aisle from them, she squirmed and made small talk excitedly with him. Bud was fine with that since it gave him a break from the chatter. He looked out the window as the trees and fields blurred by, broken only by the occasional building or body of water.

Bud had high hopes for the school year. He was back on speaking terms with Teresa, so he was willing to tolerate Gregg and her other friends. As he worked to repair his friendship with her, he hoped to convince her that he was someone she could trust. He would be able to take shop with Smitty again, so the monotony of classes would be broken up a little. Bud enjoyed working with his hands, and shop was relatively easy for him since he spent so much time helping Buck in the garage and on the farm.

Even the teachers would be new this year, so Bud hoped he had the opportunity for a new first impression and might not be stuck with his troublemaker reputation for the whole year. He didn't share his hopes with anyone for fear that speaking them aloud would somehow crush them to dust in their fragile state. Instead, he fostered them gently in his mind, being careful not to linger over them too long and smother them.

Everything went smoothly, even more so than Bud had hoped, for the first few weeks. He stopped an upperclassman from tormenting Gregg in the hall one day, for which both Gregg and Teresa were thankful. Teresa's friends seemed to have started a buzz among the freshman that Bud was a pretty great guy. A number of them looked up to him, which made him feel important, even though Smitty liked to tease him by calling him "King Wizard" in a snide manner. Bud would just laugh it off though, and suggest Smitty was jealous because he didn't command an army of loyal freshmen too.

Other than seeing each other in shop class, Bud and Smitty didn't hang out much anymore. Smitty had his license now and was always offering to pick Bud up on weekends to go somewhere, but Bud had other things on his mind. He was either doing school work in an effort to keep his grades up, or spending time with Teresa trying to win her over. A couple months into the school year, Smitty finally called him out on it.

"How come you never want to hang out anymore, Bud?" Smitty asked. "Too busy being King Wizard to spend any time with your best friend?"

"No, no, nothing like that," Bud said. "It's just that Pa and Gran got pretty sore when I got suspended last year, and my grades dropped really low. I'm just trying not to mess up too bad this year so they'll stay off my case."

"We could still hang out though. You're always with that girl, Teresa. You like her or something?"

"No," Bud chuckled nervously. "Nothing like that. We're neighbors and friends. We've known each other forever, so I guess we're pretty close. And we see each other every day walking to and from the bus."

"Okay, because if I thought you were replacing me with some chick I'd change your name from King Wizard to King Pimp," Smitty said with a wry grin.

"Reese couldn't replace you Smitty, she doesn't have your way with words," Bud said, cracking a smile.

"Ha! Okay then King Wizard, when are we going to hang out?"

Bud thought about it. His birthday was coming up, and he'd be turning sixteen. He'd be going for his license pretty soon, and hopefully he'd get it before Christmas break.

"Tell you what, Smitty," Bud said. "After I get my license, I'll take us for a ride into Augusta. We'll see what's happening down that way. How's that?"

"I could drive us into Augusta right now, Bud."

"Yeah, but it's more fun for me once I can do it," Bud said mimicking steering a car.

"You drive like that and there's no way they'll give you a license," Smitty said laughing. "Fine, after you can drive, we'll go. But no more excuses! And if you bring that chick too, you better find one for me. I'm nobody's third wheel, got it?"

Bud laughed and nodded. The two were agreed on a plan. Now they just needed to wait until Bud's birthday rolled around and he went for his license.

As his birthday approached, Buck and Maggie asked Bud what he would like to do for it. Bud said that he didn't really want anything, but he would graciously accept a batch of Gran's sugar cookies. Buck had other ideas.

November the 28th fell on a Sunday in '76. It was still breakfast when there came a knock on the Marshall's front door. Bud
was sent from the table to answer it. When he opened the door,
there stood Teresa in her Sunday best holding a package and
smiling.

"Happy birthday, Brandon," She said.

"Thanks, Reese," Bud said gazing into her beautiful hazel
eyes that were highlighted by her deep purple dress.

"I have to run, we're going to church soon. I'll see you later?"

"Sure."

She flashed him another smile and ran off towards her house.
Bud shut the door and mindlessly stumbled back to his chair carrying the package she had given him, still lost in her eyes.

It was Maggie that woke him from his daydream by asking
what it was he was carrying. It was only then that he truly noticed
the package. He opened it on the table. Teresa had given him a
book: *The Great Gatsby*. After breakfast, he headed upstairs to his
room and began reading it.

Bud did not put the book down again until he had read the
entire thing. Maggie came looking for him at lunch, but he didn't
hear her enter his room or ask him if he would like to eat. She
finally abandoned her efforts and retreated down the stairs.

He had been lost in Fitzgerald's work, trying to understand
why someone would write so beautifully about things so ugly.
When he finally put the pages to rest, he was angry. He crashed
down the stairs and out the front entry of the cape on his way to
Teresa's house. He rapped on the door, and when Jim answered
Bud said he needed to see Reese, right away. When she came to
the door he stumbled over his thoughts, losing some of his anger.
She was dressed simply in jeans and a light blue cotton shirt, but
the effect on Bud was like a cool shower on hot embers. He regained his lost heat and steadied himself.

"Why did you give me that book?" he asked.

"I thought you would enjoy it," she said simply.

"What a horrible book!"

"Horrible? I thought it was fantastically written. Didn't you think the language and symbolism were wonderful?"

"Who am I supposed to be?"

"What?"

"In the novel. Who am I supposed to be? Am I Gatsby? Am I Tom? Am I supposed to be Nick? I bet you think I'm George, don't you?"

"Brandon, I don't think you're any of them. Why do you have to be one of them?"

"How should I react, Reese? I told you when we were little that I wanted to be great. You give me *The Great Gatsby* to read. Why wouldn't I think I'm supposed to see myself in that book? But it's horrible! It's just horrible! There's nothing good in that book at all. No one is great."

"Yes," she said. "Yes, I remember you saying you wanted to be great when you grew up. It's not a good book because it's a nice, happy story, Brandon. It's a good book because of how it's written. And if it shows you that just trying to be great doesn't mean things will always be perfect, then I'm glad I got you the book. Gatsby wants to be great for the wrong reasons, and he goes about it the wrong way. I hope you take the time to read the story again someday and try to see what makes it special."

Bud stood looking at her, angry and embarrassed. He had let his emotions get the best of him again and he had run off without stopping to think.

"A good book should have a good story and a happy ending," he said.

"Maybe," Teresa said. "But life isn't always like that. And maybe, just maybe, Brandon, a good story can be like life sometimes. Maybe it can be full of bad things and sad people who don't get everything they want. Maybe sometimes the ending has to be one that we feel is wrong. Then it feels more real."

"I don't need it to be real. I have enough real." He looked down at his shoes and shuffled them on the porch before slowly looking back up. "But thank you for thinking of me on my birthday," he said.

He turned to go, but she reached out and touched him lightly on the shoulder stopping him.

"Happy Birthday, Brandon," she said taking her hand back.

He nodded and walked slowly back to the house and up to his room. Lying on his bed with tears in his eyes, he hoped his story would turn out better than Gatsby's. When he made his way downstairs for dinner, he was greeted by the sweet aroma of Maggie's sugar cookies, and suddenly the world was right again.

After dinner and cookies, Buck slid a small, brightly wrapped package across the dinner table.

"Happy Birthday, Bud," Buck said, his eyes twinkling in the artificial light.

"I told you both I didn't want anything," Bud said.

"That's true," his grandfather said, the twinkle gleaming just a bit brighter. "But there is something you may need."

Bud tore open the bright paper and lifted the lid on the box inside. There, gleaming in the lamp light, was a key. Bud looked up at his grandparents, confused. The two were beaming back at him.

"Come on," Buck said rising from the table.

Bud followed his grandparents outside and over to the garage. Buck raised the garage door and there it sat: A 1951 Ford F1 truck. Bud's mouth fell open.

"You got me a car?" he asked amazed.

Again, his grandparents just smiled. The truck was beat up and rusty, but Bud could tell it had been red at one time. The tires were worn, and the passenger–side mirror was missing. It was the most beautiful vehicle he had ever laid eyes on.

"Needs a little work," Buck said. "But we'll get her cleaned up. Here, fire her up."

Buck handed Bud the key and opened the driver–side door for him. Bud climbed in and sat behind the wheel. He took a deep breath, pressed down the clutch and brake, and put the key in the ignition. With one turn the 239 cubic liter flathead V8 roared to life, shaking the old truck's frame. Bud grinned from ear to ear. In that moment, he felt the world was his for the taking.

Buck climbed into the passenger seat and talked Bud through putting the truck into gear and getting it moving. Bud stalled several times, but eventually got the hang of it. Buck had him drive down the dirt lane and back a few times until he could do it without stalling. Then he had Bud park the truck in the driveway.

"Bud, this is your truck to use, but it's still ouahs," Buck said. "If you don't treat it right, we can take it away. Undahstand?"

Bud nodded.

"You can drive it up and down the lane like we've been doing, but not any closah to Bakah Street until you have your license. Okay?"

"Can I take Reese for a ride?" Bud asked.

Buck smiled and nodded.

Bud sprinted for the Peterson's and knocked on the door. He apologized to Jim for interrupting dinner when he answered the door with his napkin tucked in the collar of his shirt, but said he needed to see Reese.

Moments later, Teresa came to the door looking confused.

"Brandon, what's the matter? Why are you out of breath?" she said.

"First, let me say I'm sorry for earlier. I really do appreciate you getting me the book, Reese. I got upset and took it out on you, and that wasn't right."

"Don't worry about it, Brandon. I wasn't mad. Books are supposed to make you feel something."

"Right, I just felt bad. But that's not why I'm here. Look," he said motioning back towards his driveway.

Teresa leaned out her door and looked where Bud was pointing.

"Brandon! Did you get a truck?"

Bud nodded proudly. "Wanna go for a ride?" he asked.

"But you don't have a license yet, do you?"

"Just down the lane, just to try it out."

"Let me ask my dad," she said and hurried back into the house.

She quickly returned and the two ran to the truck and climbed in. Bud started it up and then, being careful not to stall in front of Teresa, took her for a ride down the lane and back. He had never felt more important than on that short drive. The whole trip was less than a half of a mile and took less than five minutes, but Bud couldn't help noticing that Teresa was smiling the whole way.

"That was wonderful," Teresa said when Bud had parked back in the driveway. "I can't wait until you have your license and we can go anywhere we want to go!"

"Me either," Bud said, as his stomach did backflips at the prospect of driving Teresa around town.

Bud spent his free time after that in the garage with his grandfather, working on the truck. They tuned the engine, did some cosmetic work, and painted it fire engine red. Bud polished it for hours until he could see his reflection smiling back on the hood.

Three weeks after his birthday, Bud got his driver's license. While he had plans with Smitty over Christmas break, he wanted to ask Teresa to go for a ride with him first. He thought she would appreciate being ahead of Smitty in line for going somewhere with him. When he asked her though, she finally decided it was time to fulfill her promise to Mabel.

"I appreciate the offer Brandon, really I do," she said. "And I definitely want to go for a ride with you someday, but what if you took someone else first?"

"Someone else?" Bud said confused.

"Sure. What about Mabel?"

"Mabel? Like your friend Mabel? Why would I take Mabel for a ride before you or even Smitty for that matter? She's your friend, not mine."

"I know that, Brandon, but you two seem to get along well. Don't you like her?"

"She seems nice enough, I guess."

"Do you think she's pretty? I mean, do you like her?"

"She's cute — What's all this about anyway Reese?"

Teresa sighed deeply. She bit her lip and then just put it all out there for Bud.

"Look, Mabel likes you, okay? It would mean a lot to me if you would, I don't know, take her on a date or something and just give her a chance."

"A date? You want me to date your friend?"

Bud was crushed. Teresa was trying to pawn him off on one of her friends when he just wanted to be with her.

"Maybe you'll like her if you spend some more time with her," Teresa offered.

Bud furrowed his brows and pursed his lips in thought.

"Once," he said. "Once, you got really mad at me for kissing a girl that I wasn't sure I really liked. Now you want me to go on a date with one of your friends that I'm sure I don't like, at least not in the way you're supposed to like someone you date. Is that about right, Reese?"

"I know, but she really likes you. Can you just give her a chance? For me?"

She looked up at Bud with those beautiful hazel eyes, and his chest ached. He took a deep breath and relented. He would take Mabel on one date, but was adamant that if he didn't feel anything for her, he wasn't about to take her on a second. Teresa thanked him and told him where Mabel's locker was so he could ask her. It would mean more coming from him, she said. Bud didn't really care how much it meant to Mabel, but because it clearly meant something to Teresa, he agreed.

That's how, on that very Saturday night, Bud found himself driving with Mabel in the passenger seat. Her ample chest bounced along with the bumpy back roads as they made their way to the movie theater in Augusta.

Bud bought tickets to see *King Kong*, along with refreshments, with money he had earned working on the farm. He sat in the dark theater, with Mabel clinging on to him at every scary moment in the movie. It should have been a sixteen–year–old boy's dream evening, but all Bud could think about was that he was there with the wrong girl.

The ride home was miserable for Bud. Mabel sat, babbling on about the movie and how scary it was. When they arrived at Mabel's house, Bud walked around and opened her door for her. He walked her to the front steps of her house and said goodnight, hoping that would be the end of things. Mabel leaned in for a kiss goodnight. Bud stopped her by lightly putting his hands on her shoulders and standing her back up.

"I'm sorry, Mabel," he said. "I can't kiss you. You seem like a nice girl and you're very cute, but I just don't feel like that about you, and it would be wrong for me to pretend to."

Mabel's eyes widened, and her face turned bright red. She stammered searching for words.

"I didn't say anything about a kiss anyway," she said. "I don't know what kind of a girl you think I am, but I'm not like that. I think you have the wrong idea, and I don't think we should see each other anymore."

She turned and walked inside, shutting the door in Bud's face. Bud let out a deep sigh and went home. The next afternoon, Teresa laid into him.

"Brandon, what did you do to Mabel?" she asked him when she found him working on his truck in the garage. "She called and said you embarrassed her horribly, and that she can't believe I'm even friends with a boy like you!"

Bud explained as best he could what had happened. He said he had been polite all evening, had bought snacks and the tickets, and had walked her to the door. It was when she had leaned in for a kiss that he had felt the need to put a stop to things.

"I couldn't kiss her, Reese," he said. "It wouldn't have been right. I don't like her like that. I let her down as gently as I could. I'm sorry she was embarrassed. I didn't want that."

Teresa softened throughout the story. She realized she had put Bud in a tough spot.

"The whole night," Bud continued, "all I could think is that I was there with the wrong girl. I should've been there with you."

He reached over and gently took her hand. She looked up into his deep blue eyes, and seeing his expression, she realized what he meant. She pulled her hand away just quickly enough that Bud realized he had stepped too far.

"Brandon," she said. "We're friends again. I think it's safe to say that, but I'm not ready or prepared to be anything more than that. I think it's best if we just keep things the way they are right now."

"Of course," he said quickly. "I wasn't trying to... I just meant that I would rather have been there with you, is all."

Bud lowered his head. He had laid his cards on the table and he knew it. Teresa just wanted to be friends, and he was going to have to live with that.

"Hey," she said causing him to lift his eyes. "I do care about you. But right now, I need you as a friend. If we were ever something more and it didn't work out, I could lose you as a friend. We did that once, and I'm pretty sure neither of us enjoyed it. Let's not do anything that might ruin our friendship again, okay?"

What she said made sense. Bud didn't want to lose Teresa's friendship again, and dating would make things complicated, especially if they ever broke up. He nodded in agreement, eliciting a smile from Teresa that eased his pain and embarrassment.

"So, how about a ride to the bookstore?" Teresa said.

"Absolutely," Bud replied. "For you? Any time."

# 20

**S**mitty stood by the side of the road as the cold wind swirled around him causing him to shiver. It was Christmas break, and Bud should've been there to pick him up ten minutes ago. He didn't want to go back inside because his parents were fighting again, and he certainly didn't want to listen to any more of that. He just needed to get away for a while.

Finally, Smitty heard the rumbling of an engine, and Bud appeared driving his bright red Ford truck down the street. Smitty's eyebrows went up. It was the first time he'd seen Bud's truck; and with all the restoration that Buck and Bud had done on it, it looked almost new.

Bud pulled in the driveway and Smitty jumped into the passenger seat.

"Pretty nice truck, Bud," he said.

"Thanks, Pa and I have put a lot of work into it. She was in rough shape when I got her, but the engine ran pretty good, and after a tune up and some cosmetic work she's better than I could've hoped for."

Bud backed out and headed towards Augusta. The two boys drove the back roads from Mt. Vernon to Route 27. Bud had ridden those roads many times before, but saw them with new eyes as the one behind the wheel.

For teenage boys, the first car represents rebellion and freedom. For Bud though, it had been a way for him and his grandfather to spend some more time together. He was proud of his truck and intended on taking very good care of it for a long time to come.

The boys got something to eat and then walked along the bank of the Kennebec River down off of Water Street. They talked about school, cars, music, and movies until Smitty finally turned the conversation to the inevitable topic of girls.

"So, you took that Mabel chick to the movies, huh?" Smitty asked.

"Yeah," Bud said not wanting to go into details.

"You get anywhere with her?"

"Nah, it wasn't like that. She's just a friend of a friend."

"She's cute though, huh? Big boobs," Smitty said holding his hands up in front of his chest.

"I guess."

"What's the matter, Bud? You don't like boobs?"

"I like boobs as much as the next guy, okay? It just wasn't like that. I don't really want to talk about it. I only went to the movies with her because she's a friend of a friend. That's all."

"Friend of a friend? You mean that Teresa chick that lives next to you, right?" Bud nodded but didn't say anything. "You like her?" Smitty asked. Bud shrugged and looked away. "She's a pretty girl," Smitty said. "A little brainy for my taste, but hey, you like reading and stuff. Why don't you ask her out?"

"Because we're friends," Bud said.

"Friends," Smitty said treating the word like a bug that had flown into his mouth and he needed to spit out. "Guys can't be friends with chicks, Bud. Either the girl is into the guy or the guy is into the chick. Friends just never works, believe me."

"Well, it works for us," Bud said dismissively.

"All right, don't get your panties in a bunch. I was just giving an opinion. Maybe it works for you two. But if you'll take some advice from me, either you need to date this girl and see if it goes anywhere or plan for her to stop being your friend when she finds a different guy she likes. No guy she dates is going to want her hanging around with you, even just as friends."

Bud didn't say anything. The idea of Reese dating someone else gave him a sour feeling in his gut. Smitty was wrong anyway; Bud was sure of it. He and Teresa would always be friends, she had said so, and she wouldn't lie.

It was starting to get late, so Bud suggested they head back to Mt. Vernon. Smitty agreed but said he wanted to make a quick stop at Shaw's Supermarket first. Bud asked him what he was stopping for.

"You'll see," was all Smitty said.

Bud drove to Shaw's, and Smitty hopped out and walked towards the store. Instead of going inside, he stopped and stood waiting. Bud watched through the window of the Ford wondering what in the world Smitty was doing as he approached another man. The two had a conversation and Smitty handed the young man some cash, pointed at Bud and then made his way back to the truck as the man went inside.

"What was all that about?" Bud asked.

"Just wait, okay?" Smitty said. "Just hang out here for a few minutes."

The two sat in silence, but not for long. Fewer than five minutes passed before the man came out of the store with a paper bag and made a bee-line for the truck. Smitty rolled down his window, and the man handed him the bag.

"Thanks," Smitty said.

The young man nodded and then headed back into the store.

"Here you go, Bud," Smitty said pulling a six pack of beer from the bag. "I gave the guy extra cash and said he could keep the change if he'd pick us up a six pack."

Smitty handed Bud one of the beers and twisted the cap off of one for himself. Bud looked at the beer and then handed it back to Smitty.

"I can't, Smitty," Bud said. "I'm driving."

"Oh, it's no big deal. You'll be able to buy it in a couple years. Besides, one's not going to hurt."

Bud thought about it, but he certainly didn't want to get caught by the Augusta police drinking and driving.

"Okay, but not until we get back to Mt. Vernon," Bud said.

In the time it took Bud to drive back down Route 27 and take the back roads to Mt. Vernon, Smitty had already downed two of the beers. He told Bud to pull down a camp road on the east side of Minnehonk Lake. The summer folks had left, and their camps were vacant for the winter. Bud parked the Ford in front of one of the abandoned buildings, and Smitty handed him one of the remaining beers.

Smitty grabbed another for himself and the two boys twisted of the caps and clinked the bottles together. Bud took a long swig. The beer had warmed quite a bit sitting on the floor at Smitty's feet, which gave it an off–putting taste. They sat and talked some more as they finished off the last four beers. Bud then instructed Smitty to get rid of the bottles because he didn't want Buck finding them in the truck. With both hands full, Smitty climbed out of the pick up and tossed the empties beside the camp. There they'd be lost until the owners came next summer.

Bud drove Smitty home and then turned the truck back towards Readfield. From there he'd take Route 41 to Winthrop and finally 133 through Wayne. Then it was just a right turn on Baker Street and finally down the dirt lane to his home. He took his time since the beers had given him a slight buzz, and he didn't want to put the truck into a ditch by accident in the dark.

The drive was uneventful, and he pulled into his own driveway a little before eleven. He walked upstairs and poked his head into his grandparent's bedroom.

"I'm home," he said.

"Have fun?" Maggie asked.

"Sure," he answered.

"G'night Bud," Buck called as Bud turned to go.

"Night Pa, night Gran," Bud said.

As he got ready for bed, Bud thought about the fact that he'd gotten away with drinking and driving home afterwards. He felt very guilty, especially after what his grandfather had said about taking the truck away if he didn't treat it right. He knew that what he had done wouldn't be considered "treating it right."

Bud tossed and turned for several hours thinking about what he'd done. He wrestled with the proposition of coming clean and telling his grandparents. Although he wasn't sure what that would accomplish besides clearing his conscience. Buck would take the truck away for sure. Ultimately, he decided that since nothing had gone wrong, he would just keep the whole thing to himself and he made a vow never to drink and drive anywhere again.

The next day, a little before lunch, Smitty showed up. He asked to speak to Bud outside. Bud agreed, but said he couldn't talk long because he was driving Gran into town to do some Christmas shopping.

Smitty was visibly upset. He told Bud that his father had smelled the beer on his breath when he walked into the house the night before, and had beaten him with a belt as punishment. He showed Bud the welts where the leather had marked up his back. Bud winced as he saw the red marks. He could sense the pain from the leather of every strike.

"I left, I'm not going back," Smitty said.

Bud was getting ready to ask a question when his grandmother walked out of the house and made her way to the truck.

"Ready, Brandon?" she asked.

"Just a second, Gran," Bud answered.

Bud turned back to Smitty as his grandmother opened the passenger door to climb up into the Ford. As she did so, a beer bottle that Smitty had apparently missed rolled out and landed on the ground in front of her.

Bud's heart stopped as she stooped to picked it up. His perception of the world blurred over the next several minutes. He stood dejected in the driveway as his grandparents questioned him and Smitty about the bottle. Bud knew he had no choice but to own up to his mistake. Their reaction was going to be far worse than if he had done it before his grandparents had discovered it on their own. As Bud was preparing himself for the onslaught, Smitty spoke.

"That's mine, Mr. Marshall, Mrs. Marshall," he said. "I bought some beer in Augusta yesterday before we drove home and drank it in the truck. Bud told me I shouldn't, but I didn't listen to him."

"You're saying Bud didn't drink any?" Buck asked.

"No. Bud said he wouldn't because he was driving," Smitty said.

Bud realized that for the second time in their friendship, Smitty was going to cover for him. He stood barely breathing, trying not to make any sudden movements that would betray the truth.

"Well," Buck said, "I'm going to have to call your father about this."

"He already knows. That's what I came here to tell Bud. I'm going to live with my aunt in Readfield for a while. My father doesn't really want to deal with me anymore."

He eyed Bud as he spoke and Bud understood. Smitty had made the decision to go to his aunt's house to live in order to get away from his dad.

"In that case," Buck said, "it's probably time you got going."

Smitty nodded and said goodbye to Bud. He climbed in the car and drove off, leaving Bud in the driveway with his grandparents. Buck sighed and looked from Bud to the truck.

"I was going to tell you," Bud said. "But I was afraid you would take the truck away."

Buck shook his head. He reached up and stroked his beard thoughtfully while eyeing Bud up and down.

"I'm taking the truck away for two weeks," Buck said.

Bud knew there was no point in arguing. Two weeks seemed like a light sentence to him anyway, considering what it could have been had his grandparents found out he had been drinking as well.

"What about shopping?" Bud asked.

"Park the truck in the garage and I'll drive us into town in the car," Maggie said.

Bud walked solemnly over to the truck and backed it into the garage.

"You don't actually believe he wasn't drinking, do you?" Maggie asked her husband.

"I believe Bud has a very loyal friend," Buck said. "I'm glad no one got hurt, and I hope this was enough to scare him from doing it again."

"But if you think he's lying—"

Buck shook his head, stopping Maggie mid-sentence. "When someone gets the wrong answer, it makes no sense to ask the question again right away," he said. "Give him a while. He was wrong this time. We'll see how he does with the question next time."

Bud would have liked to be able to drive his truck over Christmas break, but instead he was stuck inside helping his grandmother with preparations. As usual, the Marshalls and Petersons would be getting together on Christmas Day for a meal, but this year, the Steins and Mr. LaVerdier would be joining them too.

Christmas arrived in glorious splendor. The world around the farm was dusted with white overnight, and small innocent flakes fell throughout the day dotting the sky with wonder and promise.

Teresa and Bud exchanged gifts as always. Bud gave her a copy of *Lord of the Flies* which he had read in school that year. He knew she would appreciate the chance to read it in advance of her sophomore English class. Teresa always liked to have a leg up academically. She gave Bud a copy of *Watership Down*. She chuckled when he looked puzzled at the bunnies on the cover.

"Trust me, Brandon," she said with a huge smile on her face. "You'll like this one a whole lot more than *The Great Gatsby*."

"It has a happy ending then?" he asked.

"The happiest I can think of, as far as something that has to end."

The party was warm and festive. Maggie and Nancy chatted with the Steins in the kitchen. Malcolm LaVerdier and Buck sat in chairs by the fire and talked about their times in World War One and Two. Bud tried to listen in several times, but each time he got close to them they deftly changed subjects. He still hadn't gotten around to asking his grandfather about "The Big Red One" that Mr. LaVerdier had mentioned his first time there. He felt sorry now that the older men felt he shouldn't be included in their discussions of war. Surely, he was old enough now to understand what happened, wasn't he?

Instead, he spent his time with Teresa, pretending in his mind that they were more than just friends and that his girlfriend and her family had come to a Christmas party at his house. She was wearing a satin Christmas dress that was black with red and green dancing along the edges of the hem and sleeves. Her auburn hair was pulled back in a ponytail that swung absentmindedly behind her head, occasionally reflecting the glow from the fire or the lights on the tree.

Bud realized he was the happiest he had been in a long while. His thoughts briefly turned to Smitty, who was probably sitting alone with his aunt at her house in Readfield. Leaving his parents behind must be lonely, Bud thought looking around at the room full of people he cared about.

Being alone in the world, or as near as Bud could understand being alone, was one of the worst feelings he could imagine. He had felt something similar when he had spiraled into depression not so very long ago. Spending a little more time with Smitty seemed like a good idea, just in case he was feeling something similar to what Bud himself had been through. He wanted Smitty to feel as good as he felt in that moment.

Teresa fetched each of them a mug of warm apple cider from the kitchen. She returned, handing one to Bud, and her smiled warmed him as much as the fire ever could have. The two friends sat on the floor, shoulder to shoulder in front of the fire, and discussed everything and nothing all at once. Teresa leaned close and lay her head on Bud's shoulder.

"I'm so glad we can share Christmas together again," she said. "I hope we can keep doing it for years to come."

Bud could think of nothing he wanted more.

# 21

The Christmas break from school was over, and the two kids were driving back to Maranacook High school for the first classes of the new year. Bud was glad to have the truck back after his punishment for keeping from his grandparents the fact that he'd allowed Smitty to have alcohol in it. Buck had been gracious enough to allow him to drive to school and to allow Teresa to ride with him. Buck thought that Teresa would be a good influence, and she most certainly was. She would tell Bud when he was going too fast or if he wasn't paying enough attention to the road. She was one for law and order, which is one reason why she found the plot of *Lord of the Flies* abhorrent.

"I can't believe they have you read that in school," she said. Bud explained the major themes and what she could expect from class discussions when she had to read it her sophomore year.

*Watership Down*, on the other hand, Bud had found extremely enjoyable. It had opened his eyes to a new way of looking at greatness, leadership, and what it means to be "important" to others. He enjoyed discussing books with Teresa more than his other schoolmates. They tended to remain on the surface when analyzing books for themes, while Teresa was far more willing to delve deeper into what a book might mean on a more personal level.

The new year brought new hope and new promise for Bud, who had decided that he needed to be there for Smitty while he was adjusting to a new living situation. They had a shop class together, so they would see each other often. It was just a matter of finding things to do together outside of school that didn't result in either of them getting into trouble. Where Teresa was into law and order, Smitty was more into testing the limits. Unfortunately for Bud, it wouldn't take long for Smitty to test his resolve in helping him to find a new, and more positive path in life.

It was early February when Smitty came walking quickly up to Bud in the hallway before classes. He fidgeted nervously, looking over his shoulder to make sure no one was too close or listening.

"Hey, Bud, check it out," he said slyly holding up a plastic bag.

"What is it?" Bud asked not getting a good look.

"Joints. Weed, Bud. I've got four of them. We can smoke one after school if you want."

"Where'd you get that?"

"My brother knows a guy whose cousin lives in Lewiston. He hooked us up," Smitty said.

Bud had zero interest in smoking a joint, especially after the near fiasco with the beer bottle in his truck. He was about to say as much to Smitty when the bell rang for class.

"I've got to run, Bud," Smitty said. "If I'm late for Math again, Mr. Hanson is going to get me expelled for sure. One more screw up and Principal LeVeque will kick me out. He said so. Here, put this in your locker. I don't have time to go back to mine. I'll get it after school."

He shoved the baggie into Bud's hand and hurried off down the hallway. Bud chased after him calling for him to wait, but there were too many bodies for Smitty to hear him over the cavalcade of footsteps, so he returned to his locker. He had just opened it when Drake Goucher bumped into him, causing him to drop the baggie at his feet.

"Oooops," Drake said smiling. "Better be more careful, Bud."

Bud quickly bent over to retrieve the baggie and shoved it into his locker, but not before Drake got a quick glimpse of the contents. Bud shut the locker door, gave Drake a menacing glance, and headed off for his own class.

The period wasn't quite halfway over when he was summoned to Principal LeVeque's office. His heart leaped as he made the walk down the hall, terrified that he already knew what was coming. Sure enough, when he entered the office, Principal LeVeque was sitting at his desk with the plastic baggie and the four marijuana joints that he had retrieved from Bud's locker.

"Have a seat, Mr. Marshall," LeVeque said. Bud sat down across the desk from him eyeing the bag. "This was found in your locker, Mr. Marshall," LeVeque continued. "As I'm sure you know, being in possession of drugs here at school is a violation of the rules."

Bud sat, not moving and not speaking.

"Is that a safe assumption, Mr. Marshall?" LeVeque asked. Bud nodded. LeVeque waited for the young man to say something, but when Bud didn't and just stared at him, LeVeque continued. "What exactly do you think I should do in this situation—"

"It's not mine," Bud interrupted.

"It's not yours?"

"No."

"It was in your locker." Bud again just sat and stared at the principal. "Mr. Marshall, if it's not yours then how did it get into your locker?" LeVeque asked.

"I was holding it for someone, but it's not mine. I didn't even want to hold it for them, but they walked off before I could give it back," Bud said.

"Then whose is it, Mr. Marshall?"

Bud was getting very tired of being called "Mr. Marshall." The moniker had a condescending nature every time the principal used it. He made up his mind then and there that no matter what the principal said, Bud wasn't going to rat out his friend. Smitty had twice taken the fall for him in similar situations. Bud didn't want to see him expelled, not when he had run off from his parents' house to live with his aunt. Certainly not when he thought Smitty might be battling depression or other demons Bud could only guess at. He again sat and stared refusing to speak, but now his attitude was lighter and more carefree, the burden of caring what punishment happened to him was gone.

"I'll ask again, Mr. Marshall. If these drugs aren't yours, whose are they?" LeVeque asked.

"I'm not going to tell you," Bud said calmly.

"And why not, Mr. Marshall?"

"Because unlike the person that told you those were in my locker, I'm not a snitch."

"The individual who alerted us to the possible presence of drugs in your locker has an appreciation for rules, Mr. Marshall."

"No, they have a desire to get me in trouble," Bud countered. "Nothing more."

"Maybe it's time I called your grandparents in here. Perhaps that would make you more cooperative."

Principal LeVeque's threat was empty. Bud knew his grandparents were getting a call regardless of the outcome of the meeting. He smiled broadly and called LeVeque's bluff.

"I think that's a fantastic idea," he said.

Bud sat in a chair in the corner of LeVeque's office for several hours, waiting for his grandparents to arrive. Lunch came and went, but Bud wasn't allowed to eat anything. He was allowed only a cup of water that the secretary would fill for him at the water fountain. The psychological warfare that LeVeque was waging was having little effect. As the time wore on, Bud became more convinced that what he was doing was right.

When Buck and Maggie arrived, the principal led them into the office and gave them chairs on either side of Bud. He related the events thus far to them and showed them the plastic baggie containing the marijuana.

"He claims it isn't his, but he refuses to tell me who it actually belongs to," LeVeque said.

"Is this true, Brandon?" Maggie asked.

"Yes Gran, it's true that those are not my drugs. I don't use drugs, and I never have," Bud said.

"Then why don't you tell the principal whose drugs they are, Bud?" Buck said.

"Because I broke the rules, Pa," Bud said. "It's against the rules to be in possession of drugs, and they were in my locker."

"Well now, Mr. Marshall," LeVeque said. "If that's the only problem, I'm sure we can overlook your violation if you were to provide us with the name of the individual who gave them to you. You've been doing well in bringing up your grades, and I've had no trouble from you since the unfortunate incident early on in your career here. It would be a shame for you to sully all your hard work for someone else's rule breaking."

"But the individual who gave them to me is not in possession of drugs, and therefore isn't violating any rules," Bud said matter-of-factly.

Buck sensed immediately where his grandson was going, and a quick look at Maggie told him that she did as well. The glance between the two of them was all that was necessary. They had both come to the same conclusion: Bud felt he had done nothing morally wrong but had been put in a situation where he had broken a rule. They knew he was going to be loyal to the friend who had been loyal to him, and he was ready to accept his punishment.

"It is also a violation of school rules to bring drugs onto school property," LeVeque offered.

"Why?" Bud asked.

"Excuse me, Mr. Marshall? Why?"

"Yes, why is it a violation to bring drugs onto school property when it's already a violation to be in possession of them on school property?" Bud asked. "It seems that a rule forbidding possession of them is sufficient. Are you suggesting that bringing them onto school grounds is worse than possessing them on school grounds?"

"No, I'm not suggesting one is worse than the other," LeVeque said.

"It seems that you are," Bud said. "You said that my violation could be overlooked if I provide you with the name of the individual who brought them onto school grounds. Why would you do that if you didn't view the other violation as a worse one?"

"It seems you have no interest in cooperating, Mr. Marshall," LeVeque said.

"Bud, I don't want you to be difficult," Buck interjected. "I don't think Principal LeVeque wants you to be in trouble if you did nothing wrong."

"That's true. At the end of the day, we are trying to prevent students from using drugs in school," LeVeque said.

"Then neither possession or bringing drugs onto school grounds needs to be against the rules," Bud offered. "Only using them while on school grounds should be."

"Mr. Marshall, I'm not about to change the rules to suit your semantics," LeVeque said. "Ultimately, we are trying to prevent drug use on school grounds and—"

"You've done that," Bud interrupted. "You have the drugs. No one will be using them on school grounds. You say you'll forgive my violation if I tell you who brought them. I wonder if you would be as forgiving if I were unable to tell you."

"Excuse me?" LeVeque said.

"Suppose someone put those drugs in my locker without my knowledge? Would you be willing to forgive the violation then?"

"Mr. Marshall, how would we know if you're lying about someone putting the drugs there without your knowledge?" LeVeque asked.

"So, if someone tells you they suspect there are drugs in Drake Goucher's locker tomorrow, you'll check, and when you find them he'll be punished as I am?" Bud asked.

LeVeque's eyes narrowed. He could sense he was in dangerous waters with this young man, but he wasn't about to tolerate being made a fool of.

"Mr. Goucher is an upstanding student. If he were to be framed by having drugs placed in his locker —"

"You would immediately believe him because of his reputation," Bud interrupted again.

"Mr. Marshall, I don't appreciate being interrupted."

"But that's what you're saying," Bud continued. "You're saying that certain students, because of their reputations, are exempt from the rules. Others, because of bad reputations are always assumed to be guilty. I just happen to fall somewhere in the middle, and if I'm willing to provide you with a name that falls further into the bad reputation category you'll have found a bigger problem than you think I am who you can punish. I'll be honest Principal LeVeque, I think your system is unfair. The person who you think has a great reputation is one that I know to be one of the worst human beings in this school. He's cruel, vindictive, mean, selfish, and makes it his business to build himself up by tearing others down. I could give you a name for who gave me those drugs. Sure, I could. But I won't. Because even if you found the name I gave you to be a perfect example of someone with a bad reputation, I know that individual to be a loyal friend."

Principal LeVeque listened as his face reddened with each word. He had heard enough and was going to put an end to the discussion.

"Mr. Marshall," he said. "I'm giving you one last chance to give me the name of the individual who brought those drugs onto school grounds and gave them to you. If you don't tell me, I'll have no choice but to punish you with a week's suspension."

"Very well," Bud said calmly. "The person who brought those drugs to school was Drake Goucher."

"I don't appreciate you making this into a joke, young man!" LeVeque burst, no longer able to keep his calm.

"It's my word against his," Bud said coolly. "He is the one who gave you my name, isn't he? It shouldn't come as a shock that the two of us don't get along. It makes perfect sense that he would frame me in order to get me in trouble. But it doesn't matter that it's my word against his, does it? There's only a handful of names you would have accepted on my word, and those would have to be students with worse reputation than me. I refuse to play that game, Principal LeVeque."

"Game? You think this is a game?" LeVeque asked irritated.

"It is a game. It's the kind of game that Drake is great at. Build your reputation by ruining other people's. I'm not about to play it, though. I've worked hard to improve my reputation, and I've done it on my own. A year ago, you wouldn't have listened to a single word of me claiming those drugs aren't mine. It's a testament to what I've done that we're even still here having this discussion. I'm not about to build myself up more by tearing someone else down. If that means I have to face discipline for violating the rule of possessing drugs on school property, then that's a reality I accept."

Buck drove Bud's truck while Bud rode in the passenger seat. Maggie drove the car. Bud had received a week's suspension for being in possession of the marijuana. Grandfather and grandson rode in silence most of the way home before Buck spoke.

"For what it's worth, Bud," Buck said, "I think I can speak for both your grandmothah and I when I say we believe you. Not that Drake brought the drugs to school, but that they weren't yours."

"Thanks, Pa," Bud said. "I wasn't going to smoke any. I didn't even want to have them in my locker, but he walked away before I could give them back."

"Smitty?"

Bud nodded.

"I had to cover for him," Bud said. "He covered for me about the beer. I should have told you, but I drank some too. I'm sorry, Pa."

"I'm glad you decided to tell me," Buck said.

"I suppose you're going to take the truck away again," Bud said.

"Why? Are you going to do it again?"

"No."

"Then I think having to be stuck inside with your grandmothah and Me in the middle of February for a week is punishment enough. I already took the truck away for the beeah. I will say this, Bud, I don't think you treated Principal LeVeque very well. He was just trying to do his job."

"I didn't treat him well? What about how he treated me?"

"Do you think his poah treatment of you means you can treat him badly in return? Don't think you won any favahs in there or proved a point to your principal — You didn't. You made him look foolish, and he won't forget that easily. You may think the rules are written poorly or unfairly and that the system is set up for some people to succeed and others to fail, but that's life. Don't think that shoving Principal LeVeque's nose in his system's failyahs is going to get you anywhere — It isn't."

"So, I should have just ratted Smitty out?"

"I'm not saying that, Bud. It's fine to stand up for a friend. And in this instance, you had technically broken a rule. Just don't get in a habit of covering for friends when it gets you in trouble you wouldn't othahwise be in. True friends won't ask you to anyway."

"Smitty wouldn't do that."

"I hope not, Bud. There are folks who want help when they're in a bad place in life. Then there are some folks that just want to drag othahs down into that bad place so they have company. The trick is figuring out which person is which before you look up from trying to help them and find out you're in that bad place too. Only time will tell if you got it right today, but I don't blame you for wanting to help a friend."

Bud's grandfather never ceased to amaze him. Every time he spoke, it was like listening to the knowledge of a man that knows the meaning of all things. Bud figured, since Buck was talking, this was as good a time as any to ask one of the questions that had been festering for some time.

"Pa," he said. "Mr. LaVerdier said once that I should ask you about 'The Big Red One' and your time in the first World War."

Buck looked over at his grandson and let out a long sigh. "Well, Bud, that's a difficult story to tell — and I imagine, to listen to," he said. "Someday I'll share it with you, but I don't think today is the right day for it, okay?"

"All right, Pa," Bud said. Bud knew that if wasn't the right day to talk about World War One, it certainly wasn't the right day to talk about his father's suicide, so Bud didn't ask. They rode the rest of the way home in silence.

Teresa wasn't too happy about having to take the bus alone to and from school for a week, and when she heard the story about how Bud had acted in front of Principal LeVeque, she was mortified.

"What were you trying to prove, Brandon?" she asked.

"Prove? I don't know. I guess I just wanted Principal LeVeque to know that I'm on to the game and that I'm refusing to play by his rules. Maybe I'm just trying to prove to myself that I'm starting to understand."

"Understand what?"

"That greatness is about more than how others see you. It's being true to what's right, being true to your friends and the people you care about, and being a leader when being a leader is difficult instead of when it's easy."

"You think you were a leader today?"

"Maybe... Sometimes maybe being a leader is as simple as refusing to follow."

Bud pulled out his notebook that night and added some of the things that Buck had told him. Underneath where he had written "Do it for yourself" he added two lines: "Do it for someone else" and "Do it because it's right."

When he returned to school from his suspension, Smitty was quick to praise Bud's resolve not to rat out a friend. Bud said it wasn't a big deal and that Smitty had already done as much for him on two occasions. The story of Bud's meeting with Principal LeVeque was the buzz around school. No one was sure how word of what had been said got out, but Bud became a sort of cult hero for how he had stared down LeVeque and refused to break.

Regardless, Bud kept his head down and focused on his schoolwork. Every time he walked by the office he could feel Principal LeVeque's eyes following his every step. He felt like one foot out of line, and the principal was going to make an example of him. However, Bud made sure to be very careful. He was determined not to give LeVeque the chance, and was succeeding wonderfully.

Weeks of treading carefully wore on, and the end of school was less than a month away. The weather was warming quickly as summer approached. Bud felt like he was going to escape the year with only minimal drama for once. That was, until he found himself in the locker room one day and overheard some of senior boys, including Drake, talking on the opposite side of a row of lockers.

"It's almost graduation and I need to get laid," Drake was saying.

"Just pick a girl, Drake. You can have any one you want," another boy said.

"It's not that easy, Dave. I want a sure thing, you know? The last thing I want is to go the summer before college without getting any."

"Well then, what are you going to do?" a third boy asked.

"I think I'm going to go after that freshman chick. The one everyone says is really slutty. I figure freshman slut being asked out by a senior... that's a sure thing if there ever was one."

Bud's heart was in his throat. He had a horrible feeling he knew exactly who Drake was talking about.

"You mean Teresa Peterson?" Dave asked.

"That's her," Drake answered. "Brownish hair, good body, decent boobs, I wouldn't mind getting some of that."

The boys all laughed and made disgusting rude comments about Teresa. Bud's blood was steaming now. It took every ounce of his energy not to run around the lockers and lay into Drake right there. Thankfully the senior boys all moved on from the locker room, leaving Bud to stew in his anger. Bud planned to talk to Teresa on the ride home and give her a heads up about Drake and what he was thinking.

After school however, Teresa ran up to Bud and told him she had another ride home and would see him later. She ran off before Bud could say anything. Bud knew that spelled trouble. He spent the entire ride home trying to think of how to explain things to Teresa. He parked in his driveway and sat in the truck. Drake Goucher dropped Teresa off in his Pontiac Firebird as Bud watched through the truck's windshield. After Drake had turned around and driven back up the lane, Bud got out of his truck and walked over to Teresa's.

"What was all that about?" Bud asked when Teresa opened the door.

"Oh nothing," she said. "Drake just offered to give me a ride home. I thought it was nice of him so I said 'okay.'"

"Reese, can I talk to you for a minute?"

"Sure, Brandon."

Taking her by the arm, He led her down off the porch and started walking down towards the stream. He waited until they were down on the bank below his house and walking along the edge before continuing.

"Reese, I don't think you should be hanging around with Drake Goucher," he said.

"Brandon, don't be ridiculous. He's a great guy. He's a good student and a fantastic athlete. He's one of the most admired guys in the whole school."

"You don't know him like I do."

"Okay Brandon, I know you might be a little jealous—"

"I'm not jealous, Reese, I heard him talking to these other guys—"

"We're just going to a movie, it's not a big deal."

"You're going out with him?" Bud stopped walking and turned to her grabbing her arm. She snatched it back away from him angrily.

"Yes, he asked me to a movie."

"Reese, you have no idea what he's actually thinking."

"Brandon, honestly this is all so ridiculous. We're just going to one movie, it's not like we're—"

"Reese, he thinks you're a slut!"

The word echoed and lingered in the air for what felt like eternity. The change in Teresa's face was immediate. Bud could see the anger rising in her inch by inch. She brushed past him and started to stomp back to her house. Bud turned and yelled after her.

"And it's my fault."

She stopped walking and turned to look at him.

"It's my fault, Reese. It's all because of what I did to you in middle school. Please, you have to listen."

She slowly walked back up to him.

"Ok, Brandon, I'm listening," she said.

"I heard him talking to some of the other senior guys saying how he wants to get laid, and that he was thinking of you because you have a reputation as... well... because you have a reputation."

Teresa's face didn't change. She had the same look of indignation from when Bud had first used the word.

"I just don't want to see you get hurt," Bud said.

"You think I'm a slut, Brandon?"

"No! Of course not."

"You think I would have sex with Drake Goucher?"

"No."

"Then you have nothing to worry about. Drake will find out plenty fast that I'm not a slut. If you're right and all he's after is sex, he will soon learn that he's got the wrong girl."

"Reese, I just think it would be best if—"

"I'm done discussing this, Brandon. My personal life is none of your business."

She turned and walked off, leaving Bud standing by the edge of the stream. He had been hurt by her final words. He realized that he had used poor tact in broaching the subject, but he and Teresa had always discussed everything together. Part of the problem was that he had suggested that he liked her as more than a friend. Bud knew that. He also knew that he was going to have to keep an eye on her and Drake just to make sure that she was safe. She might not know Drake Goucher, but Bud did.

# 22

**K**eeping an eye on Teresa and Drake was turning out to be more difficult than Bud had anticipated. Buck was insistent that Bud start working on the farm on weekends which kept him busy, and when Teresa left with Drake in his Firebird there was nothing he could do anyway.

Drake had taken Teresa out several times, both to the movies and to dinner in Augusta. Any time Bud questioned Teresa about it, she just waved him off and said that Drake was a perfect gentleman. School was almost out, and Bud knew that once summer vacation hit, he would be stuck working on the farm almost every day. Looking out for Teresa would be near impossible then.

For Teresa, the whole experience had been surreal at first. An attractive popular guy was paying attention to her and seemed to like her. As school drew to a close however, she became aware of a shift in her perception.

Drake and Bud were a study in contrast. Any time Bud had been around a group of other guys he acted slightly different from when he was around her alone. It was as though he were trying to impress them. Teresa always felt that he came off as fake, like an actor playing his part on the stage. But the Bud she knew in private, even the one that had made her mad from time to time, always seemed genuine.

Drake, on the other hand appeared to Teresa to be the opposite. He seemed more real when he was around his friends than when the two of them were alone. At times, even Teresa felt as though when she and Drake were together they were both acting out their prescribed roles in some grand production. None of it had the authenticity of life that she felt when she was around Bud.

When the school year ended and Drake graduated, Teresa realized that he would be heading to college in the fall. It made little sense to continue a relationship that she didn't feel was destined to go anywhere serious. While it had been nice spending time with Drake, and he always treated her well, deep down she missed spending time with Bud. Eventually, she made up her mind to break things off with Drake, but she wanted to do it in the nicest way possible.

Drake on the other hand, was growing impatient. He felt like he had put in ample time with Teresa for her to start rewarding him with more physical contact. To this point, she hadn't even kissed him; even after he had spent untold money on food, movies, and gifts for her. He was growing tired of waiting and playing the nice guy. With only summer vacation between him and leaving for college, he was going to have to press the issue.

Bud was working full time on the farm. With Buck growing older and slowing down, he had delegated much of the work to Stanley and to Bud. Buck took on more of a managerial role, which put less physical strain on him. He was good at organizing what needed to be done, and although his pride had taken a hit, he relegated himself to lighter tasks that were easier for him to handle.

Bud kept an eye out for Teresa and Drake, but they very rarely stayed around the farm. Drake always seemed in a hurry to get her into the Firebird and go somewhere else. Bud would catch a glimpse of the car pulling in and leaving from time to time, and his heart would always sink as he watched the dust on the lane settle after they were gone. Sure he was jealous, but he was also worried about Teresa and missed her friendship dearly.

It was a brutally hot July day when things would finally take a turn. Bud was working in the barn with Stanley. They were loading the first bales of hay into the loft, and they were sweaty from the heat, causing the hay to stick and itch at every opportunity. Bud heard the sound of the Firebird come down the lane and park in the Peterson's driveway, as well as the sound of the door slamming shut after Drake got out.

Up on the front porch Drake met Teresa, and the two sat to talk a little. Drake suggested they go somewhere more private where they wouldn't be interrupted. Secretly, Teresa hoped that he was planning to break up with her so that she would be spared the deed of initiating it herself and agreed. Of course, Drake hoped for a different outcome entirely and wanted privacy in hopes of increasing the level of intimacy.

Bud saw the two of them pass by the barn walking towards the stream. After making an excuse that he needed to get some air, he made his way to the door to watch them. As he feared, they turned and made to follow the stream up towards the waterfall. Bud couldn't believe that Teresa would take Drake to the waterfall. She would stop before that, he thought. She would have to. The waterfall was their place, and Teresa wouldn't ruin that by taking someone else there. Once the two were just out of sight, Bud made a dash for the bridge to the woods on the other side of the stream. He made to follow them from the secrecy of the trees and see exactly where they were going.

Teresa was reluctant to take Drake to the waterfall, but she didn't know of another private spot. She had made up her mind to break things off if Drake didn't first, and she certainly didn't want a scene on her front porch. This way at least things could be done in private away from prying eyes. She would make it quick, Drake could leave on his own, and she could sit and collect herself before returning. Neither she nor Drake were aware of Bud mirroring their walk from the seclusion of the forest.

Once Bud was convinced that Teresa was taking Drake to the waterfall, he sprinted ahead. He wanted to get across Baker Street before them and find a hidden spot from which he could observe them without being seen. He found a large bush growing around a small poplar some ten yards from the bank. The bush was even with the end of the little pond where it shallowed and returned to the stream. He wouldn't be able to hear the two talking if they sat on the log on the other bank, but he would be able to watch.

The two arrived and sat on the log just as Bud had assumed they would. Sure enough, he couldn't hear anything, but by appearances the conversation hadn't started all that interestingly.

If Bud had been able to hear, he would have known that they were just discussing Drake leaving for college. Teresa was steering the conversation towards how hard it would be to date being so far apart. Drake kept redirecting it back to the two of them and how much Teresa meant to him.

Alarm bells kept ringing in Teresa's head. Her sense of the whole situation being a charade in some grand production was growing. She tried to suggest, lightly, that perhaps it would be better to end things now before they got too serious.

From behind the bush, Bud could sense tension growing between Teresa and Drake. He was barely breathing, trying not to make a sound and straining his ears to listen, all to no avail. Drake took Teresa's hand and looked at her saying something in a manner that seemed almost pleading to Bud. Teresa snatched her hand away, and the change in Drake was evident. He became agitated, and while Bud still couldn't make out any words, Drake's voice had gotten louder.

Drake had told Teresa he loved her, which sounded so hollow and fake that Teresa had recoiled in surprise. Now he was angry and demanding to know why she had been playing games with him. He wanted to know why she had pretended to like him when she didn't. He demanded to know if it was a set up. Had Bud put her up to it?

Teresa was angry at the accusations and tried to defend herself. It was when Drake used the word "slut" and implied that there was no other explanation for why a girl "like her" would deny him a more physical relationship that Teresa realized Bud had been right all along. She rose, told Drake that it was over, and turned to walk back to the farm alone.

Bud saw Teresa get up to leave and almost let out a sigh of relief, but before he could Drake jumped up and grabbed Teresa's hand. He pulled her back and forced her into an embrace and began trying to kiss her. Coals inside of Bud began to glow hot and red, and he had to restrain himself from rushing out from his hiding place. His breathing increased, and his grip on the small poplar tightened.

Teresa fought against Drake and managed to push him away. She reared back and slapped him hard across the face. This enraged Drake further and he struck back, knocking her to the ground. He stood over her menacingly as she backed away on all fours with fear in her eyes.

Bud's knuckles were white, and the coals in his gut had burst into a flame that was rising through him. Every muscle was tense from the exertion of remaining stationary, while every fiber of his being called out for him to move. He grit his teeth as he watched

Teresa back helplessly along the bank until she was almost even with his place on the other side.

A wicked smile came over Drake's face. He said nothing, but instead leapt onto Teresa, pinning her onto the ground. She struggled, but he struck her again and then put one hand over her mouth to muffle her screams. She squirmed underneath him as he worked to pull her skirt up over her hips. He used his free hand to punch her in the gut, causing her to lose her breath. She gave up her fight and resigned herself to her fate as tears began to gather in the corners of her eyes.

When Drake started to unbuckle his pants, Bud's restraints were loosened. He sprang from his hiding spot with the fury of a storm rising on the horizon. He leapt down from the bank and splashed through the stream just below the little pool. Drake looked up just in time to meet Bud's hands as they grabbed him and tossed him like he was no more than a bale of hay.

Bud knelt down and helped Teresa into a sitting position. He wiped the gathering tears from her cheeks and helped her to smooth out her skirt back down over her legs. He was about to help her to her feet when Drake slammed into him from behind.

Teresa retreated up the bank away from the stream as the boys grappled. Drake landed an elbow to Bud's lip, causing it to split and blood to gush out over his shirt. Drake had surprised Bud with his counterattack, but Bud was larger and had grown exceedingly strong from working on the farm. It didn't take long before the larger boy had control of the fight on the ground and was on top of Drake and holding him down.

The adrenaline was fueling Bud's rage as he struggled to hold Drake, who was still squirming and jostling for a better position. When Drake grabbed Bud's arm and sank in with his teeth, what remained of Bud's restraints fell to the ground. He cried out in pain and anger and his eyes widened as he turned the full force of the raging fire within him onto Drake.

The world went dull, losing both color and sound. Bud was aware only of the muffled thudding from his beating heart as it echoed within his skull. He grasped around the ground for something to return the pain from the bite on his arm back onto Drake. His fingers finally grasped a rock the size of a small melon near the edge of the pool.

Drake was still fighting as Bud raised the rock with his right hand and brought it smashing down into the side of his head. With every ounce of strength he had, Bud raised the rock and brought it down again. There was no sound, and Bud was feeling rather than seeing. He raised the rock and brought it down again. Bud had no sense of how many times he raised and lowered the rock, and he left time and space until the dull thudding of his heartbeat was replaced by Teresa's high–pitched screams.

Bud stopped with the rock in mid–air still in his hand. He looked up at Teresa who was pale and shaking, her eyes wide with terror. She covered her mouth, silencing the scream that had awoken Bud from his rage–induced trance. She backed away slowly a few steps down the edge of the stream and then turned and ran back towards the farm.

It was only then that Bud realized Drake was no longer fighting. He was no longer squirming. He was no longer moving. Bud looked at the rock in his hand, only now aware of its weight, and saw blood smeared and splattered on both it and his arm. He looked at the water of the still pool beside him and saw his reflection, specked with blood. He reached up to wipe it from his brow with his left hand, but instead he only smeared it down the side of his face. He became aware of the metallic taste in his mouth, unsure if it came from his split lip, or from the same source as the splatter that was all over him.

When he looked back down at Drake, the boy was unrecognizable. Bud had smashed in his skull at the left temple. Blood was streaming down the side of his face and along the bank into the pool, sullying it. The crystal water was turning red as the blood spread towards the middle where the current finally whisked it off down the stream. Bud turned on his knees, retched, and vomited on the bank.

That was where the sheriff and the paramedics found him, sometime later. He was sitting there on the bank of the pool, hugging his knees. On his face, hands, and arms, blood was drying brown in the hot sun, except for where his cheeks had been washed clean by his tears.

Drake Goucher was declared dead at the scene. The sheriff only managed to get four words out of Bud.

"He was hurting her."

# 23

**B**ud sat next to his grandfather in the cold grey room. Across the table, his grandmother sat next to the defense attorney, avoiding eye contact with her grandson. For everyone else, things had been moving quickly, but for Bud, waiting in a cold cell at the Maine Youth Center in South Portland, the time had seemed to drag on slowly.

Bud's lawyer explained that Drake's parents wanted him tried as an adult, and they were pushing for a conviction of murder in the first degree. The attorney didn't think they would be able to get a conviction, though. He was confident. Of course he was confident, Bud thought. After all, he wasn't going to be the one on trial.

Buck asked procedural questions about how things would progress when they went to trial, and Bud's defense attorney answered each one dutifully. Maggie sat quietly with her head down, not speaking.

It was all very straightforward according to the attorney, who spelled it all out as though he were describing directions to the supermarket.

The prosecution would try to present the case as though Bud had a plan to attack Drake and had waited in the bushes to do so. They would use Bud's prior history with Drake as an example of how Bud had motive to commit the crime. They would counter Teresa's testimony that she had been attacked by no fault of her own, by bringing up the fact that she had voluntarily led Drake to a secluded spot and by pointing out that she has a certain reputation. Bud shuddered at the thought of Teresa's name being dragged through the mud all over again.

The defense's strategy was similarly simple. Bud would tell his side of the story: how he had overheard Drake in the locker room, all the prior incidents of Drake's violence against him, wanting to protect Teresa, and Drake attacking her and subsequently himself. Then they would have Teresa corroborate her part of the story. Ultimately, the defense attorney felt the prosecution wouldn't be able to prove premeditation beyond a reasonable doubt, and Bud would be cleared of the charge of first degree murder.

Buck seemed unconvinced, as he sat just rubbing his beard and offering the occasional question.

"The only other option is to settle," the attorney said. "They're offering to not charge Bud as an adult and to lower the charges to manslaughter. Bud would remain in the Maine Youth Center until his 18th birthday, and then face two years of probation, during which he would have visits from a probation officer twice per month — and if he committed any crime in those two years he would be subject to jail time. If he committed any further violent acts in those two years, even so much as a bar fight, he would face ten years in prison."

Buck shook his head, as that seemed unacceptable to him. "Is Teresa willing to testify on Bud's behalf," he asked.

Bud looked up at the defense attorney sharply, expecting to hear that she wasn't.

"Yes," he said. "Teresa is willing to testify."

"Does she know that they're going to call her a 'slut?'" Bud asked exasperated.

Maggie looked up at Bud with shock in her eyes at hearing her grandson use the word "slut" so harshly.

"She is fully aware of the direction the prosecution is likely to take in cross–examination, yes," the attorney said.

Bud dropped his head, embarrassed. Such a stupid comment that he had made so long ago, and it simply wouldn't go away. He felt so bad that he had once again put Teresa in such a position. Now her reputation would be put on trial along with him. It wasn't fair. It wasn't right. And Bud knew it.

"I want to settle," Bud said.

The three adults in the room looked at Bud. Buck reached over and put his arm around his grandson.

"Are you sure, Bud?" Buck asked.

Bud nodded. Bud's attorney protested, saying it was unnecessary for Bud to accept the plea when he felt it was likely they could beat the charges he was facing. He explained that Drake's parents had let their grief get the better of them and had over-reached on the charges for revenge. It was foolish to accept a manslaughter plea. He couldn't understand why Bud would want to settle.

"Teresa did nothing wrong," Bud said. "I can't sit in a court room while the whole room... the whole town... the whole state practically, questions her reputation. She doesn't deserve that. She's been through enough. We all have."

The decision was made. Buck patted his grandson on the back and gave him a big hug before he left. Maggie still didn't say anything. Bud's attorney said he would let the prosecution know and get the paperwork done. With that, Bud returned to his cell in the Maine Youth Center where he had been since the day of the incident.

Sixteen months, Bud thought as he looked around the cell. He would be released on his 18th birthday. He knew he would never be able to return to high school, but he would be able to work towards his GED while in "The Center," as he called it. Bud felt that sounded better than "jail."

He spent his days reading or doing work towards earning his GED. Days all felt the same, so judging the passage of time became difficult. Bud did so by counting the number of books he had read, and the number was steadily climbing. He read literature, philosophy, history, the Bible, and anything else he could get his hands on.

Bud's time in The Center was broken only by his visits from his grandparents. Bud would ask how things were on the farm and how Teresa was doing. Maggie never talked much and seemed distant and reserved. Feeling his grandson needed something to help occupy his mind, Buck would do his best to bring news.

Buck and Maggie neglected to tell Bud that they had tried to attend Drake's funeral service. The Goucher's had asked them to leave and escorted them from the church. Buck had said he understood and looked at them with kindness in his eyes, but he was met only with anger and rage from Drake's parents. Maggie was distraught over the affair, saying they had done nothing wrong and just wanted to pay their respects. Buck said to his wife, "You don't know how someone will react to losing a child. I won't blame them for their grief. We all handle it differently."

Bud would never talk about how things were in The Center when Buck pressed him with questions. Sometimes, when his grandparents would come, bruises on Bud's face would tell them enough. Bud never fought back when the other inmates beat him. The guards had to stop every fight. Reading and doing schoolwork were not popular pastimes for an inmate to have in The Center.

And so, all of them would exchange niceties and bland information, Bud trying not to upset his grandparents and them trying not to further burden their grandson. Nevertheless, Bud was glad for the company and to see them whenever they got a chance to visit.

One visit in late September, Bud asked about Teresa. Buck told him that she hadn't returned to Maranacook High School that year. She had been receiving cruel phone calls from some of the other students, blaming her for Drake's death. Teenagers don't usually need a reason to pick on someone. Give them a reason and they'll be relentless.

Teresa and her parents felt that rather than put up with it, they would enroll her in Kents Hill School, a private institution for grades nine through twelve. Teresa would be living on campus and attending classes there. Kents Hill School was between Wayne and Mt. Vernon, so Teresa wouldn't be far from home if she needed anything.

Bud couldn't blame Teresa for not wanting to put up with the inevitable stares, name calling, and general nastiness she would have to face in returning to Maranacook High School. He was rather glad that he would never have to deal with it himself. He didn't look forward to having to return to his hometown in general when his time in The Center was through. If repairing his reputation from middle school had been difficult, it was going to be nothing compared to repairing it after this. Bud knew it would probably never happen. He had resigned himself to that.

Buck and Maggie wouldn't be returning to visit again until near Bud's birthday, so he steeled himself for the longest stretch of his life without seeing any friends or family. Bud had experienced loneliness before, but nothing like what he felt during those weeks at The Center. He redoubled his efforts in working towards his GED and he was making exceptional progress. It was amazing what one could accomplish when there was nothing else to do.

As the time came near for the visit from his grandparents, Bud found himself growing excited. He needed to see a friendly face and get some news from back on the farm. Just to hear his grandfather's voice again and to look into his deep blue eyes would bring Bud comfort and strength for the next stretch alone.

When the time came however, only Maggie showed up. She walked in with a tired, sad look on her face, and Bud immediately sensed trouble. When Maggie sat down across from Bud and looked into her grandson's eyes, she burst into tears. Through her sobs, she gave Bud the news that his grandfather had passed away.

Bud couldn't believe it. Maggie had to be wrong. He would have heard something. Bud just kept shaking his head in disbelief. Buck couldn't be dead. He simply couldn't be.

Once Maggie composed herself, she was able to explain to Bud that it had just happened. Buck had come down with pneumonia again. At first, Maggie had assumed he would be down for a few weeks and then be back up and around like he had before. As the days went on and Buck worsened, she grew more worried. When things didn't improve, Maggie had him admitted to the hospital. She hadn't slept since he had passed away late the previous night.

Bud was still reeling from the news, but when Maggie said the funeral would be held in only a few days, Bud said he wanted to be there. Maggie shook her head and told him she had already made the request, but it had been denied. Bud wasn't going to be released, even under custody, to attend the funeral. Her eyes welled up with tears again as she passed Bud a letter that his grandfather had written him when he was admitted to the hospital.

"I'm sorry," she said. "Buck forgave you immediately for what you did. It's been harder for me."

With that, she turned and left Bud alone again. He spent the afternoon trying his hardest to get leave to attend his grandfather's funeral. He spoke to administrators, yelled at guards, and demanded to make phone calls. He was denied at every turn. Criminals don't get sympathy.

He sat in his cell that night, clinging to the letter Buck had written him. That was when the realization that he would never again see or speak to his grandfather finally hit him. He opened the envelope, addressed simply: "To Bud," and began reading the letter. The tears from his eyes fell on the pages, smudging the ink as he read.

*Dear Bud,*

*You once asked me about my time in World War One. I figured I should write it down, since my strength is leaving me. I don't know that I'm ever leaving this hospital bed, and you deserve to know.*

*I'm not going to go into specifics, because the horrors of that time are still all too real. What you need to know is that I have also taken life. I'm not proud of this fact and I don't feel heroic or noble for it. No, killing is not glamorous, even in war. It is always ugly. I killed because it was expected of me, and one time in particular still haunts me to this day.*

*One of my friends, my brother in arms, had been killed by the enemy. I call him the enemy because that's all I knew about him. I'll spare you the details, as I'm sure your incident is still too fresh in your mind for such things, but I looked into his eyes before he drew his last breath. I don't know that young man's name, but his face still visits me in my dreams.*

*I feel bad about what I did, but not why I did it. Maybe that's why I have never blamed you for what you did to Drake. When someone we care about is hurt, or threatened, our sense of duty and the desire to protect or defend those that matter to us overpowers everything else.*

*I gave you a gold pocket watch on your first birthday that belonged to another soldier that died that day. By his death, I lived. I kept the watch as a reminder that while time can heal wounds and mend broken relationships, only death can erase what we have done from our memory.*

*You will never escape what you did, so there is no use in trying. You will either accept it and be able to move forward, or it will consume you. Please accept it. Not all actions in life are either right or wrong, black and white. There are fields of gray in which the things we do can be both horrendous and righteous. You are stronger than you know.*

*I love you Bud. I have tried to show you that, but I doubt I ever said it enough. There is nothing left that I can teach you. The rest you will have to learn on your own. If this is the end, please know that I will always be with you and your grandmother in spirit. She will need you now, so please forgive her for not being able to forgive you. She can't possibly understand the way I can.*

*I hope that I did well by you. It's a terrible thing, a child growing up without a father. No replacement can ever suffice, but I did the best that I could. I hope you know that.*

*All my love,*
*–Pa*


Bud sat on his bed and cried all night. The next day he requested to send a letter. He sat with pencil and paper and put down his thoughts. Then he folded the paper carefully and put it in the envelope. He was allowed to mail it. He just hoped it would reach his grandmother in time.

Maggie stood by the door of the church and welcomed everyone as they came. It was November 29th, the day after Bud's 17th birthday, and she was going to bury her husband. Car after car filed into the small church lot until people were forced to park along the side of the road. The weather was gray and cold, and a sharp wind was blowing out of the North. There had been no snow, so the land was brown and cheerless.

Maggie was about to turn and head inside to take her place at the front of the church when two stragglers came walking up. It was Mr. and Mrs. Goucher, Drake's parents. Maggie eyed them, her face unchanged as they walked up.

"Maggie," Mr. Goucher began. "First we need to say we're sor—"

"If you're here to pay your respects to my late husband, you better hurry inside and find a place to stand because we are about to begin," Maggie said cutting him off. "I'm afraid all the pews are likely full at this point."

The Gouchers nodded and walked past her into the church. Maggie took a deep breath and went in herself, escaping the cold for the time being.

The service was simple but warm, which was fitting considering the man. At length, Maggie rose and made her way to the podium to read the eulogy she had prepared for her husband.

"We are here to celebrate the life of William Patrick Marshall," she began glancing up at the multitude of sad faces in the crowd. "Of course, most of you knew him only as 'Buck.'"

At this point, Maggie paused and looked up again. She caught a glimpse of the Gouchers standing in the back of the crowded church and then looked back at her notes trying to find her place. Her eyes then drifted to the Petersons, Jim, Nancy and Teresa, sitting next to her empty seat. She stumbled and fidgeted for a few seconds. Finally, she folded up her paper and looked up at the crowd.

"I was never very good with words," she said. "Looking now at what I've written, it seems entirely inadequate for the man we are here for today. I think, if you'll all be patient with me, I would like to read some words by someone else which seem to better represent my husband's life."

Maggie stepped down from the podium, walked over to her seat where her purse was sitting and retrieved an envelope. She then returned to the podium, pulled out several sheets of paper, smoothed them out and began to read.

*"Dear Gran,"*

Teresa's head lifted and her eyebrows rose as she instantly realized whose words Maggie would be reading. Her heart began pounding out of her chest as she thought of all those people who knew what Bud had done and were probably repulsed by being forced to listen respectfully to his words. Her eyes shifted from side to side trying to catch a glimpse of everyone's reactions as Maggie continued.

*I have exhausted every administrative avenue I can think of to be there with you today, all to no avail. Not surprisingly, people in my current situation don't garner a great deal of sympathy.*

*I know you won't be alone. Everyone knew and respected Pa, so I'm sure the whole town will show up for his service.*

Maggie paused and looked up at the faces staring back at her. Truly, the whole town was there. She saw the faces of Mr. Pratt the mill owner, and Mr. Weiss, who had been town manager for a number of years. Malcolm LaVerdier was there, wearing his dress uniform and a solemn expression. The Steins were there, and Stanley the handyman. Obviously, the Petersons were up front, and even Principal LeVeque had come to pay his respects. She saw numerous others who had brought their cars for Buck to work on, or for whom he had performed handyman services. There were so many lives in that room that her husband had touched. She took a deep breath before continuing.

*Maybe saying they knew Pa isn't the right way to express it. I don't think even I truly knew Pa. I was acquainted with him as well as anyone, except you of course, but the letter of his you gave me made me realize there was so much about him that I didn't know.*

*It saddens me to think that if it weren't for my actions I may have learned so much more about him. I guess that's the way with losing loved ones, we never realize how much more we wanted to say, or to ask, or to do, until it's too late.*

*I don't know if Drake's parents will come to the service or not. No one would blame them if they didn't come. Certainly, I would never blame them. It would take more courage than I know that I would have in their situation to do so.*

Maggie stopped reading to glance up at the Gouchers standing in the back of the room, who were now looking around nervously for eyes turning their way.

*But if they do come, please relay a message for me if you get the chance. Tell them I'm sorry. I'm sorry for what I did, but not for why I did it. I know the reason for doing something can never excuse the act itself, but I will never be sorry for trying to protect someone I care for deeply.*

Teresa shifted in her seat and tried to look again out of the corner of her eyes to see if people were looking her way. As far as she could tell, everyone was fixated on Maggie behind the podium. She settled back again to listen.

*That does not excuse my actions. It doesn't excuse the fact that I took someone away from them. I wish every day I could take that back, and losing Pa has only deepened that regret for me. It has made me realize the depth of the thing I stole from them. Yes, their son is gone, and that would be bad enough, except I took something more. I took from them one of the same things that has been taken from me. I took their chance to say goodbye.*

*Pa wrote that it's a terrible thing, my growing up without a father. Somehow, I think going on as a father or mother without your child must be worse. There are so many things I want to say to Pa, or to ask, or to learn from him. I cannot fathom the depths of those feelings for Drake's parents.*

*For me, there is an emptiness that feels like it will never be filled. There is a desperation and an anger that won't subside. There is a need that will never be met.*

*Pa once told me that life is never easy, but you should never let the hard times change you. That is something I have struggled with my whole life and it is harder today than ever before.*

*I pray the Gouchers are able to find peace with their loss. If they could find peace, that would give me hope for myself where today I can find none. Today the world looks bleak and cold, like a winter that will never end. The only way I can think to go on is to honor Pa's memory by living by the words he taught me.*

*I find myself asking what Pa would say were he here to give me advice. I think he would say that you never know when spring will come and you have to weather the harsh times with a resolve to carry on. He would say that no matter how far away it may be, eventually spring will come. And when spring comes, those that have stood strong in the face of the deepest of winters will be better for it.*

*Pa taught me that the greatest thing a man can do is love another with all his heart. If that is the measure of greatness in a man, then you and I are a testament to Pa's greatness. But you and I are not alone in that regard, Gran. As you look around the church at Pa's service, I hope you can find comfort in the knowledge that so much of the love that Pa shared is represented in that room. The family, the friends, the everyday and important men and women of our town: all of those people will be there because Pa was the greatest of men, one who gave every bit of himself for others.*

*So, I will try to live each day, from this one forward, as Pa would have lived it. I will try to stand unchanged in the face of the adversity the world throws at me. I will try to give more of myself for others. I will try to be soft at heart and live by his example of greatness.*

*I'm so sorry Gran, for all of the troubles I gave the two of you over the years. I have so many people I need to apologize to and my only hope is that I live long enough to get to all of them. I know the day will be hardest on you and the only person capable of comforting you is the one we lost. Please know that all my love and prayers are with you today and always.*

*−Brandon*

Tears were streaming down Maggie's face as she folded the letter up and returned it to the envelope. She stepped down from the podium and made her way back to her seat where she sat down next to Jim Peterson. Jim put his arm around Maggie and leaned close to her ear.

"Buck would have loved that," he said through his tears.

After the service, the Gouchers waited for Maggie outside. When she emerged from the church, the two walked up to her. Mrs. Goucher took her hand, and Mr. Goucher spoke looking her in the eye.

"Your grandson is right," he said. "Buck truly was a great man."

Maggie laid her husband to rest that afternoon under a sunless sky. At his head a simple marker was placed.

*William "Buck" Marshall*
*Husband, Father, Grandfather, Friend*
*1898 − 1977*

# 24

**B**ud sat alone in his cell in The Center. He hadn't seen his grandmother, or anyone for that matter, since she came to tell him his grandfather had died. It was getting close to Christmas, and he wondered sadly when she might return. Bud had less than a year remaining in The Center before he would be released on probation.

The solitude gave Bud lots of time. He had time to work towards his GED, time to read, and plenty of time to think. Bud thought about his grandfather and all the things he had shared. If he had his notebook, he would have written down everything he could remember, lest he forget. Bud thought about the funeral and his grandmother. He wondered how she was holding up with everything that had happened. She must be lonely, but then the Petersons would see that she had company. And of course, Bud thought about Teresa. He wondered if she had been at the funeral. He imagined she must have been. She wouldn't miss Buck's funeral even if it potentially meant awkwardness for herself.

With the thoughts swirling in Bud's mind like a constant maelstrom of worry and wonder, he knew exactly what the phrase "stir crazy" meant. He was sure he was headed for a breakdown if he couldn't get some news from back home soon. It was three days before Christmas when Maggie finally arrived again for a visit.

They sat across from one another, at first saying nothing at all. Bud thought his grandmother looked terribly sad, and he wished horribly to be out of that place and back home so he could grieve with her. She looked up into her grandson's deep blue eyes, eyes that reminded her so much of her husband, and took a deep, exhausted breath.

"I hadn't forgiven you," she said. "Your grandfather forgave you almost immediately, Bud. But I couldn't. I didn't. Not until I read your letter." Bud looked at her, but didn't speak. He swallowed, choking back a tear. "I don't know how to explain what happened in that church when I read it out loud," Maggie said.

"You read my letter at the church?" Bud asked.

"Yes, I read it at the funeral instead of my eulogy. I wasn't going to, but when I stood to give it your words just seemed so much more fitting than mine. There was an entire room of people grieving for your grandfather, while still mad and confused over what you had done. But after I read your letter... After, it was like a great water had washed away the anger and all that was left was sadness. I couldn't find a single eye without tears as I look around the church. It felt to me like you had channeled your grandfather's words, as though he had written that letter himself. I don't know if the Gouchers have forgiven you, but I have."

"I don't deserve your forgiveness, Gran. Not yet, anyway. But I do look forward to trying to earn it when I finally get out of here."

"I'm glad to hear it." Maggie smiled as she said it.

"Was Teresa there?" Bud asked apprehensively.

"Yes, she was, Brandon," Maggie answered. "I didn't get a chance to talk to her. Her parents took her back to Kents Hill School right after the funeral."

"This whole thing is probably as hard for her as for anyone."

"Your grandfather felt you had saved her a great deal of hardship when you prevented her from testifying. I remember him saying it. I didn't understand at the time, but with the rumors and rumblings around town, I understand now."

"What rumors?"

"I've overheard people saying that Teresa invited that boy to the waterfall. Like she was asking for what happened. Like it was her fault."

"That's ridiculous!" Bud exclaimed.

"I know, I know. I'm sure to set anyone straight that I catch saying it, believe me. But had there been a trial and the prosecution impugned that lovely girl's reputation, I can only imagine how much worse the rumors would have been. You did a good thing to save her from all of that."

"No, not a good thing," Bud said. "It would have been my fault. I started rumors about Reese way back in middle school. I know now that rumors and reputations don't die easily. I don't suppose Reese will ever forgive me. I wouldn't blame her. I hope she can escape the rumors though, and find serenity somewhere."

Maggie showed Bud his Christmas present, though he wouldn't be allowed to keep it in The Center. She hadn't had time to buy him anything, and what good it would have done to buy him something while stuck in The Center, she didn't know. Instead, she gave him the gold pocket watch that Buck had initially given him on his first birthday. Bud looked at the inscription on the back.

"What does '*Tempus Edax Rerum*' mean Gran?" He asked.

"I don't know, Brandon," she said. "I suppose you'll have to find that out for yourself."

Bud was refreshed by his grandmother's visit, and he rededicated himself to accomplishing something while he was in The Center. He continued working towards his GED while also beginning a study of Latin so that he could learn the meaning of the words inscribed on the watch. By the time Bud's grandmother visited again around Easter, he was excited to tell her that he had learned the meaning of the Latin phrase.

"Time, devourer of all things," Bud told his grandmother.

"That sounds like something your grandfather would have wanted you to have, yes," Maggie said.

Bud wrote letters home as often as he could, but he didn't receive many in return, and Maggie simply couldn't visit as often as he would've have liked. While Bud didn't want to admit it to himself, his grandmother was getting old as well. Buck's death had taken a toll on her mentally as well as physically. She had aged noticeably in the months since her husband's death. Bud knew Jim Peterson was watching out for her, but his desire to get home and do it himself was ever growing.

He wondered if he should write a letter to Teresa, but thought better of it. Bud had made up his mind to let her make the first move. She would do things in her own time, if ever.

Summer hit and it was oppressively hot sitting in a lonely cell. Bud completed his GED in August, and the sense of accomplishment was what he felt he needed to make it the rest of the way through his sentence. Bud looked back on his life, all he had done, all he had learned, and wondered if he should be writing it all down. It seemed like too monumental a task sweating through the hot days in his cell. Instead, he continued just to read whatever he could get his hands on. While some would find reading *Crime and Punishment* ironic, Bud was simply glad to have an escape.

It was late August when Bud received a new visitor: Smitty. Bud sat across from his friend and beamed brightly at having the chance to talk to someone. Bud's face wore fresh bruises from a run–in with some of the other inmates in The Center, and Smitty eyed him dubiously.

"What's the other guy look like?" he asked.

"Oh, these?" Bud asked, pointing to his face. "There are a few guys here that don't really get along well with others, if you know what I mean."

"I hope you gave as good as you got."

"Nah, I'm just trying to lay low and get out of here without getting into any more trouble."

"So, you just take the beating and don't fight back?"

"Basically," Bud shrugged.

"I could never do that," Smitty said. "After what you gave Drake, who deserved it by the way, I would think everyone in here would be afraid of you."

"Three more months and it won't matter. What have you been up to?"

"I graduated, somehow. Now I've got a pretty good set–up with that guy in Lewiston. The one that took care of things for my brother. You remember?"

Bud knew exactly what Smitty was talking about. He was talking about the person that had gotten the marijuana that Bud had gotten into so much trouble for having in his locker. Smitty was working with a drug dealer.

"I know who you mean," Bud said.

"Yeah, well I've got a good thing with him. I pretty much own all of Readfield, Mt. Vernon, Manchester, Winthrop, Wayne, and Fayette. Anyone wants something, they go through me."

"What's your aunt think about it?"

"Her? She's oblivious. She thinks I've got a job at a hardware store. I moved out a couple months ago and got my own apartment in Winthrop. Yup, things couldn't be better."

"You be careful, Smitty," Bud said. "I of all people know how fast a good thing can turn bad. Don't get in over your head."

Bud was glad to have had someone to visit with, but the idea of Smitty selling drugs concerned him. Any contact with someone like that while he was on probation would land him right back behind bars. He knew he was going to have to end his friendship with Smitty when he got out of The Center.

After Smitty's visit, Bud spent the rest of his time in The Center without any more visitors. Later in life, if anyone asked Bud about his time there, he would answer that he had earned every minute and would say nothing more about it. Those were the toughest months of his life since the time he spent in deep depression. Thankfully for Bud, he had grown mentally tougher, or his time in The Center likely would have left him a broken shell of his former self.

It's one thing to experience boredom or loneliness. It is another thing entirely to live those things. Bud didn't make any friends in The Center, and he didn't want any. His goals were to get his GED, and do his time on his best behavior so he could return home and start rebuilding his life. He spent every moment of every day planning for his time outside The Center. When the day came though, it was far less than he had imagined it to be.

There was no celebration. There was no fanfare. His few belongings that were confiscated from him when he entered were returned to him, and he was escorted from the property. Maggie was waiting in her car parked nearby on the curb. Bud walked over, placed his few things in the back seat, and climbed into the front passenger seat next to his grandmother.

"Hi Gran," he said.

"Hi," she replied. "Ready to go home?"

Bud nodded. They rode in silence up Interstate 95 to Augusta, where Maggie exited and took Route 202 west towards Winthrop. Bud peered out the window at the businesses and homes as they passed them. Maggie turned down Main St. in Winthrop, drove through the town and turned right onto Route 133. For over an hour and a half, they rode in complete silence from the Youth Center until Maggie made the right–hand turn onto Baker Street and approached the little dirt lane they lived on.

Bud stared straight ahead as they passed the place where the stream from the waterfall passed through the culvert under the road. He didn't dare look to his left towards where the water left the small pool for fear of seeing Drake's body floating in the little stream. He knew it was ridiculous, but he wasn't ready to face that place again.

Maggie turned down the dirt lane and eventually, into the driveway of the small two–bedroom cape that was their home. They parked and walked inside. Bud dropped his things on the stairs to take them up to his room later. Maggie motioned him into the kitchen and had him sit at the table.

Still neither said a word as Maggie prepared tomato soup and grilled cheese. Bud had said nothing, but somehow his grandmother had known that it was the perfect meal, considering the chill outside and in his heart.

Sometimes it's impossible to find the right thing to say, and so it's better to sit in silence than try to fill the void with meaningless words that are ill suited for the moment. So it was for grandmother and grandson, sitting and eating their first meal together without Buck there to share it with them. There were a million things they could have said, but they both knew it all could wait. Instead, they let both the joy and the sadness of the moment consume them.

Bud savored every drop of the rich soup as it warmed him from within. It felt right to be home, but wrong without his grandfather. When Maggie was done eating, she rose and began to wash the dishes at the sink. Bud had finished as well, and he sat watching her. The image was wrong. His mind registered conflict and a wave of panic rushed over him demanding that he either flee or right the situation.

Bud stood and carried his dishes to the sink. He gently took the sponge from Maggie's hand, giving her a reassuring look. He proceeded to wash each item in turn and handed them to his grandmother to dry. When they were done, he wiped a tear from her cheek, kissed her where it had been, and made his way to the front door.

Bud threw on one of Buck's old jackets, still hanging in the hallway, and walked outside and down the front steps. He strode over to the Petersons, took a deep breath, mounted the stairs, and knocked on the front door. Jim opened it and smiled when he saw Bud.

"Bud, you're home," Jim said.

"Hello, Mr. Peterson," Bud said.

"You can call me Jim, Bud. You know that."

"Ok Jim… You had an arrangement with my grandfather for him to work on the farm. He hired me to do some of the lesser chores, but over the years, I took on more and more responsibility from him. I know I've made some mistakes, sir, but if you would give me the chance, I would like to try to take his place running the farm for you. I wouldn't expect you to pay me what you used to pay him, where I'm just starting out in his position and all. I'd be happy to start at whatever pay you feel is fair. I understand if you say 'no.' It won't be a good image around town for you to hire me, so I certainly won't blame you if you don't. All I can promise is that those days are behind me, and I want nothing more than to rebuild a life and prove to people that I've grown as a person."

Jim waited patiently for Bud to finish speaking. He looked into the young man's eyes: deep blue eyes like his grandfather's.

"Well, Bud, I sold off most of the new acreage after your grandfather died. It was just too much for Stanley to manage on his own, and I'm afraid I'm not a lot of help myself. Never learned to manage my own farm it seems."

"I understand," Bud said. "Thank you for listening, Jim."

"Wait, Bud," Jim said stopping Bud as he was turning to leave. "I didn't say, 'no.' I think we can work you back in along with Stanley. I had wood delivered this year since your grandfather wasn't around to cut any, and I sold off most of what we could cut anyway. There's a lot left to be split and stacked in the barn. Why don't you start by doing that tomorrow, and we'll go from there? Okay?"

"Thank you, sir," Bud nodded. "I'll start first thing."

"And, Bud? Be sure to stack some under your shed for Maggie and yourself."

Bud thanked Jim again and headed back home to unpack the few belongings he'd brought back from The Center. Jim shut the door and turned to find Nancy, looking at him from the hallway.

"You hired him?" Nancy asked.

"Yes, I did Nancy," Jim replied.

"Why Jim?" She sighed. "Why? I know he protected Teresa, but what he did to that boy was just horrible. How can we have him around the farm?"

"He did protect Teresa, you're right. I think people deserve a second chance sometimes." Jim sighed. He let a sadness wash over him that he had been fighting since the day Buck had been buried.

"Buck Marshall was my friend," he continued. "He never said so, and he never would, but I think he felt like he failed with

Paul. I think Bud was his second chance. Maybe Bud won't work out, and I'll have the hard job of letting him go. Maybe he isn't deserving of a second chance at all. Maybe I'm just putting our family in a horrible position. But you know what, Nancy? There are some things I just don't want to believe. I don't want to believe that Bud is a bad person. I don't want to believe that he's a lost cause. I don't want to believe that... that—"

"You don't want to believe what, Jim?"

Jim took a deep breath and steadied himself. "I guess I just don't want to believe that my friend, Buck Marshall, failed a second time," he said. "So I'm going to do everything I can to see that he didn't."

"What do you think Teresa will say about it?" Nancy asked.

"We'll cross that bridge when we come to it."

Bud climbed the stairs to his bedroom. He put his things away and began tidying up. On his dresser, he found the gold pocket watch his grandfather had given him on his first birthday. *"Tempus Edax Rerum,"* the inscription greeted him. Tomorrow he would begin his long road to rebuild his life. He stooped and reached under the dresser, pulling out his old notebook and the *Alice and Jerry* reader. He sat the rest of the afternoon, writing everything he could remember from the things his grandfather had taught him.

Before he closed his eyes that night, Bud reflected on the last year and a half. The dark whispered the words etched on the watch, "Time, devourer of all things." He hoped it was true, in a way. There were so many mistakes to make up for, and so much that he wished he could change. In time, he hoped to forge a new direction.

No one gets a road map for life, and each of our choices leads us down a different path. Some paths are well traveled, and it's easy to find your way. Others are bumpy, rough, and unpleasant. Sometimes we make choices that lead us down roads from which there is no coming back. In such cases, we forge ahead and hope we can find the way. It was in that circumstance, that Bud Marshall found himself. There was no going back from the choices he had made. He could only hope now to clear his way forward.

# 25

**"You** what?!"

Teresa was home for Christmas break and had seen Bud watering the horses in the paddock. When she asked her father what he was doing, Jim had no choice but to tell her they had hired Bud to run the farm. Teresa was beside herself.

"He knows the farm," Jim said. "Quite frankly, he's a far better worker than Stanley, and he and Maggie are going to need the money."

Teresa stood, mouth agape, staring at her father. "I can't come home for summer now," she said.

"Now, Teresa, you're overreacting," Nancy said.

"Am I? Am I really, Mom? Do you have any idea what people will say to me? 'Oh, your ex–boyfriend's murderer is working at your farm?' I can't possibly be here." Teresa was red in the face from anger.

"Teresa, I don't think it will be as bad as all that," Jim said.

"It will be," she said. "That's why I couldn't go back to Maranacook. Now it's why I can't be home this summer. Mom, you need to call Aunt Beverly and see if I can stay with her."

"In Rhode Island?" Nancy asked.

"Yes. Please Mom," Teresa said. "I can't be around him. Not yet."

"What about the Christmas party?" Jim asked. "The Steins will be there, and Mr. LaVerdier. Your mother and I are going. Are you saying that you won't?"

"No, I won't," Teresa said. "You'll have to make some excuse for me. I can't see him."

"Teresa, he saved yo—" Jim began.

"I know!" Teresa cut in. "I know, Dad. I know what he did. I'm thankful that he saved me, but everything else is... still too vivid." She stared off into nothingness, recalling the moment. "The pool, the blood, the rock in Brandon's hand... and worst of all, the look in his eyes... Lifeless, vacant, sort of detached... I'm terrified that if I see him again I'll see those eyes looking back at me. Please. I'm not ready."

Christmas Day, Bud was nervous to have company, but Maggie had insisted on maintaining tradition. Bud understood, he just didn't want to be the center of attention. When the Petersons arrived first, he was rather relieved that Teresa hadn't come with them. Jim made some excuse about her not feeling well, which Bud felt probably wasn't entirely untrue if she felt anything like he did about the prospect of being face to face with her again.

The Steins arrived a few minutes later, and Mr. LaVerdier came shuffling in last after he had seen everyone arrive from his window across the street. He took up his normal chair in the corner of the room and watched everyone else mingle. Bud weaved in and out of conversations, trying to be as polite as possible all while wondering exactly what the others thought of him.

Mr. LaVerdier had had enough of watching Bud scurry around like a lost and wounded puppy and called him over to have a seat nearby.

"How are you doing, boy?" LaVerdier asked.

"I'm doing all right," Bud answered.

Malcolm LaVerdier shook his head and lowered his voice. "Now, now, that's a fine answer for the likes of them," he said motioning towards the other guests. "I expect you to spare me the polite bull shit, boy. I expect the truth. How are you doing?"

The direct tone irked Bud, who wasn't used to being treated so harshly by folks outside of The Center. Everyone thus far had treated him gently, like a delicate thing perched on the edge of a table they were afraid to make fall and break.

"Quite frankly, Mr. LaVerdier," Bud began, "I don't give a damn what you or anyone else expects. My life, if you hadn't noticed, has been a steaming pile of manure the last year and a half or so. Considering that, I'd say I'm doing all right. In fact, I'm probably doing better than all right. I'm back home with my Gran, I have a job that's earning us some money, and I've got a chance to try and turn my life around. I don't know what you expect me to say. You want me to say that I'm tired? Tired of having to expect funny looks from people? Tired of being sad and feeling alone? Tired of wondering if I'm actually the monster everyone seems to believe I am? Fine, I'm tired. But I don't have the luxury of sitting back and doing nothing about it if I want to improve my reputation in this town. So I'm going to tell everyone that asks that I'm all right, and then I'm going to go ahead and prove it to them."

"That was a better answer," LaVerdier said smiling. "But you're lying to yourself."

"Excuse me?"

"You said you don't give a damn what anyone expects from you, but you intend on changing your reputation. Seems to me you care a great deal what people expect."

"I just want their expectations for me to match my own," Bud said.

"That's a good way to ensure that you'll never be happy again," LaVerdier said. "You can trust me on that one."

"People treated you worse than you felt you deserved to be?"

"No, people treated me like a hero." Malcolm LaVerdier looked down at his shoes. "I'm no hero."

Bud looked at the old man sitting in the corner of the living room. He had shrunk suddenly and looked small and worn against the cushions of the chair. Bud immediately felt a kinship with Malcolm LaVerdier that he never had before. Here was a man who had seen and done unspeakable things in World War II, and to this day he was still paying the price for it.

"Am I a hero Mr. LaVerdier?" Bud asked.

"Boy, I think it's time you called me 'Malcolm,'" LaVerdier replied.

"And it's time you called me 'Bud.' Am I a hero, Malcolm?"

"Do you feel like a hero, Bud?"

Bud didn't feel like a hero. He was tormented by the thing he had done, by the life he had taken, and by the reality that there was no going back. He didn't answer the question, instead asking another of his own.

"How do you get past it?" Bud asked.

Malcolm LaVerdier held up his hands and stared Bud in the eye.

"Clearly," he said, "I'm not the one to ask. If I had been in your situation where everyone saw me as the monster I felt like, I could have withered happily away in misery. Instead, I was forced to avoid people to escape the adoration. Solitude was the only solace from the demands for heroic war stories of vanquishing the enemy. You have a different problem. You want to convince others, and yourself I expect, that you aren't the monster — that the good intentions for your actions are enough to even out the evil of the actions themselves."

"You don't think they are? You think I'm the monster?"

"Believe me, Bud, I had that debate with your late grandfather. He said something that made the most sense to me of anything anyone ever has. I wish I had met him just after the war and not so late in life."

"What did he say?" Bud asked.

"He said, 'We are each the monster, and we are each the hero sent to destroy it. It's just a matter of who wins.'"

"And for you, the monster won?"

"Bud, I never even attempted the battle. Now, will you tell me the story of what happened that day?"

Bud sat with Malcolm LaVerdier and for the first time since he had done it for the authorities, recounted the entire event from when he heard Drake's car come down the lane, to when he was put in the back of a patrol car. Mr. LaVerdier sat with his eyes closed listening to the retelling of events. He didn't move or speak until Bud was finished.

"Thank you, Bud," LaVerdier said when the story was over. "I know that was hard for you." Bud nodded. "If you'll take my advice, never tell it again — At least not in specifics. If you must tell it, only tell it in generalities. Such things can only be understood by those who have lived it. Do you want my opinion?"

"Yes, please," Bud said.

"Drake let the monster win. But then, as I told your grandfather, I don't think some people are born with the hero at all."

"And what about me, Malcolm? Am I the monster, or the hero?"

"That," the old man said, "remains to be seen."

Bud sat that night thinking of his conversation with Mr. LaVerdier. He realized the old man had been right about one thing. Bud couldn't control whether or not his reputation changed, so he shouldn't care what anyone else expected or thought of him. All he could control was what he thought of himself. He was determined to prove to himself that he was the hero and not the monster.

As Bud lay in bed, listening to the cold December winds blowing outside, he planned his first steps towards a brighter and happier future. He didn't want to end up like Malcolm LaVerdier, avoiding the world and wallowing in the regret of past deeds. What was done, was done, and so what was to be done in the future was all that needed to matter.

Bud awoke with renewed vigor and a fresh perspective on his life. He attended to his work on the farm happily, enjoying the simple act of doing. He finished his tasks early, and then set to fixing up the garage so that he could resume his grandfather's work as a mechanic.

His old Ford truck was parked in the garage now, but it would need some work before he could start it and move it outside. The prospect of building his own future, as Buck had done, filled him with purpose. Bud had made the decision to be happy, whatever that meant for him. Right now, that meant he just needed to start living again.

The winter passed and spring broke, renewing the world around the little dirt lane. Bud was happy with his work on the farm. He had done such a good job that Jim and Nancy saw no need to keep Stanley on any longer. Bud was sorry to see him go, but Stanley held no ill will towards the Petersons. With Jim's recommendation, he got a job at a large commercial egg farm.

Bud was left running the farm on his own, but he enjoyed the work and needed the money since he hadn't had any business repairing cars in Buck's old garage. Bud didn't know if people were reluctant to give him the business, given his reputation, or if he simply hadn't gotten the word out.

Bud had expected that he would bump into Teresa at some point that summer when she returned from Kents Hill School, but Jim informed him that she was going to be staying with her aunt in Rhode Island. She had gotten a summer job at a restaurant on the coast and would be gone until school began again in the fall.

The situation left Bud with mixed feelings. On one hand, he was relieved that he could avoid the awkwardness that was inevitable in seeing Teresa again. On the other hand, he missed her and wished he could apologize for all that he had put her through. He had the feeling that Teresa was avoiding him, and his working on the farm was only making things more difficult for her. He asked Jim if he should find another place to work so as to make things easier for Teresa.

"Don't you dare, Bud," Jim said. "If you quit I'll be forced to find someone else to run the farm, and no one's going to do it as well as you. Teresa's got her own things to work through in her own way. She knows this is her home, and when she's ready to come back, she will."

"Jim, I need to ask you a question," Bud said.

"What is it?"

"Why are you still running this place as a farm anyway? You must have made a good deal of money selling off the newer acreage. You could get a decent amount for the remaining animals. You could even sell some of the hay fields if you wanted to. Why keep running it?"

"It's a fair question, Bud. I don't really know to be honest. It's true we don't need to run it for the money anymore. Nancy and I have enough to last us the rest of our lives living here. I guess I keep it going just because we always have been. It would be strange not to."

"I just hope you aren't keeping it running for me," Bud said.

"No Bud, we wouldn't—"

"Because I would be okay Jim. I would find something else."

"Bud, I know that."

"I just wanted to make sure."

Bud realized after the conversation that he was done being treated gently. The only way he was going to convince the people who cared about him that he was okay, was to begin acting like it. He desperately wanted to get a car repair business off the ground to show Jim that he was telling the truth. He would be okay without his job on the farm. The opportunity wouldn't come until later that summer.

Deborah Stein wanted to drive into Augusta to do some shopping, but the car wouldn't start. She tried calling a few places but couldn't get anyone to come to the house to work on it. Exasperated, she called Bud. She knew he had helped Buck in the garage for years, and asked him if he would come take a look at the car. Bud said he'd be happy to do it.

The car was up and running in under thirty minutes, and Mrs. Stein was thrilled. She told everyone she knew how great Bud was as a mechanic, and how he'd even come to her house to work on her car. Before he knew what was happening, Bud had mechanic jobs rolling in. There were plenty of folks who wanted someone who was willing to come to their house, rather than take their car to a garage. Bud was happy for the opportunity.

Gas prices were high, so Bud charged extra for house calls, but he had no lack of work. Jim was understanding and let him make his own schedule for working on the farm so long as he got all the work done. Things weren't out of hand yet anyway. There were still many people around town who were reluctant to give Bud the business given his prior record, but his reputation as a mechanic was beginning to overcome those hesitations.

Bud's newfound business success was forcing Jim to reconsider all of his options. If Bud was going to be busy as a mechanic, it would mean he'd have far less time to work on the farm. Perhaps selling some of the land and animals wasn't a terrible idea.

Jim wasn't sure why he was holding on so tightly to the idea of keeping the place a working farm. After all, times had changed and commercial farms were able to undercut him on pretty much everything. His farm was more of a novelty for locals who didn't feel like making a drive into town, or who just wanted to support a member of the community. He decided to give it a year and see where things lay next summer.

When fall arrived, Teresa returned to Kents Hill School without spending so much as a single night in her childhood home. Bud still hadn't seen her since the incident with Drake, and he was beginning now to doubt he ever would. She would go on to be successful at whatever she chose to do, he knew that. Leaving their small town behind and escaping the horrors that she had lived would be the easy thing to do.

Bud on the other hand, was determined to make his home right where it had always been. No one was going to force him to leave. The probation officer, who visited every two weeks, liked to remind Bud that he had to toe the line, but he was also impressed with how well the young man was getting on. It was unusual for someone to readjust to society so fast and with so much determination.

Bud charged ahead towards the future he saw for himself. Every so often, he would pause and look over his shoulder, just to make sure that trouble wasn't too close behind. He always had the sneaking suspicion that life was determined to make things difficult for him. But then, he would tell himself it was just para-noia to think that way and he should be glad for the progress he was making. There was nothing he could do anyway. Life would throw at him whatever it chose to.

# 26

**B**ud and his grandmother arrived home one evening shortly before Bud's nineteenth birthday to find a state police car sitting in their driveway. Bud parked, and he and Maggie got out of the car. The state trooper did the same and met them at the front steps.

"Can we help you, officer?" Bud asked.

"I hope so," The man answered. "And it's Nichols, Trooper Nichols."

"Why don't you come inside, Trooper Nichols?" Bud said, motioning him towards the door.

Nichols nodded and followed Bud and Maggie through the door. Bud shut it behind them, and Maggie went to put a few things away in the kitchen as Bud led the trooper to the living room and offered him a seat. The trooper declined, saying he would prefer to stand. Bud sat on the arm of the chair, and Maggie came and stood in the doorway to the living room.

"I'll be brief," Trooper Nichols began. "Earlier today the state police conducted a drug bust of an individual you know, a Chad Smith. Usually goes by the name 'Smitty.'"

"Yes, I know him," Bud said.

"When was the last time you saw him?"

"He visited me when I was in the Maine Youth Center in South Portland."

"You haven't seen or spoken to him since?"

"No, sir," Bud shook his head.

The trooper looked hard at Bud before continuing.

"Mr. Smith wasn't in his apartment when officers entered by force. We did confiscate a rather large quantity of illicit substances. We believe Mr. Smith is on the run and may seek aid from people he knows."

"I haven't heard from him, sir. I wouldn't be able to help him anyway, it would violate my parole."

"Yes, I know that, Mr. Marshall. We feel he may try to contact you anyway."

"Why would he contact Brandon?" Maggie asked from the doorway.

"People on the run have a tendency to contact anyone they trust. In Mr. Smith's case that list is extremely short as far as we can piece together. We're just covering all of our bases. You haven't seen him?"

"No," Bud said.

"What if I told you we found his car abandoned a short distance down Baker Street from the turnoff to your dirt road?"

Bud looked shocked.

"Would you mind if I looked around the property a little bit?"

"No, not at all," Bud and Maggie said together.

"Thank you, I'll do that before I leave." The trooper pulled a card from his pocket and handed it to Bud. "If he contacts you, Mr. Marshall, I would appreciate it if you would let us know," he said.

Bud nodded and said that he would. Trooper Nichols thanked them, and Maggie showed him to the door. Bud sat holding the business card, wondering what Smitty was going to do.

It wasn't fifteen minutes later when there came a knock at the door. Bud glanced confused at Maggie and then made his way down the front hall to answer it. When Bud opened the door, there was Smitty looking nervously around the dark.

"Smitty?" Bud said loudly. "What are you doing here?"

"Shhh, not so loud," Smitty said. "That statey left a few minutes ago. I waited to be sure he's gone, but I still don't need you screaming my name to the whole neighborhood."

"Smitty, what are you doing?" Bud asked quieter.

"What do you think I'm doing? I'm trying not to get arrested. Aren't you going to let me in?"

Bud stood in the doorway, blocking Smitty from entering. He looked hard at his friend, but didn't move.

"You know I can't," Bud said.

"What do you mean you can't?"

"It violates my parole, Smitty. I could go back to jail."

"If I get caught out here I'm going to jail. You want that? I thought you were my friend, Bud."

"I am your friend, but you need to understand the position you're putting me in. They found your car, they know you're probably looking for me to help you, what do you expect me to do?"

"Just let me hide here until morning so I can figure stuff out. Then I'll be out of your hair, okay? You have to help me, Bud."

Bud stood weighing his options. He knew the authorities suspected that Smitty would come to him for help. For all he knew they were still watching the house right now. Smitty may have watched the trooper leave, but that didn't mean he wouldn't be driving around the area.

"I'll help you, Smitty," Bud said.

"Thanks, Bud," Smitty said and tried to move into the house. Bud stopped him from entering with his hand. He looked sadly at his old friend and then spoke with as much conviction as he could muster.

"I'll help you by waiting ten minutes before I call the state police to let them know you were here."

Smitty's face morphed from relieved to confused, then shocked and finally angry.

"You low–down dirty piece of shit!" Smitty said. "Some friend you are! After all the times I covered for your ass and you can't do me one little favor? What a lousy excuse—"

"This isn't a little favor, Smitty," Bud cut in. "And if you were any kind of friend you wouldn't have asked me to violate my parole and risk jail time for your mistake. Maybe if I hadn't gone to juvey we could've built something together and stayed out of trouble. Who knows? Maybe we could've started a garage to fix up cars together. It doesn't matter now. What's done is done. You messed up. I can't help you any more than you could've helped me after I killed Drake. This is your mistake. You're going to have to own it."

"Fine way to treat a friend," Smitty said disgustedly.

"Nine minutes, Smitty. I suggest you get going."

Smitty turned and walked down the steps without looking back. Bud shut the door and locked it. When he turned, Maggie was standing in the hallway.

"I'm very proud of you, Brandon," she said. "You did the right thing."

"I hope so," Bud said. "I just destroyed the one friendship I had left in the world, probably."

"No, not the only one, I'm sure. Besides, he's the one that destroyed it. I think you know that. Do you want me to call Trooper Nichols?"

"No, Gran, I need to do it."

Bud waited eight more long minutes before calling the number on the card the trooper had given him. He relayed the information that Chad Smith had just come to his house asking for help and had been turned away. Trooper Nichols got the word from dispatch and turned his cruiser around, returning to the Marshall home.

The trooper thanked Bud and Maggie for calling it in and then began a search of the area. Smitty's car was still where he had left it, so the trooper assumed he was on foot. He returned to the Marshall house, thanked them again, and asked that they forward on any additional information if and when they had it.

Bud never saw Smitty again, and he never learned what became of him. The decision to turn his friend in bothered Bud for some time after that, and he knew he would probably second guess it for the rest of his life, but there was no knowing how things would have gone had he chosen another path. With Christmas approaching, the doubts about his actions were replaced with the question of whether or not he would see Teresa.

Bud went back and forth on whether or not he should get her a gift, and if he were going to what would be appropriate. They had always purchased books for one another when they were younger, but he needed the right book. Making the right choice was imperative. Bud spent hours in book stores all over Maine, browsing the shelves and talking to sellers about their favorite novels and what would make a good gift. He finally found what he thought would be appropriate after a tip from one bookstore, and a long drive to Boston, Massachusetts. He purchased the book, planning to give it to Teresa if she came over on Christmas Day.

The anticipation built as Christmas morning arrived. Bud had wrapped the book in white paper with silver snowflakes and tied it with a red ribbon. As the Steins and Mr. LaVerdier arrived, Bud greeted them, but looked past them trying to catch a glimpse of the Petersons. When they arrived, Jim and Nancy were alone. Teresa wasn't with them.

Bud was deeply disappointed, but told himself that he shouldn't have expected any differently. He welcomed Jim and Nancy and showed them into the living room. Then he went and retrieved the gift he had purchased and brought it over to them.

"I got this for Teresa," Bud said. "Would you do me a favor and see that she gets it?"

"Of course, Bud," Jim said. "I think she wanted to come, but just can't bring herself to do it."

"I understand. Will you tell her that? Tell her I understand and that I don't blame her. And tell her I'm not upset. I just thought this gift would be something she would like. There are no expectations attached to it."

Jim nodded and took the gift for Teresa. Bud spent most of the remainder of the gathering talking to Malcolm LaVerdier. The old man was impressed with how well Bud's car repair business was going. He suggested the young man needed to make it official and get a business license, put up a sign and do some advertising around town.

Bud said he would consider all of it. He expressed that it would be difficult to grow too much more in the confines of the small garage his grandfather had built, but it would be good to have a steady clientele.

The party was pleasant enough, and everyone had their fill of food and drink. Malcolm LaVerdier made an excuse and left first, quite a bit earlier than everyone else. That left Bud sitting alone in the corner of the living room while the others chatted. Jim kept glancing over at the young man wishing there were some way he could persuade Teresa to give him another chance. When the time came to leave, Jim put his arm on Bud's shoulder, held up the gift for Teresa, and nodded.

"She'll be headed back to school after the new year," Jim said. "And she's already decided to return to Rhode Island for the summer. Keep your chin up though, Bud. I don't think she's as much angry as she is scared and confused."

"I don't know whether to be encouraged by that or not," Bud said.

Bud sat by his window that night looking out at the bare landscape. There was no snow on the ground that Christmas, which made the whole affair seem less joyful. He hoped that Teresa wouldn't be upset that he had bought her a gift. He was trying to give her space to work through what she was feeling, but his sense that she was gone from his life forever was growing.

Over in the Peterson house, Teresa was doing something similar. She was sitting, looking out her window and holding the book Bud had given her: a first trade edition of *East of Eden*. When her father had handed her the package and told her it was from Bud, she had sighed loudly.

"Before you get upset," her father said, "you need to know that he said this comes with no expectations. He just thought you would like it, so he got it for you. Also, he wanted me to tell you that he understands why you don't want to see him. He's not upset, either. I genuinely think he just misses you. It must be hard for him too, going through all of this alone."

Teresa had taken the gift up to her room to open it. When she had unwrapped the copy of *East of Eden* her mouth fell open. Steinbeck was one of her favorite authors and the first edition had probably cost Bud a great deal. She was both moved and angered that he had done such a thing for her. She sat at the window, tears welling in her eyes, torn in two by the knowledge that she had a true friend just next door and the realization that the thought of seeing him still terrified her.

Despite what Bud had told her father, Teresa knew this gift was purchased with Bud's hopes of seeing her at Christmas. She

realized, sitting looking out her window at the frigid world behind the panes of glass, that the only way she could escape was
not to return home at all. This place would forever be tainted by
the memories of what happened, and Teresa felt she needed
space and a lot more time before she could face them.

When Bud didn't hear anything from Teresa and he realized
she had returned to school, he knew that meant he wouldn't hear
from her at all. He was saddened, but knew Teresa had made her
choice. She no longer wanted him as a part of her life.

Bud put on a brave face and continued working on the farm
in between fixing up cars in his garage. He thought a lot about
what Mr. LaVerdier had said about making his business official.
He decided when summer arrived, he would do just that and try
to build a real company.

It was early that spring, when Malcolm LaVerdier died unex-
pectedly. The church volunteers found him when he didn't
answer the door when they came to deliver food from the pantry.
The old man's dog had died a few years earlier, and no one knew
if he had any living relatives.

Bud attended the small funeral and saw Mr. LaVerdier buried in the Veteran's Cemetery in Augusta. He stood, listening to
the playing of taps, wondering if Malcolm would find the whole
ceremony appropriate or not. In any case, there was nothing Bud
could do about it.

A few weeks later, a lawyer contacted the Marshalls about
Mr. LaVerdier's will. It seemed that whether Malcolm had relatives or not was largely irrelevant. He had no money to speak of,
and his only possession was the yellow trailer house and the land
it sat on, both of which he had willed to Bud. Along with the will,
Malcolm had left a note.

*"Sell the house, if you can. Use the money. Don't give up the fight.
The hero needs to win."*

Bud managed to sell the trailer, though he didn't get a lot of money for it, and had it hauled off the land. The location, he thought, would be a perfect spot to build a new garage with several bays to open a car repair business. He would need licenses and a change in zoning to make the lot commercial property, but he figured it was worth a shot. He wasn't even sure he had enough money to build what he needed. Getting a loan would likely prove difficult, but he was determined to try.

When summer arrived, Jim shared the news that Teresa was leaving for college straight from her aunt's house in Rhode Island and wouldn't be coming home first. In fact, she didn't intend on coming home for Christmas either. The whole family was going to spend Christmas at her aunt's. He and Nancy had made plans to take a few days in August to see that she got settled into the dorms at UMASS Amherst, where she would be studying to become a nurse. They wouldn't see her again until Christmas in Rhode Island.

This relieved Bud of both distractions and excuses. He needed to start building his own life, and a business of his own seemed the right way to go about it. He set about getting the required licensing and zoning to put a garage on the land Mr. LaVerdier had left him.

The business license and the zoning change turned out to be the easier parts of the puzzle to complete. Getting the loan to build a garage was proving more difficult. Bud visited several banks, but with no credit he was unable to secure a business or construction loan. What he had received from the sale of the trailer was only going to get him part way to what he needed.

Bud could see what he wanted sitting in front of him, but he couldn't find a way to reach it. He was putting as much money away from his work as he could while still paying his grandmother's as well as his own bills, but at the rate he was going, it would be several years before he had saved enough to build anything. Every time he looked across the dirt lane at the empty lot, it made his stomach turn. The frustration was slowly wearing him down.

# 27

It was Maggie who finally suggested a potential solution to the problems Bud was facing finding money. She offered to sell her car, which she never drove anymore and let Bud use that money. She also offered what little savings she had left from when Buck was working. Those two sources of money, plus what Bud had from the sale of Malcolm LaVerdier's trailer would get him much closer to putting up the structure he wanted for his garage.

Bud determined that to get him the rest of the way, he would need to sell his Ford F1 pickup and find something else he could fix up. After Maggie sold the car, he used the money to find an old junker to get running again. He found a 1968 Chevy C10 stepside pickup that was all rusted out and wouldn't run. He bought it cheap, and had it delivered to the house.

He put the old Chevy in the garage and spent every spare minute working on getting it running and fixed up. By late summer, he was able to get it working. He still needed to do some body–work and replace a few parts, but with the new pickup working, he was able to sell his '51 Ford. The money gave him enough to build the garage he wanted. He decided to tell Jim that he would work on the farm through winter, but next summer he was going to focus solely on the business.

Jim listened as Bud explained that he was going to be finished working on the farm. Bud offered to stay on in the spring until he had trained someone new, but Jim waived him off.

"No, Bud," Jim said, "I think you were right. It's time for us to cut back on what we're doing with the farm. I imagine we'll sell off most of the animals this fall. We'll probably keep one or two of the horses to ride if we want and at least some of the hay field acreage, but we'll leave things so we don't need to hire anyone new. That is, if you're willing to give me hand now and then still, just as a neighbor?"

"Of course, Jim," Bud said. "I'm always here to help."

"Glad to hear it. So you have enough money to get your repair business up and going now, huh?"

"I have enough to build the garage itself. I'll move what I have for tools from the old garage over there to start and add to it as I go."

"Wouldn't you rather just get everything set up how you want from the beginning?"

"I would, yes," Bud said, "but I don't quite have enough money for all of that right now. I'll have to add on as I go."

"What if I loaned you the money?"

"Jim, I couldn't ask you—"

"You didn't," Jim cut in. "I'm offering. With what we sell I'll have some extra cash on hand. I'll loan you what you need to get set up properly and you can pay me back. We'll set up a schedule that works for both of us."

"That's very kind, but I don't know if it's a good idea borrowing from a friend."

"I'll just give you the money if you prefer," Jim said, smiling slyly.

"A loan would be very kind, thank you, Jim."

"Good. After all Buck did for us over the years, I consider this paying his good will forward."

Bud thanked Jim again and was about to leave when Jim stopped him.

"One more thing, Bud," Jim said.

"What's that?"

"I'm giving your grandmother a special gift for Christmas this year, but I'm afraid we're going to have to start on it early."

"Start on it?"

"Yes, I'm having oil burning furnaces and baseboard heaters put in both our house and in yours — No more storing all that firewood every year. We only need as much wood as we want for the fireplaces."

"That's an awful big gift Jim, I'm sure she'll appreciate it."

"Well, I figure oil prices are starting to come down, and it's time we simplified life a little bit where we can."

"Thank you. You're a good friend and a good neighbor. I hope I can repay you someday."

Bud broke ground on his garage two weeks later. He was going to have three automotive bays, an office, and plenty of room to store all the new tools he now planned to buy. Construction was going to move quickly once the foundation was complete, and Bud planned to be open by late fall. He had already chosen a name for his business that he hoped Buck would have liked: "Marshall Automotive."

The oil furnaces went in the two houses in September, with baseboard radiators to replace the old wood–fired ones. Maggie was overwhelmed by the gift, and kept saying that Jim and Nancy had done far too much for her. Bud was glad to see her smiling again. She hadn't had many reasons to since Buck had passed away, and it made him happy to see her filled with joy again.

Bud was delayed a little in opening his garage from when he had hoped due to helping Jim in the two houses. He had handed out flyers to all of his current customers for them to give to friends and family. He hoped they would spread the news. He imagined seeing lots of new faces when he was able to open the doors.

The big day finally arrived, and "Marshall Automotive" opened in 1980 on Bud's twentieth birthday. His loyal customers turned out to be his best salesmen. Folks came from neighboring towns when they heard the quality work that Bud was doing out of his garage. He was busier than he would have ever imagined, and it was rare if one of his garage bays was empty for more than a couple of days. Bud's reputation as a car–repair man had finally surpassed his other reputation, at least insomuch as many folks were at least willing to have him work on their vehicles.

Bud was looking forward to Christmas so he would have an excuse to take a break for a couple of days. He was working himself ragged and was even considering hiring another mechanic so that he wouldn't feel like he needed to turn any business away. Paying Jim Peterson back wasn't going to be a problem in the least if things kept up their current pace.

When the holidays arrived, Bud got the day of rest he sorely needed. The Christmas gathering was held early that year, so Jim and Nancy could attend before heading out of town. It had dwindled from past years to just Bud, Maggie, Jim, Nancy and the Steins. That was okay with Maggie as she was slowing down in her old age, and fewer people meant less food to prepare. The conversation revolved mainly around Bud's new business venture. Everyone was excited for the young man. Jim and Nancy were invested in his success with the money they had loaned him, which Nancy privately wasn't too thrilled about. The Steins were customers of Bud's and raved about the work he did. Maggie was glad to know that Bud was building himself a new future.

Towards the end of the party, Bud snuck off to a corner by himself and sat looking out a window at the frosty world outside. He thought about his grandfather and Malcolm LaVerdier and wondered what exactly they would think about his auto–repair business. Then he thought about Teresa. He wondered if Jim had told her what he was doing, or that he had loaned Bud the money for the tools and supplies. As he was deep in thought, Jim saw him sitting alone and walked over to him.

"Buck would be proud of you," he said as if reading Bud's thoughts. Bud nodded and kept peering out the window. "I told Teresa what you're doing and that you're really busy. She's happy for you."

"What did she say?" Bud asked.

"I believe her exact words were, 'Well I'm happy for him, but I hope he's still finding time to read.'"

"Yes, that sounds like her," Bud said smiling. His smile sank into a slight frown as he turned back to look out the window. "I don't suppose she'll be coming back. I can't imagine this place can offer her anything other than bad memories."

"She may yet, Bud. Maine is Teresa's home, and after a while she may discover that the great wide world out there that seems full of new beginnings and opportunities has little more to offer than had she stayed right here."

It was kind of Jim to try and cheer Bud up, but he didn't need it. He wasn't sad so much as hopeful. He hoped Teresa found what she needed and didn't have to come back. Happiness for her seemed so far away in Bud's mind. If he didn't have a mind to fight for himself, he too might have chosen to try and escape.

Business picked up again a little after the new year, and Bud stayed busy enough to pay the bills. He felt bad leaving his grandmother alone in the house all day. She was slowing down tremendously and seemed tired all the time. He would often return to the house for lunch and find her asleep in a chair with scattered pictures of her and Buck when they were younger on her lap. Bud knew how loneliness could wear on a person.

It was during the March cold snap that year, that Maggie got sick and had her fall. She had been upstairs in bed nursing her cold, but felt like she needed a hot cup of tea. She stumbled and fell down the last few stairs, breaking her hip. Nearly an hour later, Bud found her laying on the floor in pain.

The doctor patched her up and said she needed to take it easy for a while. He also said there was to be no more going up and down stairs until she was fully recovered. Bud made up a bed downstairs for her and made sure to check in as regularly as he could.

By the end of March, Maggie's cold was better, and she was physically feeling a bit more like herself. It would be several weeks still before she was up and moving around, but at least the illness had passed. That made the morning that Bud couldn't wake her all that more of a shock.

The fall and illness had taken their toll, and Maggie had passed in her sleep a few days before April. Bud was devastated, and he closed the garage until he could handle her final arrangements.

Maggie had a will naming Bud as her sole heir and leaving all of her and Buck's inheritance to him. He owned the house and all of their belongings. Bud made preparations for the funeral and purchased a headstone that would be placed at her head, right next to Buck's. The frost had thawed enough that a plot could be dug, and Maggie could be buried right away.

Jim and Nancy helped out where they could. Nancy especially was helpful with many of the arrangements, including seeing that Bud had food every day and making sure he was eating it. The two worried about Bud's mental state. Losing Buck, Malcolm LaVerdier, and Maggie all in less than five years was bound to take its toll. Not to mention the fact that his best friend, Teresa, hadn't spoken to him in all that time.

Bud, meanwhile, didn't have time to consider the depths of his grief as he managed Maggie's affairs. It wasn't until the day of the funeral that the full extent of what he had lost hit him. He stood at the doorway greeting those that had come to pay their respects to Maggie. He kept waiting for a face he thought would arrive, but never came. It was Nancy that gave him the news. She walked up behind Bud who was standing by the door, still waiting several minutes after they should have begun the service.

"Bud," Nancy said, "Teresa's not coming. She sent her respects, but she had exams that she couldn't get out of. She's very sorry."

"Oh, of course," Bud said.

"We should probably start the service now."

"Right... Of course, you're right."

Bud sat wondering how Teresa could miss Maggie's funeral. Surely there must have been a way to reschedule her exams for something like this. Then he thought he was being selfish and that Teresa would have come if she could have. None of it was important in that moment anyway, so he pushed the thoughts from his mind. Today was for his grandmother. Bud took a deep breath as he stood to give the eulogy.

"We are here to celebrate the life of Margaret Louise O'Shea Marshall. Most of you knew her simply as Maggie. I knew her as Gran. She was my grandmother, but the only mother I've ever known. She was kind and loving, quiet but stern. To know my grandmother was to love her. I will remember her warm smile, her generous heart, and her sugar cookies. I could stand here and proclaim her virtues for hours, telling stories of all the traits that made her wonderful. But it was her simple nature and her uncanny ability to see to the heart of those around her that made her so special. And so, I am going to keep this brief. I will miss her, as I'm sure all of you present will as well. I take comfort in the thought that she has found her way back into the loving arms of the man she spent her life with, my grandfather. No two people could have done a better job teaching me what it means to love. Although I am sad that my time on earth with them has ended, I am happy that their time together can resume. I love you Gran. I will miss you. Thank you for all that you did, for all the love that you gave, for all that you taught me, and for the life that you shared with me and with all of us here."

Bud stood by Maggie's grave long after everyone else had gone. He looked at the two headstones of his grandparents, letting his grief wash over him, like he had the water from the falls at the pool when he was younger. He felt utterly alone in the world.

The choice to carry on after losing those we love is not an easy one. Finding happiness in a world of sorrow can be difficult. Everything Bud saw, reminded him of his grandparents. Every item, every room, every smell, evoked memories of times they had shared. Bud found himself spending more and more time at the garage to escape the memories.

He poured himself into his work. He decided not to hire any additional help, rather choosing to spend extra hours finishing everything on his own. The result was he was making a good deal of money, but he had no time to himself. He didn't even have time to realize that he was miserable. It was a phone call in the heat of August that woke him up.

Mrs. Stein called from a pay phone in town. Her car had broken down on Route 133 and she didn't know who else to call. Bud told her he would be right there. He put a sign on the door, grabbed a few things, and drove off towards town. He picked up Mrs. Stein and drove to her car, parked on the side of the road just outside of town.

Bud opened the hood and quickly assessed the problem as a simple case of overheating. To fix the problem, he filled the radiator and the car started right up. Mrs. Stein was overjoyed and demanded to pay him on the spot for his trouble. Bud said it wasn't necessary, of course, but she insisted.

"You should offer this as a service," Mrs. Stein said.

"Offer what?" Bud asked.

"Saving stranded motorists."

"Oh well, Mrs. Stein, not every fix is as simple as a dry radiator. Sometimes I need the car in the shop to actually fix it. It can take time."

"What about a tow truck?"

"Yes, but those are expensive. I can't afford anything like that just yet, but maybe someday."

"Someday soon I should think as well as you're doing."

"Thank you, Mrs. Stein. Things are going pretty well at the shop."

"That should make you happy," she said smiling.

The phrase caught Bud off guard. He nodded and said he should be going. Mrs. Stein thanked him again, climbed into her car, and headed for town. When Bud climbed behind the wheel of his pickup, he just sat for several minutes running the words through his head.

That should make you happy, he thought. Bud realized he wasn't allowing anything good to penetrate the bubble he had put around himself. He smiled for the first time since Maggie's death, put the truck in gear, and drove back to the garage. The next day, he put an advertisement in the paper for a mechanic position.

Bud knew he could either be happy, or he could be sad. The choice was up to him. He could work himself into the ground, burying his grief under a mound of car parts and grease, or he could build a business that he could be proud of. He sat down that night and wrote out a five–year business plan. Within five years, before his twenty–sixth birthday, Bud wanted a tow truck and at least three employees working under him. He wanted to be able to take on a more managerial role, having built his business into something self–sustaining.

Buck had taught Bud not to be afraid of hard work. He never had been in the past. Accomplishing something he put his mind to was something Bud had always been able to do. He purchased books on business and read into the wee hours of the morning. One week after placing the ad, Bud hired his first employee. For the first time in his life, Bud was somebody's boss. He allowed the tiniest feeling of importance to creep into his being. He held it close for a second and then let it go.

"You have a long way to go, Bud Marshall," he told himself. "Do it for yourself. Do it for somebody else. Do it because it's right."

# 28

**B**ud beat his timeline by over two years. The May sun of 1984 was shining bright in the sky as Bud looked on his new tow truck glistening brightly in the driveway of his auto repair shop. He had painted both the tow truck and his Chevy C10 dark green, and both sported white letters on the doors reading "Marshall Automotive" and the business phone number.

Marshall Automotive now had three full–time mechanics that worked for Bud. The loan Jim and Nancy had given him had been paid off last Christmas. Bud had given them an envelope with the remaining balance in it. That very night, Nancy had apologized to Jim for her misgivings both about hiring Bud for the farm and loaning him the money for the garage.

"You were right about Bud, Jim," she said. "I was so worried about what people in town might think, or say. I was terrified that we were loaning money to him and no one would go to him for work because of what he had done. But you saw something in him that I couldn't see. The looks and comments around town don't matter at all compared to what that young man has done. I doubt anyone could've turned their life around the way he has."

"I think I know one other person who could have," Jim said in reply.

"Who's that?"

"His grandfather."

The garage was, in fact, very popular among the local population. No one could talk about car troubles without someone mentioning Bud's business.

"You should go see Bud Marshall."

"Bud Marshall, isn't he the kid that—"

"Yeah, yeah, that was a long time ago. He's a good guy. Completely turned his life around. Besides, he's the best mechanic in Kennebec County. You're not going to find anyone that does better work for a better price in Central Maine, I can promise you that."

The conversation was repeated all over the area. Bud had lucked into a great business situation. Gas prices had continued to fall, and the economy was surging. People had more money to spend, and they were driving a lot more. Put those together with Maine's notoriously rough roads and Bud had the perfect recipe for lots of business.

As a manager, Bud was much like his grandfather. He demanded his employees work hard and do the best job they were capable of. If a mechanic didn't know how to do something, Bud taught him how. Once he felt an employee knew how to do it right, they were expected to perform that task correctly from then on.

When one mechanic made a mistake on a job, Bud refunded the customer's money and then spent the entire night working on the car himself to make it right. He also gave that mechanic a second chance. When the same mechanic once again screwed up, this time on some routine maintenance, Bud fired him on the spot. He then covered the extra work in the shop himself until he found a mechanic to replace the one he fired.

He wore the same overalls as all of his employees, with the same simple name badge on the breast reading only "Bud." He was a leader by example, and those that worked for him said he was tough but fair. He paid his employees well and was understanding if they had family troubles or similar issues that required them to take time off. Bud would simply pick up the slack until they returned.

If folks hadn't known better, they would have thought the dirty mechanic they met when they brought their car to Marshall Automotive was just another employee instead of the owner and proprietor. Bud knew all of his customers by name, and he treated them with respect and made sure they were happy with their experience. His business motto was, "We'll make it right," and that was the driving focus of how things operated.

Bud was standing and admiring the new tow truck when he heard a voice behind him.

"You the owner of this place?" the voice asked.

Bud turned and his face lit up.

"Reese!" he exclaimed.

Teresa was standing there, leaning on one leg with a hand on her hip. Her hair was short and pulled back, and she was wearing a knee–length cotton skirt with blue flowers and a blue blouse. She was barefoot and smiled out of the corner of her mouth.

"I'm impressed, Brandon," she said admiring the truck and the building. "When Dad said you had started a garage... I don't know... I guess I pictured something more... modest. This is a serious operation."

"Thanks, Reese," he said. "But what are you doing home?"

"I just graduated college. I have a few days before I start work and I decided it had been too long since I'd been home. I came to see Mom and Dad before I get sucked in to being a nurse full time. When I saw this place," she motioned at the garage, "I knew I had to come say, 'hi' and get a close up look."

"That's great! Let me show you the place."

Bud showed Teresa around the garage and told her everything he had done to get it up and running. Teresa shared that she had taken a nursing job at Massachusetts General Hospital and had an apartment in Boston. Bud finished the tour and the two returned to the front of the building.

"It's good to see you, Reese," Bud said. "It's been a rough few years. It was lonely after Gran died..." His words drifted off.

"I'm really sorry I wasn't there, Brandon," Teresa said.

"It's okay."

"No, no it's not. Maggie was important to me too. I should have found a way to be there, regardless of... well, of everything else."

"I don't blame you, Reese."

"I know you don't. You never have, Brandon. I was wrong though. I haven't handled things very well. I want you to know that I'm going to try to do better. After all," she said looking around at Bud's and her two houses, "this is home."

Bud smiled at her and nodded.

"I have to run, Brandon, but I'll be home at Christmas this year. I'll see you then, okay? I'd say 'take care of yourself,' but by the looks of things you've already done that."

Bud looked back at the tow truck and the garage he had built.

"I'd say I'm gaining ground for once, rather than losing it," Bud said.

"Well, that's a start," she said. "Bye, Brandon."

"Bye, Reese."

He watched her walk away across the dirt lane and up the steps to her house. He let out a deep sigh and walked inside to his office.

The summer was extremely busy. The town took over the dirt lane, paved it, and extended it to connect to the Pond Road that ran along Pocassett Lake into Wayne. It was now called Hales

Road, and Bud had a new address to deal with. He had to redo all of his business information, but the connection to Pond Road cut over a mile off the drive into Wayne, and the paved road meant things would be better maintained and more regularly plowed in the winter.

Bud turned twenty–four that November. In the six years since he'd left The Center he felt like he had gotten his life back on track. He was no longer "that boy that did that horrible thing," but rather the "best mechanic around." He hadn't tried to convince anyone that he was changed. He had just set a goal and worked towards it.

As he took stock of things on his birthday, he thought he needed a new goal. He pulled his old notebook out and began writing. He didn't have any particular subject in mind, but rather just let his thoughts flood onto the page. He read back over all that he had written and realized a few things.

First, Bud realized that he was happier than he had been in a long time. He had, as Buck would have said, weathered the storm and come out stronger on the other side. He enjoyed his work and looked forward to growing his business.

Second, he recognized that although he was happy, he was still lonely. This was a difficult realization for Bud to reconcile with his happiness. In the past, loneliness had pushed Bud into a state of depression. Now, he was lonely, but he was happy.

This led Bud into his final realization: that he wanted companionship. He had no real friends to speak of. He talked to his employees, and to Jim and Nancy, and to his customers, but he had no social life to speak of outside of those interactions. He was happy with life, but not content. He wondered if building some friendships would help to fill that void.

Bud knew that as a child, Teresa had filled that part of his life, and then Smitty as a teenager and adolescent. Since neither of them were an option any more, Bud would have to find someone new. It would be easier said than done in a small Maine town, but Bud wasn't going to force things anyway. He decided just to be open to the possibility.

As for goals, Bud set several new ones that day. He set a goal to have the new tow truck paid off within three years. Once that truck was paid off, he would consider buying a second one if he felt there was enough demand. He also set a goal to read a book every month. Through his writing he realized that he hadn't read anything other than business books in some time. He still had a love for reading and felt the desire to dive into some new books. Bud's final goal was to become more involved in the community. The end game with his final goal was to meet new people and eventually fill his desire for companionship. He decided to attend some town meetings as a start and go from there.

Bud wrote his goals on a piece of paper he tore from the notebook and taped them next to the bathroom mirror where he would see them every day. He hoped the constant reminder would be enough to initiate his desire to succeed and drive him to accomplish them.

As the year drew to a close, Bud's attention turned to Christmas. Nancy and Jim had invited Bud and the Steins to their house for a Christmas Day meal. The tradition seemed appropriate to continue, and Bud thought both Buck and Maggie would want him to go, so he agreed. He also knew that Teresa was going to be home, and the brief meeting they had had that summer gave him a glimmer of hope that they could again be on friendly terms.

He wanted to get her a book, as they had always done for each other, but he was absolutely lost as to what it should be. He was in the middle of reading the book to meet his goal for the month of December, but he didn't think *A Clockwork Orange* would be an appropriate gift. Bud, himself, was having difficulty with the subject matter and imagery in parts of the novel. He went back and forth in his mind on the matter right up until a few days before Christmas. Forced to make a decision, he did so.

On Christmas Day, Bud took a deep breath and walked over to the Peterson's farmhouse. Teresa met Bud at the door and welcomed him inside. There was a glowing fire in the fireplace, and the house smelled of cinnamon and pine. A tree was decorated in the corner of the room, and there were Christmas knick knacks on every available inch of flat real estate. Bud held up the gift he had finally decided to give to Teresa.

"Merry Christmas," he said.

"Oh, Bud, thank you," she said. "You didn't have to get me anything."

"It's Christmas."

"You're right, here," she said handing him a thin, brightly wrapped gift. "Open yours first."

Bud opened the bright paper. Inside was a copy of *Jonathan Livingston Seagull.*

"Have you read it before?" Teresa asked. Bud shook his head, no. "I hope you like it. I think you will. It's a first edition."

"Thank you, Reese. I'm sure this was far too much money."

"I doubt it was any more than the first edition of *East of Eden* you gave me. Thank you, by the way."

"You're welcome. I don't know if I want you to open my gift now. It seems almost silly compared to this," he said holding up the Richard Bach story.

"I'm sure I'll love it."

Bud handed her the package and she slowly removed the paper. Inside was a dirty worn old copy of an *Alice and Jerry* learn–to–read book. Teresa's heart skipped a beat as she realized what Bud had given her.

"It may be a little late to return it to you," Bud said. "And I'm afraid it's a little worse for wear. Maybe you never intended to get it back anyway, but I thought you should have it. Open the cover."

Teresa opened the book and saw the words she had written when she was only a little girl.

To Brandon,
    *This book will help. Friends forever.*
      *Love,*
        *Teresa*

Underneath her message, Bud had added one of his own.

Reese,
    *It helped more than you will ever know. Forever is a*
    *long time, but not long enough for me to apologize for*
    *all that I've put our friendship through. If I could do*
    *it over, I know I could get it right.*
      *Love Always,*
        *Bud*

Teresa wiped a single tear away and closed the book. She looked up at Bud and into his deep blue eyes. The look that she had feared she might see in those eyes was nowhere to be found. Instead she saw only the little boy who lived next door, the boy who had been her best friend all those years ago. She pulled Bud into an embrace, wrapping her arms around his neck. Bud responded, putting his arms around her and holding her.

"Thank you, Brandon," she said. "This is the greatest gift you could have given me."

"It's just a worn out old book, Reese."

"No," she said breaking off the hug and holding him at arm's length so she could look back into his eyes. "No, it's so much more. It says everything I needed to hear."

She hugged him again and wiped another tear from her cheek. She composed herself and led him into the dining room where everyone else was gathered to eat. Bud enjoyed a meal with the closest thing he had remaining to a family, and he couldn't think of a better way to spend the holidays.

The next day Teresa headed back down to Boston to her job at the hospital. Bud returned to his work in the garage, but promised Teresa he would look in on her parents regularly. Both of them felt refreshed and renewed in a way they couldn't explain and didn't care to understand. They just both knew that they were going to be okay, whether together or apart, from that day forward.

# 29

It was March when Jim first mentioned it to Bud. Nancy had been extremely tired for a while, was short of breath, and now she was having aches and pains and was complaining about her vision. It was nothing that Nancy said anyone needed to worry about, but Jim wanted her to see a doctor.

Bud asked if Jim had mentioned it to Teresa at all. Jim said he hadn't. He didn't want to needlessly worry her, especially when she was still getting into the flow of her job at the hospital.

"I think you need to talk to Teresa," Bud said. "If you don't tell her and it's serious, she'll be very upset. If it's nothing, she'll respect that you kept her in the loop. Besides, working in a hospital, I'm sure she knows plenty of people that could be of help."

Jim took Bud's advice and told Teresa about the problems plaguing her mother. Teresa insisted they go to a doctor immediately. Nancy was hesitant, insisting it was all nothing and she was just worn out. But eventually she relented and went to see a doctor.

Things didn't go as smoothly at the doctor as the Petersons had hoped. Before long they found themselves at the hospital. There were tests and referrals and more tests. The prognosis wasn't good. Nancy had stage IV metastatic breast cancer. It was already in her bones, lungs, liver, and brain. Her options were severely limited. Teresa insisted that her mother come to the hospital she worked at for treatment. Jim agreed and drove his ailing wife to Boston.

Bud said he would look after the farm while Jim and Nancy were away. Jim would return periodically to check on things, but Nancy was going to stay down in Boston for the length of her treatment. Bud did his best to be reassuring and supportive.

"You two go do what you need to do," he said. "Reese will see that you have the best doctors, I'm sure of it. Don't worry about a single thing up here. I can manage the farm and the house well enough. When you both get back, things will be exactly as you left them."

Jim thanked Bud, and Nancy gave him a big hug. It would be a lot of work for Bud to manage both the Peterson farm and his own business, but the Petersons were like family, and Bud was going to do everything in his power to make things easier for them. Jim said he would keep in touch and shook Bud's hand before getting in the car and driving away.

The next month was extremely trying for everyone involved. Nancy underwent cancer treatment, which by all accounts was not going well and was taking its toll on her. Bud was exceedingly busy both at his business and on the farm, and he was determined to stay true to his goal to be more involved in the community. He was attending town meetings regularly and trying to learn what he could about how things in local government ran. He met several people at the meetings and even struck up friendships with a few of them. One of these friends happened to be Gregg, the young man who Teresa had grown close to all those years ago in school. Teresa had been right, of course, and he and Bud got along well discussing books and other shared interests.

It was an afternoon in late April when Bud was going to attend a town meeting about work that needed to be done on the town boat launch. He thought about skipping it, because Teresa had contacted him saying that she needed to return to the farmhouse for a few things for her mother. Bud was sorry he wouldn't be there to see her, but he decided to stick to his routine of attending.

At the meeting, the board of selectmen announced that per the estimate they had received from the state, they only had enough in the budget to account for half of the cost to repair the boat launch. The launch and docks had fallen into disrepair, and the state would not allow them to be opened to the public without the repair work being done. Mr. Stevens, chairman of the selectboard, was making a motion to raise property taxes to account for the difference when Bud spoke up.

"Who else did you get quotes from?" Bud called out from the audience.

"Mr. Marshall, if you want to make a comment you'll need to wait until the chair recognizes you."

"Well, you called me by name so I guess you recognized me just fine," Bud said to chuckles in the room.

"That's fine, Mr. Marshall," Chairman Stevens said, trying to quiet the crowd. "The chair will recognize you. What did you ask?"

"Who else did you get quotes from for the work besides the state?"

"No one, Mr. Marshall," Chairman Stevens said, looking at the other members of the board. "The state would see that all work would be done to code."

"Yes, but couldn't someone else do that?"

"In theory, Mr. Marshall, but you're asking someone to coordinate a number of different contractors. That would take time, and this needs to be repaired so that it can be used this season."

Bud started asking particulars on what work needed to be done and what the quotes had been for each line item. Finally, chairman Stevens was exasperated, called Bud to the front of the room, and handed him the notes on the work to be done.

"I don't know what you expect to accomplish, Mr. Marshall, but here are all the particulars," chairman Stevens said. "Now, if you will kindly let us proceed—"

"Is James Prescott here tonight?" Bud called out, interrupting him. James raised his hand and said, "Yes," from the back of the room. "What would you charge the town for 10 yards of concrete that we could form into blocks for the base of the launch?"

Teresa had retrieved all of her mother's things that she had requested and returned to the car in the driveway. The car was driven by a smartly dressed young man in his mid–twenties with dark hair that he had slicked back and parted neatly. The young man's name was David Reynolds, a hot–shot young lawyer in Boston, and Teresa's new boyfriend.

They left the house and were driving through town when Teresa spotted Bud leaving the town hall. She called for David to pull over, and the two got out.

"Brandon!" she called, running over to him.

"Hey, Reese," Bud said. David gave a funny look at Bud when he called Teresa by a nickname, but both Bud and Teresa ignored him. "How's your mom doing?"

"Not well. She stopped treatment yesterday, it was just too much for her. I came up just to get some of her things to make her more comfortable. We just wait and see where it goes now."

"I'm sorry," Bud said, and he meant it. Then Bud turned and looked at the young man with Teresa. He was quite the contrast to Bud, standing there in his work overalls with the name patch on the breast. "Hi, Bud Marshall," he said to the stranger, extending a hand.

"Oh, Brandon, I'm sorry," Teresa said. "This is David, my boyfriend."

"Pleasure to meet you," David said shaking Bud's hand and then wiping it not so subtly on his pants.

"Where are you coming from?" Teresa said to Bud.

"Town meeting," Bud answered.

"You were at a town meeting?" David said incredulously looking at Bud's attire a second time.

"Bud!" Gregg called running up to the other three. "That was amazing! Oh, hey, Teresa. Good to see you back in town. I heard about your mother, I'm so sorry. My thoughts and prayers are with you guys."

"Thank you," Teresa said.

"You should've just seen Bud," Gregg said, continuing. "He just made a fool of the entire selectboard."

"What?" Teresa said.

"Well, not really a fool," Bud said. "They were insistent that they didn't have the money to repair the boat launch, I just—"

"He just made it work right then and there," Gregg cut in. "He started calling on businessmen there in the room and getting quotes to have the work done by them instead of the state. In less than ten minutes, Bud had cut the cost almost in half. Chairman Stevens ended up putting Bud in charge of the entire project just to get him to shut up!"

"Very impressive, Brandon," Teresa said. "Sounds like you're a pretty important guy around here these days."

"I don't know about important," Bud said, "but I hate to see them spend money they don't have to and give work to folks outside of town when we have businesspeople right here that could do it. I imagine I can get some people to volunteer some of the work and get the cost down under budget. Probably get it done faster than the state would have too."

"So you think you know more about it than the selectmen?" David said.

"David, don't be rude," Teresa said slapping his arm.

"No, it's okay, Reese," Bud said. "The board is full of very successful people, but I read somewhere that we learn more from our mistakes than our successes. If that's true than I figure I've learned more than all of them combined."

"Heck, then you should be the chairman, not Stevens," Gregg said, chuckling.

"But that's the problem, Gregg," Bud said. "I'm horribly overqualified."

Gregg laughed out loud, and even Teresa smiled. Only David was unimpressed with Bud's quip.

"We need to get going, Teresa," David said.

"Yes, well thank you for looking after the farm, Brandon," Teresa said, turning away.

"Good to see you, Teresa," Gregg said. "And you... other person."

"Sorry, Gregg, this is my boyfriend David," Teresa said as David pulled her by the arm, leading her towards the car. "He's very happy to have met you," she called back over her shoulder.

"Boyfriend?!" Gregg exclaimed. "Better treat her right or you'll have to answer to Bud, and that didn't turn out so well for the last one."

Bud gave Gregg a look that would have silenced the wind, and Gregg knew he had stepped over the line.

"What?" he said. "The guy's clearly a jerk."

"Jerk or not, that was uncalled for. You have no idea what Reese has or hasn't told that guy. She's not going to have a very pleasant ride back to Boston."

Teresa tried to avoid explaining, but David was insistent. He wanted to know what Gregg had been talking about. Teresa relented and by the time they reached the Kittery bridge, she had recounted as much of the story as she was willing to tell.

"That guy's a murderer, and he's out walking around?" David asked.

"He's not a murderer, David," Teresa said.

"He killed a guy!"

"He accidentally killed a guy who was attacking me."

"Still, he should be behind bars."

"He did his time and his probation. As far as I'm concerned he's no more dangerous than you are."

"That's absurd, I would never kill anyone."

"Even if they were attacking me?"

"Whatever, Teresa, the whole conversation is ridiculous. I don't want you near that Bud, or whatever you want to call him, anymore. Is that clear?"

"I'm sorry. At what point did you start telling me who I can or cannot be around?" Teresa asked.

"When you started hanging around with killers. Honestly, the whole thing wouldn't have been a problem if you just hadn't led the guy on in the first place."

"What did you say?"

David didn't answer. Teresa folded her arms across her chest and refused to speak to him the rest of the way to Boston. David later apologized, saying that he had spoken out of frustration and hadn't really meant it. The tension lessened between the two of them, but remained. It was a stressful time anyway, as Nancy's condition deteriorated.

Teresa watched sadly as her mother slipped away. Nancy passed three weeks after Teresa returned from Maine. She was going to be buried back home in Maine, and Jim began preparations to move her body and for the funeral. Teresa said she would be home for the service, and David agreed to go as well.

Bud had the farm exactly as Jim and Nancy had left it, as he said he would. He had prepared several meals and left them in the refrigerator and freezer so that Jim wouldn't have to think about getting things to eat for a few days. He offered to do anything else Jim needed. Bud was exhausted from working the farm, his business, and starting work on the boat launch, but he carried on without complaining.

The funeral was a quiet affair with mostly family and a couple dozen close friends. David sat up front next to Teresa and her father. Bud sat a couple of rows back, wanting to give the family their space. After the service, Nancy was buried in the nearby cemetery, the same that Buck and Maggie had been laid to rest in. After everyone else had left, Bud lingered and made his way over to his grandparents' grave.

"I'm sure you know already," Bud said kneeling in front of the two headstones, "but we lost Nancy. It's been a rough go lately. Things are hard. Maybe everyone reaches a point in life where you're saying, 'goodbye' more than you're saying, 'hello,' but that doesn't make it any easier when it comes. I wish I had you two here to talk to, but I know you're up there somewhere. Take care of Nancy until Jim's time comes, will you? Tell her I'll take care of him the best I can down here, and Reese too, if she'll let me. I suppose she has David to do that now, but tell Nancy I'll be here if she ever needs me."

Bud stood at the two graves for quite some time just listening to the breeze and feeling the sun on his face. The chickadees sang in the nearby branches, and it gave the place a pleasant air, rather than the gloomy one he would've expected. Finally, he said good-bye to his grandparents and walked back towards the church. When he came to the front door, he found Teresa sitting on the bottom step, crying.

"Hey, Reese," he said, walking up to her. "Anything I can do?"

"Oh, Hi Brandon," she said, looking up and wiping her tears. "I'm okay. I mean, not okay, but I'm as well as I can be—"

"I understand," Bud said sitting next to her.

"I could use a ride home."

"Sure, but where's David, or your father?"

"Dad left before we did, or before David did, I should say. David had run down the street to the general store to use a phone to check in at work. When he came back, he said he needed to go back to Boston. Something came up on one of his cases, and he had to go right away."

Bud was shocked that David had just left Teresa sitting on the steps of the church crying so he could drive back to Boston. Couldn't he have at least driven Teresa home first? The whole thing seemed preposterous to Bud, but he felt the best thing to do at that moment was worry about Teresa and let her worry about David.

"Come on," Bud said, "let's get you home."

Bud stood and reached out his hands to help Teresa on to her feet. They walked towards Bud's dark green Chevy C10, parked on the side of the road, but Bud just kept walking past it.

"Isn't that your truck?" Teresa asked.

"Sure is, but a day like today calls for a long leisurely walk home."

"It's like five miles!"

"And we have all the time in the world and thousands of tears to cry before we need to be there."

"What about your truck?"

"I'll get a ride down with one of the mechanics tomorrow and pick it up."

They walked slowly, side by side, down the edge of Route 133 until they came to the Pond Road. They turned right and walked along the side of Pocasset Lake. Neither spoke until they turned left towards home on the new extension of Hales Road.

"It's amazing how things change," Teresa said.

"Yes," Bud said looking at her.

"Thank you for this, Brandon. I didn't realize how badly I needed time to clear my head. This walk is perfect."

They walked on together. Teresa would stop periodically to look at an animal or bird, or comment on a new house. When they came to what had been the "new acreage" on the farm so many years ago, she was amazed to see a road for a housing development that was being put in. She shook her head and kept walking.

Once they came to the farmhouse, Teresa stopped and stood on the side of the road looking out at the farm and the woods beyond. Bud stood beside her silently, following her gaze across the land. She stopped when her eyes began following the water upstream and she turned her attention back to the house.

"I'm moving home," she said.

"What?"

"I'm moving home," she said again turning to Bud.

"Reese, you have a life down in Boston—"

"And I have a home here," she said interrupting. "I can't leave Dad here all alone. I'll get a job up here, in Augusta or Lewiston or something. There are plenty of hospitals in Maine I can work at."

"What about David?" Bud asked. Teresa frowned and looked down at the ground. "I'm sorry," Bud said, "that's none of my business. I just figured you'd want to be near him."

"We broke up, Brandon."

"You what? When?"

"When he left for Boston, I told him that if his job was more important than me and my family on today of all days, then we should just end things right then and there."

"What did he say?"

"He called me selfish. He said I couldn't possibly understand how much work it takes to become really successful. He said if I can't appreciate the work he's doing and how much he's sacrificing to build a better future, then I'm ungrateful."

Bud looked at Teresa as tears started to well up in her eyes. He wanted to reach out to her and to pull her close. He wanted to hold her and protect her from the ugliness of the world. Bud knew all too well the feelings of pain, anger, and sadness that would tear someone to pieces if they let them.

"Reese," he said, "he's wrong. You're neither selfish, nor ungrateful. You are one of the most selfless and generous people I know. You have a kind heart, too kind — forgiving me over and over is proof of that. He's a terrible fool."

She turned to hug Bud and collapsed in his arms. He held her tightly as she erupted in tears. The weight of the day had come crashing down on her in an instant, and she had lost the will to fight it any longer. Bud held her for several minutes and then helped her into the house. He took her upstairs and helped her lay down in bed.

Jim was waiting when he came down. Bud explained what he could and said he would be next door if either of them needed him. Bud left, crossed the road to the garage, and told his employees that he would be taking the rest of the day off. Unless there was an emergency, they weren't to bother him. Bud sat down in the living room and cried tears of his own, both for Nancy and from sheer exhaustion. He went to bed without dinner and slept the entire night.

He knew the new day would bring a new world: one without Nancy, but one with Teresa returning home. He would have to spend the next few weeks on the boat–launch project, as well as helping Jim and Teresa settle in — not to mention running the garage. He would have slept for ages to prepare himself for the work to come, but time waits for no one, and the dawn would come heedless of his approval.

# 30

The next several weeks, Bud didn't have a minute to himself. He would rise at 4:30 a.m., get himself showered and dressed, have breakfast, and head over to the garage to ensure everything was ready for the day. He would leave instructions for his employees, and when the first arrived, just before six, he would head out.

Bud would cross the road to the Peterson's farmhouse and check on Jim, who was alone until Teresa moved all of her stuff back home from Boston. He made breakfast and made sure Jim didn't need anything else before heading into town.

Once Bud was satisfied that Jim was settled, he would walk back to his house, get in the truck, and drive to the boat launch. The rest of the morning was spent coordinating work on the launch and dock to make sure things were being done correctly and efficiently.

Lunch was a chance for Bud to swing back by the garage and deal with any issues that had cropped up during the morning. Once he was satisfied there, he would go back to the farmhouse and make lunch for Jim and himself. He would eat with Teresa's father, keeping him company for as long as he could manage.

One more stop at the garage before he headed back into town would ensure that his employees were on top of things for the afternoon. Work at the boat launch lasted until four 4:45 p.m. when everyone went home for the day. Bud would then return to the garage and close out the evening there. He would often stay in the office until close to seven o'clock, dealing with phone calls, messages, and future appointments.

With work complete at Marshall Automotive, he would head to the farmhouse one last time to make dinner for Jim and himself. He would keep Jim company until nine o'clock or so before excusing himself for the evening. Then he would finally make his way home and collapse for the night, only to rise and do the dance again the next day.

When Teresa returned home, Bud helped her move her things back into the house. He maintained his routine, adding Teresa to the meals so that she would have time to settle in before having to worry about anything.

The boat launch and dock were completed two days after Teresa got home. The whole project was finished to code, ahead of schedule and at less than half of the amount the state had quoted for the work, partially thanks to the fact that many of the local business people wanted to stick it to the selectboard and had charged their cost for materials or barely over that, and Bud had enlisted a large number of volunteers donating time and labor for free.

That night at dinner, Bud kept nodding off, barely able to keep his eyes open. Jim or Teresa would say his name, or nudge him gently and his head would snap up, his eyes wide with confusion. Eventually, exhaustion got the best of him and he fell asleep in his mashed potatoes. Jim shook his head and looked at Teresa.

"And I always thought Buck would be the one to work himself to death. At least the potatoes broke his fall," Jim said.

Teresa rolled her eyes. "Will you help me get him home? I'll get him cleaned up and into bed," she said.

Jim nodded, and the two of them managed to each grab Bud under an arm and hoist him to his feet. He stirred and half stumbled with Jim and Teresa's help to his house. They shuffled him up the stairs to the bedroom and laid him down. Jim left Bud and Teresa there and went home.

Teresa took off Bud's shoes, and got a warm washcloth to wipe his face. As she wiped the potatoes from his forehead, Bud stirred and looked at her.

"Teresa, what are—"

"Shhh," she said. "You fell asleep. Dad and I got you home and into bed. Just relax now."

Bud moaned, and closed his eyes.

"Thanks," he mumbled.

"Poor, Brandon," she said. "You've been working so hard looking out for us, and the town, and your business, but no one's been looking out for you. Just rest now. Dad and I are very lucky to have you in our lives. I never really realized how big a part of the family you've always been until now."

She leaned down and kissed him gently on the forehead. Bud hadn't heard a single word. He had already fallen into a deep, dreamless sleep.

Bud awoke in a panic. The sunlight was streaming through his window and the clock in his bedroom said it was after seven o'clock in the morning. He shot out of bed and tripped over his shoes. Confused, he grabbed them and started pulling them on as he stumbled towards the stairs. He raced down them and towards the front door, desperate to get to the garage.

People will be waiting, he thought. Customers, employees, no one can get in. Why didn't anyone come to the house? Surely they did. I slept through the knocking. His thoughts raced as fast as he did trying to get to the door, when a voice from the kitchen stopped him.

"Brandon!" the voice called. "What are you doing?"

Bud turned to see Teresa looking at him, confused. She was wearing one of Maggie's old aprons, gingham blue, and was standing at the stove. The smell of bacon cooking penetrated the panic Bud felt, and he regained some of his senses.

"I have to go open the garage," he said. "I'm horribly late. Wait, what are you doing here?"

"Brandon, it's Sunday. You don't have to open today. I turned off your alarm last night so you could sleep and came over this morning to make you breakfast."

"Oh… thanks."

He wandered into the kitchen, and she guided him to the table and sat him down. Teresa had prepared eggs, bacon, and toast. She handed Bud a cup of coffee, placing the sugar and cream on the table.

"Now," she said, sitting across from him, "we need to discuss how hard you've been working lately."

"I'm fine, Reese, really. It's no big deal. I'm just doing what needs to be done."

"Brandon, you fell asleep in your mashed potatoes last night." Bud looked down embarrassed and Teresa chuckled. "It's okay, it was cute. Dad and I appreciate everything you've been doing for us, but it's time for you to let us handle some things again."

"I just know how hard it is—"

"Yes, we're sad, but we're not broken. We pretty much knew what was coming, and we had a chance to say our goodbyes. We will always have a sad spot in our hearts for Mom, but we'll be okay. As for you though, you're worn out. Don't try to protest, Brandon, Dad and I agree that you need to slow down a little bit. So, once a week on Sunday, you are going to take the day off completely. No work, no meetings, no going here or there or wherever. You will rest, take a walk, read a book, or just sleep in."

"Reese, I appreciate the concern but I really don't think—"

"This is not a discussion, Brandon. You want to help Dad and me?"

"Of course, but—"

"Then we need you healthy and energized. Now, what would you like to do today? I plan on starting my search for a job tomorrow, but today, I'm all yours."

"All right Reese," Bud said, smiling. "I see you've made up your mind on this, so there's no sense in my fighting it, at least not today. Let's start by eating this wonderful breakfast you made, and then how about we just take a drive?"

Teresa agreed, and the two of them sat and ate their breakfast together. Bud retreated back up the stairs, showered, and put on fresh clothes. Less than an hour from when Bud had stormed down the stairs in a fit of panic, the two of them were climbing into Bud's dark green C10 pickup to take a drive.

"Where would you like to go?" Bud asked.

"Anywhere you want to take me, Brandon," she replied, leaning back leisurely. He started the truck, and they drove out Hales Road, turned on Pond Road, and then north on Route 133. Bud followed it into Livermore Falls and then took Route 17 through Jay before turning west where it met Route 2. They drove through Rumford and past the hospital there, which Teresa noted as they drove by. They continued through Bethel and into New Hampshire.

Bud got an idea as they approached Gorham. He turned south and asked Teresa if she would like to drive up Mt.

Washington. She thought that sounded wonderful. They ascended and took in the views from the peak. The sun warmed their faces in the cooler air at the top of the mountain. The warmth spread to their hearts, and they smiled as they took in the beauty around them.

On the return drive, they stopped only briefly for lunch. When they got back to the cape on Hales Road, Teresa thanked Bud and walked home to join her father in attending the late afternoon service at church. Bud spent the rest of the afternoon and evening sitting and reading.

Teresa and Jim had been right. By the end of the day, Bud felt fully refreshed and ready to face another week. He decided to listen, and that one day a week to catch his breath didn't seem like a bad idea. Besides, if he could spend that time with Teresa, it would be all the more enjoyable.

The sun continued to rise and to set. Teresa got a job as a nurse at the hospital they had passed in Rumford. It was a long drive that put a lot of wear and tear on her car, but she joked that she knew a good mechanic that would see that the vehicle was in good enough shape to make the trip.

Teresa's schedule meant that she wasn't always available to spend Sundays with Bud, but whenever she could, she gave her free time to him. That summer, there was one stretch when there were several Sundays in a row that Teresa had to work. When she finally got a Sunday off in late July, she promised to spend it with Bud.

When Bud asked Teresa what she wanted to do that day at breakfast, she suggested they just go for a walk and stay close to home. It was too hot to think of doing much else.

After she returned from church that morning, they strolled from the house and inevitably made for the shade of the woods on the other side of the stream. They crossed the bridge by the old cattle wade and entered the woods at the top of the slope on the other side. From there, the two friends continued their leisurely walk along the forest floor.

The sunlight shone in patches through the leaves, projecting bright spots onto the ground. The woods were silent but for the sound of the birds, the occasional rustle in the undergrowth, and the sound of their footsteps.

Quite a way into the woods, they came to a fallen pine tree, it's roots standing in the air like a hand calling for them to halt. Teresa walked around the roots and sat on the trunk, motioning for Bud to join her.

"The woods are beautiful," she said. "And quiet. I love how peaceful it all is."

"Yes, it is peaceful. I can't come in here without thinking of Pa. I used to help him cut firewood — most of it we did in the other woods," Bud said, motioning towards the east side of the farm. "They're building houses over there now — it's actually kind of sad. I wonder what he would think about all that."

"He was a great man, your grandfather."

"Yes, he was," Bud said, sighing. "He had a way of looking at things. I think he learned from everything around him. You know, one time when I was being the troublemaker I was back then, he taught me a lesson about life from the trees?"

"What lesson was that, Brandon?"

"Well, he asked me to look around first, asked me what I saw. So I said, 'trees.' 'What kind of trees?' he asked. I said all kinds. Then he told me there were two kinds of trees: deciduous trees, the ones that change color in the fall and lose their leaves — and evergreen trees, the ones that stay green year–round. Deciduous trees are changed by the world around them. When the weather gets too harsh, and the nutrients they need too scarce, they shut down and go dormant. They basically die inside, waiting for the world to improve. But the evergreens won't be changed by the world. Pa said they rely only on their character to survive, that the evergreen is 'resolute.' So, being a young man who thought he knew everything, I said, 'sure, but deciduous trees are hard woods, and evergreens are soft woods. Aren't hard woods stronger than soft woods?'"

"What did he say to that?"

"He said I was right. Deciduous trees are harder at heart, but softer on the outside." Bud stood and walked over and peeled some bark off of a nearby birch tree and carried it over to Teresa before sitting back down next to her. "'But,' Pa said, 'look at what happens to hard woods in a wind storm: they break.'" Bud put his hand on the bark of the pine tree where they sat. "Evergreens may be rough on the outside, but they're soft at heart. A storm has to rip an evergreen up by its very roots to destroy it. Pa said if a man can be like the evergreen, soft at heart but unwilling to be changed by the world around him, he could get through just about whatever the world threw at him. But if he is hard at heart and lets the world dictate how he should be, eventually he will either succumb to pressure or break under the strain."

"Sounds like he was a very wise man," Teresa said, putting her hand on Bud's shoulder.

"He was. I think I was fortunate that I knew him when I did. The man I knew was the result of a lifetime of learning. All that wisdom was gained from years of mistakes and questions, I'm sure. He once told me that the greatest thing a man can do is to love another with all of his heart. Remember when we were younger, and you asked me what I wanted to be when I grew up? I told you I wanted to be great."

"Yes, I remember. I told you that you needed something to be great at."

"I know what that something is now," Bud said, turning to look in her eyes.

"What do you want to be great at, Brandon?"

"I want to be a great husband and father. I want to be a great teacher for my children, like my grandfather was for me. I want them to learn from all that I have learned and all the mistakes I've made, so that maybe they won't make them themselves. I want to love and guide them to an easier life than I've had. I want what my grandfather had: people to share my life with and to give all of my love to."

In that moment, Teresa no longer saw the man that owned an auto repair business and that the town had entrusted to rebuild the boat landing. She saw instead the little boy who didn't know how to read.

"That is a wonderful and noble goal, Brandon. But I think you need to forgive yourself first for the mistakes you've made. How can anyone move forward with regret?"

"I don't think I know how to do that, Reese."

"Come with me," she said standing and taking his hand.

Teresa led Bud from the woods and back across the bridge. She turned and began walking up the bank of the stream. She stopped at Baker Street and looked both ways for cars before leading Bud on across the road. When they hit the other side, Bud stopped her.

"Reese, I can't... I can't go back there," he said.

"Yes, you can. We can, together."

She pulled his arm and led him on up to the waterfall and the pool below it. Bud's heart pounded as they approached the spot neither had been to since that fateful day. Bud took a deep breath as he surveyed the scene. There was no body, no blood, no sign of the struggle that had happened. The log on the bank was covered with moss, and the whole place looked smaller than Bud remembered it. Teresa turned to face Bud, and she had tears in her eyes.

"I'm so sorry, Brandon," she said. "I'm sorry I brought him here. I shouldn't have, this was our place. I didn't want to, and I should have listened to my gut. I'm sorry I didn't believe you when you told me what he wanted… what he was like. It's my fault."

"No, no. No, Reese," Bud said. "It was my fault. I started the rumors about you. Your reputation was my doing. Had I not done that, he never would have thought he could get what he wanted from you. I was the one that went too far. He's dead because of me, not because of you. You did absolutely nothing wrong. This place is all horrible memories now, we should go."

"No Brandon, we need to take it back. You saved me here, right here," she said pointing to the ground. "For all the mistakes we both made, you saved me from something horrible right here. I am extremely grateful for that. You protected me."

"You shouldn't have been in the situation, Reese, and it was my fault you were."

"Regardless of whose fault, both of ours, I think… I was in the situation. But you followed us, you kept me safe. Why, Brandon? Why did you follow us?"

"I didn't want you to get hurt."

"Why? Why did you need to protect me?"

"Because, Reese, because it was my fault."

"No, Brandon. Why? Why did you have to protect me?"

"What do you mean 'why?' Because I cared about you, because I care about you."

"Say it, Brandon. Say the word. Say why you had to follow us, why you felt the need to protect me, and why you care so much that you might be at fault. It's the same reason I care that it might be my fault. The same reason why I feel guilty for bringing him here. Say it, Brandon."

She looked deep into his eyes: those blue eyes that twinkled when the light hit them just right. They were sad and beautiful and spoke the words as he said them.

"Because I love you, Reese."

She grabbed him and pressed her lips to his. Bud felt the warmth of her kiss as it radiated through his body. He reached out and pulled her closer into his body, letting the emotion of all their years wash over him. Joy, sadness, pain, and exhilaration surged through him all at once. Teresa broke off the kiss and stepped back.

"And this," she said, "is our place."

She kicked off her shoes, pulled her cotton sundress up over her head and tossed it on the nearby log. She turned from him and undid her bra, throwing it on top of her dress. Then she slowly slid off her underwear and turned to face him in all her perfect innocence.

"Ever since the summer I realized I loved you, I was terrified for you to see me like this. I was afraid you would reject me, or that I wouldn't be good enough." She walked up and pulled Bud's shirt off over his head. She embraced him again. "I'm not afraid anymore, Brandon. I love you. I have always love you."

"Reese, I—"

"Shhh," she held a finger to his lips. She knelt down and removed his shoes and socks. Then she stood and undid his pants, pulling them along with his underwear to the ground. He stepped out of them, feeling the light summer breeze on his naked body. She smiled and took his hand, leading him down to the pool. They both gasped as she guided him into the cool water.

Teresa pulled Bud over to the waterfall, which was still strong from the spring and summer rains. They stood under the water, and she pulled him in for another kiss. With their bodies pressed together and wrapped in a loving embrace, they let the water wash the pain and horrors of the place away.

"Our place?" Bud asked.

"Our place," Teresa said.

As they lay on the bank, drying their naked bodies in the hot July sun, Bud felt content. He rolled over and looked at Teresa lying next to him and beyond her to the place where he had saved her. It all seemed so long ago now, as though in another lifetime. She rolled and looked at him and seemed to read his mind.

"It's done, Brandon, it's all over," she said. "All we can do now, is move forward to what comes next."

"And what comes next?" he asked.

She smiled. "Greatness," she said, pulling him in for another kiss.

# 31

**H**appiness is a choice we each must make. So often we think, if only I had this or that, or if only such and such would happen. Then magically happiness will appear as a knight on a white horse to save us from the muddling emotional discomforts in life, which will suddenly cease to exist.

Reality is a different prospect all together. Suffering is an indispensable part of living, and without it there is no being. It is each of us that makes the choice whether to be happy or whether to dwell in the darkness that would consume our souls if we let it.

As Bud and Teresa sat at dinner with Jim that night in the Peterson farmhouse, they basked in the warmth of the happiness they had chosen. Even Jim could feel a change in the air, as though they had been living under a blanket, but hadn't noticed the stifling nature of it until it had been lifted and the freshness swept in.

Jim watched as his daughter and the boy from next door gazed at each other throughout dinner. He knew something had changed and a long-awaited event had come to pass. When

Teresa said goodnight to Bud at the door and they both said, "I love you" to each other, his suspicions were confirmed.

As she turned, a bright smile on her face, she met her father's gaze, and the grin that suggested he knew and understood.

"I suppose it was inevitable," he said.

"What was?" she asked.

"That the two of you would both discover that the answer to so many of the questions you were asking was right next door all along."

Teresa blushed, but smiled at her dad. Her happiness had lifted his spirits as well. Teresa and Bud's love reminded him of when he fell in love with Nancy, and how happy they had been. A tear rolled down his cheek as he returned her smile. She walked over to him and wiped it away.

"Why are you crying?" she asked.

"So many reasons," he said.

It would be wrong to say that the next couple of months were easy. They were not. They were happy times, but trying. Teresa's new job had her working long and odd hours, which meant she was often out of sync with Bud's time at the garage. They ate meals together when they could, and every free moment they had together was filled with joy.

When they walked in town together, however, people gave them sidelong glances and muttered under their breath. While Teresa and Bud may have moved on from the incident with Drake that had happened all those years ago, the wind still whispered rumors of scandal.

It was harder on Teresa than Bud, since Bud had already reestablished himself within the town. Teresa had essentially been nonexistent since the day the incident occurred. She had been in private school, in Rhode Island, or away at college. The town didn't know her in the same way they knew Bud, and it was upon her that they cast their dispersions.

Here was a girl, by all accounts, that had seduced a boy and brought him to a quiet spot. There, by the serenity of a waterfall, she had refused his advances, causing him to strike out against her. Bud had arrived to defend her, and had killed the boy accidentally in the process. But had it all been a ruse to gain the attention of the boy next door? Had the evil siren finally won her prize? Would this crafty seductress claim another victim in Bud Marshall?

Those were the rumors that folks pondered when Teresa walked by. Bud was not oblivious to the murmurs that bubbled beneath the surface of otherwise innocuous interactions. A simple question, or the tone of a phrase said in a certain way, tipped Bud off that people were skeptical of Teresa. On more than one occasion, Bud felt compelled to defend the woman he loved. He did so as calmly as he could manage, never raising his voice, but speaking sternly and with all the authority he could muster.

"Teresa is a better person than I am," he would say. "If I could manage to grow a heart half as good as hers, I would consider myself a saint."

While Bud's words carried weight in the small town, some people still wondered if Teresa was somehow tricking him. Neither of them let any of the gossip interrupt their happiness, however. In rediscovering each other, they had rediscovered the joy of young children playing in a grassy meadow without a care. No minor annoyance was going to lessen their enjoyment of the moments they shared.

In Bud's free time, when Teresa was working, he would read or write in his old notebook. He would jot down thoughts, poems, or anything he felt he wanted to remember. It became like a journal for him, which he gladly shared with Teresa when she had time to read it.

She loved his writing, and his poetry. She told him that in another life he could have been a great author or poet. He would laugh and call it ridiculous, but she would insist: a little more practice and he could truly be great. Bud was glad for the compliment, and it encouraged him to continue writing his thoughts.

Teresa had less time for such pursuits than she would have liked. The hospital in Rumford kept her very busy, and the little free time she did have she preferred to spend in Bud's arms. While summer lasted, they would find a shady spot beneath a tree or on the bank of the pool and just enjoy being together. They discussed books, and poems, and dreamt about the future.

Teresa turned twenty–four as the leaves changed color and fell to the earth. The air turned colder, and her and Bud's time together moved indoors and either under a warm blanket on the couch, or on colder days, in front of a fire.

On Bud's twenty–fifth birthday, the first snow fell from the sky. The landscape turned as white as a blank canvas longing for someone to paint.

It was over Christmas that Bud approached Jim. Teresa was working at the hospital, which was fine because Bud wanted to talk to her father alone. The two men sat down together for lunch, Bud took a deep breath, and broached the subject he had been wanting to discuss for several weeks.

"I want to talk to you about, Reese," Bud said.

"Mmmm?" Jim sounded through a mouthful of food.

"I would like to ask your permission to marry her."

Jim swallowed his mouthful of food, and looked at Bud. He picked up his glass and took a long, slow drink of water. He set it deliberately back down on the table and wiped his mouth with a napkin.

"Well, Bud," he began. "I would think by this point you would have realized that my permission doesn't mean a whole heck of a lot when it comes to what Teresa does or doesn't do." He smiled broadly and then began to laugh. Bud started laughing too.

"I suppose I did know that, Jim," Bud said.

"Bud, you have always been like family. Personally, I would love nothing more than to have you as a son–in–law, but that's not for me to decide at this point. If you've got the gumption to ask my daughter to marry you, by all means you have my blessing to do so."

"Thank you," Bud said.

"The question is Bud, are you prepared for what her answer will mean, in either case?"

"Jim, I have lived in sorrow and solitude for long periods of my life. I have seen some of the lowest points that any living man can weather. Reese brings joy and sunlight into my life like no one else. I've seen what life is without her. I'm prepared for that possibility. What I'm not prepared for is to let another chance, another minute, pass by without grabbing onto the greatest thing to have ever walked through my life. I've waited too long, and had accepted the reality that it may never happen. Now that it's within my grasp, I'm not going to let it slip through my fingers without so much as a fight."

"Yes, I'd say you're ready," Jim said as he laughed again. "Also, what you just said to me… I'd go with that when you ask her."

Bud proposed to Teresa on the first of the New Year. He got down on one knee where the puddle had been so many years ago, and held up the diamond ring he had bought.

"I've made more mistakes in life than I care to think about or admit, one of the very first right here in this spot. I'd hate to know that by not asking to spend the rest of my life with you, I'd made an even worse one. Just by the fact of who you are, and what you make me feel, I am a better person. You have always seen beyond my errors, forgiven me, and encouraged me to be the person I am inside. I am no longer content imagining a life without you in it. Reese, will you marry me?"

She took his hand and raised him to his feet. She looked up into his blue eyes that twinkled even in the dim January light. She took his cheeks in her hands, and kissed him firmly on the lips.

"Yes, Brandon, I will marry you," she said. "As long as you promise to be the boy who couldn't read. And the boy who sat in his room and learned to read to prove that he could. And as long as you'll be the boy who shares books with me, and wishes for my happiness, and protects me, and defends me. As long as you promise to be the boy I know and love, and have loved for as long as I can remember — and the boy who loves me in return, I will marry you."

"That is the only boy here," he said taking her hand and placing it to his heart.

"Promise?"

"Promise."

They embraced and shared a deep and passionate kiss. When they told Jim the news, he channeled Bud's grandfather Buck on the night he learned Nancy was pregnant with Teresa as he just smiled and said knowingly, "Well, that's wonderful news."

Wedding preparations began soon after that. Teresa insisted that they be married at the farm, and Bud was happy to agree. He suggested they build an arch down near the barn, and guests could be seated on the hill leading down so that they could all see. In this way, the backdrop would be the stream and the woods behind the farm. To Teresa, it sounded like a wonderful suggestion.

Bud chose Gregg to be his best man, as Jim would be giving Teresa away and Gregg knew both Bud and Teresa. Teresa thought long and hard about a maid of honor, but had trouble deciding. It was Bud that suggested her childhood friend Mabel. Teresa thought it might be awkward for her, where she had once been on a date with Bud and he had ended the relationship, but Mabel jumped at the chance when Teresa offered it.

Teresa and Bud had images of a small ceremony with a few friends and family, but when word of the engagement made its way into town, folks began telling Bud how excited they were, and how they couldn't wait for their invitation.

Bud would shrug when he had to tell Teresa of yet another person excited for the wedding. He would suggest that they didn't have to invite everyone in town and he could just tell everyone they were keeping things small.

"No," she'd say. "It's the price I pay for having such a great and important fiancé."

She would say it playfully, and Bud knew she was teasing. There was once a time he would have let such things go to his head, but now the only person whose opinion mattered was the one he was going to marry. Teresa didn't really mind that the wedding would be larger, and she found some pride in the fact that her future husband was so well respected around town. When the invitations finally went out, there were well over 250 people invited.

The Marshall – Peterson wedding was going to be one of the largest to–dos in that small town in quite some time. Some were coming to see if the rumors about Teresa were true. Others were coming because they liked and respected Bud Marshall, and they saw an invitation to his wedding as an honor. Most people were coming because it was likely to be a huge party that everyone would be talking about and no one wanted to be left out.

The wedding date had been set for June 28th, 1986, a Saturday. No alternative plans had been made in the event of rain, so everyone involved crossed their fingers, hoping that the weather would be pleasant enough for an outdoor wedding.

# 32

As he stood behind the house, Bud could look down towards the stream and the archway. He had crafted it out of pine logs from the forest beyond. There were hundreds of white chairs directed towards it, and a huge tent had been erected to the west with tables for the reception after the ceremony.

It was the evening before the wedding, and the sun was just beginning to set. As it fell it cast a red glow that crept down the length of the stream. To Bud, it looked like a red wash of blood flowing down from the little pool upstream and slowly filling the pond. The large tent blocked the light from hitting the chairs, casting them in a dark and ominous shadow.

Bud began to shake. It started in the fingers as the memories that he had driven down deep inside himself, memories that he thought he had moved beyond, flooded back. His heart began to race and his knees weakened. He would have collapsed if Teresa had not walked up behind him and taken his hand.

"You're cold," she said. Then she felt his hand trembling. "Are you okay?"

Bud said nothing, but continued to watch the red from the setting sun spread across the pond until it was dark crimson in the fading light.

"Brandon?" Teresa said, trying again to rouse him. "Are you okay?"

"So much blood," he said.

She looked at him, concerned that he wasn't feeling well. The look in his eyes filled her with terror. It was the same detached look she'd seen that day by the pool when he took Drake's life to protect her. She dropped his hand and stepped back. This shocked him back into the world and he turned, seeing her look of concern.

"Huh? No, I mean yes — I'm okay, Reese."

"Brandon, what's wrong?"

"It's just, I know we said it's over, but it's not, not for me. It will never be over. I don't know if this place is right. Are we right? Maybe, maybe somewhere else..."

She took a step forward and put her hand cautiously on his arm. "Would it matter where it was, Brandon? Would somewhere else make it all go away?" she asked.

Bud looked back down at the stream. The light had faded and the water was dark, but no longer red. "No," he said. The horrors were in his mind and nowhere else. There was no escape.

"Do you love me, Brandon? Do you want to marry me?" Teresa asked.

"Yes," he said taking her hand in his. "I love you and I want nothing more in this life than to marry you and be your husband and the father to your children."

"Will you still want to live here? With all that's... happened? Will you want our children to grow up here?" she asked, motioning at the farm, the stream, and the woods.

"This is home. There is both joy and pain here for me, but for them the canvas will be blank. They will create their own memories. There is nowhere else I would want to go."

"Good. Then tomorrow we will add new memories of joy, and paint over some of the pain."

"No, not over it," he said. "It is part of the picture, forever. We will paint around it with joy until it is just an ugly dark spot surrounded by light and happiness. If we cover it the stain will show through and sully the beauty above it. I tried to cover it, to forget, but it is still there. There is no sense trying to hide it any longer."

She stood on her toes and kissed him gently on the cheek. "I'll see you tomorrow," she said and left him standing in the fading light.

Bud stood for a while longer as the air cooled and the fireflies began to dance along the hill below. When he heard the first call of the owls, he headed inside for the night.

Teresa sat on her bed, thinking about the look she had once again seen in Bud's eyes. It had been fleeting, but the slightest measure of fear and doubt crept into her mind. But then, she thought, her touch and voice had called him back from the abyss. She realized that Bud needed her help to navigate the darkness. She pulled out a piece of paper on which she had written her vows, and began making a few changes that better suited what she hoped to be as a wife for her new husband.

The sun rose bright and beautiful on a new day. Any concerns about the weather were proved needless as the temperature would reach the mid–eighties and not a drop of rain would fall.

Bud dressed in an old suit of Buck's that his grandmother had kept, and he hadn't the heart to throw away. It was tan, and he paired it with a white collared shirt and a blue tie that made his eyes shine brightly. He put on a polished pair of brown shoes and then made his way outside to aid with the arrival of the guests.

The wedding would begin in the early afternoon, and guests started arriving around two. Jim was there with Bud to greet everyone and show them to their seats. Mabel was in the farmhouse helping Teresa get ready, and Gregg parked cars along Hales Road once the garage parking lot had been filled. Bud had closed the garage for the day, and all of his employees were eager to attending the wedding.

Bud was pointing the musicians in the right direction when he heard a commotion up by the road. He could see that Gregg and another man were having an argument, and their voices were growing louder. Concerned, Bud asked Jim to deal with the musicians so he could go see what all the fuss was.

He made his way over to the commotion to see Gregg, standing face to face with Drake's father.

"What's the problem here?" Bud asked walking up. His face grew concerned when he saw it was Drake's dad making all the noise.

"He wanted to see you," Gregg said. "I told him you were busy and he wasn't invited."

"I have every right!" Drake's father yelled.

"I'll take care of it, thank you, Gregg," Bud said sending Gregg to help the other guests. "Mr. Goucher, what can I do for you?"

"How dare you!" Drake's father said. "How dare you disrespect my son like this! Getting married in the very place you killed him, and marrying the girl who told all those lies about him!"

The man was clearly drunk, and Bud didn't appreciate him talking that way about Teresa.

"Sir," Bud said as calmly as he could, "this is my home and I will be married here if I choose to be."

"No! You will not disrespect my son again!" Drake's father got real close to Bud and put a finger in his face. "That little whore isn't going to get away with this either."

Bud could smell the liquor thick on the man's breath. His heart began to pound harder as his anger grew.

"Sir, I won't have you talking about Reese that way. I am going to kindly ask you to leave," Bud said.

"What are you going to do, huh?" Drake's father said poking Bud in the chest. "You going to kill me too? Are you going to kill me like you did my son, you miserable son of a bitch? Are you going to have that dirty slut of yours make up lies about me too?"

Bud's blood pressure rose and his heartbeat pounded in his head. His anger was building to a boiling point.

"I've asked you nicely not to talk that way about Reese, and I don't appreciate you in my face either. Kindly step back and please remove yourself from this property, or I will have to call the sheriff."

"Yeah? You call the sheriff! I'm not going anywhere, and I'll get in your face all I want to, you murdering piece of shit."

Drake's father shoved Bud backwards with both of his hands. Bud managed to stay on his feet, but his anger was enflamed even more, and his face reddened. He took a deep breath to try and calm himself. He was about to tell the man to leave again when Jim ran up.

"Bud, everything okay?" Jim asked.

"Call the sheriff please, Jim. This man refuses to leave our property despite being asked nicely several times. He's just here to cause trouble," Bud said turning to Jim.

As Bud turned back to face Drake's father, he caught the man's fist to his jaw. Bud staggered back, and the man lunged at him. Bud sidestepped him and he fell on the ground unable to maintain his balance in his inebriated state. Bud felt the urge to jump on him, to hit him back, to release all of his anger. His body tensed, ready to spring – but he didn't. He stopped and took another deep breath putting his hand to his sore jaw.

Jim grabbed one of the man's arms, and Gregg came running up, having seen the whole thing from a distance. Gregg grabbed the other arm, and the two looked at Bud.

"Take him over to the garage," Bud said. "I'll call the sheriff and he can pick Mr. Goucher up there."

Jim and Gregg led the man off, and Bud turned towards the farmhouse, which was closest, and walked in the front door. He stopped in the hallway, shaking, and tried to calm himself. Mabel came down the stairs and saw Bud standing there.

"What's happening, Bud? We heard yelling," she said.

"It's nothing, Mabel. You can tell Reese that everything is okay, just a rowdy drunk causing a bit of a stir. I guess he started celebrating a little early," Bud said, trying to force a smile.

Bud didn't want Teresa to know now that Drake's father had been the cause of the ruckus. He would tell her later, after the wedding. For now, he wanted her mind at ease. He went to the phone and called the sheriff.

The sheriff came and picked up Drake's dad, took brief statements from Jim, Gregg, and Bud, and excused himself. He said he would be back if he needed more information, but he understood they had a wedding to get to and didn't want to keep them longer than necessary.

Bud's stress level was elevated, and he clearly wore the incident in the expression on his face. Jim suggested they go sit in Bud's house for a few minutes to collect themselves. Bud left Gregg in charge of things, and walked to the cape with Jim.

"Are you okay, Bud?" Jim asked, as he sat down at the kitchen table, handing Bud a glass of ice water.

"Yes, I'm all right. It's just the things he said about Teresa — about me," he paused. "I'm okay."

"He was just drunk, Bud."

"No, he was in pain. He hasn't forgotten, and neither have I. We all have specters that haunt us in the quiet moments when the dark closes in, and we lose where we are. For some of us, they're worse than for others. I can't blame him for what he's going through."

"You're a better man than I am, Bud," Jim said shaking his head.

"No, I'm not, that's the thing, Jim. I've just lived through the darkness."

"But you didn't hit him back. That took a great deal of restraint. More than I think I would have had if I were you."

"I've been down the other road. I know where that leads," Bud said, looking away into the ether of the past. "I'll never go there again, not unless I have no other choice."

Bud took another sip of water and told Jim he was all right to head back out. Most of the guests had arrived, and everyone was settling into their seats for the ceremony. Gregg and Bud took their places by the arch, and Jim went to get Teresa. A few minutes later everyone was in their places, and the musicians began to play.

Mabel came down the aisle first, wearing a short yellow dress. She carried a small bouquet of spruce and white roses. She bobbed slightly, smiling as she came.

The musicians stopped as Mabel took her place on the opposite side of the arch from Bud and Gregg. They began again a few seconds later with the bridal march.

Jim walked side by side with Teresa from the porch on the farmhouse. They turned and began down the aisle between the hundreds of guests gathered. Everyone stood and watched father and daughter walking arm in arm.

Teresa wore a simple white strapless dress that hung to her lower thigh and flared at the bottom. It was tied at the waist with a white satin ribbon. In her hands she held a larger version of the spruce and white rose bouquet Mabel had carried. Her auburn hair, which was pulled up and ringed by small white flowers, shimmered in the summer sun. She walked barefoot and smiled broadly when she saw Bud waiting by the arch.

The service was short and beautiful. Bud and Teresa chose to read vows they had written themselves. Each had labored to find the right words, and neither had heard what the other would say until that moment, standing in the sun by the banks of the stream. The minister asked Bud to go first.

"I stand here today in the presence of God, our family, and friends to commit my life, my heart, and my very being to you. If I am to be judged, by powers mortal or immortal, let them say I am of meager quality, lesser character, and wholly inadequate to receive the blessings of your love. For such judgements, I could fault neither man nor God, for I have measured myself and come to similar conclusions. But I pledge here and now to spend every moment, from this to the end of time, working to amend that deficit. Loving you has been my greatest challenge, and my greatest success. It wasn't until I lost my fear of walking the world alone, that was I able to see your footsteps beside mine. I loved you before I knew you, and I will love you through eternity."

The guests were moved by Bud's words. The minister turned to Teresa and asked her now to speak her vows to Bud. Mabel handed her a folded–up piece of paper, and Teresa apologized to the guests for not being able to remember her words as Bud had. People chuckled, and Teresa took a deep breath before beginning.

"I believe in you, the person you will become, and the couple we will be together. I release who I was alone, and become a new person with you. With my whole heart, I take you as my husband, acknowledging and accepting your faults and strengths, as you do mine. In fear and in doubt, I will be your foundation. In darkness, I will be your light. In despair, I will be your hope. Neither the crumbling of mountains, nor the falling of the stars will diminish my love. The earth may stand still, the sun may cease to shine, the sands in the hourglass of time may stop falling, but my love for you will persist. When the wind whispers, it will whisper my hopes, my fears, and my dreams to you. When the rain falls or the sun shines, they will nourish our bond. When the birds sing, they will sing only of my love for you. When the wolves and coyotes cry, they will cry that we are resolved only to each other, forsaking all others. When eternity echoes, it will echo our story, and all who hear it will know and understand. Today I pledge myself to you, for together our greatness is untold."

The wedding guests sat in awe of Teresa's words. If they had been moved by Bud's, they were stunned by hers. None now could doubt the love she felt, nor her commitment to the man she was marrying.

After they had finished their vows and exchanged rings, the minister announced them as husband and wife, and they kissed. The cheers and applause resonated through the woods, and up the stream to the small pool by the waterfall. They sounded on the banks of Pocasset Lake, and down the length of Baker Street. They reverberated through town, and into the cemetery near the church. Joy and happiness spread across the countryside with the proclamation of love.

Afterwards, the guests moved into the large tent for the reception. The warmth and excitement followed them there. It was during dinner that Teresa asked Bud about the yelling outside her house before the ceremony. Bud told her only enough to settle her curiosity, not wanting to ruin such a wonderful day. Towards the end of the meal, Jim rose clinking a fork on his glass.

"I believe it's customary for the father of the bride to say a few words," he said. "I have known Bud almost his entire life. I remember vividly the night he came here to live with his grandparents. I have watched him grow alongside my beautiful daughter, Teresa, and have always felt like he was part of the family. I am glad today that we make that official. Bud, if Maggie and Buck were here today, I have no doubt that they would be extremely proud of the man you have become, and the things you have overcome and accomplished. I take comfort knowing that you are a man of strength, wisdom, and courage. I know Teresa will be safe with you, and you likewise with her. I cannot think of a better man, living or imagined, for my daughter to have married. Teresa, it is a father's joy to watch his little girl grow into a smart, capable woman. My only regret is that your mother couldn't be here today to see you married. You have her stubbornness, but also her capacity for forgiveness and love. I wish you both joy, love, and comfort, wherever life leads you. Cheers."

"Cheers," said all of the guests assembled.

There was dancing, and drinks, and general merriment through the evening. When it was time for the celebration to end, the party gathered on Hales Road to wave goodbye to the newlyweds. Mabel and Gregg had decorated Bud's Chevy C10 pickup with "Just Married," and the typical accouterments of tin cans.

Teresa looked back out the window as they drove towards Baker Street. She smiled at the image of the throngs of people waving, her father at the front, smiling with tears in his eyes. She turned back to look out the front window as Bud made the left onto Baker Street, then she slid over and lay her head on his shoulder.

Neither was sure what the future might hold, but they knew that together, they could conquer just about anything. For now, they had planned a honeymoon and some time alone, away from the trappings of the past. As they crossed over the spot where the stream passed through a culvert under the road, they both looked west towards the pool and the waterfall.

"Our place," Bud said.

"Our place," Teresa agreed, and she kissed him on the cheek.

# 33

"I don't want to leave," Teresa said.

She had walked out of the bathroom wearing only a tee shirt and, climbed up next to Bud on the bed. They had spent two weeks in the little lakeside cabin on Moosehead Lake, but it was time for their honeymoon to end and for the couple to return home.

"Well, I don't either, but I have a business to get back to and you have your job at the hospital. We can't leave them high and dry forever. What would the world ever do without us?" he teased, kissing her on the lips.

"The world will survive. Besides, I don't want the world. I only want you."

The two weeks of solitude had been a glorious respite from the realities of life. They had kindled the fires of their passion in an effort to make up for lost moments. Now, it was time for true married life to begin.

"And you have me," Bud said, kissing her again.

When they arrived home, Jim had left a gift on the table: the deed to the farm signed over to them along with a note.

*Hey Kids,*
    *Hope you had fun. We'll talk about this when you get back*
*from the honeymoon.*
                    *Love, Dad*

"You can't just give us the farm, Dad," Teresa said later that evening after they had all sat down to dinner together.

"Of course I can, it's mine to give. Besides, what's one old guy going to do with a big old farm anyway?" Jim said.

"Where are you going to live, though?" Teresa asked.

"I thought I'd purchase a lot in that new development down the road and build a little place just for myself," he said.

"That's ridiculous, you're not doing that," Teresa said adamantly. "I won't hear of it."

"This is not a negotiation, Teresa," Jim said, smiling. "I'm giving you the farm, and that's that. It is Mom's and my wedding gift to the two of you. If she were still alive, she would agree with me."

Teresa sulked at her father's invocation of her mother. It was one thing to argue with her dad face to face, but she couldn't very well argue with the dead. She looked angrily at Bud for support. He didn't want to get in the middle of an argument with father and daughter, but this was his wife now. He quickly had an idea that he hoped would satisfy everyone.

"Then you'll have to move into my place," Bud said.

"Your place?" Jim asked.

"Well, Pa and Gran's old place, sure. If we're moving in here, I won't need it. It's smaller than your house, so it shouldn't be more than 'one old guy' can manage," Bud said, smiling.

Teresa looked at Bud and raised an eyebrow. He looked back at her as if to say, "Well, what's wrong with that?" She thought for a minute and figured it was as good an arrangement as any, and so turned her attention to her father, waiting for his answer.

"All right, kids," Jim said. "If you don't mind having me next door, I will move into your house, Bud. But I will not accept it as a gift. The deed stays in your name, and you will charge me rent."

"Deal," Bud said.

"What!" Teresa said, outraged. "Rent? You're going to charge my father rent?"

"Yes, I am," Bud said with the slightest glimmer in his eye. "That's what he wants, so that's what I'm going to do. Jim, I will want your one–dollar rent payment on the first of each month, and I expect it to be on time."

"Now wait just a minute—" Jim started to say.

"Now, I agreed to charge rent, but I did not agree to an amount," Bud said interrupting. "One dollar, and not a penny less, Jim."

Bud was very pleased with himself, and sat with a big grin on his face. Jim was frustrated, but had to chuckle anyway. Meanwhile, Teresa rolled her eyes at the two men in her life, and wondered what she had gotten herself into.

There was a lot of moving over the next few days. Bud and Jim did most of the work as Teresa had to return to her shift at the hospital in Rumford. By the end of their first week back, Bud and Teresa were fully moved into the farmhouse, and Jim was settled in the two–bedroom cape that had been the Marshalls'. The swap was a little odd for the two men who felt like they were living in someone else's house, but Teresa had no problem remaining in her childhood home.

It was only a week later when Teresa sat Bud down at the dinner table and told him she was pregnant. She had been feeling tired and nauseous, and her breasts were sore, so she got checked out at the hospital. Sure enough, there was a baby Marshall on the way.

Bud was overjoyed that before the next summer arrived in full, he would be a father. When they told Jim the news, he was thrilled as well. Later that evening, Bud and Teresa lay in bed discussing the future.

"I think I want to take time off from nursing," Teresa said.

"You mean until after the baby?" Bud asked.

"Yes, but also for a while afterwards if I can. It's difficult hours, and I would want to be home with the baby for a little while after it's born anyway. I was thinking maybe I could stop when I'm around 20 weeks and stay home, well, indefinitely."

"Reese, I will support you in whatever you want to do."

"Do you think we make enough money for me not to be working?" she asked.

"We have plenty of money. Don't even worry about that. Jim gave us the farm, the garage is doing very well, we have quite a bit of savings, and I'm getting regular rent payments from your father."

The last comment made Teresa roll her eyes. "I'm serious, Brandon. Could we make it on what your automotive business brings in alone? Even with a baby?"

"Yes," he said. "We would have more than enough. How long are you thinking about staying home?"

"At least until the baby starts school."

"This baby, or...? What if we have more children?"

"That's why I'm asking about our finances, Brandon. I want to be home with any children while they're little. At least until they start school."

"Why the sudden change? I thought you loved nursing."

"I do," she said, and let out a long sigh. "Actually, it's something you said once, or that Buck said and that you told me. 'The greatest thing you can do is to love another with all your heart.' You said you wanted to be a great father. Well, I want to be a great mother too, and I can't do that if I'm running off at all hours to be a nurse, at least not the way I want to."

"Lots of moms work these days."

"I know, and I'm not saying there's something wrong with that. It's just not what I want, not right now."

"Okay, Reese," Bud said. "You stay home as long as you want."

"And we'll be okay? Financially, I mean. Even if we're talking about several children?"

"I don't know that I've adequately represented just how well the garage is doing…"

"How well is it doing, Brandon?"

"Very," he said smiling.

Teresa gave her intention to stop working at the hospital in Rumford when she reached her 20th week of pregnancy. When Bud told her just how much the garage was bringing in each year, she was shocked. Bud wasn't wealthy by any means, but he was making far more than anyone in the area would have realized, given that he still drove his old truck and wore work clothes pretty much all the time.

Bud even said he was going to put an advertisement out to find a manager for the garage, so that he could spend more time at home with Teresa and the baby as well. He didn't want someone to take over completely, but to do enough that he didn't feel the need to rush over first thing every morning and stay until closing every night.

He waited until Teresa was twenty weeks pregnant and staying home. There was no sense in hiring someone so he could stay home if she wasn't there. Bud placed the advertisement in all the regional newspapers hoping to attract a few quality candidates. He was getting frustrated from not receiving calls or inquiries when four days later, a man walked into his office at the garage.

"Mr. Marshall?" the man said.

"Yes, that's me," Bud said, standing from the desk to shake his hand.

"My name's Cupp, Arthur Cupp."

Arthur Cupp was known across the state as a prominent businessman and philanthropist. He owned stores and factories in a variety of industries all over central Maine.

"I know of your name, Mr. Cupp. Please, sit down," Bud said motioning for a chair. "What can I do for you?"

"I'm here because I noticed your ad in one of the papers looking for a manager."

Bud looked confused at Arthur Cupp. "Why would a gentleman of your stature want to manage my garage?"

"I don't, Mr. Marshall. I'm here to see if you'd be interested in selling it."

Mr. Cupp made Bud a very generous offer and Bud said he would consider it. Cupp shook his hand and left his number, saying when Bud made a decision to give him a call. Bud discussed the offer with Teresa that night over dinner. The money was staggering to her.

"That's almost enough for us to live on the rest of our lives," she said. Bud nodded and shrugged his shoulders. "What do you think about it?"

"It's ten to fifteen years' worth of revenue as the business stands today," Bud answered. "Far more than that as far as the income we personally pull from it after payroll and expenses."

"So, we should do it, right?"

"It's hard," Bud said.

"What is?"

"How do you put a price on something you built with your own hands? Can you measure in dollars something that you've put so much of yourself into? The business would make a good steady income for us for as long as we want to run it, but is it foolish not to take such a large sum of money today? I don't know Reese, I need to think about it."

"It would give you time to spend with me and the baby. And Gregg is always bugging you to run for town manager. It would give you time to do that if you wanted. We could even start run-ning the farm again. I was raised on a working farm — not that I ever helped out much, but it might be nice for our kids to have something like that."

"Running a farm is a lot of work in itself. I suppose we could do something small like having a chicken coop, maybe a pig or two, or a couple of cows, and a small garden. I don't know that I'd want to take on much more than that anyway. There are still the two horses and we have to hay the fields every year. I'll have to think about it, like I said. It's a lot to consider. Right now, I'd like to just focus on you and the baby."

Bud hadn't had any calls or inquiries about the managerial position that he was inclined to move forward on. He felt that maybe he could promote the head mechanic and place some of the managerial duties on him for the time being to relieve a little of his workload. That would buy him some time to figure out what he wanted to do about Arthur Cupp's offer.

With Teresa no longer working, the pleasure of having her around all the time wasn't lost on Bud. He would sneak over from the garage even when he was working to see her, kiss her, and talk to the baby growing inside her. He wore his excitement on his face everywhere he went. Lying in bed at night, he would rub Teresa's ever–growing belly and dream of the life ahead.

As the leaves changed and fell lazily to the ground, Bud and Teresa embraced the changes they needed to make in their own lives. Bud painted the nursery so that it would be fresh and clean for the baby. Teresa tried her hand at knitting, attempting baby booties and a hat. They prepared for the reality of a growing fam-ily in which to share their love.

At Christmas, Jim presented them with the cradle that he and Buck had made for Brandon when he first came to live there. He had found it tucked away in the cape, and felt Bud and Teresa should have it.

When the bitter January and February winds bit at the siding of the farmhouse, Bud and Teresa stayed warm by the fireplace, Teresa's bare feet up on an ottoman. She would knit, and he would read stories aloud for her and the baby.

As spring approached, everyone prepared themselves for the newest addition to the family. Bud said that if it was a boy he'd like to name it "William," after his grandfather. Teresa thought that was a wonderful idea. When Bud asked if Teresa would like to name a girl after her mother, Nancy, Teresa said she liked the idea, but though it might be too hard for her father to call anyone by his wife's name. That made sense to Bud, and so they hadn't settled on any name should the baby be a girl.

March dragged on slowly, and Teresa was becoming more and more uncomfortably pregnant every day. Her back ached and her ankles swelled. Bud did his best to make her comfortable, but both of them hoped that the baby would arrive soon. The anticipation had begun to build beyond what either could readily tolerate.

# 34

It was late on March 29th, in 1987, when Teresa went into labor. She wanted to have the baby at the hospital in Rumford where she had worked because she knew the staff there. Bud, Teresa, and Jim all loaded into Jim's car to make the nearly hour–long drive.

Bud sat in the back with Teresa, doing what he could to help her through the pain of her contractions. It felt like Jim hit every bump there was to be found on the roads to Rumford, but Bud knew he was doing his best to drive quickly and stay calm. Bud silently wished Teresa had chosen to have the baby in Augusta, or even Lewiston. Either would have been a shorter drive, and both were bigger hospitals.

The drive was made more difficult by the steady spring showers that were falling making the road wet and the world even more dark in the fading evening light. Jim strained his eyes to see the road through the reflection of the headlights on the drizzle. He exhaled deeply when they finally pulled onto the hospital property.

Teresa knew the staff, and she was welcomed by everyone she met. She did her best to smile through the pain of her contractions which were growing ever closer together. She and Bud were shown to a delivery room where the doctor and nurses began their examinations and preparing for the baby's arrival.

Watching the news on the tiny television, Jim sat alone in the waiting room, trying his best to relax after the stress of the drive. He had purchased a cup of coffee, and was prepared for a long night ahead.

Teresa knew first pregnancies could take a long time, but she was ill–prepared for the exhaustion the whole process would mean. Bud stayed by the head end of the bed. He wiped her forehead and spoke soft encouraging words. It was difficult to watch his wife, the woman he loved, in so much pain, but he was very proud of her.

Bud made occasional trips to the waiting room to inform Jim of the progress Teresa was making. At one point in the early morning hours, Bud found Jim sitting with his eyes closed and his arms folded across his chest. Bud, thinking Jim was asleep, walked over and sat next to him just to catch his breath for a few minutes from the stress of the delivery room.

"How's it going?" Jim asked, his eyes still closed.

"Good, I think," Bud answered. "She's been pushing for a while now. I can't imagine it will be much longer. She's an amazing woman — stronger than I could have ever imagined."

"She always has been. Even as a little girl."

Jim opened his eyes and smiled at Bud. Bud smiled back and stood to walk back to the delivery room.

"Bring me the good news," Jim said.

"As soon as I have it," Bud said.

Teresa strained and pushed with every contraction. Sweat formed and rolled down her forehead faster than Bud could wipe it away. Bud was anxious, but the doctor was calm and spoke in a very measured voice. He continued to tell Teresa she was doing wonderfully, and it would only be a few more pushes.

It was nearly an hour after Bud had been out to see Jim that the baby arrived. Teresa slumped back in exhaustion and accomplishment. The doctor announced that she and Bud had a healthy baby girl. Tears welled in Bud's eyes as he looked down at his wife. She was smiling and crying.

The baby was wiped and placed on Teresa's chest to hold. Bud kissed his wife on the head as she nuzzled the baby girl.

"You were amazing," Bud told her.

Teresa smiled up at him, staring into his twinkling blue eyes.

"I love you," she said, and her face suddenly turned to anguish.

Buzzers and alarms began sounding in the delivery room. Bud looked up, concerned. The baby was whisked away from Teresa's arms as doctors and nurses swarmed around her. Bud was escorted from room in protest. All he could do was ask what was happening as he was physically moved out of the room by two orderlies.

"No! Wait! What's going on? What is happening?" he yelled.

The orderlies led him back to the waiting room, and told him he would have to stay there.

"Your wife and baby are in good hands," one of them said.

"What's happening?" Jim asked, walking quickly over.

"Something's wrong," Bud answered. "There were alarms. Teresa didn't look right, she looked in pain. It was shortly after the baby was born. I don't know what's going on. Someone tell me what's going on!"

A receptionist tried to calm Bud down as he yelled for answers, but he continued to holler, demanding to see the doctor.

"Bud, if she's sick, the doctor is busy," Jim said, taking his arm.

"I need to be in there," Bud said.

"I know how you feel, Bud. I'm worried too. Let's try to be calm together. Come, sit with me. Tell me about the baby."

Bud looked at Jim. His face was calm, but his eyes were a storm of terror. The two men walked back and sat down next to one another in two of the chairs facing the tv. Bud didn't speak for several minutes trying to compose himself.

"We have a baby girl," He said at last.

"That's wonderful, Bud. Is the baby okay?"

"I think so. She seemed to be fine. It was Teresa who looked in pain. I just wish someone would tell us something."

The men sat in silence for what felt like an eternity. When they finally saw the doctor coming towards them, they rose simultaneously. They took a few paces and met him in the middle of the room.

"Mr. Marshall," The doctor said, "can we talk in private?"

"This is my father–in–law, we can speak here," Bud said.

"All right," The doctor said nodding. "First, the baby is fine. She's resting comfortably, and you can go see her whenever you are ready."

"That's good," Jim said.

"Your wife," the doctor said, holding Bud's eye, "suffered cardiac arrest and respiratory failure. We believe it may have been an amniotic fluid embolism. We did everything we could, but we were unable to restart her heart. I'm terribly sorry sir, we lost her."

"Lost her?" Bud said. "No, no, that's not right. She can't be gone, we just had a daughter. You have to fix it!"

"I'm sorry, sir," the doctor said. "Take as much time as you need. When you're ready to see her or the baby just let the receptionist know and…"

The doctor's words faded into incomprehensible sounds. Jim's eyes were wet and red. For Bud, the world went fuzzy, and he lost his grip on the earth. He stumbled, and Jim caught him, holding him up right.

The men walked together to Teresa's side. They stood and cried together. Jim held his daughter's hand, and Bud kissed her softly on the cheek.

"Come back," Bud whispered in her ear, but she didn't move. Bud grew angry. He was angry with Teresa for leaving him, he was angry at himself for leaving her side, he was angry with the doctor for not being able to save her, and he was angry at life for stealing his happiness.

Jim kissed his daughter's hand, wiped a piece of hair from her brow and whispered to her, "Say hello to your mother. I love both of you very, very much. I'll look after Bud and the baby."

Bud's anger was quelled by his soft and honest words.

"I'll go and see the baby, if it's okay," Jim said. "I'll leave you to say your goodbyes."

Bud nodded and Jim kissed his daughter's forehead, said goodbye one last time, and walked out of the room with tears in his eyes. Once he was gone, Bud collapsed onto his wife, sobbing.

"You can't go, not without me. It's not fair. I've spent my whole life waiting for you, waiting for us. I can't spend the rest of it missing you, it's too hard. It should have been me. You're the stronger one."

He picked up his head from the bed and wiped the tears from his eyes. Teresa was gone, and this time she wouldn't return. She wasn't avoiding him because of something he had said, or something he had done. There would be no forgiveness this time. She would never again show up, no explanation needed, and fall back into their routine together. There was no need for Bud to apologize this time, but he did anyway.

"I'm sorry. I said it would take a lifetime to apologize for all I've done. I thought I had more time. Promise me something, Reese. Promise you'll wait for me. Wait for me like I waited for you. Wait for me by the waterfall. Our place."

He bent down and kissed her one last time. He lingered for several more minutes, reluctant to leave her. When he turned to go, he thought he must feel what she had felt all of those times she had been determined to stay away from him. It was the hardest thing he had ever done, but he knew it was the right thing to do.

Bud found Jim standing and looking through the glass into the nursery at the newborn.

"Why aren't you holding her?" Bud asked.

"I'm not her father," Jim said smiling, his eyes still red from the tears. "Her father should hold her first."

Bud asked and a nurse brought the little girl out for Bud and Jim to hold. She stirred and cried as the nurse placed her in Bud's arms.

"Shhh, shhh," Bud said rocking her gently. "Don't cry, baby girl. It'll be okay. Your Grandpa Jim and I are going to take good care of you. I promise, you will never lack for love."

The baby calmed and stopped crying as Bud rocked her. He handed her to Jim, who smiled as he rocked her from side to side.

"What are you going to name her, Bud?" Jim asked.

"I don't know," Bud answered. "We never came up with a name for a girl."

"She has your eyes."

"And her mother's face. I hope she has her mother's strength. Things won't be easy for her."

Teresa was buried a week later. The baby slept soundly in Jim's arms as Bud tried to give the eulogy. He broke down in tears halfway through, apologizing. Unable to continue he said simply, "She will be missed," and returned to his seat.

Bud held the baby as Teresa was lowered into the ground close to Nancy's gravesite. The baby cried as the casket reached the bottom, and Bud rocked her gently, soothing her.

On her stone, Bud had a quote engraved from her favorite novel, *East of Eden*.

> *"We should remember our dying and try so to live*
> *that our death brings no pleasure on the world."*
> — *Steinbeck*

After the service, Bud, Jim, and the baby returned to the farm-house after the service. They sat in the living room, the baby lying peacefully sleeping after her formula. Stillness filled the room as Bud looked around, taking in every object of the room. His eyes eventually settled on Jim, who was staring silently towards the ceiling deep in thought.

"I need you to move back here to the farmhouse," Bud said, shaking Jim from his thoughts.

"No, you don't, Bud. You don't need me here."

"I do, and so does she," Bud said pointing to the baby.

"What can I do? I've lost the same as you. I can't be any stronger than you can."

"You can love her — that's what she needs. She doesn't have a mother to love her. I can't be a mother, and I know you can't either, but you can be a grandfather. I've never raised a baby, but you have. I need the help — I can't do this alone, not right now. I want you here."

"All right, Bud," Jim said. "But what will you do with your grandparent's house?"

"I'll rent it out, for real this time."

"Okay, I'll start moving my stuff over. I suppose I'll move into Teresa's old bedroom."

The use of Teresa's name made Bud wince in physical pain. Tears immediately formed in the corners of his eyes and began running down his cheeks. He started shaking, unable to control his sorrow.

"I'm sorry, Bud," Jim said.

"How can I do this? How can I go on without her?"

"I don't know, but you will because you have to."

"Will I? What if I'm not strong enough?"

"You are."

"My father wasn't," Bud said, looking up at Jim with blood-shot eyes.

"You are not your father," Jim said.

"How do you know? You didn't know my father."

"I know you, and I knew your grandfather — probably just about as well as anyone other than you and your grandmother. And I know that your grandfather and your father were nothing alike, your grandfather told me that. I know you're not like your father because you are so much like your grandfather. You can't possibly be anything like your father."

"And her," Bud said pointing to his daughter again. "She will never know her mother. How can I make up for that? I can't be a mother. She needs what I can't give her."

"She needs love, like you said. You can give her that. I can give her that. You never knew your mother, and you did just fine. At least that little girl will know of her mother. What do you know about your mother, Bud? Nothing, I'd wager. I certainly don't know anything about her, and I don't think Buck or Maggie did either. We will tell that baby girl everything about her mother, who she was, what she was like, and how much we loved her. That's what's best for her. She doesn't have a mother, but she has a father. She has you. You can't be weak on this one, Bud. There is no out for you. There's no Buck Marshall to take on this responsibility for you. I'm certainly no Buck. I can't possibly do for this baby what he did for you. But I can help you. I can help you in any way that I'm able. You don't have a choice on this one, Bud; you have to be your grandfather."

"We always have a choice," Bud said.

"Maybe so. Maybe your grandfather had a choice the day you were left on that step next door, but he understood exactly what he had to do. I suppose your father had a choice too. Are you happy with the choice he made? Are you glad that you never knew him? Are you glad you know nothing about your mother?"

"Would I have been better off having never come here? Would I have been better off with him?"

"I can't answer that, Bud. Would you have been better off with him being the man he was? Maybe not. But don't try to pretend that the choice he made was noble, or made solely in your best interest. It wasn't. It was cowardly and selfish."

The words were harsh and cold in Bud's ears. Jim was angry and scared.

"You think my father was selfish?" Bud asked.

"Yes, I do," Jim said. "He cared more for his own grief than for the potential joy he had right in front of him. Did he think about how hard he was making things for Buck and Maggie when he left you here? Did he think about how hard it would be for you growing up without a mother or a father? As far as I can tell, the only thing he was thinking about is how hard it would be for him. You're right, you have a choice. Some choices are hard and some are easy. And sometimes the easy choice is the hard way, and the hard choice is the easy way. This is an easy choice, Bud, and it's laying right there in front of you. Choose joy, choose happiness, choose your daughter."

"Maybe you're right. Maybe my father was selfish. Who's to know what he was thinking or feeling. If his grief was anywhere near what mine is, I can understand the pain. I don't see how it's an easy choice when every fiber of my being is crying out in despair. I do wish I knew something of my mother, whether she were strong. I wonder how much of her I have in me. I don't even know her name."

"I don't know your mother's name either, Bud, but I know where you can go to find out; if that's something you need to do to move forward."

# 35

The sky was gray, and threatening. Bud left the records building, having received the information concerning his mother's gravesite. He climbed into the dark green Chevy and drove through Cambridge to the gates of the cemetery. The truck moved slowly between the stones until Bud brought it to a stop under the branches of an oak tree and climbed out.

The light was fading as Bud wandered through the rows of graves looking for his mother's. He had to stop and study several that were worn and difficult to read in the dim light. After several minutes of searching, he found what he was looking for. He knelt and read the name out loud.

"Mary Clarence Roberts Marshall."

Bud's birthday was etched into the stone as the date of his mother's last living day on earth, November 28, 1960. Below the dates, there was a quote.

> *"Death lies on her, like an untimely frost*
> *Upon the sweetest flower of all the field."*
> *—W. Shakespeare*

Bud recognized the quote from Shakespeare's *Romeo and Juliet*. He shuddered, thinking of the end for both Romeo and his own father, Paul. A chill ran down the back of Bud's neck and he shivered. He had far more in common with his father than he had wanted to admit to himself. In that moment, Bud knew exactly what his father must have been feeling the day he buried his wife, Mary.

Bud returned to the truck and drove until he found a phone booth. The first few drops of rain fell from the clouds as he entered it. Opening the yellow pages, he leafed through them until he found what he was looking for. Bud could only hope the store was open, and that the item he wanted would ease the pain. He deposited coins, and sure enough, a woman answered on the other end. She gave him directions on how to get to the store, and Bud thanked her and hung up. Before leaving the phone booth, he made one additional call.

"Mr. Cupp? It's Bud Marshall. Are you still interested in purchasing the garage?"

When Bud had finished the call, he walked back through the rain, which was now falling steadily. He drove solemnly, following the directions he got during the first phone call. Before long, he arrived at a small store with bright windows shining out into the storm.

He entered and bought a single item, and returned to the truck. Placing it carefully on the passenger seat, he retraced his route to the cemetery and parked under the same oak tree. Taking the item next to him, he exited the truck, and walked back to his mother's grave. Bud knelt on the wet ground, not caring how soggy his clothes were getting in the pouring rain. The wind blew, causing him to shiver. The words Teresa had spoken to him on their wedding day came back to him.

*"When the wind whispers, it will whisper my hopes, my fears, and my dreams to you. When the rain falls or the sun shines, they will nourish our bond."*

Bud looked up through the falling rain at the sky, and then down to the grave of his mother.

"You have a granddaughter," he said. "She's beautiful. I don't know what you had hoped for me, but I have done the best with what I've had. I have made mistakes, for which I am sorry and for which I have paid. I don't know if the pain I have now is further payment for those mistakes or not. I don't pretend to know the meaning of all of this. I do know that I hate finding you here like this: alone without love or remembrance. I can't imagine that you deserve it. I would have liked to know you, so that you could be remembered. There's not much I can do about that now, but for what it's worth, thank you. Thank you for bringing me into the world."

Bud lay the bouquet of flowers he held in his hand on his mother's grave. The tears from his eyes mixed with the rain flooding from the sky. He placed his hand to his lips, and then to his mother's stone. He struggled to his feet, and sloshed back to the truck to make the long drive back to Maine.

When Bud arrived back at the farmhouse, Jim was lying on the floor of Teresa's childhood bedroom in tears. Bud sat on the floor next to him and placed his hand on the man's back. Jim startled and looked up.

"Oh, Bud, you're home," he said. "Thank God. I was beginning to worry."

"No need to worry," Bud said. "There will never be need to worry again. Are you okay?"

"Yes, it's just hard being in this room with all the memories."

"Do you want the master bedroom?"

Jim sighed. "There are a few memories over there as well. No Bud, I'm fine right here. It's going to take time, for both of us I imagine. Did you find what you were looking for?"

"Yes, more than what I was looking for actually. I have a name for our baby girl."

"And?"

"I want to name her Mary Teresa, after my mother and hers."

"I think that's very fitting, Bud."

"There's another thing," Bud said.

"What's that?"

"I've agreed to sell the garage."

Arthur Cupp had read Teresa's obituary in the paper, so he knew of Bud's loss. A man of lesser moral standing would have taken advantage of the situation, but Arthur Cupp was a good man. When Bud had said he was willing to sell the garage at the originally offered price, Cupp had insisted on giving him ten percent more.

Jim was concerned that Bud was selling out of grief, and making a mistake he would come to regret. But Bud assured him that he had seriously considered selling well before Teresa had passed. Wanting to be there for the baby had cemented his decision. Between his savings, the money from the sale of the garage, and rental income from his grandparent's old house, Bud would have ample money to live and raise his daughter. Jim insisted on taking on a portion of the expenses as well, having sufficient savings himself.

Bud also bought a Honda Civic. It was time for a family car, something safe and reliable for him and the baby. He kept the truck, but he parked it beside the house and covered it for the time being. When the baby was a little older, Bud planned to begin running the farm again, but he wouldn't need the truck very often until then.

Those first few months, neither Bud nor Jim slept very much. Mary Teresa, who Bud still often referred to as "Baby Girl," was up every couple of hours. The two men tried to take turns giving her formula so the other could rest, but every cry inevitably woke both of them. They survived on coffee and hope.

The exhaustion combined with the mixed emotions of joy and grief was overwhelming. Either man could break down into tears from so little as a smell, an object, a picture, a sound, or a thought. A coo, a giggle, a smile, or precious expression could bring them back to the joy of the moment. It was enough to feel as if they aged years in only a few months.

Things improved as baby Mary began to sleep better at night. Her waking and feeding grew less frequent, and she slept for longer stretches, allowing Bud and Jim to get some actual rest.

By her first birthday, Mary was sleeping through the night with only occasional bouts of waking in the middle. Her hair had turned auburn like her mother's, but her eyes had remained a deep blue like her father and great grandfather. She had the look of her mother, which brought both joy and sadness to look on her.

She both walked and spoke early, her first word being "Dada." Bud showed her pictures of Teresa often, saying, "Mama" in an attempt to teach her the word and the meaning. It was on her birthday, with the picture of Teresa sitting at the table, that Mary had pointing at it and used the word for the first time.

Bud cried with the knowledge that he had at least succeeded in teaching her what her mother looked like. Mary would toddle around the house pointing at pictures of Teresa saying, "Mama" with each one. Bud would smile and nod, encouraging and praising her at every opportunity. She was smart, like her mother.

Arthur Cupp had taken over the garage, and Bud had rented his grandparent's house to the man Cupp had hired to manage the business. It was bittersweet for Bud, who was glad to have the time to spend with his daughter, but hated to watch the cars driving in and out of the business he'd built but no longer ran.

Bud found himself taking walks around the farm, both with Mary and by himself. He would often stroll through the woods, or along the banks of the stream up to the waterfall and the little pool below it. He half expected to find Teresa waiting for him, sitting on the log on the grassy bank by the water.

When he took Mary there, he would sit with her and tell her stories about her mother. She was too young to understand, but she would sit and gaze into her father's eyes just listening to the sound of his voice.

When he was alone, Bud would write in his notebook. He wrote whatever came to his mind, be it memories of Teresa, or his thoughts about life. He wrote things that made him happy, and things that made him sad. At times, he found himself writing directly to Teresa, asking for advice or for her help with something difficult. Other times he was writing to Mary, telling her what he hoped and wished for her and her future. It became an amalgam of all the parts of Bud's mind.

Jim was a rock through it all. His face grew worn, and whenever Bud asked if he was okay, Jim would say he was fine, but tired. The strain of holding up the world was wearing him down faster than Jim cared to admit. He still went to church every Sunday, as he had done with his family for years, but now he did so alone.

One Sunday when Mary was two, Jim returned to the farmhouse to find Bud sitting in the living room with Mary playing on the floor. Jim sank into one of the free chairs and exhaled loudly.

"You okay, Jim?" Bud asked.

"Yeah, just tired," Jim answered.

"How was church?"

"It was good. Sermon was on Job today. I found it ironic and fitting."

Bud cracked a smile, but the comment raised questions in his mind. He looked at his daughter playing on the floor and thought of Teresa.

"Jim," he said. "Would you want to take Mary to church with you?"

"Do you want Mary to go to church?"

"I'm just thinking that Teresa would have wanted her to. After all, it's something you always did as a family."

"I would love to take Mary to church Bud, but do you want her to go?"

"Why wouldn't I?" Bud asked, somewhat defensively.

"Well, you're not really a regular church goer, are you, Bud?"

"Well, no—"

"Let me ask you a question, Bud. Do you believe in God?"

It was a simple question for which Bud had no simple answer. He chose to answer the question with a question of his own.

"If you were me, would you believe in God?"

"If I were you, I would have more cause to believe in God than I do being who I am."

Jim had said it directly, without a hint of irony, humor, or doubt. Bud looked confused at his father–in–law, studying every inch of his face as though trying to find the flaw.

"But my life has been so full of tragedy and sadness…"

"Exactly," Jim said. "To not believe in God, is to believe that such a life is entirely a matter of chance. It's to believe that random events unfolded that resulted in the hardships that encompassed your life. That is an unsettling thought, Bud."

"But to believe in God is to believe that He put those hardships on me. Why would God do such a thing? Why me? Why am I deserving of such treatment? I'm not pious like Job. I don't want a test of my faith. What, 'The Lord giveth and the Lord taketh away?' The Lord never giveth to me, all he did was take. He took my mother, my father, my grandparents, my wife. What if I don't want to believe in a God that would do such things."

"Ah, but you said what if you don't want to. You didn't say you didn't believe in Him. The truth is, Bud, he gave you so much. He gave you grandparents that loved you. He gave you a chance at a life. He placed in your path a woman who loved you despite all your failings. He put Nancy and myself there to be your support as well. And he gave you the most beautiful daughter any man could hope for. Most of all Bud, he gave you no more than you were capable of handling."

"And what about my father? Did God give him no more than he could handle?"

"Your father is difficult to understand, I know. I don't pretend to know the mysteries of God or why He does the things He does. I've had my crises of faith, as any man can. I choose to believe that the things that are out of our control that happen, happen for a reason. I choose to believe that while I am incapable of understanding the reasoning of God, there is reasoning there. I choose to believe that He gives us choices in life that determine our course, and while he may already know our decisions, he provides us with the choice regardless. I choose to believe that we will be judged on those choices, and if we are judged worthy we will ascend into heaven."

"You believe in heaven?"

"I have to, Bud. I have to believe that my wife and daughter are in heaven, and they are waiting there for me. It is both a wonderfully uplifting and depressing belief all at the same time."

"Depressing?"

"It is sad to think that my wife is there just waiting, just waiting for me. I wish she didn't have to wait. How lonely that must be. But I have work here still… here on earth. But maybe heaven is a place without loneliness. That's my hope. That heaven allows for all the loneliness and sadness and despair of this world to melt away, leaving only joy. Then the waiting wouldn't seem so bad. But to think that there were no heaven? To believe that when we die, that is simply the end? That is a belief too horrifying for me to entertain. What hope would remain if I believed I would never see Nancy again? If you would never see Teresa, or Buck, or Maggie? No, I choose to believe both in Him and in heaven, because both things give me hope — hope that there is purpose beyond what we understand and hope that those we have lost we will see again."

"Did my grandfather believe in God? In heaven?"

"We never discussed it, but I think so. I suspect he was conflicted. He saw horrors in war that I can't imagine. He lost a son to suicide, but it brought you into his life. I know he believed in redemption, at least in this life if not in the next. It doesn't really matter, does it? It only matters if you believe."

"I'm not sure what I believe sometimes," Bud said. "I go through the motions of believing, almost because I feel like they're expected of me. I would like Mary to go with you to church, though. I would like her to decide for herself whether to believe or not."

"I would be happy to have the company."

After that day, Bud became more introspective. He spoke less and listened more. Often, it was only the twinkle in his eye that betrayed his thoughts as he listened to others in a conversation.

He continued his involvement in the community, attending town meetings regularly. When Bud rose to give his thoughts on a matter, people stopped to listen. His work on the boat launch had proven him to be competent, and his opinions carried a great deal of weight in the town.

Mary attended church with Jim, not understanding much about it at her young age, but glad to be spending time with "Grandpa Jim." Like her mother, she was a precocious girl with intelligence and maturity beyond her years. She was careful never to get her Sunday dress dirty and sat quietly through church, never fussing or otherwise causing disruption.

The sadness of losing Teresa never fully dissipated, but the crying subsided and was reserved for a few private moments when either Jim or Bud would let their minds wander back to memories of the past.

For Jim, these moments were usually while he was sitting alone at night in Teresa's childhood bedroom as he set down the weight of the day and collapsed, exhausted. Carrying on was wearing him thin. It was only the moments of brightness spent with Mary that kept him going despite the darkness closing in.

As he lay in bed at night, struggling to find sleep, he thought of the promise he had made to his daughter when he said good-bye in the hospital. He would take care of his granddaughter, and Bud, for as long as he could. He was tired, it was true; but he was too tired to sleep, and he still had work to do.

Bud's moments of sadness came in his time alone. When he went for a walk in the woods or up to the waterfall without Mary, his mind would wander and memories would come flooding in. His tears were not all of sadness and loneliness. There were those too, of course, but often he cried remembering the happy times he had shared with Teresa, Buck, and Maggie.

There was so much that Bud still wanted to share with Mary about her mother and grandparents and he didn't want all of it to be sad. He forced himself to focus on the good times as much as the bad and slowly he crawled his way out of the gloom and into the light.

Mary turned four in 1991, and Bud decided it was time to start running the farm again. She had grown to the point where she didn't need someone paying attention to her at all times, and Bud was ready to start doing again.

It doesn't serve to sit still for too long. One can become complacent with the monotony of life. Bud had grown up working on the farm, and many of his happy memories were there. He was determined to build similar memories for his daughter.

# 36

**M**ary loved to feed the chickens. They bobbed in and out around her feet, and she'd giggle as they ducked to and fro pecking at the corn as she tossed in on the ground. Bud had insisted that his daughter have chores, but he never called them that. Instead, he told her she would be helping him on the farm. Helping daddy was fun.

She had been working on the farm from the moment Bud had started running it again. Having recently turned five, she was spending her last summer before she would start school in the fall. June had begun sunny and warm, and the summer promised days of excitement and enjoyment.

Bud's eyes danced whenever he watched his daughter work or play, for she approached both with the same zest and enthusiasm. It was impossible for him to look at her without seeing Teresa, but the happiness of watching her grow finally outweighed the lingering pain of his loss.

Once the chickens were fed, Mary ran to her father standing in the open doorway of the barn.

"I'm done, Daddy," she said.

"Done already?" he said with a smile.

"Yes."

"You fed the rabbits and the chickens?"

"Uh huh," She said, nodding emphatically at her father.

The rabbits had been Jim's idea. He had built the small hutch on the back side of the barn himself. They were unlikely to ever eat them, but a girl having a pet wasn't such a bad thing. Bud appreciated her having something to be responsible for. Every morning Mary had to feed both them and the chickens. Bud was sure to lay the food out when he got to the barn first so that she could manage things from there.

"Well then," Bud said. "I suppose you can run along and play, but stay off the road and away from the pond and the stream."

She laughed and ran off to discover the world. Bud thought he would probably find her later sitting under the big oak reading or playing with her dolls. He knew Jim was in his usual summer spot, sitting on the front porch, and that he would keep an eye on her until Bud finished the rest of his morning chores around the farm.

Bud headed up for a break and to have some lunch a little after eleven. Sure enough, he found Mary playing under the oak, and Jim sitting on the porch watching her. Jim looked content, but tired. He had earned the weariness, Bud thought. After all, Jim was nearly sixty, and the last five or six years of his life had to have been some of the hardest.

"Up for some lunch?" Jim asked, as Bud took a seat next to him on the porch. Bud nodded and turned his attention to Mary playing under the tree. "She's a pretty amazing little girl, Bud."

"Like her mother," Bud said.

"And her father," Jim said, putting his hand on Bud's shoulder.

"Mary!" Bud called. "Let's go in and have some lunch, baby girl." He and Jim stood, waiting as Mary came running over.

Life seemed almost dull and monotonous, which was exactly what the two men preferred, given all that had happened. There was comfort in the routine, safety in the boredom, and joy to be found in the quiet.

The topic of school came up that day at lunch. Mary was excited to start kindergarten and learn all kinds of new and wonderful things. Like her parents she was already an accomplished reader, and neither Bud nor Jim had any doubt she would excel in school.

Bud's only concern was saying goodbye to his daughter every morning. How do you send the one thing you love most off into the world when everyone you've loved before has been lost? The idea of putting Mary on a bus and hoping against hope all day that she would return safely in the afternoon terrified Bud.

When Bud expressed his fear to Jim, Jim had looked him in the eye and said, "Welcome to being a parent." It wasn't a great deal of consolation, but the time was quickly approaching when Bud would have to deal with his fear head on.

Days wore on, and Bud's apprehension grew. He purchased a backpack, new from L. L. Bean, monogrammed with Mary's initials and school supplies to go in it. She carried it around for weeks leading up to her first day. The bus would pick Mary up right in front of the farmhouse, as Hales Road was a regularly traveled throughway now. There would be no walking to Baker Street for little Mary.

The first day of school arrived, and Bud sat on the porch with his daughter while she waited for the bus. He promised he would be there waiting for her when she got home, and he told her not to worry and that she would do great. Mary rolled her eyes.

"I'll be okay, Daddy. I'm excited."

So much like her mother, Bud thought.

When the bus pulled up, Mary jumped up and ran towards it. Halfway across the lawn she stopped, turned and ran back. She bounded up the steps and wrapped her arms around her father.

"I love you," she said.

"I love you too, baby girl."

She kissed him on the cheek, jumped back down the stairs, and ran to the open door of the bus. Bud saw her waving from one of the windows as the bus pulled away down Hales Road towards Pocasset Lake. He waved back and then turned away and wiped the tear from the corner of his eye.

Bud worked, but was of restless mind all day wondering about Mary. He was waiting on the porch as he had promised he would be when she arrived home safe and sound on the bus that afternoon. She climbed down the steps of the bus and ran up to him, hugging him again.

"Well? How was your first day?" Bud asked.

"Great," Mary answered. "I got to read from the blackboard. I can read more than anyone. They'll get better, but I'm way ahead. We played games. We have a class pet — a baby chick! I said that we have chickens, and the teacher let me feed it!"

Mary rambled on for several minutes, spilling every detail of her first day. Bud listened with a grin on his face. His fears had been unfounded, at least thus far. If anything, Mary was over prepared for school. He didn't want her thinking everything would be easy, but he didn't see the harm in letting his five–year–old little girl revel in the joy of her first day.

The porch scene became part of their routine. Bud would sit with his daughter in the morning waiting for the bus to come, and he would be there waiting for her when she got home in the afternoon. She would tell her father everything about her day, and he would listen, never interrupting until she was finished. Grandpa Jim would usually get a recap of the day's adventures at the dinner table each night.

Mary was never excused from doing her chores each morning. Bud expected her to rise before school in time to see the rabbits and chickens were fed properly. Then she could get cleaned up and dressed for school.

Bud's only concern was that Mary didn't seem to have many friends. She didn't complain and said that she liked the other kids well enough, and they didn't treat her poorly. She just found she didn't have a lot in common with them, and so kept mainly to herself.

Being raised an only child was something Bud had some experience with, but he and Teresa had always had each other growing up. Mary, on the other hand, had been by herself for nearly the entirety of her first five years of life, with only her father and grandfather for daily interaction. Bud didn't want her to grow up without a real childhood. He encouraged his daughter to try and make friends with some of the other children. She said she would try.

Mary tried to join in the other games the children would play, but she found them silly. Often, she could be found sitting in the shade reading a book or drawing pictures in a notebook.

One such day, when Mary had settled down against the school building at recess reading a book, another little girl came over to her.

"What are you doing?" the little girl asked.

"Just reading," Mary answered.

"What are you reading?"

"*Frog and Toad.*"

"Oh, I like those books," the little girl said, sitting down next to Mary.

The two read the book together. The girl's name was Abby, a freckle–faced redhead who wore large rimmed glasses. She was awkward, and most of the other children didn't like her. Mary had no problem sharing a book with her, and the two spent the rest of recess together.

Abby's family owned a house not too far from Mary, on the southern end of Lovejoy Pond. The two became fast friends, and when the school year ended and summer arrived, Mary made frequent trips to Abby's to swim and play in the water. It pleased Bud that his daughter had a playmate and wouldn't be alone with only himself and Jim to keep her company.

It was a Friday in September of Mary's first grade year that Bud faced his first minor challenge in parenting. Mary got off the bus, and he could tell something was wrong. She didn't run up the steps like she normally did to give him a hug, but rather walked with her head down watching her feet.

"Hey, baby girl," Bud said. "What's wrong?"

"Nothing," she said. He motioned for her to sit next to him on the porch, but she continued towards the door.

"Mary? Aren't you going to sit and tell me about your day?"

"I don't know," she said.

"Have a seat," Bud told her patting the porch swing next to himself. She sat down next to him, swinging her legs but still not speaking. "Okay, what did you do today?"

"Nothing."

"Nothing? Okay, how's Abby?"

"I don't know."

"You don't, okay. Well, run along inside then and we'll talk more at dinner."

Mary went inside and up to her room. Bud was concerned and mentioned to Jim that something was bothering Mary, and the two of them would have to try and find out more at dinner. Jim said he would just sit and listen unless he were needed. It was a father's job to most of the prodding. The three sat down to dinner, but Bud waited until they were finished before questioning Mary about the day again.

"Would you tell us what's bothering you now, baby girl?"

"It's nothing," Mary said.

"If it's nothing then you should be able to tell us."

"The other kids were making fun of me and Abby."

"Oh, is that all? Well, don't let them get to you. You and Abby just ignore them and—"

"I'm not friends with Abby anymore, Daddy."

"What? Why not?"

"The other kids said she's ugly and a loser. And if I hang out with her I'm a loser too. I'm not a loser."

"No, you're not, but you shouldn't let them tell you what to think about Abby."

"If I'm friends with Abby, none of the other kids will like me."

"Ah, I see," Bud said. "Well, baby girl, you have a choice to make. Either, you can be friends with Abby and not worry about what the other kids think and just be yourself, or you can be what all the other kids want you to be and be friends with them instead of Abby."

"I can still be me. I just can't be friends with Abby."

"Do you like Abby?"

"Yes."

"Do you think Abby is ugly?"

"No."

"Do you think that you and Abby are losers?"

"No."

"Then it seems to me that by not being friends with Abby, you are being what the other kids want you to be. You aren't being who Mary is. My baby girl, my Mary, doesn't think Abby is ugly or a loser. My Mary likes Abby."

"But everyone will hate me, Daddy!"

"Would you rather Abby hate you?"

"No, I don't want Abby to hate me."

"Well, you're going to have to choose who is more important: Abby, or all the other kids. Someone is going to dislike you. But, if you just choose to be who you are, I think eventually all the kids who you would care to be friends with will decide you're not a loser."

"I don't know what to do, Daddy? What if Abby is a loser? I don't want to be a loser. What do I do?"

"Well, you get to choose. Do you want to be the Mary that is friends with Abby and doesn't care what anyone else thinks, or do you want to be the Mary that acts the way all the other kids want you to so that they'll be your friend?"

"I don't know."

Mary had finished her dinner, so Bud told her to clear her place at the table and head up to get ready for bed.

"You get changed, brush your teeth, and climb into bed. You can read until I come up to tuck you in, okay? And you can think about which Mary you want to be."

Mary kissed her grandfather on the cheek, told him she loved him, and headed up to bed. Jim watched her go, seeing the image from real life overlaid with a hundred memories of watching Teresa do the same as a child. He smiled, peering through the weary mist of the past before turning his attention back to the present.

"Good talk, Dad," Jim said to Bud.

"You think? I don't know that I got through to her," Bud said.

"Only time will tell. She has a good dad, who is very smart and cares about her very much. I think she'll figure it out."

"She has a smart Grandpa Jim, too. Don't think I've forgotten 'the easy choice is the hard way, and the hard choice is the easy way.' I've thought so much about that the last few years. I think I understand what you mean."

"Oh, and what did I mean, Bud?"

"I made my choice, what you called the easy one. I chose to live and raise Teresa's and my baby girl. It wasn't an easy choice, not really. The hardest part about it is that I have to make the same choice each and every day. The choice I made means I never stop choosing. Had I made the other choice, what you called the hard choice, it would have been the easy way out because I would never have to make the choice again."

Jim nodded and said, "Yes, the choice in that case would mean never having to face it again. But it's not the right choice. The right choice often means having to choose over and over again."

"I'm glad you were here to help me make the right choice, Jim."

"I'm glad too. I'm also glad I knew someone like your grandfather. I never thought much about the conditions of life, the mysteries if you will, until I met him. It was when he first started working here on the farm that my eyes were opened to the world around me. We were walking the farm, and he insisted we walk through the forest on the South part of the property, even though we only used it for cutting firewood at the time. He stopped and looked and studied and took his time. When I asked him what he was doing, he said he was thinking about the trees. He was thinking about their 'character.' That was the word he used: 'Character.' It was in that moment that I realized I had never wondered about my own character, let alone the character of the trees. I had never really thought much about the world in general. I took the way the world worked as a given, never bothering to ask 'why' or 'how.' It was your grandfather who taught me to learn, not only from myself, but from everyone and everything around me. I've tried every day since that to learn a little more about the way the world works."

"Yes," Bud said nodding. "Pa was good like that. He was always teaching, even when he wasn't talking. He was a masterful teacher, making you want to learn and forcing you to think."

"You asked me once if your grandfather believed in God. Do you remember?" Jim asked.

"Yes, I remember."

"For what it's worth, I think he did."

"What makes you think that?"

"Actually, something you said in your letter to your grandmother after he died. You said he had told you that the greatest thing a man can do is to love another with all his heart. That that is true greatness."

"Yes, he did say that."

"That is God, Bud. God is love, and God is great. Don't you see? John 3:16 – 'For God so loved the world, that he gave his only begotten Son, that whosoever believeth in him should not perish, but have everlasting life.' That is the greatest act ever recorded. That God would give his Son for us out of pure love so that we could go to heaven. I think your grandfather understood this better than any man I have ever known. It's not just about sacrifice, needless or wasteful sacrifice, but about giving of yourself for the people you truly care about. It's about making that choice, the choice to love, each and every day."

"You think that's what Pa meant?"

"I do, Bud. I can see it in the way he lived. The night you came here and were left on that doorstep next door, your grandfather made a choice. He made it in a second, without hesitation. He chose to love you. But he made that choice over and over each and every day until the moment he died. That, Bud, is greatness. It is the same choice you made for my daughter, and it's the same choice you make every day for Mary."

"And the same choice you make every day for us."

Jim's eyes teared up and he fumbled with his words. "Yes, Bud, the same. It's the same choice I make... I miss my wife. I miss my daughter. It's no secret that I'm tired. I'm tired from grief and from life. I'm tired of waiting to see them. But I choose to love who I can while I can, and that's you and Mary. You were right, the easy choice is hard because you have to make it over and over. It can be exhausting."

Bud stood and walked over behind Jim, putting his hand on his father–in–law's shoulder. He squeezed it gently and bent down and removed Jim's dishes, carrying them to the sink. Jim sat in silence as Bud washed them and put them away.

"For what it's worth, Jim," Bud said, "I'm glad Mary and I are here to help you make the right choice."

Jim smiled, and Bud headed up stairs to tuck Mary in for bed. When he entered her room, she was lying and reading quietly. He waited patiently for her to reach a spot where she could stop and put the book away. When she had, he turned off the light.

"Daddy?" Mary said, as he kissed her on the forehead.

"Yes, baby girl?"

"I want to be friends with Abby."

# 37

The phone rang, and Jim answered it. It was the principal of Mary's school, and she asked to meet with Bud as soon as he could come. It was the Monday after Mary had come home despondent from the other children's treatment of Abby.

Jim walked out to Bud, who was working on the farm, to relay the message. Bud put down what he was doing and made the drive to Mary's school. When Bud arrived, Mary was sitting in the principal's office.

Bud was informed by the principal that Mary had been rude to several of the other children. He asked the principal to start at the very beginning of the story. She said that as she understood it, Mary and Abby had been sitting by the school reading a book, when several other students had approached them. Mary had stood and announced in no uncertain terms that the other children were not allowed to play with them. When the other kids had asked why, Mary had informed them it was because they were bad kids and she and Abby wanted nothing to do with people like them. She had called them all "stupid."

Bud was confused. Why was Mary in trouble for standing up for herself and Abby? He was told by the principal that school policy was not to tolerate belittling of one student by another. Calling the other children 'bad' or 'stupid' was inappropriate behavior.

"We try to live by the Golden Rule here, Mr. Marshall," the principal said. "Do unto others as you would have them do unto you."

"And when someone has already treated you poorly? Should you let them do it again? From my understanding, those kids have already called Abby names. My daughter was standing up for a friend."

"Yes, so she claims. She would have done well to inform us of that incident when it happened. The other children deny any such thing occurred."

"And Abby? What does she say happened?"

"Abby has taken her friend's side of things, obviously. Unfortunately, on my end I can only go by what I can be sure has happened, and that is what your daughter said to those children today. Neither Mary nor Abby deny any of that. I will not justify their bad behavior by supposed bad behavior of another."

"You felt the need to call me all the way in here because Mary called other students a name?"

"No, Mr. Marshall," the principal said. "I called you in here because Mary was disrespectful when she was told she was wrong in the matter."

"Disrespectful how?" Bud asked.

"She told me she doesn't care what I or anyone else thinks. She said what she did was right and that I'm wrong."

Mary looked at her father from the chair in front of the principal's desk. She looked sad and confused.

"I happen to agree with my daughter," Bud said.

"Mr. Marshall, you need to understand—"

"No, I understand perfectly. You're the one that seems confused. My daughter stood up for a friend who had been treated poorly just last week by these children. I don't know who they are. I don't know their names — But I do know their type. I know their type very well. I'm extremely proud of my daughter for taking a stand against them. If more children were able to do that, the kind of thing you're worried about would happen a lot less. I can appreciate you're upset that she called them names, and that was inappropriate, but standing up for a friend is never wrong. And Mary was right, they are bad kids, at least in what they said about Abby last week."

"I don't think you're in a position to judge any child as good or bad, Mr. Marshall. Quite frankly, I know a little about your past, and you're not the one I would choose to be the arbiter of what is good and bad behavior in general."

"Then you would be wrong again. I'm the perfect person to judge what is good and what is bad because I have a greater appreciation and understanding of the nature of both good and evil than anyone you've likely ever known. I've made poor choices in my life, yes. But I've made good ones as well. I'm proud of the choice my daughter made today. If your school had more children making the choice she did, it would be better for it. Come on, baby girl, we're going home."

Bud took his daughter by the hand and walked out of the office. After they had climbed into the car and started up the road towards home, Bud told Mary that he didn't want her calling other children names or talking back to the principal or anyone else in charge.

"But Daddy, you said I was right," Mary said.

"You were right to stand up for Abby," Bud said. "You didn't need to call the other kids names to do it, and you certainly don't need to talk back to the principal."

"You talked back to her," Mary sulked.

"She's not my principal. You be respectful, baby girl, and if you have a problem with someone then you let them know in an adult and considerate way."

"Yes, Daddy."

After Mary had gone to bed that night, Bud sat down with Jim and told him everything that had happened. He sat, listening patiently for Bud to finish the whole story before saying anything.

"Do you understand good and evil, Bud?" Jim asked.

"I think so," Bud said.

"Tell me."

"Old Mr. LaVerdier told me once that he had a conversation with Pa about it. They talked about the monster inside... the ability to commit evil. I was asking Mr. LaVerdier if he thought I was a monster for what I'd done to Drake, or a hero for saving Teresa. He said Pa had once told him that we are each the mythological monster and we are each the hero sent to destroy it. The only question was which one would win."

"The idea being, that we are all capable of both good and evil."

"Yes, and that through our choices we determine which one is winning. It's an ongoing battle, I think. One day you can make a choice in which the monster wins and on another day, it's the hero who succeeds."

"And that day with Drake, Bud — which one won that day?"

"I wish I knew. I've thought so long about it and never come any closer to the truth. It feels almost like the hero unleashed the monster."

Jim furrowed his brow and rubbed his chin. He let out a long, deep sigh, but said nothing.

"You don't agree?" Bud asked. "You think people are inherently good or evil?"

"No," Jim said. "I'm just trying to reconcile what you're saying with my belief in God."

"You don't want to believe that God gave each of us both good and evil."

"No, I don't, Bud."

"But he must have, Jim. Even Satan is a fallen angel."

"Bud, are you saying this belief you have about the nature of good and evil makes you more of a believer in God?"

"I don't know if it makes me a believer in God. It does lead me to believe that whoever wrote the Bible had a better understanding of it than most of us. Look at the story of the garden of Eden and the tree of knowledge of good and evil. Whether the Bible is divine in nature, or a collection of parables, it is infinitely profound. The garden of Eden, surrounded by a wall, is a perfect paradise. And yet, evil finds its way in through the snake that persuades Eve to eat from the tree. Even in paradise, where everything seems perfect, one must be aware of evil."

"But Adam and Eve had no knowledge of evil before they ate from the tree."

"Very true, but the evil was already there. God told Adam and Eve not to eat from that tree. Had they not, they would have had no idea that the capacity for evil existed within themselves. They would have gone on living in paradise. Once they ate, they were cast out of paradise and were now forced to make their own choices. Every day from that day forward, they had to choose between good and evil."

"So, the Bible is telling of the time when humans became aware that they had the capacity for evil? The ability to sin?"

"Yes, if you believe the Bible is from God."

"And you don't?"

"Even if the Bible isn't from God, the story in Genesis suggests that the author had a philosophical understanding of good and evil and that both are already within each of us. The story of the garden of Eden is a perfect example of that. Eden is the ideal: a perfect place with walls to keep everyone within it safe. But even there, Adam and Eve aren't safe from evil, from sin. Because the possibility of sin lay within each of them."

"That is a terrifying thought," Jim said.

"Yes, but also a liberating one, don't you think? If the nature of evil is such that each individual has the possibility of controlling it, then it isn't some external force to be feared."

"No, but it's an internal force to be feared."

"Not feared, but understood. We have no need to fear something we can control. We have the capacity for evil, but we have the choice not to act on it because we also have the capacity for good. Once I realized I had the choice, I could move forward from what I'd done. If evil was something I had no control over, just something you either are or aren't, I would have been left with no option."

"Do you think there are people who don't realize they have the ability to do good?"

"I do," Bud said. "I saw them in The Center. They had given themselves over to the monster inside. The hero may still be in them, but they no longer have any knowledge of it. I think that's what happened to Smitty too."

"Your friend when you were younger?"

"Yes. No one ever believed in Smitty. No one told him that he could be anything other than what he was. So, when he got in trouble he just believed that's who he was. When it came time for him to decide who he was, the choice in his mind had already been made for him. He was playing his part in the life that he felt had been chosen for him. Pa told me not to be changed by the world, but I don't think that means that you should never change. Sometimes choosing means change. Smitty was changed by the world, simply because he refused to make the choice for himself."

"So Smitty let the evil within himself win."

"I'm not even sure he let it win. He may not have even realized there was another choice. One has to recognize the true nature of good and evil, that they exist together within you, to be able to choose one over the other."

"And that's why you told Mary's principal that you understood that nature better than anyone she's known."

Bud nodded. He went to the cupboard and got two glasses, got some ice from the freezer, filled them with water from the tap, and brought them into the living room for Jim and himself. He sat and took a long swig from his, letting the cold radiate through his body.

"And what about those of us who don't think we're capable of great evil?" Jim asked.

"You're wrong," Bud said, and he took another swallow of his water.

"How do you know?"

"Close your eyes, Jim," Bud said. Jim put his glass on the table next to his chair, closed his eyes and leaned back. Bud spoke slowly, taking his time with each word to give Jim the opportunity to paint each stroke in his mind. "Imagine yourself along the far bank of that pool by the waterfall. You're watching your daughter sitting on the log, talking to Drake. She seems agitated and he seems angry. She stands to leave, but he grabs her, pulling her back. He kisses her roughly. She breaks off the kiss and slaps him hard across the face. He lashes out at her with his hand, knocking her to the ground. She looks stunned and frightened laying on the ground. A wicked smile crosses his face and he jumps on top of her. She starts fighting back and he strikes her again. She relents, stops fighting, and goes limp. He starts undoing his pants. You know exactly what he's planning to do. He's going to hurt your daughter, Jim. He's going to hurt a person that you love."

Jim grew more and more restless in his chair as Bud continued to set the scene. A look of pain and anger washed over his
previously peaceful face. Bud watched his inner struggle. He
didn't speak for some time, letting Jim wrestle with his feelings.

"What would you do, Jim?" Bud asked finally. "Could you
hurt that boy?"

"Yes," Jim said. "Yes, I could hurt him."

"Keep your eyes closed. Run to them. Run over and throw
him off of your daughter. Help her up Jim. He attacks you from
behind, hitting you hard. There's a lot of pain. The two of you
wrestle on the ground and you find yourself on top of him. He
sinks he teeth into your arm sending waves up pain shooting up
it and radiating through your body. Do you want to kill him
Jim?"

"Yes."

"Now, don't."

"What?"

"Don't kill him, Jim. Don't do it in your mind. Don't even
strike him. Stop yourself from doing it." Jim opened his eyes and
looked confused at Bud. "Are you finding it harder to not kill him
than to kill him?"

"Yes."

"Now you've found the monster."

Tears began to form in Jim's eyes. Bud walked over to him,
picked up the water from the table and handed it to him.

"Take a sip, Jim," Bud said. Jim raised the glass to his lips.

"Why was it so hard to stop?" Jim asked.

"It's not until we realize our capacity for evil, that being good
really means anything. Anyone can be good if they believe they
couldn't possibly do anything bad. Mary's principal has never
considered that an alternative exists to 'Do unto others as you
would have them do unto you.' For her, the idea that someone
would choose to do something evil hasn't entered her mind,

because she doesn't understand that she, herself, has that capability. Everyone that says, 'I could never do that' or 'I would never do that' hasn't truly explored the depths of their inner being. I have, and not by choice the first time. I've been to hell and seen the monster within myself. My inner hero has challenged him more than once since that day by the waterfall, and won each time. There were many times in The Center when other juveniles would taunt me, or hit me, that I wanted to strike back. I wanted to inflict pain upon them. But I didn't. I wanted to hit Drake's father on my wedding day. Again, I beat the monster back. Why was it so hard for you to stop the monster just now in your mind? Because you hadn't truly realized he was even there yet. The monster is strong, very strong. But if you can beat him in your mind, you can beat him if it ever comes to it in real life. But for those who refuse to admit that a monster even exists within themselves... Well, you just saw how hard it is to defeat in the moment."

"I think I understand now what you meant when you said the hero unleashed the monster," Jim said. "You wanted to help Teresa acting from a place of good, but because you didn't fully understand it or recognize it, the monster came out."

"Failure to recognize evil — to admit that it even exists — means that it will ultimately win. You can't fight what you don't know, or won't at least recognize is there in the first place."

They sat and finished drinking their water. Jim stood to take his glass into the kitchen, but paused on the way and looked down at Bud.

"Thank you," Jim said. "I think you just made me a better Christian."

"How's that?" Bud asked.

"'Yea, though I walk through the valley of the shadow of death, I will fear no evil: for thou art with me; thy rod and thy staff they comfort me.' I now understand where the evil lies, and with the strength of God, I will be able to defeat it. For why would I have feared evil as death approached if it weren't the evil within myself, the sin, that might keep me from heaven? Now, before my time ends on this earth, I can face that evil and overcome it. That brings me peace."

Jim put his glass in the sink, said goodnight and headed for the stairs. Bud followed several minutes later. He got ready for bed and then pulled his old notebook out and wrote down everything from the day.

The next morning, Bud walked downstairs to find Jim already in the kitchen making coffee. It was unlike Jim to rise before the rest of the house, so Bud was a little concerned.

"You're up early, Jim," Bud said.

"Yes, well, our discussion last night made me realize a few things. I realized that lately, I haven't been living as much as I've just been waiting to die. I've spent my life paying others to do for me. I've never built anything. I've never created anything. I've never made... anything."

Bud smirked and his eye twinkled in the light of the kitchen. "So, you made... coffee?" he asked.

"No. Well, yes I did. But that's not why I'm up. I want to start doing again. If I'm going to live, I want to face the monster and win. And lately my monster has been apathy. I've been content to let the moments slip by until I pass out of the world. So starting today, I want to start working on the farm with you, if you'll have me. I know it's not my farm anymore, not that it ever really was. Buck built it into anything real to begin with, and you've brought it back to life. I've merely been an outside observer. I want to be involved in the work for once. I want to bring meaning to what's left of my life, so that when I die, I can feel like I took part in living."

Bud understood what Jim was saying. Money had never been a real concern for him and Nancy, and so for him the farm had merely existed. In looking deep within himself, Jim had found the thing that he had been lacking in his life: a purpose. Everyone needs a reason to get up in the morning, or the simple act of being becomes the chore. Bud walked over to the cupboard, removed a coffee cup, and held it up for Jim to fill.

"Alright, Jim," he said, "let's get started."

# 38

Jim's age was immediately apparent when he began working on the farm. He was weak and quick to tire, but his spirits were lifted simply by attempting the work. Every night he was exhausted, but in a different way than he was used to. He was tired from the work, but he felt accomplished rather than feeling worn out simply by living.

It was several years later, after a long summer day of bringing in hay from the fields, when Jim stopped Bud in the barn before heading back up to the house.

"Thank you, Bud," he said.

"For what?" Bud asked.

"For reminding me that life is more than passing the days. Life is about setting a goal and striving to reach it. I needed a purpose with Nancy and Teresa gone, and simply living for you and Mary wasn't enough... for any of us. Thank you for helping me reach my goal of being a real part of running the farm."

Jim worked until the end of his days. It was on an April morning, shortly after Mary's ninth birthday, that Bud came downstairs and didn't find Jim in the kitchen. He had passed peacefully in his sleep. Bud smiled as he wiped away a tear, content in the thought that Jim had found peace within himself and was confident enough to face his maker and be judged for his life on earth.

Jim was buried next to his wife in the cemetery near the church in town. Mary stood with her father by the side of her grandfather's grave, wearing a black dress and holding a single white rose. Bud wrapped his arm around his daughter and held her close, knowing she was all he had left in the world.

Mary didn't cry. To Bud, she seemed oddly detached from the whole event. They drove home from the funeral in silence, and once inside Mary headed straight up to her room. Bud checked on her later and found her playing with her dolls on her bed.

"Baby girl, would you like to talk?" Bud asked.

"No, I'm okay," she said.

"Are you sure? It's a sad day. I imagine you have some questions."

"Not really, I'm fine."

Bud turned to leave, but stopped in the doorway. He watched his daughter play for several minutes. There was no joy in her movements. While the motions were there, there was nothing behind them that suggested she was even aware of what she was doing. He stepped back into her room, walked over, and sat on the end of her bed.

"It's okay to be sad," Bud said.

"What's the point?"

"What do you mean, 'what's the point?'"

"What's the point in being sad, Dad? Grandpa Jim is gone. There's nothing anyone can do about it. Being sad doesn't do anything."

"Are you sad?"

"No, not really," Mary said, shrugging.

"Remember how I've always told you that it's not okay to lie? That's not just for lying to others, baby girl. It's also very important that you never lie to yourself. 'What's the point in being sad?' The point is about living the truth. The one thing we can do with Grandpa Jim gone is to grieve, but you can't do that if you can't find the truth of your feelings. So, be honest with yourself, how do you feel?"

Mary looked up at her father and tears began to form at the corners of her blue eyes. "I'm mad," she said. "I'm mad that he left us. It's not fair. My life's not fair. Not only do I not have a mother, but now I lose Grandpa Jim too?"

Mary rolled over and sobbed violently into her pillow. Bud moved up the bed and rubbed her back with his hand. It was hard, as a father, to watch his daughter in pain and to not be able to do anything for her. He waited for her to calm down, and then sat her up and faced her, holding her hand in his.

"Grandpa Jim didn't leave us, not really," he said. "As long as we keep him in our hearts, he is always with us. The same is true for your mother. I'm sorry that you never got to know her, but I can promise you that she loved you. I could tell that from the moment she held you in her arms, for the brief time that she could. It's okay to be mad, and to be sad, and anything else you're feeling. There is an emptiness that Grandpa Jim has left in our lives, and it will take time for us to feel normal again. But as long as we love each other, we can get through it together."

"But what if I lose you too?"

Bud pulled his daughter into an embrace and held her tightly. The fear of leaving her alone in the world was real and palpable in his own heart. How does one promise something that isn't his to guarantee? How does one promise an uncertain future? Bud offered the only thing he had to give.

"I promise that I will do everything I can to not leave you for a long, long time."

"Sometimes I wish I had a mother and a father like everybody else," she said.

"You have a mother, baby girl, she's just not with us here on earth anymore."

"Yeah, but it's not the same."

"I know it's not."

Bud and Mary held each other and cried together for some time after that. They spent the rest of the afternoon sharing their favorite stories about Grandpa Jim, and Bud even shared some with Mary about her mother. Through their pain, they grew closer together as father and daughter.

Jim had willed everything he had to Bud, who was amazed at how much money his father–in–law had in savings. Either Jim or Nancy had clearly come from money. The way Buck had managed the farm, as well as selling the far acreage to developers, had either added to the family wealth, or at least kept them from cutting into what they had to begin with. Bud realized, looking at the sum he was about to receive, that he was set for the rest of his life and would surely be able to will a handsome sum to his daughter as well.

The money gave him comfort in the knowledge that even if something happened to him, Mary would be taken care of financially. He needed a will of his own, however, and to decide on a guardian to watch after Mary should anything happen. It was something he would have to carefully consider.

Bud was terrified that something would happen to him and that he would leave his daughter alone in the world without anyone. Every time he pondered the problem, he reached the same conclusion: he could trust Gregg. Gregg had been a friend to Teresa early in life, and Bud's best friend other than Jim after his wife died. When Bud asked Gregg and his wife to be Godparents for Mary, they were honored and accepted immediately. They had a family of their own, but Bud had no doubt in his mind that should the unfortunate happen, Mary would be loved and taken care of.

The second Friday in May, Mary once again got off the bus visibly distraught. This time, she had tears on her face already as she climbed the front steps where Bud waited on the porch. She was carrying a painted clay pot with soil in it.

"What's the matter, baby girl?" Bud asked.

"This," she said holding up the pot.

"What? It's lovely."

Mary had painted the pot green and then covered it with sunflowers all around the outside.

"It's for Mother's Day," Mary said.

"Oh, I see."

"One of the boys said, 'Why is Mary even bothering to paint a pot, she doesn't even have a mother?' I said that I do too have a mother, but he said not really because she's dead and can't see it anyway so what's the point?"

"Well, that wasn't very nice of him."

"I know. The teacher told him so, and he got in trouble for it. But he's right, isn't he? What good is this for Mom now?"

"I think she would love it. We'll take it to her Sunday morning on Mother's Day, before church."

"Church?" Mary asked.

"Yes. You haven't been going, and I was thinking it's time you started again. I thought I might go with you, since Grandpa Jim is no longer here to take you."

"You want to go to church with me?"

"Well, I don't think you should have to stop going, and I certainly don't want you to have to go alone. So, if it's okay with you, I'd like to join you."

"Okay. Thank you, Dad."

"You're welcome, baby girl."

Early Sunday morning, Bud and Mary drove down to the church and parked. They walked to the cemetery, and Bud led his daughter to her mother's grave. It was the first time Mary had ever been there. Bud had wanted to wait until he felt she was ready, but now he thought he had protected her for too long. Seeing where her mother was laid to rest and being able to visit the site would hopefully be good for her.

"Reese, Mary and I are here. She has something for you," Bud said.

"Happy Mother's Day, Mom, I painted this for you, and I planted a sunflower. It should grow at some point," Mary said kneeling and placing the pot in front of her mother's stone.

The two stood in silence for several minutes and then Bud kissed his fingers and placed his hand on the stone to say goodbye. Mary copied her father and did the same. Father and daughter then walked back and into the church for the Sunday service.

After church, while walking to the car, Bud heard a voice calling his name. He turned to see Mabel half walking, half running, up to him and Mary.

"Hi, Bud! It's good to see you again," she said.

"Hi, Mabel. I didn't know you were still in town."

"I wasn't. I left for quite a while there, but I'm back now. Can't stay away I guess," she giggled. "I was sorry I missed Teresa's service. I was out of the state and couldn't get away to make it back. Is this her daughter?"

"Yes, this is Mary. Mary, this is Mabel. She was good friends with your mother when they were younger."

Mary and Mabel said hello. Mabel smiled awkwardly, and then turned back to Bud.

"She's a beautiful girl. Looks a lot like her mother, except for the eyes. She definitely has your eyes."

"Thank you," Bud said. "Do you have any children?"

"No, no, not me. I wanted kids, but my ex–husband didn't."

"Oh, you were married. I didn't know."

"Yes. Didn't last long, though. We just wanted different things, you know how it is."

Bud didn't know, but didn't say so. He just nodded and said, "Sure."

"Well, it's good to see you again, Bud," Mabel said. "Maybe we could get together for coffee or dinner or something now that I'm back in town."

"Oh, well, that would be nice, Mabel, but things are a little hectic right now. Jim just recently passed away, and we're still finding our footing."

"Oh goodness, I had no idea. I'm so sorry! Well, here, let me give you my number, and if you need anything you can give me a call. And maybe when things settle down we can get together."

Bud took the paper on which Mabel wrote her number. "Thanks, I appreciate it," he said.

As they drove along the Pond Road towards Hales Road, Mary turned to her father and said, "That woman seems to like you."

"Who? Mabel?"

"Yes. You don't want to go to dinner with her?"

"It's complicated, baby girl."

"Why? You don't like her?"

"She's a very nice girl, at least she was when I knew her. But she's looking for something I can't give her. She wants a husband and a family."

"But she could be your wife," Mary said.

"I already have a wife, just like you already have a mother."

Mary said nothing until they pulled into the driveway back at the farm. Before they got out of the car she turned to her father and said, "Dad, don't you want someone to keep you from being lonely? Wouldn't it be nice to have someone to cheer you up when you're sad, or just be there when you need them?"

"I know it's hard to understand, but your mother is still that for me. When I'm afraid, she is my strength. When the world grows dim and I'm lonely or sad, she still cheers me up. I made a promise to her on our wedding day to love her forever. It's a promise I intend to keep."

"You don't have to stop loving her, Dad — but do you really think Mom would expect you to go on without anyone? Would she really want that for you, or for me?"

Mary climbed out of the car and shut the door loudly. She stomped up the front steps and into the house. Bud sat a long time in the car thinking. He wondered if he were doing the right thing by choosing not to remarry. Mabel wasn't the only choice; there were other women out there too. Perhaps Mary would be better off with a female figure in her life. Was he doing her an injustice?

Mary was approaching the time in her life when she would be going through changes. They were changes that Bud, as a man, couldn't possibly relate to or fully understand. He planned to do his best to guide her, but a woman would have a far easier time relating to Mary during puberty.

It would also provide someone to be there for Mary that she knew and was close to in the event of something terrible happening to him. Bud went back and forth, not sure if any of those were the right reasons to take another wife.

In Bud's mind, the only real reason to marry was for love. Committing your life to another is a choice not to be taken lightly. It seemed to him that Mabel had done just that, and her marriage had resulted in divorce. The last thing Bud wanted was to marry for the wrong reasons, but he knew in his heart that he would never love another woman.

That night, Bud tucked Mary in to bed and explained to her that while he understood she was having a hard time with the loss of her grandfather on top of not having a mother around, he couldn't simply take another wife to replace the one she had lost the day she was born.

Marriage, he explained, was something very serious, and he would be doing himself and Mary a disservice by not treating it that way. He had made a vow to Teresa, in front of God and all of their friends and family. That was a sacred thing, and not something to be abandoned on a whim.

Mary listened to her father's explanation with a sour look on her face. She was frustrated, angry, and confused. It wasn't fair that the other kids had mothers and she didn't. Why couldn't her father see that he wasn't being fair to her? Didn't he love her?

"So I'll never have a mother," she said.

"You have a mother, baby girl."

"No, I don't! She's dead! And you love her more than me! I hate you!"

There were few things at that point in Bud's life that could have reduced him to nothingness. The words, "I hate you," from his daughter did just that. For several seconds he couldn't breathe or see. He was staggering in the dark, grasping for a hand, an arm, anything to hold him up. It was the memory of Teresa that finally lifted him back to reality. He saw her face in the face of his daughter, angry and disappointed in him. He found fresh air and sucked it greedily into his lungs and smiled.

"You are so much like her, you know?" he said. "There are only two people I have known that could break me with those words: her and you. It's true, I've never loved anyone more than your mother... not until you. If I could grab hold of the earth and spin it backwards to the moment when she first held you in her arms and freeze time I would. I would live in that moment, that perfect moment when I had both of you, forever. But I can't do that, baby girl. All I can do is be the best father I can be for you. Even if I married someone else... Even if I married Mabel, or any other woman, I couldn't replace the mother you lost. She was as wonderful and unique as you are. I couldn't love another woman as much as her any more than I could love another child as much as you. But if you want, I will go to your mother's grave with you every Sunday — and I will wait while you talk to her for as long as you want to. You can tell her your hopes, your fears, and your dreams. And she will listen, for as long as you want to talk. And I promise you, she loves you as much as I do, which is more than anyone has ever been loved throughout all of human history. Beyond that I can't promise you a mother. I'm sorry the world stole her from you. I can't tell you why it happened or provide you any comfort for such an unjust act. The world isn't fair. That's a lesson everyone has to learn eventually. I'm sorry you had to learn it the day you were born. I can tell you from experience that the world, in all its injustice, doesn't get to choose how you respond. You get to choose, and if you'll take my advice, you'll choose to find strength and courage when the world treats you unfairly. Because the other option is to choose to play the victim, blaming every trouble of your life on the circumstances beyond your control. I promise you that people who do that never amount to much. But my baby girl, the Mary I know, is destined for greatness."

Mary looked up at her father with wondering eyes. Her anger had slowly melted away as she realized her pain was mirrored in the pain of her father. Tears filled her eyes and she lunged forward and wrapped her arms around him.

"I'm sorry, Dad," she said. "I don't really hate you. I could never hate you. I love you."

"I know, baby girl," he said. "I know. I love you too."

The sunflower in the pot Mary had placed on Teresa's grave grew and bloomed over the Sundays to follow. On each one, Mary stood at the grave and recounted her week for her mother. Bud waited patiently at a distance, being sure to give his daughter her privacy.

When Mary had finished, they would switch places and Bud would talk to his wife for a few minutes. He would tell her his struggles and successes and just how much he missed her. He concluded each time with the same words: "I loved you before I knew you, and I will love you through eternity."

# 39

**M**ountains are not reduced to dust by the acute force of even the harshest storms, but rather by the persistent and continuous wear of time, wind, and water. That is how meandering rivers carve canyons of solid rock, and how towering peaks that scrape the heavens are reduced to waste and rubble.

And so it was, given the time and constant pressure, Gregg persuaded Bud to run for town manager. Mary was fourteen was and going to be entering high school, and Bud felt he could afford the time away from home. With overwhelming support, Bud was elected and took his place leading the small town in 2001.

Mary was proud and excited that her father had a place of prominence in the local community. Her dad was someone everyone was going to look to for leadership and decision making. Bud had regular meetings to attend every other Tuesday night with the board of selectmen, as well as scheduled meetings with others throughout the week. Mary made a point of going with him to the Tuesday night meetings whenever she could. Many of the other meetings, however, she was left on her own at the house.

The last several years, Mary had found herself spending a lot of time at Abby's home on Lovejoy Pond. Abby's mother had taken it upon herself to help guide Mary through the more confusing parts of female teenage development. Bud was glad his daughter had an adult female she could turn to with questions that he felt inadequate to explain. Abby had developed physically before Mary which, while somewhat disappointing, gave Mary a close friend to be an advanced guide to the changes she would soon be making.

Starting at Maranacook High School was a double–edged sword. While Mary received some notoriety from her dad's position as town manager, not all of it was good. Since Maranacook combined students from the primary schools of several nearby areas, not all the kids were from Mary's town; and so not all of their parents had the benefit of knowing Bud personally. The story of Bud, Drake, and Teresa wasn't so distant in the past that everyone's parents had simply forgotten about it. More than once, Mary heard comments wondering how her town could have selected a murderer as town manager.

Mary had a basic understanding of what her father had done. He had sat her down before she entered the Maranacook Middle School in an attempt to get ahead of the inevitable gossip. Children in middle school are somewhat less privy to the discussions of adults, and so the rumor mill regarding her dad had been relatively quiet during her three years there, and she hadn't heard talk like she heard now in the high school.

While her father hadn't shared details, Mary knew enough to know that what her father had done may have been wrong, but it was for a good reason. He had done his time in the juvenile center in South Portland, as well as his probation, and while he could never take back what he'd done, he was trying to make up for his mistakes. She wasn't ashamed of her father, but the whispers behind her back had a grating effect.

After two weeks of ignoring comments, Mary decided that she ought to say something to her father. When she got off the bus, Bud was sitting on the porch, waiting as he always did. Just like usual, she sat down next to him and began telling him about her day. At first, she only mentioned classes, what she was learning, and the work she had been assigned

"And there's one last thing," she said looking at Bud out of the corner of her eye. "It's not really even worth mentioning."

Bud raised an eyebrow. "It sounds like it is. What is it?"

"Some of the kids, not ones from around here, mind you, but some of them keep talking about you. They keep asking how our town could have made a... well, a murderer the town manager."

Bud nodded. He wasn't at all surprised that talk of what he had done eventually infiltrated Mary's world. He was sorry that his becoming town manager is what likely tipped the scales. Perhaps anonymity would have been a more prudent path, but he wasn't one to sit still, and not being involved offered him zero opportunity at absolution within the community.

"Do you think your father is a bad person?" He asked. "Be honest with yourself, now."

"No Dad, you're a wonderful person. I know you're not perfect, but you try and you do everything for me that you can. Now you're doing what you can for the town. What you did may have been horrible, but why you did it — why you did it wasn't. I don't think you're a bad person."

"Well, then that's all that matters to me. I know that doesn't help you with what the other kids are saying, but you need to know that it doesn't bother me. If you're worried about my feelings, don't. If you're worried about how what I did affects how others see you..." Bud took a deep breath, and sighed. "Well, I'm sorry, but it probably will. It's not fair, it may not be right, but it is reality. Some people, many people actually, are going to judge you by who your parents are. All I can do for you is to keep trying to show people that the image they may have of who I am isn't right. I'll keep trying to show them the person that I know myself to be. And you just keep doing the same for yourself. Eventually, either people will recognize who you are, or you'll stop caring what they think."

"That's all you can do, huh?" Mary said looking somewhat disappointed. It all sounded like a lot of work with an uncertain outcome to her. The idea that one could spend years working to show the world the person they truly are and that others wouldn't see it anyway was disheartening.

"We could go into town and get ice cream," Bud offered his daughter with a smile.

"Ice cream?" She said. "How's ice cream going to help?"

"Don't you like ice cream?"

"Yeah, but—"

"Good, let's go."

Smiling at the absurdity of the idea that getting ice cream would be some kind of cure–all for the situation, Mary climbed in the car with her father. They drove into town to the ice cream stand, and each ordered a sundae. The sunlight shimmered on the water as the two strolled down Main St. to where it flowed from Pocasset Lake under the road and into Androscoggin Lake. Father and daughter sat on a bench by the edge of the water, enjoying a mild September evening together.

Mary was about to thank her father for the ice cream when another man walked up and began talking to Bud. They began discussing town matters. Mary tuned the man out as he rambled on angrily about how poorly the town was being managed: taxes, regulations, and on and on. Her father was listening politely to the man's concerns and doing his best to answer his questions. Mary sensed the man relax as the conversation with her father continued. Eventually, he thanked Bud and went on his way.

"He seemed upset," Mary said once he'd gone.

"Yes, they usually are at first," Bud agreed. "No one wants to talk with the town manager because they're happy with how things are going. They want to talk to the town manager because they feel something is wrong."

"Doesn't that get old, Dad?"

"Well, yes and no. I work for them, baby girl. It's my job to listen to their concerns and take them into account when making decisions that affect the whole town. I have to do my best to serve everyone's interests."

"That sounds impossible. How can you possibly make everyone happy?"

"I can't make everyone happy. I probably can't really make anyone truly happy, but I can do my best not to make anyone unhappy."

"How do you do that? Not make anyone unhappy?"

"By not doing anything I don't think we have to do. It would be easy to say that the town should have this or that — but everything costs money, which means taxes. If we're going to spend folks' tax money, I think it should be on things that we need to spend it on and that benefit all of us together."

"Like what?"

"Well, for example plowing the roads. One of the items that gentleman was upset about was that plowing costs are increasing this season. Once I explained that much of the increased budget cost was due to the increase in fuel prices, he understood."

"Sounds like town manager is a lot like head of the complaint department, Dad."

Bud laughed. "In some ways, yes it is. I spend quite a bit of my time resolving disputes, explaining decisions, and addressing the concerns of townspeople. I suppose I've earned that. For years, I was one of the townspeople in the meetings complaining and asking questions."

After they finished their ice cream, they returned to the car and drove home. Mary had seen a different side of her father that evening: one where he put the concerns of others above his own. She felt she could handle a little gossip from people ignorant of who her father was if her father could handle the constant barrage of people around town clambering for his attention. Murderer? The idea would be laughable to anyone who knew her father and saw how calmly and patiently he had dealt with that irate individual.

Later that week, when Mary once again overheard someone talking about her dad, she decided to be proactive.

She turned to the individual and said, "You're not very smart, are you? First of all, you don't know my father at all. If you did, you'd know he's nothing like what you're describing. But if he were, do you think it would be smart to go around talking about him like that? You think it's a good idea to taunt and mock murderous criminals? Oooh, doesn't sound so smart to me. You should probably find something else to talk about, because right now you sound like a complete idiot."

Mary walked off smiling, very pleased with herself. She was excited to get home and tell her dad how she had handled the situation. When she got off the bus, her dad was waiting for her on the porch, but there was a blonde woman standing and talking to him. She was tall and athletic, with blue eyes, and a pretty face. Mary walked cautiously up the stairs, catching part of the conversation as she passed.

"I just don't see why we have to do it now," the woman said.

"Well, Ms. Pruitt, if we don't update the equipment, the fire department won't have the proper tools to do their job. I for one, don't want to be responsible if they're unable to adequately fight a fire or rescue an individual in trouble."

"But wouldn't it be acceptable to wait until—"

"Excuse me, I'm sorry, Ms. Pruitt, my daughter's home from school. Pardon me for just a minute."

Bud walked over and kissed his daughter on the cheek.

"I'm sorry, baby girl, this will only take a minute. I'll catch up with you about your day as soon as I'm finished, okay?"

"Yeah, of course," Mary said. "I have homework I should get started on anyway. I'll be up in my room."

"All right, I'll come up as soon as I'm done."

Mary walked up to her room, frustrated that she couldn't talk to her father like she normally did. Her dad didn't come right up either. He stood talking to Ms. Pruitt for the better part of two hours. By the time she left, it was time for him to start making dinner. He poked his head into her room and apologized again and said they could talk over their meal. Mary just waved him off. By that point, she didn't feel like talking.

When dinner was ready, Mary was more interested in the woman on the porch than what she had initially wanted to tell her father.

"Who was that woman?" she asked.

"Sue Pruitt. Nice enough woman, but she seems to find something she needs to discuss every single week. It's enough to drive you crazy."

"She was here a long time."

"I'm sorry about that. She's a talker."

Mary decided to let it go. She told her father about her day, and he was proud of her for handling the kid at school, but he warned her not to even appear like she was making threats against anyone.

"I know that's not what you were doing," he said, "but taken the wrong way, it could seem like you were threatening that your dad might kill anyone that said something bad about him."

Mary rolled her eyes, but she understood what her dad meant. She said she would tone it down just a little next time, but hoped she wouldn't have to deal with the situation again anyway.

The next week went by smoothly enough. Bud was able to meet his daughter on the porch and have their usual talk, and Mary's week had gone by without anything too traumatic — for a teenaged girl anyway. Sue Pruitt did interrupt Bud on the farm one day while Mary was at school. She also kept him late after the Tuesday meeting asking questions, but Mary had stayed home anyway so it didn't really affect her. The only real trouble Mary had was with her friend Abby.

Abby had developed from the freckle–faced nerd into a busty, fair–skinned, and very attractive young woman. She was garnering the attention of quite a few high school boys. It didn't bother Mary that boys were interested in her friend, but she was a bit jealous of the lost time. With her father so involved with his duties as town manager, Mary would have liked to spend more time with Abby, but she was too busy going on dates. On one particular Friday, Mary suggested the two girls get together that weekend to hang out, but Abby said she couldn't because she was going out with a tall sophomore boy with "dreamy eyes."

Mary returned home discouraged, and joined her dad on the porch and to share the news of the day with him. She was just getting to the disappointment with Abby when a car pulled up. Sue Pruitt got out and waved at the two of them. Mary was rankled by the sudden arrival, crossed her arms over her chest, and scowled.

"Hi, Sue, what can I do for you?" Bud called from the porch.

"Sue? You call her 'Sue' now?" Mary asked, disgusted.

"She told me I should call her 'Sue,'" Bud said. "Be polite."

"I just wanted to bring you this apple pie to thank you for taking the time to answer all of my concerns the other night," Sue Pruitt said, climbing the front steps and handing Bud a box. "Also, we're having a pot luck tomorrow night to raise money for the library. I was hoping you might make an appearance — maybe say a few words about the importance of keeping the library open."

Mary rolled her eyes, but Bud said, "I'd be happy to."

"Wonderful," Sue said. "Okay, well, I can see you're busy so I'll leave you alone. I'll see you tomorrow night."

"See you tomorrow," Bud nodded as Sue tread back down the stairs and drove off in her car.

"Really, Dad?" Mary said. "Another night with Sue Pruitt? What, does she like you or something?"

"I'm sorry, a pot luck for the library is something I should at least pop my head into. Sue is just an interested citizen like myself."

"Yeah, interested in my dad. How old is she anyway?"

"She's a bit younger than me — probably mid to late thirties."

"So, she likes you."

"She doesn't know me Mary, not beyond being town manager anyway."

"She's single?"

"Yes, as far as I know she's not married."

"Do you like her?"

"Not in that way Mary, no. She's a nice enough woman, but to be honest, the incessant questions and concerns from her are very tiring."

Mary was sure this was all a part of Sue trying to get closer to her father. Who could blame the woman? Her dad was an important man in the town, handsome, and well off. He was a catch if there ever was one. Mary suggested the questions might stop if her father asked Sue Pruitt out on a date, but Bud wanted nothing to do with that. He didn't think Sue was interested in him in that way, and he certainly wasn't interested in her.

Insisting that her father start dating certainly wasn't going to work. Relenting, Mary shifted the subject to Abby and all the boys that were becoming interested in her.

"It's not that I mind her dating, it's just hard to find time to spend with her anymore, and with all your meetings—"

"You are left all alone," Bud said, finishing her sentence.

"Yeah. It's fine, I can entertain myself. I've always been good at that. It would just be nice to have someone to talk to."

"I'm sorry, baby girl, this town manager thing has taken up far more of my time than I ever realized it would."

"I'm not saying this to make you feel bad, Dad. I think it's great that you're the town manager. You're doing important stuff, and you seem to be good at it. I watched that man the other day start off so frustrated, and after talking to you he seemed content, almost happy. I just don't want Abby to leave me behind."

"If Abby is a true friend, she won't do that. You're at that age though, where guys and girls take a more serious interest in one another. If boys are interested in Abby, I'm sure she's enjoying the attention."

"I think sometimes she's more interested in the attention than the boys," Mary said, rolling her eyes.

"Let me tell you something your great grandfather told me a long time ago. We were in the forest cutting firewood, and he asked me to look around and tell him what I saw. So, I told him trees, of course. He asked me what kind of trees, and I said there were all kinds. Then he told me there were two types of trees: deciduous and evergreens—"

"Dad, I learned about this in science class a long time ago."

"Oh, well then, how about you tell me the difference between the two."

"All right. Deciduous trees are the ones that change color in the fall and lose their leaves for the winter. When it gets colder or dryer, they have less capacity to photosynthesize food so they store their nutrients in their roots and go dormant for the winter. One of the first chemicals to be turned into a stored nutrient is chlorophyll, which makes the leaves green, and that's why they change color. Evergreens typically have finer leaves, in the shape of needles, which are better suited for hard climates, so they continue to produce food year–round and remain green."

"Very good, baby girl. Now your great–grandpa compared these two types of trees to people — said we're essentially the same. There are people that when the world around them changes, they'll react to the world and are changed themselves, just as the deciduous trees are. Especially when times get hard, they'll shut down and go dormant until the world around them improves. Other people trust to their own character to get through the hard times. These people are like the evergreens, who refuse to be changed by the world."

"Sounds like Great–Grandpa was an interesting guy. What did you say when he told you that?"

"Being the obstinate youth I was, I pointed out that deciduous trees are hard woods and evergreens are soft woods. I suggested hard woods were stronger than soft woods. Your Great–Grandpa said I was right — deciduous trees are harder, but only at their heart. He reminded me what happens to a deciduous tree in a strong wind storm: they break. While evergreens may have a rough exterior, they are soft at heart — and as a result a storm has to tear them up by the roots to kill them. He said that if I could be like the evergreen, hard on the outside but soft at heart and rely on my character to survive — If I refused to be changed by the world around me, I could get through anything life throws at me."

"So," Mary said, thinking, "you think Abby is letting the world change her?"

"Only Abby could say for sure," Bud said. "She's going through changes physically, hormonally, and emotionally as it is.

I don't know what it's like to be a young girl, but I'm sure it's a confusing time regardless. My point in telling you the story, is that this time could be tough on you as well, and I don't want you to let it dictate to you who you are. That's a choice that you, and you alone should get to make."

"So, supposing I know who I am, or who I want to be, how do I make sure I stay that person?"

"Through your choices, baby girl. Through those decisions you make every day. Sometimes you'll get it right, and other times you'll get it wrong. If you let your heart and truth be your compass, you shouldn't get lost. But if you have questions, you can ask. I can tell you choices that I made that I regret, and others that I'm pretty sure I got right. Recognize, though, that you're capable of making the worst choice imaginable. If you can admit that to yourself, it will help you to avoid it and rather make the best choice available. Usually, we fall somewhere in between the two with a choice that is neither wholly good or wholly bad."

"But hopefully we're closer to good than bad, right?"

"Hopefully. The great thing is, if you get it a little wrong today, you get to choose again tomorrow. If you get it too wrong though... then you might be out of choices. That's why it's important to realize that you have it within yourself to make those kinds of horrible decisions. Each of us can commit evil."

"Evil?" Mary said her eyes widening. "That's a strong word, Dad. I don't know about evil."

"You need to, because evil is within each of us. Remember the story of the Garden of Eden. Both Adam and Eve already had the capacity for sin, for evil, within themselves. Until they ate from the tree of knowledge of good and evil, they didn't know it. Once they did, they could never again live in paradise on earth. Don't neglect that knowledge, because it is that knowledge that gives you the power to choose good rather than evil."

"Wow, you got all this from Great–Grandpa?"

"Well, no. The last part I've learned through a lot of poor choices — choices I hope to keep you from ever making."

Mary looked at her father with new eyes. The two of them sat on the porch together letting the sun sink in the West. Once it had departed, Mary followed her father inside, steadfast in her resolve to make the right choices and be the person she wanted to be: a person like her father.

# 40

**M**ary expanded her group of friends over the coming years. She didn't abandon Abby as her closest and dearest, but in the cases where Abby was otherwise occupied by boys, Mary had other classmates with whom to spend time. She never sought popularity, but it seemed to find her nonetheless.

Bud had once had the thought that being a leader was sometimes as simple as refusing to follow. Mary was learning first-hand how that could prove true. She was focused on her studies and had a small group of close friends, but she was friendly and courteous with everyone, and so everyone enjoyed being around her.

One night, when Bud came home from a meeting, he found strange cars parked along the road in front of the farmhouse. He walked in the front door to find three other kids in the living room with Mary. The three seemed to be arguing and Mary was sitting with an indignant look on her face, but when she saw her father, she stood and spoke over the others.

"My dad's home guys, so we'll have to quit for tonight and pick things up tomorrow during study hall," she said.

The other kids agreed, said their goodbyes and began to file out of the house. Mary shut the door behind them, turned to her dad and said, "I hope you don't mind me having our group get–together here. I knew you'd be at your meeting, so we wouldn't bother you."

"No, that's fine," Bud said. "Who were they?"

"Sorry, the larger boy is Patrick, the smaller is Mark, and the girl's name is Denise. They're all in my English class. We have to do a group project together," Mary said, rolling her eyes.

"Oh? Why don't you come sit at the table and tell me about it?"

Father and daughter made their way into the kitchen. Bud got himself a glass of water and offered one to Mary, but she waved him off. They then sat down across from one another at the table.

"It's just this ridiculous thing," Mary continued. "Mr. Seward put us all in groups to do a group presentation for the book we're reading."

"What book?" Bud asked.

"Fahrenheit 451. The whole thing is stupid. We're supposed to come up with a book as a group that we think should be banned from reading in school, and do a presentation supporting our choice. It kind of misses the point of the entire story."

"And what does the rest of your group think?"

Mary shrugged. "They seem fine with it. They just can't agree on a book."

"Did you suggest a book?"

"No, mostly I just sit, listening to them argue. I asked Mr. Seward if I could be on my own and argue for not banning any books, but he said I couldn't. We have to work in groups, and we have to pick a book."

"You don't want to work in a group, baby girl?"

"No, not with them. They're fine kids, but we're never all going to agree on anything. Forget the fact that I think the whole thing's stupid and don't want to pick a book at all. Mark thinks we should pick the Bible, and argue based on keeping religion out of school. Obviously, I disagree with that, and so does Denise. She suggested the Satanic Bible, saying everyone would have to agree that's worse. Patrick wants to do something like Mein Kampf that's already been banned in places, because it will be easier. It's just a bunch of back and forth and we aren't getting anywhere."

"Sounds like someone needs to take control of the group," Bud said.

"Probably, but I don't know who."

"Why not you, baby girl?"

"Me? I don't even want to do this stupid thing. I don't want to pick a book at all. Why would they listen to me?" Mary asked.

"Because you understand the theme of the book, and probably have the best chance of the four of you of placing this project within that context. It's not about liking the kids you're working with, or thinking them capable. It's about making the group come together for a common purpose. You know the car garage across the street that I used to own?" Mary nodded. "When I was running the garage, I had to get everyone to work together. I didn't necessarily get along with all of my mechanics all the time, but I led by example and gave them a common goal to work towards."

"But dad, I don't agree with banning books at all. If you can justify banning one book, someone else can justify banning a different one. Reading an idea in a book doesn't mean you have to agree with it. In fact, reading about things you disagree with can help you to clarify what you think. Words have the power to say whatever we want them to say. If you start banning books because you don't like the way the words are arranged then you might as well—" Mary stopped mid–sentence, as a look of realization came over her face.

"Yes?" Bud asked.

"I've got it dad. Thanks," she said, jumping up from the table. She half–ran to the other side, kissed him on the forehead, and headed for the stairs. "Goodnight, Dad. I love you."

"Love you too, baby girl. Goodnight," he said, smiling.

Several days later, Mary arrived home beaming. Bud was waiting on the porch, like always and greeted her smile with one of his own.

"You seem happy today, baby girl," he said.

"We gave our group presentation today."

"Oh? Let's go inside and get out of the cold. You can tell me all about it."

Once they were settled in the living room Mary began, the words flowing melodically from her lips. "It was amazing. We asked Mr. Seward if we could present last, saying our presentation would be best after everyone else's. He agreed, so we sat listening to other groups justifying the banning of several different books for all manner of reasons. Then we stood up. Patrick began by holding up our book, the unabridged dictionary, and then slamming it down on the desk in front of him. This book contains every single word that exists in every novel that has ever been banned, burned, or suggested to be subject to either. Every foul and dangerous idea that has ever been written has been formed by combining the words that are callously defined in earnest on these pages, he said. I wrote that part," she said, proudly. "The class' eyes were wide for the whole thing. We took turns speaking, and I went last. I concluded our presentation by saying that the point wasn't that the dictionary, or any book, should be banned. It was instead that if you justify banning a book for the words written in it, you can justify the banning of words and ideas themselves. I said that was the lesson of Fahrenheit 451, and that if we want to travel that road, our group feels we should jump to the chase and ban every word and its definition right from the start. Mr. Seward loved it. He said he had planned on making the point we made in our presentation in a class discussion after all the groups had finished, but that we had done his job for him. It was absolutely perfect, dad."

"The unabridged dictionary? I wonder who came up with that," Bud said, smiling. "How did you convince the others?"

"I don't really know. I think I was just so enthusiastic about the whole thing when I suggested it to them in study hall that they just kind of climbed on board immediately."

"I'm very proud of you, baby girl. You found a way to stand up for what you believe in, and speak the truth. And you did it with such conviction that you convinced your group to support you, and managed to do what your teacher asked of you at the same time. When I was around your age, my defiance to what I disagreed with was not nowhere near as subtle or well crafted. I assume you all received an "A" on this project?"

"Actually, an "A+," dad," Mary said.

Bud nodded. His daughter had always been quiet and polite, saving her inner–most concerns for either Abby or himself. That, along with her constantly smile and the twinkle in her eye, led others to believe that she was the eternal optimist and never complained. Bud was glad to see her confidence grow as a result of taking a larger and more direct role in a group.

As her sixteenth birthday approached, Mary hinted to her father that it might be nice to have a car. It would be much more convenient than taking the bus to and from school, or having to rely on friends to get places. Bud pretended not to notice when she dropped subtle reminders, but on her birthday, he surprised her with a used Subaru Impreza.

Bud said he would fix the car up for her and make sure that it was running well and looked good on the outside. He offered to do general maintenance such as oil changes, but it would be Mary's job to pay for gas and oil. She already got a small allowance for doing her jobs around the farm, but she would need to get a part–time job to supplement that income if she wanted to drive anywhere other than just to school and back.

She considered the ice cream shop, which would be perfect for summer, but wouldn't provide her a chance to work during the winter. Eventually, she settled on applying at the small general store in town. She got the job, and began working a few hours after school two days a week and one full weekend day to begin. All in all, it only added up to about fifteen hours, but it would provide her with plenty of gas money with some left over for what her father called "fun stuff."

Mary was a hard worker, thanks to all the chores she had been responsible for on the farm while growing up. Working at the general store provided her with a discipline and time management that she had lacked working basically on her own at home. She was stubborn, like her mother, and liked to do things her own way. It took time for her to grasp that when working for a manager or superior, one had to do things the way they wanted it to be done.

Meanwhile, Bud was busy with his duties as town manager. Both Mabel and Sue Pruitt made a habit of taking as many of Bud's free moments as they could manage. There was always a fundraiser, or a dinner, or a meeting they corralled him into attending. Mary was glad to have the distraction of working, and she tried to plan her schedule in concert with her father's so that they would be away on the same nights. She found it frustrating that he was gone so much, but she managed the best she could.

It was during a rare dinner together before Mary's high school senior year that she subtly expressed her frustration to her father.

"It's nice to actually be able to sit down to a meal at home with you for once," she said.

"Yes, it's been difficult, hasn't it?" Bud answered between mouthfuls.

"I'll be starting my senior year soon."

"I know. I can't believe how fast the time has gone. Are you excited?"

"I guess. I'm sure it'll go fast. Before we know it, I'll be headed off to college."

"That's true. I hadn't really thought about it. A year from now it will be almost time to say goodbye."

"And then we won't be having any dinners at home for a while. I suppose I'll be home around Christmas, and maybe in the summer if I don't get a job wherever I end up. Still, we won't be seeing much of one another, not that we do now anyway."

The realization of how much Bud had been neglecting his daughter struck him in the chest. He looked at Mary, now nearly a grown woman, and sadness swept over him at the moments he had missed. He had always been waiting on the porch when she got home from school, but the time they shared there had dwindled to a few pleasantries before they headed their separate ways. They also still attended church together, visiting Teresa's grave every Sunday beforehand. But that didn't afford them much time to talk and connect with one another like they used to.

"I'm sorry, baby girl," he said. "I haven't been a very good father lately."

"You're a wonderful father," she said, shaking her head at him. "You have a lot to do for the town. I understand that. I just wish we had more time. There's just never enough time."

"We're going to make time this year. Before you leave for college, we're going to make time."

At the next town meeting, Bud resigned as town manager. It took everyone by surprise when he presented his letter to the selectboard. He agreed to stay until the board had found a new town manager, and long enough to see that person settled. When Mary found out, she was livid, but Bud explained that he had done his service to the town, and now it was someone else's turn. It was time for him to do a better job serving his family, before it was too late.

Father and daughter once again began having regular meals together. Bud had one year — one year before his daughter headed out into the world. There was so much still to tell her, so much to teach her, and he was running out of time. He wanted their remaining time to be memorable, and so he began scheduling outings with her during her time off.

They spent their time together that fall pumpkin picking, laughing together as they got lost in a corn maze, and enjoying the splendor of the changing leaves from the "Height of the Land." When winter arrived, they went to the movies in Augusta, ice skated hand in hand on Lovejoy Pond, and tried to learn to ski together at Sugarloaf Ski Resort. After spring arrived, they took leisurely walks through the woods, went to a sugar shack to see maple syrup being made, and took a trip to the museum in Boston.

In June, Bud watched proudly as Mary marched with her graduating class at Maranacook High School. She graduated near the top of her class and had been accepted to Columbia University in New York where she planned to major in English and Comparative Literature. Their time together was dwindling, and Bud felt like he needed to find something truly meaningful for their remaining outings together.

It was a week after graduation that Mary came downstairs to breakfast, prepared to spend the day with her father. As they sat and ate, she asked her dad what he had planned for the two of them. Bud told her she'd just have to wait and see. When they had finished eating, Bud grabbed a small bag and led his daughter up to the pool below the waterfall.

Bud set the bag down by the log and then sat himself, motioning for Mary to join him. She looked around in wonder at the little clearing to which her father had led her. The trees on either side and the bank of earth and stone that the waterfall cascaded over gave the impression of walls and made the place feel safe and serene. She sat on the log next to her father, still marveling at the splendor of the land around her.

"It's beautiful," she said.

"Yes it is," Bud said looking around. "This was your mother's and my place, but I doubt she'll mind me bringing you here. I first came here with another little boy that used to live on our street. We played and splashed in the little pool there. After he moved away, I brought your mother. We were still just children back then. This is where I taught her to swim. We would sit on this log and read books together. We would lay on the bank and talk about anything and everything, sharing our hopes and dreams for the future. We shared our first kiss here. And right there is where I took the life of the one who was trying to hurt her."

Bud said it all very matter–of–factly, and the effect on his daughter was obvious. Her face turned from pleasant to shock in an instant.

"Why did you bring me here, Dad?" Mary asked.

"I brought you here because it's a very important place for me. Some of my happiest and most awful memories happened in this spot. When I come here, I feel more deeply than anywhere else in the world. I feel joy and sadness, anger and love, fear and hope, all together simultaneously. This is where I am most human. This is where I am most honest. I brought you here because this fall you are going off into the world where I can no longer be there to protect you. I want you to be able to ask me anything, or tell me anything, and have my answer be real, and this is where I can do that."

"What do you want me to ask?"

"Anything you want."

"Do you regret killing that boy, the one who was going to hurt Mom?"

Bud chuckled, which startled Mary enough that she moved away from her father slightly. "Regret?" he said. "Regret is a funny thing, baby girl. I don't regret saving your mother from being raped by that monster. And yes, he was a monster, but he was also a human being. I do regret that I took his life. I regret that I let my own monster come out in my rage and destroy that young man."

"But you said he was a monster."

"He was. In that moment he definitely was, but so was I. Do you think I'm still a monster?"

Mary looked into her father's eyes, deep and blue but in that second full of sadness and pain. She studied his face and saw the lines of care and worry, his smooth skin cracked and broken by the years. In his questioning expression she saw that he wasn't asking her the question as much as he was asking himself.

"No Dad," she said, "you're not the monster anymore."

"Thank you, baby girl. That brings me comfort, but again, also sadness. If I could defeat the monster within myself, then surely that boy could have too had he been given the opportunity. Would he have? Only he could have known for sure."

"I can't believe that happened right here," Mary said. "It's so peaceful and feels so safe. It doesn't seem possible."

"It feels peaceful and safe because you are. All that is here is what you bring with you. When you bring peace, you will find it.

Bring love and joy, they are here. If you bring evil, then evil will find you."

"I could never bring evil here."

"You're wrong, baby girl," Bud said shaking his head. She looked at him doubtfully. He stood and walked to the edge of the water and picked up a small stone. He tossed it and watched it sink to the sandy bottom, sending ripples across the surface. "We each have both good and evil within us. Until you recognize your capacity to do evil, you will never fully realize your ability to do good. What good is morality if you don't have the choice? You do have the choice, in everything you do. Know it, and it will make choosing good all the more virtuous."

"You sound like someone who has finally found God, Dad."

"You sound like a daughter that still has hope for her father's soul," he said smiling at her. "Found God? I haven't really spent much time looking. I've been too busy trying to find myself. Maybe with you gone and with nothing left to do, I'll have time to look now. Who knows?"

"I worry about leaving you here alone," Mary said.

"And I worry about you going off alone."

"You don't need to worry, Dad, I'll be fine. There'll be plenty of other people around. I'm sure I'll make lots of friends and be perfectly safe."

"That's not really my worry, baby girl. I worry that with all those new people, and all those new ideas, that everyone will try to change you. There'll be friends and teachers and all manner of people telling you what to think, and what to believe, and who you should want to be. I just hope I've taught you well enough how to think, that when someone else tells you what to think, you'll know better than to listen. Like your Great-Grandpa said, the world will try to change a person if they let it. You have to be stronger than that."

Mary walked over and kissed her father on the cheek and said, "I am, I had a good teacher — the best."

The two of them spent the better part of the day by the waterfall. Mary's father had packed lunch in the bag he'd carried, and they made a picnic on the grassy bank. She breathed the clean, fresh air and listened to the water as it splashed into the pool. She felt like she never wanted to leave.

"Who owns this place, Dad?"

"You know," he said, "I've never bothered to find out."

"You should."

"Why? Do you think they'd mind us coming here?"

"No," Mary said smiling up at her father. "I think you should buy it."

"Buy it?" His face was pure amusement. "What would I do with it?"

"Keep it just like this, forever. I'd hate to see the owner ruin it by cutting these trees and building a house or something."

Bud hadn't thought about the possibility of the owner deciding to do something with the land. Of course, his daughter was right. Someone owned it and could do whatever they wanted. He nodded and agreed to look into buying the property to preserve it.

Overall, Bud was happy with the day when they finally walked home in the late afternoon. His daughter had asked him many questions about her mother, grandparents, and great grandparents. Bud had answered everything as honestly and thoroughly as he could.

The summer passed too quickly after that. Bud and Mary went camping, hiking, and spent time on the lakes. When it came time for Mary to go to school however, Bud still wasn't ready. Time, the devourer of all things, he thought as he helped Mary pack her Subaru for the drive to New York.

Bud insisted on following her to Columbia in his own car, to see her settled into her new living arrangements. The next morning, she waved as he pulled away from the curb to drive home, leaving her to begin her solo journey into life. Bud had promised himself he wouldn't cry. He had given her the tools and the knowledge, and it was up to her to use them. That evening, when he pulled onto Baker Street, he parked on the side of the road, and walked to the waterfall.

There was a full moon which lighted his way along the path. As he came upon the pool, it seemed to glow in the moonlight. He stood, letting his mind wander where it may through the fields and over the years. Through the misty spray, he could see Teresa standing under the water of the falls. She was smiling and beckoning for him to join her. He smiled as the warmth of her being coursed through him.

"Our baby girl has left for college," he said out loud. "I've done the very best I can, I hope you approve." The vision nodded and moved out of the water towards him. "I wish you could have been here. She's such an amazing girl — young woman, excuse me. It's all gone so fast, and now here I am alone again." In the moonlight Teresa shook her head, no, and drifted ever closer. "Somehow, I knew you would be here, because I need you. I haven't come here enough. Only here am I able to truly see you anymore. Everywhere else you have faded, but here you're still whole and real. I never want to leave. I want to stay here with you forever." She came very close now and touched his heart with her outstretched hand. He felt her enter his body like a cool drink of water. Then she was gone.

He knew he couldn't stay, not yet. There was work left to be done. He just didn't know what it was. When the time came, he would see her again. He shook the ghost from his mind, and returned home to the farm. He called Mary, and said, "I'm home."

# 41

The tractor tipped over. Bud had made the mistake of trying to take a shortcut. He had tried to skirt along the bank of the pond instead of going around and using the bridge. It was foolish, and Bud knew it. Now he was pinned underneath the John Deere and his leg was in tremendous pain. It was probably broken. Mary was away at school, so all Bud could do was yell and hope someone would hear him.

Thankfully, the driver of a car going by on Hales Road saw the tractor lying on its side and stopped to investigate. The driver was a kindly old gentleman, who hurried up to the garage across the street to get help.

It took three men to lift the tractor enough to slide Bud out from underneath, which was extremely painful. One of the mechanics had called an ambulance, and Bud was rushed to the hospital in Augusta. His leg was badly broken and he would have to be in a cast and remain mostly immobile until it had healed.

Mary wasn't very happy when she received the phone call explaining what happened. She had been concerned about her father being alone, and this justified that worry in her mind. She said she was coming home.

"No, baby girl," he said, "there's nothing you could do now anyway. I'm just going to be laid up at home. Gregg said he'd check in on me and take care of the farm chores that can't stand to wait. You stay where you are. I should be up and around a little bit more by the time you're home for Christmas."

As soon as Mary had hung up the phone call with her father, she looked up Gregg's phone number and called him.

"Hello?" Gregg said, answering.

"Gregg?" Mary asked.

"Speaking."

"It's Mary, Bud's daughter. Dad gave me your number for emergencies and stuff."

"Sure Mary, what's up?"

"You heard about Dad and the tractor…"

"I did… horrible."

"I need to ask you a favor. Dad said you're going to check in on him until he's up and around."

"Of course, I'm not about to leave him high and dry without help."

"Do you have a pen and paper handy?"

"Um… sure, around here somewhere," Gregg said, pulling out drawers and rooting around for a pen that still functioned. "What for?"

"I have a list of things to run through with you that you'll need to do for dad."

"A list?"

Mary began listing off chores that Gregg would need to be sure to handle as long as her father was unable. She stressed that Gregg needed to make sure that her father was eating properly, that the animals were tended to, that there was plenty of stuff to read around the house to keep her father occupied, and that under no circumstances was her father to attempt any work before the doctor cleared him to do so.

"He'll try to do work, Gregg, if you don't stop him," Mary said. "My father is incredibly hard working and he doesn't know when to stop sometimes."

"Yes, I've realized that about him," Gregg said.

"I really wish he wasn't all alone in that house."

"I'll make sure he has some company each day."

"Thank you, Gregg. My father is very lucky to have a friend like you."

When she hung up the phone, Mary felt better about the situation her father was in. At least she knew there was someone she could call to get updates on her Dad's condition. Her father would always say he was "fine," even if he really wasn't, and it was a long time until Christmas.

Sitting with nothing to do, was akin to torture for Bud Marshall. He read and wrote in his notebook a lot. There was nothing that interested him on the television, so he took to doing crosswords just to have something to occupy his mind during the long daytime hours.

Gregg was good about coming first thing in the morning to see the animals fed and spend a little time with Bud before he had to leave for work. He would always make a point to return in the evening on his way home and check in again for an hour or so. Bud was grateful, but hated that it took Greg away from his family.

When Mary arrived home for Christmas, she gave Bud the lecture he knew was coming. She wanted him to be more careful, not to take any silly risks, and to keep a cell phone on him at all times for emergencies. She also made what Bud thought was an outlandish request in that he sell the farm and retire early. He had the money to do so, of course, but just the thought of having nothing to do drove him stir crazy. Then Mary made her final plea.

"And it would be nice," She said emphasizing the word 'nice' as though Bud would be doing her a favor, "if you would at least consider dating."

"Dating?"

"Yes, Dad, dating. I really hate the idea of you alone in this house all the time. Doesn't it get lonely? You're still a young man, and there are plenty of women who would be very lucky to have you as a husband."

"I'm not that young baby girl. I'll be fifty in a couple of years, you know? And yes, it gets lonely sometimes, but as long as I have work to do on the farm, I'm occupied and just fine. Sitting around with this cast on my leg with nothing to do has been the hard part. Once I'm healed up and can get back out there doing stuff, I'll be okay."

"Please, Dad, just think about it, okay? How about Ms. Pruitt? She seemed to like you."

"You mean Mrs. Anderson. She was married last year."

"What about that other woman? Mabel."

"Moved away, I believe. I haven't seen her in quite some time. She's not really my type anyway."

"Well, who is your type, Dad?"

"Your mother is," Bud said smiling. "I know, I know, not what you want to hear. I understand, baby girl. I'll think about it, okay? If you want the truth, I probably should have done it when you were much younger. But I wasn't ready then, and now I think I'm too old and it's just silly."

Mary didn't think it was silly for her father to have companionship, but she let the matter drop for now. She repeated her thought about selling the farm, but Bud wouldn't hear of it. He changed the subject by handing her a gift wrapped in red and green Christmas paper.

"It's not Christmas for a couple days, Dad," Mary said.

"I know. Open it."

Mary tore slowly into the colorful paper which concealed a thin box. She opened the box to find a deed: a deed to a piece of property. It was in her name.

"It's the land with your mother's and my waterfall," Bud said. "I bought it for you. I trust that you'll keep it safe."

"This is wonderful, Dad, but you could have left it in your name."

"I know I could have. And one day you'll own the farm and your great–grandparent's old house: all of it. But I wanted you to have this now."

"Thank you, Dad. I promise I'll always keep it safe."

Mary returned to school after the holidays, and Bud hobbled around on crutches for a while longer. The injury kept him sidelined for longer than he would have liked, but with the rest over the winter and some rehab work, he was up and around by spring; although he walked with a bit of a limp for the rest of his life.

He put a lot of thought into what Mary had said about dating, but he just couldn't seem to bring himself to try. Every time he thought about it, he couldn't figure out where to start. He didn't think men his age should be hanging around bars, and internet dating wasn't his thing. Just carrying the cell phone as Mary had insisted felt awkward and foreign. He was a man of a different age and time who wished he could go back to when things were simpler.

Although he was less involved than in the past, Bud did make a point to continue going to town meetings and to church on Sundays. It was more an exercise in routine than in anything else. He didn't want to stand still for too long, for fear that he would find himself stuck there with no purpose.

The goal he had set to be a great husband and father seemed distant and lost in the past. His wife was dead and his daughter had left the nest. Bud was left adrift in a sea with no port to even search for. When the tenants renting his grandparents' old house didn't renew their lease, he had an idea.

Bud was going to completely remodel and renovate both the old cape and the farmhouse. He would start on Buck and Maggie's old cape, and when that was finished, he would move in there temporarily while he worked on the farmhouse. When Mary asked him why he was doing it, he brushed her off and said it was just for something to do. Secretly though, he hoped to do what Jim had done and give her and her future family the farm, and move back into the cape himself. That way he would always be close to Mary and her family.

Over Mary's four years in college, Bud pursued his new goal. He slowed the amount of work he did on the farm, selling off most of the animals and equipment. He kept a few laying hens and the garden, and he continued to hay the fields in the summer. For the most part, his focus was turned to the renovations of the houses.

Bud gutted the cape and opened up the floor plan. Downstairs, he created an open–concept floorplan with kitchen, dining, and living areas all in one big space with new, large windows facing south towards the stream. There was also a half bath and a small sitting room, with its own picture windows that looked out at the farmhouse next door and to the barn and stream below. Upstairs, Bud kept the two bedrooms and remodeled the bathroom. The place was practically brand new by the time he'd finished.

When he moved on to the farmhouse, Bud kept the layout as it was. He opened up the wall some from the kitchen to the dining room and created an arched door from the dining room to the sitting room. Upstairs he remodeled the bathroom, enlarging it slightly by stealing some space from the hall closet.

Both homes got new or resurfaced hardwood floors and radiant heat. Bud bought all new appliances, and vinyl siding to bring both houses up to date.

By the time Mary graduated from college in 2009, the project was complete. When Bud asked Mary what her plans were now that she had her degree, she said she was going to move home for the time being until she found a regular job. Bud shook his head no.

"You can't move home," he said.

"Why not?" Mary asked, a little hurt.

"Because," her father said handing her a set of keys, "you have your own place now. I'm giving you the cape. A grown woman should have a space all her own. I just hope you like the neighbors."

She laughed and gave her dad a big hug. The house was everything a college graduate could hope for. It felt clean and open, and the views from the sitting room down towards the stream and forest to the south were stunning.

Mary eventually got a job working for a real estate company out of Winthrop. The commute wasn't too bad, and it afforded her some flexibility to pursue a career in writing.

Though her father was once again left without a project or goal, he was happy to have his baby girl nearby once again. At first, he found contentment in just taking a walk or reading a book, but as time went on, the lack of purpose began to eat away at him.

Bud found himself going to the waterfall more and more often. Occasionally, when she had the time available, Mary would go with him. Bud would sit and talk to himself, or to Mary if she were there, just reminiscing about all the things that had happened in his life. Often, he would bring his notebook and write everything down that he could remember.

When Mary would go with him, he would tell her about the books he and Teresa would read together. Mary was fascinated by the stories and would sit with her eyes closed, picturing the two of them together as children reading on the bank.

"What was Mom's favorite book?" she asked once.

"*East of Eden*," Bud said. "I still have the first edition that I gave her as a gift one Christmas. It's where the quote on her tombstone comes from too."

"And what's your favorite book?"

"*Watership Down*, probably."

Several weeks later, Bud walked up to the pool and found a stone bench on the bank near the log that had always been there. It was granite, about three feet long, and was engraved on the top. It had two quotes: "Nearly everybody has his box of secret pain, shared with no one," and "My heart has joined the Thousand, for my friend stopped running today."

Tears filled his eyes as he recognized the quotes from *East of Eden* and *Watership Down* and the significance for him and Teresa. Mary came walking up behind him, smiling. She had seen him go and had followed him.

"I hope you like it, Dad," she said, startling him. He turned to face her, his eyes red and watery.

"It's beautiful, baby girl, your mother would have loved it."

The two stood without talking for several minutes. Bud seemed lost in thought as he looked down at the granite bench. Finally, Mary broke the silence.

"I worry about you, Dad. You've been coming here a lot. I don't know that it does you good to dwell so much on the past and never look to the future. If you need to talk, I mean really talk, I'm here to listen."

"Thank you. Yes, I know that you're right. I try so hard to find things to look forward to, but so often I find I'm just looking back. I don't think it's any secret that I still miss her." He bent down and ran his hand over the rough etching on the stone bench. "I wish so much that she could be here to help me. Loving her was my purpose in life. When she died, it became raising you. Now, look at you — you're all grown up. I am a man without direction or reason for being. I did all those renovations on the houses, thinking that would fulfill me, and it did for a short while. Now I feel like I'm left searching again."

Mary walked over and wrapped her arms around her father, holding him in an embrace. She whispered in his ear, "If you need a purpose, let's find one for you together. I still need my father."

"I know you do," Bud said. "I'm not going anywhere. And if you're willing to help me, I'm willing to try to look ahead rather than behind."

They sat on the bench together, and Mary shared her vision for the future. She wanted a husband and children. She painted a picture of being able to stay home with the kids and write all the beautiful things her father had taught her. She imagined the children playing on the farm and learning to feed the animals as she had as a child. She told her father she wanted a husband as strong and loving as he is: one that loves her the way Bud loved her mother. She hoped they could do together as a family all the things that she and her father had done together: camping and swimming, skating and playing.

"And you could bring them up here to the waterfall, and read stories with them like you did with Mom," Mary said.

"I'd like that."

Bud was excited by the prospect of the future that Mary had in mind. It filled him with hope that he could comfortably make the transition from being only a parent into being a grandparent as well. He didn't tell her his plan to give her the farm if and when she got married though. That was something small he could look forward to.

Perhaps that's the key, he thought to himself. Little things to look forward to. I don't need some grand goal or purpose, just something small and not too far away. I'm getting too old for giant leaps anyway. Small steps and just keep moving.

# 42

"**W**hat's the young man's name again?" Bud asked his daughter, putting his hand to his chin mocking a curious demeanor.

"I told you his name, Dad," Mary said rolling her eyes.

"Yes I know, but remind me."

"Stephen. Stephen Holmes."

"Right, right, and he's a doctor?"

"Yes, Dad."

"And this makes, what? Three dates? No, four now."

"They're not dates," Mary said laughing at her father's ridiculous antics. "We're just having coffee after his shift, so I'll be home a little later than normal. We're friends."

"Well, he sounds like a very nice young man, I'd love to meet him sometime."

"Not with your behavior, no thank you. The poor guy would be terrified with you making those ridiculous faces and acting like a fool."

"I have no idea what you're talking about," Bud said, throwing his hands wildly into the air.

"Fine, that's fine, Dad. You act like a fool and scare off the first nice guy I've met since I got home. That's fine."

"I'm teasing, baby girl. I'm glad you've made a friend. I hope things work out, and if they do, I'll behave when you decide it's time for him to meet me."

It was early November when Mary asked her father if it would be okay for Stephen to join them for Thanksgiving. Bud thought that sounded like a great idea and offered to have it at the farmhouse. Mary agreed, but informed her father she wanted to try cooking the turkey herself.

Bud had been feeling run down, but the prospect of a family Thanksgiving lifted his spirits. He wanted to make a good impression on the young man Mary was bringing home, so he made sure to clean the farmhouse from top to bottom. He got quite sore, and found himself having dizzy spells as well. Chalking it all up to turning fifty next year on top of years of hard manual labor, he tried to put it out of his mind. Bud decided after the house was clean that he would take it easy until Thanksgiving, just in case he was coming down with a bug.

The next two weeks, Bud mostly stayed in bed. A slight fever and night sweats convinced him that he'd come down with a flu bug. It frustrated him that it had to come on with Thanksgiving on the horizon. He promised Mary that he'd be better by the time Thanksgiving Day arrived, and he'd be ready to host her and Stephen.

When he woke up Thanksgiving morning though, he still felt awful. He was feverish, tired, and ached in his joints. Putting on a brave face, he readied himself to share a meal with his daughter and her boyfriend.

Bud wasn't very hungry, but he did his best to be polite and eat what he could from the delicious turkey his daughter had prepared. As Mary cleaned up from the meal in the kitchen, Bud got a few moments alone with Steve.

"So how did you and my Mary meet?" Bud asked.

"Through a mutual friend at her work, actually."

"And you work in Winthrop too?"

"Part of the time, yes. I split my time between the facility in Winthrop and the hospital in Augusta. I rent a place to live in Winthrop."

A wave of dizziness came over Bud, and his head swam. Mary's boyfriend noticed the change, and a look of concern came over his face.

"Are you ok, Mr. Marshall?" he asked.

"Yes, fine, Stephen. Thank you. I've got a bit of a flu bug I'm afraid. I've had a bit of a fever for a couple weeks, and I get nights sweats and all the fun stuff. Just got a little dizzy there. I'll be all right though. And you can call me 'Bud.'"

"Okay. You can call me 'Steve,' sir. Did you say it's been a couple weeks?"

"Yes, I'm sure I'll be over it any day now. I had hoped to kick it before today. It's destroyed my appetite. I've lost five or ten pounds already."

Steve looked concerned again and furrowed his brow. He cocked his head and asked, "Have you had any fatigue? Joint or bone pain?"

"Well sure, a little. Nothing that anyone my age doesn't experience, I suppose."

"Have you seen a doctor?"

"No, like I said it's just the flu. I'm sure I'll be over it soon."

"I think you should see a doctor just to be sure," Steve said as Mary walked into the room.

"See a doctor for what?" she asked.

"Oh nothing, baby girl. I've got a bit of the flu, that's all. I've been tired and run down. Steve's just looking out for me, I think."

"If Steve thinks you should see a doctor, maybe you should go," she said. She looked at Steve and he nodded. "Just to be safe."

Bud looked at Mary and her boyfriend. It seemed to Bud that Steve was just trying to look important in front of his daughter. His first impulse was to brush them off and wait out the illness. As he looked in her eyes though, he saw her concern. If it would ease her mind, Bud resolved it would be best to go and see someone.

"All right, kids," he said. "I can see the old man is overruled here. If you two think I need to get this checked out, I will. Can I come to your office in Winthrop, Steve?"

"I think it's best if we have you go to Augusta. They're better equipped to run tests if need be."

Early the next week, Bud was answering questions and being poked and prodded. When he had agreed to go see someone, he figured he wouldn't actually ever have to. He thought his symptoms would clear up in the next couple days and he'd be vindicated in his belief that it was just a bad flu. When they didn't however, he began to get a little worried himself. As the day at the hospital wore on and more and more tests were ordered, his apprehension grew.

After far more time than Bud had planned to spend at the hospital and more tests than he could remember, Bud received the bad news. He was diagnosed with Acute Myeloid Leukemia, a cancer of the blood. The oncologist recommended three–week cycles of chemotherapy over several courses to last about six months. Bud was still relatively young, so his prognosis was fairly positive for a complete remission.

That evening, Bud walked up to the waterfall and sat on the bench his daughter had placed there. He stared off into the distance just listening to the sound of the falls until the cold air penetrated the light jacket he had worn. He walked back slowly,

410 Thomas J. Torrington

taking in every inch of ground, picturing every time he had tread that weary way before. He imagined walking it with grandchildren, taking them to splash in the pool on a hot summer day, and reading to them on the grassy bank. Life, he thought, is a tragedy.

Gregg showed up at the farmhouse the next evening. Bud showed him to the living room, where he had a fire going. He offered Gregg a drink, which his friend refused, and the two sat, just watching the flames tickle the stone.

"Bad news travels fast in a small town," Bud said to the silence.

"Mary called me. You all right?"

"You mean, other than the cancer?"

Gregg caught a twinkle from the fire in the corner of Bud's eye as he looked over. "Other than the cancer," he said.

"I'd like to say, 'I'll live,' but there are no certainties at this point. Let's just say I'm taking it in stride."

"Is there anything I can do, Bud?" Gregg asked. Bud shook his head slowly. The two friends sat in silence again for several minutes.

"Do you believe in God, Gregg?" Bud asked at last.

"No," Greg answered. "I've seen no proof that there's a God. Do you?"

"I'm starting to."

Gregg's eyes widened and his lips parted as he gave Bud a look of incredulousness.

"You don't think I should?" Bud asked, chuckling at Gregg's facial expression.

"I would think you of all people wouldn't think there's a God. What with the way your life has been from the moment you were born until now."

Bud nodded. "Yes, hard to believe any God would want what my life has been to happen to anyone."

"Exactly."

"Better to believe it was all just some randomness of the universe. Some happenstance of immaterial fate, chance — not design, nothing that anyone could control. Is that about right, Gregg?"

"Well, yes but—"

"Better to believe that my mother died giving birth to me randomly. That my father committing suicide and casting me off on another was just an unfortunate consequence of it. My lies about my best friend in the world defaming her character, and then those lies leading to my killing of another human being were a cruel twist of fate. Reese's death giving birth to my daughter — and now my cancer which may take my life just as I was looking forward to the possible future of grandchildren of my own to love, and every other bad or unfortunate thing that has happened to me were all a matter of bad luck rather than of some supernatural design?"

"You want a reason," Gregg said in a somber tone.

"I don't want a reason, Gregg, I just want there to be one. I don't need to know what it is, just that it's there and that all the misery and sadness aren't some lousy roll of illusory dice."

"And what good could you possibly think a God would have for putting you through all that misery?"

Bud thought back on his life, to the moments that stood out. His face grew into a broad smile.

"Can you see the beauty in the world, Gregg?"

"Sure, I guess."

"Really? The simple wonder of sharing a glass of lemonade and sandwiches with your best friend as you lay in the sun and read a good book together? The profound joy of sitting in the woods and talking with a person you admire, and learning from the knowledge they have to share? The unexplainable warmth and happiness of watching your daughter get off a school bus and run to your waiting arms for the hug she's waited all day for? Can you see the beauty in sitting in a chair in front of a fire talking to a good friend and appreciate every word, every second, for how precious it truly is? Because I can."

"To hear you talk about it, I'm beginning to."

"That's the gift God has given me, Gregg. For all the misery and horror of my life, I can see the undeniable truth — it isn't the grand, spectacular moments in life that truly matter any more than it's the most horrific. It's the simple, everyday magic of love, friendship, and family that carry us forward. The depths of my pain have made them that much brighter and more apparent."

Gregg nodded and sat back in his chair, and his thoughts wandered through the years. He tried to linger on the simple moments, rather than the grand, spectacular events like his wedding and found it difficult. He had let them slip out of memory, rejecting them as inconsequential. Bud, on the other hand, seemed to be able to recall the tiniest details of insignificant times in his life. Gregg realized he couldn't see the beauty. If he could, he would remember.

Bud just sat watching the fire, his hand to his chin with a contented grin on his face. It seemed to Gregg the very essence of the moment was being drawn towards and into his friend from all around the room. From time to time, Bud would close his eyes for a few seconds and his smile would grow. This was what savoring life looked like.

"When do you start chemo?" Gregg asked, regretting it immediately as the effect was to pull Bud out of the contented state he had been in. He looked up with almost a start and seemed to shake his head before taking a deep breath.

"Two days," he said. "The acute leukemia is very aggressive. The oncologist wanted to start right away, but I asked for a few days."

"How long will it last?"

"Three courses over six months, and then we'll see."

Mary and Steve took turns driving Bud to and from his chemotherapy treatments in Augusta. Bud maintained a cheerful demeanor, even when he had to ask for the car to be pulled over to be sick on the side of the road. He took the time with Mary to tell her stories from his life, stories he thought she ought to hear. When he was with Steve, he took the time to get to know him and ask him questions about his life.

Steve had a kind soul, as far as Bud could tell. He had gone into medicine from a desire to help people. Treating patients was the only thing that kept him doing it, because the administration and politics of the hospital weren't to his liking. He and Bud got along well as hearing about it reminded Bud of dealing with the politics of being town manager.

They were driving home one day between Christmas and New Year's, and Bud was looking even more green than normal. Steve asked if Bud wanted him to pull over, but Bud waved him off.

"I'm okay, Steve, but thank you. I'll let you know."

"All right. This probably isn't the best time to talk about this, but we don't get much time together alone outside of the car—"

"You want to marry my daughter," Bud said, smiling at Steve through the nausea.

Steve laughed. "Yes, sir, I do."

"I appreciate the 'sir,' but really, you can call me 'Bud,' Steve. Now, I assume you're telling me this because you want to ask for my permission."

"Yes, sir — uh, I mean, Bud. Your permission, your blessing, would mean a lot."

"Well Steve, I'll tell you what Mary's grandfather told me when I asked for permission to marry her mother. At this point my permission doesn't mean a whole heck of a lot, but if you've got the gumption to ask my daughter to marry you, by all means you have my blessing to do so."

Steve proposed to Mary on New Year's Eve, and she happily accepted. Bud was very happy for the young couple and told Mary so during their next trip to the hospital together. He wished them happiness for many years to come.

"I was thinking, Dad," Mary said.

"Mmmm?"

"I'd like to have the wedding on the farm, like you and Mom did."

"That would be lovely, baby girl. Whatever you'd like."

"I'm thinking July."

"This July? That seems soon to me. Will that be enough time to get everything ready?"

"Yes, I think if we do it on the farm, we should have enough time to get everything together."

"I hope you're not hurrying on my account," Bud said furrowing his brow. "I plan on being around whenever you have the wedding, so no need to rush."

Mary laughed. "Maybe I'm just excited to be married. Did you ever think that could be the case?"

"Oh, well then, by all means."

Wedding plans began, and chemo treatments continued. Bud's treatment of induction chemotherapy would conclude in May, and if he was in remission, he would begin consolidation treatment to help prevent any cancer relapse. He hoped to have all his treatment finished by the time the wedding rolled around in July, and maybe even have a little of his hair back.

While Bud wanted to take a more active role in the wedding plans, he wasn't much help while going through cancer treatments, especially as the day got closer and he was dealing with the longer hospital stays of consolidation therapy. He would simply listen to his daughter as they drove in the car, and bask in the glow of her excitement. He offered advice only when he was asked, and even then, kept his answers vague and open ended.

This was going to be her day, and he wanted her to have exactly what she was picturing.

# 43

**A**s Mary peered out one of the windows of the cape, it seemed to her that the setting sun cast off golden rivulets and sparkling diamonds on the surface of the stream. The glimmer passed by the bottom of the hill below the two houses, and finally ended, filling the pond with amber honey. Then she saw him sitting there; the lonely silhouette of her father was cast against the evening sky, hunched and small. She wondered what he was doing out of the house and why he was sitting on the crest of the hill. Deciding she had better check on him, she made for the front door.

Bud heard her coming, her bare feet brushing the blades of grass with each step. "Hello, baby girl," he said. "Sit — join me." She sat next to her father and turned to study him. His eyes were cloudy and tired as they started listlessly into the distance. His hair was just beginning to grow again, and he was covered on top by a light fuzz. A mild summer breeze blew out of the south and met their faces, gently cooling the evening air.

"What are you doing, Dad?" she asked, looking down on the farm. The chairs and tent were all set up and ready for the wedding. They had been placed in much the same position as when Bud had married Teresa years before.

"To tell you the truth, I was on my way to the waterfall. This is as far as I got. It would seem the pain and fatigue from my treatment are still too great for me to walk as far as I would want to."

"Which is why you should be resting. May I remind you that I expect you to walk me down the aisle tomorrow." She had said it only teasing as an encouragement, but Bud's face soured.

"Tomorrow? What will tomorrow bring, I wonder? We sit precariously perched upon the precipice of the future. Inevitably, we fall," he said. Mary's face darkened and her eyes narrowed. Bud saw the change as he turned to face her. His eyes cleared and came once again into focus. "I'm sorry, baby girl. Yes, of course I'll be ready to walk you down the aisle. Now, sit with me and enjoy the evening for a while, won't you? And then you can help me back to the farmhouse."

"I don't like it when you talk like that, Dad. It's been happening more and more lately."

"Nothing to worry about, trust me. Just the ramblings of a tired old man. I blame the chemo. I'm getting better though — I can feel it. Before you know it, your dad will be tossing hay bales into the barn just like he used to."

Bud was in complete remission. The doctors had taken some of his bone marrow, frozen it, and placed it in storage. There was always a chance of relapse, and cancer–free marrow of his own was a hedge it case it happened.

The sun cast its final rays upon the world, and the stream ceased to sparkle. From the forest, the unmistakable call of a barred owl echoed into the night. The gathering twilight gave birth to dozens of fireflies dancing on the hill below them. Bud closed his eyes and drew a deep breath, releasing it slowly.

"I would have liked to sit by the waterfall tonight. I imagine it's quite peaceful. Such things will have to wait for me to rebuild my strength though."

"And you will, Dad," Mary said, placing an arm around him. "You haven't been out of treatment all that long. The doctors said it might take time. You've been through a lot. And I'm proud of the way you fought and how strong you've been through it all. I can't imagine if you weren't here for tomorrow."

"Well, if I'm going to make it all the way down there," Bud said nodding towards the chairs set up for the ceremony, "I had better get some rest. Otherwise, you may have to carry me down the aisle." He laughed and Mary smiled.

"Maybe we should have a wheelbarrow handy. You know, just in case." She helped her father to his feet, and walked him back to the farmhouse and up the stairs to his room. They both knew the following day would be a challenge for Bud, both mentally and physically, but both were determined to make it a success.

When the sun rose on the third Saturday of July in 2010, the day grew warm. There was hardly a cloud to be found, and the guests would have only temperatures in the 80's and bright sunny skies to contend with. Mary had gone to the farmhouse early to get ready for the ceremony. Steve's parents had agreed to help with much of the planning, as Bud was unable to with all the medical care he was receiving, and now they helped keep everything organized.

When the time came, Bud summoned all of his strength and made the walk with his daughter from the farmhouse and down to the archway in front of the stream. The warm sun beamed down on his nearly bald head and beads of sweat ran down his forehead. He wiped them away with his handkerchief.

Mary was dressed in a beautiful white strapless wedding gown that flared below the waist. It had a long train that flowed behind them as they walked. She held her father's arm, supporting him more than once on their march down the hill.

Bud gave his daughter's hand to Steve, announcing his intention to give her away in marriage, and then found his seat, sitting quickly to relieve the pain in his joints and the exhaustion of the walk.

The ceremony was brief, and Mary and Steve exchanged traditional vows. As they kissed for the first time as husband and wife, Bud wiped away a tear and smiled as memories of the past flooded into his consciousness.

The guests filed out for cocktails and music as the wedding party gathered to take pictures. When Mary looked for her father, he was nowhere to be seen. She sent his friend Gregg to go and find him for the photos. Gregg found Bud still sitting in his chair with his eyes cast to the west up the length of the stream towards Baker Street.

"Hey, Bud," Gregg said, "ready to take some pictures?"

"I was hoping to avoid them, Gregg, if I'm being honest."

"What, why?"

"I'd rather not be remembered looking like this," Bud said waving his hand around his head.

"Don't be ridiculous, Bud. Mary is going to want you in those pictures regardless of what you look like. Come on, I'll help you over there."

Bud reluctantly broke his gaze, and let Gregg help him to his feet. He fought through the aches and pains to smile for the pictures, and then asked Gregg to help him to his seat in the reception tent. He sat sipping a glass of water and listening to the bustle of merriment all around.

During dinner, Bud pulled himself up, ignoring the protests of his body. He steadied himself and took a deep breath before picking up a knife and tapping it gently on the glass in front of him silencing the guests.

"It's customary for the father to say a few words, and I'll do my best to keep it to just a few," Bud said, eliciting a laugh from the other tables. "It was... just over 24 years ago when Mary's grandfather stood in very nearly this exact spot the day I married her mother. He expressed a regret that Reese's mother could not be there that day. It's a regret that I sadly echo today, that my wife, Mary's mother, is not here with us to celebrate in person. I believe however, that she is here in spirit and that she would be just as proud and happy for Mary and Steve as I am. I need to thank Steve's parents, Paula and Mark Holmes, for all the help they have given our children through the planning and preparation leading up to this moment. I'm afraid I've been far less help than I would have liked, although my wallet has served its purpose." The crowd laughed again. Bud took a sip of water and turned to face Mary and Steve before continuing.

"Steve, I am blessed now to call you my son–in–law. A father wishes many things for his daughter: happiness, love, security — and you fulfill so many of those for Mary. We are gathered to celebrate the start of your journey through life together. You'll receive more advice than you could ever use, but I'm going to offer you some from my own experience. Today you chose to love each other for the rest of your lives. It is a noble, laudable choice that couples have made throughout all of human history. Those couples that have successful marriages, recognize one very important fact about that choice: that you make it over and over each and every day. Every morning that you wake up, you get to choose each other all over again. Love is not chance, it is that choice. And like all important choices, do not make it lightly. Accept that loving each other requires work, commitment, and often self–sacrifice — but in doing so you build something greater than either of you could ever hope to be without the other." Bud paused and took another sip of water.

"I'm afraid today has taken a lot out of me. That's the sad reality of my recovery, that I am unable to carry on as I used to. For all of you it may prove beneficial, since I'm going to stop rambling and wrap this up," Bud said, causing the crowd to chuckle again. "Where was I? Ah well, it doesn't matter. Steve and Mary, I know that whatever life throws your way, you can find strength and comfort in one another. Trust in one another and the love you share and you will find greatness. Let us raise our glasses to Mr. and Mrs. Holmes." Bud held his glass in the air as did the guests gathered throughout the large tent. "To greatness," he said and he took another drink.

"To greatness," the guests said.

Bud sat, taking a deep breath and trying to relax his sore body. Mary pushed back her chair and made her way over to her father.

"Are you all right, Dad?" she asked.

"Yes, baby girl, I'm fine. Would you and Steve help me back up to the farmhouse? I think the day has fully worn me out, and I should head to bed."

"Okay, Dad."

Mary went and got Steve, and together they helped Bud out of his chair and back up the hill to the farmhouse. Bud stopped them at the crest of the hill, and turned back to look at the tent below them and the stream beyond.

"It really was a beautiful day, and I'm so very happy for the two of you," Bud said. "I'm glad I could be here to see it."

"So are we, Dad," Mary said. "Come on, we'll help you upstairs."

"Do you think I'll ever be able to get back up there? To the waterfall, I mean," Bud said, his eyes drawn back up the length of the water.

"Of course, Dad, your strength will be back before you know it."

"I hope so. Listen you two, I would like to give you your gift now. I know you're leaving tomorrow on your honeymoon for a week, and I want you to have it before you go. I don't know that I'll be awake before you head out in the morning."

"It can wait until we get back if you want," Steve said.

"No Steve, I think I'd like to do it now if you both can take a minute." Mary and Steve nodded. "Join me in the kitchen — I'll make it quick," Bud said.

They helped Bud up the front steps and into the kitchen of the beautifully renovated farmhouse. The three sat down, and Bud slid a manila envelope across the table to the newlyweds.

"Inside is the deed to the farm," Bud said. "I'm giving it to the two of you, if you'll have it."

"Oh, Dad!" Mary said. "You don't need to do that. Where will you live?"

"Well, I'd like to live next door in my childhood home... If you'll let me."

"Of course, it's yours."

"Well, technically it belongs to you Mary, and now to Steve as well, I suppose." Bud looked at his son–in–law and smiled.

"We'd be glad to have you next door," Steve said. "And I'm honored that you would give us the farm. I can't think of a better place to live."

Mary nodded and said, "Okay Dad, if that's what you want."

"It is, very much. Now help me up the stairs, and you better get back to your party."

The newlyweds helped Bud climb the wooden treads and sat him on the edge of the bed. Mary thanked him for a braving the day, and kissed him on the cheek. They left him there, smiling, and returned to their guests.

Bud rose carefully and opened the bedroom windows. He lay in bed and listened to the muddled din of the wedding party. As the music began for Mary and Steve's first dance, he drifted off to sleep.

Bud wandered the banks of the stream in the foggy shadow of his dreams. As the guests danced, Bud stood on the grassy bank listening to the melody of the water falling into the pond. Teresa emerged again, from the depths of memory, and joined him to dance on the bank. Safe in each other's arms, they swayed to the music of their souls. Discomfort and exhaustion washed from Bud's being as boundless love renewed his spirit.

He awoke sometime after nine in the morning to the sound of workers disassembling the tent and gathering the chairs. His body felt stronger than it had in as long as Bud could remember since he got sick and he felt like he practically glided down the stairs to the kitchen. A note on the table from his daughter and son–in–law contained their goodbyes as well as all of their honeymoon contact information. They had also left him a piece of cake in the refrigerator. Bud made himself a late breakfast and with his renewed feeling of strength, began planning in his mind to move his things over to the cape before they returned home. He would get Gregg to help, and make it a surprise for the couple when they got back.

There's nothing like a wedding to remind us of who and why we love, he thought. Over the next several days, Bud's belongings were moved into the cape and Mary's things over to the farmhouse. Gregg was happy to help and enlisted several other able bodies as well. Bud did better than he thought he would, although he had to stop frequently to rest. He mostly directed the others as to which items needed to go and where they should be put in each house.

It was the day before Mary and Steve were scheduled to arrive home, that Bud finally felt ready to make the walk to the waterfall. It was cloudy but warm, and he sat on the bench and spoke out loud to Teresa for close to an hour, telling her everything about the past six months, his illness, and the wedding. Bud made the walk back without having to stop and rest a single time. He was still sore and tired, but the strength was returning to his limbs. He felt, finally, like he was on the real road to recovery.

# 44

**B**ud still couldn't work. Though he was in far better shape than he had been in a long time, his joints still ached as a side effect of the chemotherapy, and he still found himself getting tired too easily. He had regular doctor visits to do follow–up tests, and thus far things looked promising.

Mary and Steve returned from their honeymoon tan and happy. They were both pleasantly surprised to find Bud had moved everything into the farmhouse for them while they were gone. Steve gave up his apartment in Winthrop, and while the drive was significantly longer for him, he enjoyed the peace and quiet of the farm during his off time.

Summer waned and the crisp fall air drifted in from the north. The trees turned burnt orange began to release their leaves to the forest floor. Bud walked to the waterfall often, as the weather allowed, regaining his stamina with every step. By the time the snows of winter flew, he was feeling almost normal again. He wasn't as strong as he had been earlier in life, but the aches from the chemo treatment were gone, and the fatigue he felt was more a product of age than anything.

When Christmas came around, Steve and Mary joined Bud at the cape. Bud sat in the living room as shadows from the fire danced along the walls. He imagined he could see the shapes of people from Christmas gatherings long ago. Buck and Malcolm LaVerdier were chatting in the corner, Jim was talking to the Steins, Nancy and Maggie were carrying food and drinks, he and Teresa were playing on the floor, talking in the hall, or sharing a quiet moment alone.

Those were happy times, but in reflection they brought not only smiles, but tears and sorrow for what was lost. Today wasn't the day to linger in the past however, so he shooed the specters from his mind and returned to the present. There was life still in the house and new memories to be made. Reflection would have to wait.

Bud sat and chatted with Mary and Steve as the lingering scents of cinnamon and nutmeg wafted around them. The young couple wanted to run the farm. Mary was going to quit her job to stay home full time so she could write and take care of the day–to–day chores. Steve would keep his current job, but help out during haying and any larger projects that demanded an extra set of hands.

It all sounded wonderful to Bud, who loved the farm and was happy that giving it to his daughter and her husband had proven to be the right decision. He offered to help out where he could, knowing that right now he would be limited to light work, but as time went on, he hoped to take on heavier tasks. For now, he could at least serve as a resource of information and knowledge.

The prospect of movement and activity returning in full supplied hope to Bud at a time in his life that seemed uncertain. His cancer was in remission, but he didn't feel safe. Routine and frequent doctor visits to check for more cancer meant dread lingered over his shoulder, taunting him and daring him to look back. He needed something to run towards, rather than away from, and Mary and Steve growing the farm was just that.

Life however, has a way of ignoring the plans of mere mortals and dictating reality in ways that render our own desires inconsequential. That's not to say that all happenstances are bad, but even the happiest chances can alter our own designs. It was early in the spring of 2011 when Mary learned she was pregnant with her and Steve's first child.

Bud was thrilled to say the least, but Mary's ability to handle farm work would be limited by pregnancy and raising a baby. Sadly, plans to return the farm to its former glory were placed on hold, and the status quo meant only the small garden and handful of animals would remain.

"I could take on a little more work maybe," Bud offered one rainy spring afternoon while he sat watching Mary knit in the farmhouse living room.

"That's thoughtful, Dad, but Steve and I wouldn't want to burden you with more work than you need to take on right now."

"It's not a burden, really. It would be good to have some real work to do."

"Don't you think you should just be taking it easy?"

"Maybe just a couple of cows, and a pig? A horse or two? You really ought to have a horse. Just think of your son or daughter learning to ride! Oh, wouldn't that be fun, baby girl?"

"It all sounds great, but I don't think it's the right time. Maybe after the baby is grown a little."

"Right, of course. That's probably for the best." Bud let the subject drop. He went about his days and weeks in monotonous routine. At least Reece would be happy he was finding the time to read. Rain or shine, he took a walk every day to the waterfall along the banks of the stream. When the weather was pleasant, he would bring his notebook and sit on the granite bench and write whatever came into his head.

His medical checkups and cancer screenings had become part of the routine as well. Bud had never taken them for granted, but because he had been in remission for nearly a full year, the phone call still caught him off guard.

The word "relapse" is the last one any cancer survivor wants to hear, and when Bud's doctor used it on the phone, it was like ice upon his heart. He had the words repeated several times, but they never improved to his ear.

It was June when Bud started chemotherapy for the second time. It seemed to him like he had just managed to forget the nausea and sick feelings from his first treatment when he had to start again. He was put on a more aggressive schedule than during his first bout with cancer, and he was monitored and tested constantly. The hope was that they had caught things early enough that complete remission would again be the outcome.

Mary was despondent at the news of her father's relapse. She sat and cried for hours at a time, wondering if it were her fear of losing her father alone, or the changing hormones from the pregnancy that were the primary cause. She decided it was probably both, and each fed off of the other.

"I should have let you do more on the farm," she said to her father one day, driving him home from treatment.

"You think mucking out horse stalls would've kept the cancer away?" Bud asked, forcing a smile before motioning her to pull over so he could be sick on the side of the road. She rubbed his back, gave him a sip of water, and helped him back into the passenger seat.

"I took away something you wanted to do," she said as she pulled back into traffic on Route 202. "Mentally it had to have a negative effect on you. Doctors are always saying that you need a positive mental attitude to beat cancer."

"To beat it, yes baby girl. Not to prevent it."

"Why would preventing it be any different? When you beat it this time, you can do whatever you want on the farm. We'll stuff that barn so full of animals—"

"That I'll be swimming in manure?" Bud said, laughing.

"Well, you know what I mean."

"Yes I do, baby girl, and I appreciate it. One step at a time though. You shouldn't be getting so worked up as it is. You have a baby growing inside you that you need to think about."

Before the one–month mark of Bud's induction chemotherapy treatment, his oncologist hit him with more bad news. Bud's leukemia wasn't responding to the treatment. His doctor believed it had become resistant to the induction chemotherapy, which wasn't unheard of in cases of a relapse. Bud was given options, none of which sounded too promising.

The recommendation was for Bud to undergo a bone marrow transplant, something the oncologist referred to as hematopoietic cell transplantation or HCT. He would have radiation treatment that would eradicate all of his existing marrow, including the cancer cells, from his body. The doctors would then introduce new bone marrow stem cells in the hopes of re–growing cancer–free marrow.

The procedure was fraught with risks. Bud would spend a period of time in the hospital without any bone marrow, making him susceptible to deadly infections. An allogeneic transplant, using marrow from another donor, may not be accepted by his body, causing further complications. If Bud chose autologous treatment, using the marrow of his own that he had frozen, it was far more likely to be accepted by the body, but increased the chances of another relapse.

Bud listened to his doctor explain the options, the risks, and the chances of complications. He then stood and walked to the window in the doctor's office, looking out at cloudless summer sky.

"If I do nothing?" Bud asked.

"You have acute myeloid leukemia, Bud. You wouldn't last long without treatment: A couple weeks, a month maybe."

"If I continue the chemotherapy?"

"You have refractory disease — your cancer is resistant to the chemo. It wouldn't help."

Bud turned and faced the doctor, nodding. "So, a transplant is really the only option. It's just a matter of whether I go with my own marrow, or that of a donor?" he said.

"Yes."

"What are the chances of survival with each?"

The oncologist leaned back in his chair, exhaling. He meshed his fingers and tapped his thumbs together. He clucked his tongue and said, "It's tough to say for sure. If your frozen marrow is cancer–free and you can avoid another relapse, your chances are higher going that route. Unfortunately, there's no knowing if you'll have a relapse until we do the transplant."

"Can you give me a number, doc?"

"With this type of therapy, the chances of achieving full re-mission and living beyond five years — it's anywhere from five to forty percent."

"That's kind of a big range," Bud said irritated.

"Well there are a lot of variables and we—"

"What is your recommendation?" Bud was clearly getting ag-itated, and his doctor's face softened.

"Ok Bud. I think we should radiate your marrow, clear it all out including the cancer. Then we do the transplant. We'll check for an allogeneic match, and in the event we don't have one that I feel is perfect, or close enough to it, we'll definitely use the mar-row you have frozen. Otherwise, you make the call. I wish I could tell you that one way or the other is a sure thing, but there are too many variables. The positives on your side are that you're still fairly young, and we caught this early in the relapse stage so your blast percentage is still low. Is there anything that you don't understand or that you want me to explain again for you?" Bud shook his head. "Do you want to proceed with the HCT?" Bud nodded. "Good, let's get to work then."

With no perfect donor matches available, Bud chose to use his own frozen marrow. He faced the treatment with determined resolve. The radiation treatment was quite similar to the chemo treatment Bud had gone through before. He experienced nausea, vomiting, and a general feeling of being ill. The treatment itself caused him some pain in his bones and joints, which were treated with general pain killers.

When he was having a bad day, he would lay with his eyes closed, picturing the water falling over the rocks into the little pool and listening for the melodic splashing it made. If he focused hard enough, he could see Teresa laying on the green bank in the sun, smiling up at him. When he was finally released from the hospital after a successful transplant, he asked Mary and Steve to drive him straight to the waterfall.

Mary helped him make the walk along the bank, while Steve waited with the car on the side of Baker Street. Bud had Mary help him down onto the bench, and then he asked her for a few minutes alone. After she had gone, he broke down into tears, the first tears he had shed since learning he had relapsed, and he spoke aloud to the wind, "I don't know how much more I can take."

He let the tears flow freely from his eyes, releasing all of the pent–up emotion he had stored for months since he had received the phone call from the oncologist. When he had nothing left, he called for Mary, and she and Steve took him home.

The transplant team visited Bud twice a week to monitor him for complications or a second relapse. If there were no complications after three months, they would reduce their visits to monthly, and after a year to every other month. Bud was told that his chances of relapse would decrease significantly after twelve months. He only made it until September.

Bud sat in the hospital bed after another round of tests, watching the leaves blow off of the limbs of the trees outside his window. Mary was pacing around the room, talking incessantly about the marrow donor program and how she couldn't believe out of all the people available, there wasn't a perfect match for her father.

Bud pulled his eyes from the window and focused them on his daughter walking back and forth. She had a stubbornness and a strength that Bud had only ever seen in one other person.

"Mary," he said, "please stop for a minute."

"What, Dad?" she said, continuing to pace.

"Please, baby girl, stop and listen for a minute." She stopped walking and came to the edge of his bed.

"Yes, Dad?" she said.

"Take me home."

"But, Dad—"

"Please, Mary, take me home. I don't want to do this anymore."

"Dad, you have to keep fighting," she said tears welling up in her eyes. "You can beat this."

"No, baby girl, I'm afraid this time I have been torn up by the roots."

# 45

They placed his bed in the sitting room so that he could look out the windows towards the farm, and down to the stream behind the barn. At first, the world outside was full of color. Orange, red, and yellow danced in the wind. But as time passed, the land grew brown and barren.

Bud filled his days by writing in his notebook. He felt that time was short, and he needed to get everything from his mind down on paper before it was too late. Gregg would visit and bring him classic car magazines to read, but Bud neither had the interest or the energy to look at them. When he wasn't writing, he was napping or gazing out the window, lost in memory.

Mary spent her free time sitting in a chair at her father's bedside. She would read and knit while he wrote in his notebook, get him food that he barely ate, and try to keep him hydrated as best as she could.

On one cold, November morning, she brought him breakfast, kissed him on the forehead and told him she would be back after Steve left for work. Bud looked more tired and worn even than usual, and she worried for a second that he wouldn't be alive when she returned. Her fears were needless, because he was sitting up in bed propped up on some pillows when she returned.

"Dad," she said, "you haven't touched your breakfast. You need to eat."

"Baby girl, I need you to do me a favor. Upstairs in my bedroom closet, high up on the shelf, there's a cardboard box. I need you to get that for me and bring it down here." He patted the bed beside himself.

"But your breakfast—"

"That can wait. This can't. Please."

Mary sighed and left the room. She climbed the oak treads of the stairs and went into her father's bedroom. Opening the closet, she found it, a medium–sized cardboard filing box. It was so heavy that she nearly dropped it pulling it down from the shelf. She half carried, half dragged it down the stairs and into the sitting room where her father lay.

"What is in this? It has to weight thirty pounds," she said grunting and lifting it onto the bed beside her father. His eyes danced in the morning light coming through the window as he opened it.

"Oh, lots of things — things worth keeping, and remembering," he said pulling items from the box. "Aha," he said at last pulling out a small cloth pouch. "This is where we'll begin."

"Begin?"

"I assume you're able to spend the whole day with me?"

"Yes," Mary said. "Steve is at work until this evening, so I was going to stay here. Just like I always do."

"Wonderful. In that case, I have a few things for you. I want to give them to you while they're still mine to give."

"Dad, I don't think—"

He raised a finger and clicked his tongue at her. "You will at least humor your sick father today."

"All right, what is it, Dad?"

Bud opened the pouch and slid the gold pocket watch that Buck had given him out into his hand. "This," he said, "was your great–grandfather's. I don't know the full story, because he never got the chance to tell it to me, but it first belonged to a soldier he met in World War One. He gave it to me on my first birthday, but I didn't really even know anything about it until after he died. He and my grandmother held it for me until then. It is time I passed it on to you." Bud handed her the watch, which she turned gently in her hands.

"It's beautiful, Dad."

"Yes, sadly it doesn't work anymore. I don't know that there isn't some repair shop that wouldn't be able to make it run again, but to this point I doubt anyone has tried to find one. These days they'd probably tell you it isn't worth the hassle. Read the inscription."

Mary turned the watch over and read the words out loud, "*Tempus Edax Rerum.* What's it mean?"

"It means, 'Time, devourer of all things.'"

"That's rather depressing, Dad," Mary said, pursing her face.

"Mmmm," Bud said, thoughtfully rubbing his chin. "Perhaps, but it doesn't say all good things, it says all things. In so much as time devours, it devours both good and evil. It devours pain as well as joy. I always viewed it more as a reminder to live for this moment, right now. Because in an instant, it's gone."

"You don't have to give this to me now," Mary said, extending the watch in her hand.

"I want to," Bud said, closing her hand around the watch with his. "It is mine to give, and I would rather do it now while I am still alive to do so. My strength has left me. Mary, it won't be long now."

Her lip quivered and she turned her face away from her father, clutching the watch to her chest. "I'm not ready for you to go," she said.

"What have I always told you, baby girl?"

"That we don't get to choose what happens. We only get to choose how we respond to it."

Bud nodded, smiling. When Mary turned back to face him her eyes were wet with tears. Her father reached over and wiped them away with his hand.

"I won't tell you not to cry, or not to be sad. Grief is an enviable thing, baby girl. Remember that. For loving someone so strongly and so deeply that the loss of them cleaves your heart in two, is preferable to having never loved anyone so much to begin with. Now, I need to rest for a while, and then we will talk some more."

Mary excused herself, wiped her face to dry her. She returned and sat by his bed as he slept, browsing through the items in the box she had carried down for him. By the time he opened his eyes again, it was near noon. She had brought him fresh food, which he left untouched on the bedside table.

"Now, where were we?" he asked.

"You gave me Great–Grandpa's watch."

"Yes, of course. Well, what else do we have in here?"

"I wanted to ask you about this," Mary said holding up a worn and dirty book. "It's an old *Alice and Jerry* learn–to–read book that both you and Mom wrote to each other in."

"Oh yes, that was your mother's first gift to me. I couldn't read and she gave it to me to help me learn. I was horrible to her, thinking she was making fun of me." Bud chuckled, wincing with the effort. "I threw mud at her, messing up her Sunday dress. She didn't speak to me for some time after that. My, your mother was stubborn when she wanted to be. I gave it back to her years later, having written a note for her. I think it won her over."

Mary ran her hand over the worn cover, thinking how much it must have meant for her father to save it for all those years after her mother had given it to him.

Bud pulled out other books, one by one, from the box. There were copies of *Stuart Little, Charlotte's Web, Watership Down* and *The Great Gatsby,* all of which showed signs of being read many times. It can be easy to tell a book that is special in the eyes of its owner. A well–loved book is worn and dogeared with the grime of fingers from many turnings of the pages.

"This one," Bud said, handing Mary *The Great Gatsby,* "was a source of some debate between your mother and me. She thought this was a great work of literature. I on the other hand, hated it. I was incensed that she had even suggested I read it."

"Really, Dad? You didn't like *The Great Gatsby?*"

"I still don't. I can appreciate the writing. I'll just leave it at that."

From the box, Bud next pulled first editions of *East of Eden* and *Jonathan Livingston Seagull.* He explained the significance of each as he handed them to his daughter.

"The stories that touch us, that truly move us, the ones that we read over and over again regardless of the number of times we have read them before — those stories are the ones that speak to our souls. There's something truly human about them. Through them we explore the depths of Hell and the pinnacle of Heaven," Bud said, straining to raise his hands towards the ceiling.

"Heaven?" Mary said, raising an eyebrow. "I didn't know you believed in Heaven, Dad. In all those years of going to church with me you never seemed like a true believer."

"I believe there is a higher power at work, baby girl. I don't know what it is, and if some folks want to call it 'God,' I'm just fine with that. As for Heaven, I know it exists. Your Grandpa Jim and I once discussed it. He believed in Heaven, but at the time I wasn't so sure. I had just lost your mother, and I was in a very dark place. From such places it can be difficult for the light to break through. But since then, I have seen it. I have witnessed

Heaven with my waking eyes. I have seen your mother beckoning me, welcoming me with open arms. Heaven is real, and it is only by our choice that we don't spend our mortal hours there."

"And what choice is that, Dad? How can we live here in Heaven on Earth?" Mary asked.

"It is every choice, baby girl. I have tried to teach you that every choice matters. Every choice is one between absolute good and absolute evil. Many of the ones we make fall somewhere in between, but the possibilities for both are there. I have grown to realize that evil is easy to understand — evil is found in those conscious actions that cause unnecessary suffering for another. Good however, is a little more complicated than I think most people realize. Good isn't as simple as not being evil. No, good is more proactive than that."

"How do we choose to be good then, Dad?"

"You have to accept that there is going to be suffering — that you are going to face struggles. Find a way to turn that hardship into something positive for someone else. That is the lesson of Christ, as well as I can understand it. That is the true nature of love — to sacrifice something of yourself for someone else. Choose that love whenever you can, but especially with those that matter the most to you. In those small moments of love and understanding, the grace and beauty of Heaven are open to you. I have made many poor choices in my life. I have tried to guide you to make better ones, and you have. I hope as a result of learning from my struggles, that your struggles and the struggles of your children and generations to come will be lessened. I am so proud of you and the woman you have grown into. I am thankful that your choices have been better than mine. That is all a father can wish for, that those that come after him can do better and be better and live fuller than he has. I have no doubt that you will."

Mary could see that her father was getting tired again. She smiled and brushed his cheek with her hand. She said, "If you need to rest, Dad, we can continue later."

"Yes, perhaps I should. One more rest and then we can get to the most important thing," he said.

Bud lay his head back down on the pillow and closed his eyes. His breathing was shallow, and his heart beat was weak when Mary checked his pulse. It was hard watching her father diminish and she just hoped he wasn't in too much pain.

She sat in the chair at his bedside the entire afternoon, perusing the other books from the box. There were works of philosophy, history, and classic literature. Many of them had notes scribbled in the margins in her father's handwriting. Bud had bookcases full of things to read, but these books had clearly held deeper meaning for him, and he had kept them away from the rest, as though to keep them safe.

As the hours passed, Bud continued to sleep. The shadows lengthened, and Mary worried that he might not wake before she had to leave to make dinner for Steve and herself. Her father still had not touched any of the lunch she had made for him, so she found no cause to prepare him anything for dinner. The sky grew dim, and Mary heard Steve's car pull into the driveway next door at the farmhouse and the door shut. She pulled the covers up over her father and left him for the time being.

"How is he doing?" Steve asked as Mary walked into the house.

"I think we are losing him, or at least he seems to think so," she said, her eyes downcast.

"Why do you say that?"

"He's giving things away," she said, holding up the gold pocket watch. Steve took it and studied it before handing it back.

"Probably worth quite a bit. It's definitely old."

"Pre–World War One according to Dad."

"So, you think he's preparing for the end?"

"I'm afraid he is, Steve. He seems more worn down and tired than usual. He's sleeping now. He's been sleeping most of the day. I'll make some dinner and eat, but then I'm heading right back over there. The little he's been awake, he's wanted to talk."

"Hmmm, that's not like him, is it? Usually he just sits and writes or stares out the window."

"Yes, and talking seems to be taking a lot out of him. Anyway, let's grab dinner and then I'll go back over."

Mary ate quickly, not wanting her father to wake without her there. She left the dishes for Steve to wash, threw on a jacket, and made her way back over to the cape and the sitting room where her father lay. When she walked in the room, Bud was sitting up holding his notebook on his lap, but his eyes were closed.

"Dad?" she said alarmed.

His eyes opened and he smiled at her. He said, "I knew you'd be back soon. How's Steve?"

"He's good. You startled me."

"Oh, I'm not gone yet, baby girl. I have one more thing to share with you before I go," he said, patting the notebook and smiling. "I have done my best to share all my knowledge with you as you grew, but I'm sure I've forgotten a few things or left them out. Everything I could hope to teach you can be found within these pages. I've written my hopes, my dreams, my observations of life, and many of my stories — some of which you know and some of which you don't. I'm afraid they're fractured and scattered, many written without context or out of sequence of time. What I'm saying is, it's a jumbled mess. I've been trying to put everything in order, or make notes to tell you what a thought or story is in reference to. I had hoped to put everything neatly where it belongs, maybe even write it into my life's story — though I doubt anyone other than yourself would ever care to read it, it's terribly sad and tragic most of the time, but there are happy moments too. Listen to me, I'm rambling now."

Bud lifted the notebook gingerly from his lap and extended it to Mary. She took it and opened it, leafing through the pages of handwritten text.

"What would you have me do with it, Dad?" she asked.

"I would have you read it and remember your father fondly. I would have you understand both where you come from, and where you are going. I would have you learn from all that I have learned and pass that on. I wrote this for you. I started long before I knew you would exist, or that I would want you to have it. Please, take it. Whenever you feel you need me, turn to it. '*When the wind whispers, it will whisper my hopes, my fears, and my dreams to you. When the rain falls or the sun shines, they will nourish our bond. When the birds sing, they will sing only of my love for you.*' Those were your mother's words to me the day we were married. They are all I have left to give and all I can promise to you."

"Thank you, Dad," Mary said. "Is there anything I can do for you?"

Bud waved her closer to the bed. When she came near, he placed his outstretched hand on her swollen belly.

"I wish I could have lived to meet my grandchild," he said. "That, it seems, is not my choice. Something you could do for me? It seems presumptuous even to ask... "

"Anything, Dad, it's okay."

"If it's a boy, name him 'William.' But call him 'Buck.'"

"I think we could do that," she said, taking her father's hand in hers.

"Thank you. Then my work on this Earth is done. The success or failure of my life will be for the future to determine. I have done my best, baby girl. I did my best for you. I have given you what knowledge and tools I had, and I hope that you can do better with them than I did. I go now to meet your mother. Even now I can see her, calling to me through the curtain of this world. She's waiting for me. Waiting by the waterfall — Our place."

Bud Marshall died in November 2011, just shy of his fifty-first birthday. His daughter was by his side, holding his hand. The weight of his life fell away and he embraced the promise of forever. Outside the window, the first few snowflakes of the season were just beginning to fall.

# 46

The younger boy chased the older along the wrought iron fence, laughing. Their father called for them to be careful not to dirty their Sunday clothes. He stood under a sentinel pine, holding the baby girl. She was less than eighteen months old and squirmed restlessly, wanting to get down. His wife was kneeling in front of the two granite headstones. He liked to wait outside the cemetery because he knew how she liked her privacy when she spoke to them.

She rose at last, kissed her hand, placed it atop each stone in turn and then headed back to where husband stood under the majestic evergreen, calling for the boys to come and join them. She patted the baby girl on the head and kissed her husband on the cheek, thanking him for waiting patiently. The boys came running up, laughing. The younger held up a bright red leaf that had fallen from a nearby oak.

"Oh, that's a beautiful one," she said. "Let's save that one, and we can iron it between two pieces of wax paper and put it in your scrapbook."

The older boy scoffed, "I saw it first, he should be thanking me."

"I'm sure we can find plenty of others if you want one too," she said kindly.

He looked up and past his mother at the white pine standing above them. His face shifted from frustration to curiosity. "Mom," he said, "how come some trees change color and lose their leaves while others always stay green?"

She knelt down, zipping his jacket against the cold. As she did, the gold watch she kept on a chain around her neck broke free from the collar of her dress, and danced in the crisp air. It had long since stopped working, but she wore it as a reminder that every moment is precious. She smiled, and the early morning light cascading through the bare branches of the trees twinkled in her deep blue eyes.

"Well, Buck," she said, "let me tell you…"

The End

For the first twenty years of his adult life, Thomas J. Torrington made a career as a golf teaching professional.

Now he has transitioned into a life as a writer of literary fiction stories that explore the depths of the human condition.

When he's not hitting 300-yard drives, he's hitting the ski slopes with his wife and two young children, or otherwise enjoying the outdoors near his home in rural Maine.

Made in the USA
Middletown, DE
11 September 2024